HONEY CREEK FAREWELL
A Novel of the Civil War

Gary McGhee

PublishAmerica
Baltimore

ISBN: 1-4241-3876-0
PUBLISHED BY PUBLISHAMERICA, LLLP
www.publishamerica.com
Baltimore

Printed in the United States of America

*This book is dedicated with love to
my mother, Ollie Bee McGhee,
who inspired my love of genealogy
and to Aunt Nellie McGhee,
who was the caretaker and nurse to
my great grandmother, Mary Elvira McGhee.*

I wish to thank my cousin, Leona Durham, an excellent genealogist, whose research helped me immeasurably in putting this work together.

For all my distant cousins, who research the McGhee line, thank you. This includes Richard McGhee, Else Tyler, and James Shope who were always generous in sharing information.

Jim McGhee is a fine Civil War historian from Missouri who generously shared research about the 16th Missouri Infantry (C.S.A.) with me. Thank you, Jim. Your kindness was a great help.

Thanks to my daughter, Kim, and granddaughter, Jennifer, who read the first draft of this work and gave me both encouragement and suggestions for improvement. Thank you. I listened.

Thanks to Joy and Cathy for their help and encouragement also. Yes, Joy, there's an epilogue.

Finally, but certainly not least, a special note of thanks to my wife, Patricia, who has always believed in me.

Table of Contents

Part I

Prologue

Missouri, 1862…Perhaps the worst place to live during the Civil War. Union forces occupied this state that tried to remain neutral, and Confederate armies tried to free it of Union control. The greatest horrors came from guerrilla bands, some Union loyalist and others Confederate sympathizers. Brutality was commonplace as civilians suspected of being loyal to the wrong side were murdered and businesses and homes looted and burned. Even children were not spared as these partisan bands committed unspeakable atrocities against the people of Missouri, and the land became a killing ground soaked in the blood of innocents.

Chapter One
Honey Creek, Missouri
January 1862

A dozen guerrillas hide within the tree line on a slope overlooking an idyllic, pastoral scene. Smoke curls from the chimney of the large farm house and drifts lazily toward the men waiting to spill the blood of its inhabitants. Frost on the roof top of the home reflects the early morning sun, just now beginning to break through and burn off patches of fog lying on the land like a threadbare blanket. Hoar frost covers the corn stubble and pasture grass, once luxuriant green, but now dormant beige. As the sun's rays do penetrate, the hoar frost winks tears of thawing as if nature knows of the blood bath to come.

These warriors who wait are hard men, men whose humanity has already been stolen by a monotonous litany of revenge and brutality throughout bloody Kansas and Missouri the past four years. And now, their eyes, those windows of the soul, reflect the unflinching, cold emotion of fanaticism, and anyone suspected of being loyal to the other side is marked for death. An eye for an eye—good enough reason for living or killing. So, as the breaths of their horses steam and shroud them in a cloak of fog, these hard men, these young men, these old, young men wait.

"That's Burton's place all right," Captain Quigley said, his voice flat. "Traded and ate with 'em a while back, fore he up and died in '57. Never liked his attitude. He and his squaw-man brother accused me of cheating on a business deal."

"Cap'n, you sure they be on the rebel side? I hear they're neutral."

The captain gave the youngest of his recruits, just a boy with peach fuzz on his chin, a cold stare. "They say so, but they ain't. They be from Georgia, and I don't have time for cowardly fence sitters anyway. Why, their half breed kin all follow that sorry Cherokee son-of-a-bitch, Stand Watie, and they ain't but a stone's throw from here over in Indian Territory. The Confederates done made that Injun a general in their army. Think of it boy, a Cherokee general. Why, if the rebels win, he'll probably be governor of Missouri. Ain't that just fine. Wanna be takin' orders from Injuns and breeds?"

"No, sir, guess I don't."

"Cap'n, people coming out," one of the other men cautioned.

Captain Quigley lifted the binoculars to his eyes. Four young people came out and walked toward the neatly stacked firewood a few yards from the house. One carried a rifle, and after leaning his weapon against the wood pile, he began stacking firewood into the outstretched arms of his brother and sisters. As his three siblings carried logs back to the house, the older one retrieved his rifle and headed toward the south side of the woods a short distance away.

"Looks like Newt growed a tad," the Captain chortled. "Abe, take this youngster, make your way to those woods and find him. We'll take care of the rest."

"Cap'n, we don't havta shoot the women, do we?" The peach fuzz youngster asked.

"Listen boy, you're gettin' on my nerves with all these questions. You done forgot the bodies of women and younguns we found up north slaughtered like sheep by rebels? Don't have the belly for this, then git."

"Sorry Cap'n, I got the stomach. Me and Abe'll take care of that Newt fella." The youngster turned his horse back into the woods and followed Abe.

"How many inside?" One of the other men asked.

"Half dozen, no more, but only three boys, and one's already in the woods. Gone huntin,' I suppose." Then with a cackle added, "Trouble is, we're huntin' him. All right men, we'll wait a few minutes for Abe and Jimmy boy to track Newt, then we go in."

"Those MacEver wemmen purdy, Capt'n?" one of the men asked as he spit. Some of the others laughed, but there was no humor in his question or in his eyes—only cold malice.

"They ain't dog ugly, but them horses in the corral be more important. Kill the other livestock, but we take the horses. We got good men waiting for 'em. Old Burton always kept good stock, and there be gold hid too. Don't forget."

The Captain drew his sword and held it at ready. "Let's make short work of this. We got us a long ride back north."

"Capt'n, look. Someone's coming out again."

Another figure came out the door and walked toward the wood pile. With the hood of the coat up, it was hard to tell whether the person was a boy or girl.

"Franklin, think you can make that shot from here?" Captain Quigley said in a tone sounding more like a command than a question.

"No problem, Sir." With that, Franklin, the best sharpshooter in the company, dismounted and took up a kneeling position to aim his rifle at the target 100 yards away.

"It's a girl, Ca—" The sentence was never finished. The Captain's cold stare at the man next to him was all it took to close the subject.

"Rest of you get ready. Soon as Franklin hits his target, we charge. You boys remember what them rebs did up in Newton County. Burn everything. Save the horses."

With bright blue eyes and reddish blonde hair, neighbors said Florence MacEver was the prettiest of Burton's girls. At seventeen, she was already turning heads in Pineville, where they would go once a month to shop, visit kin, and attend Sunday services at the Methodist Church. Florence daydreamed about their last trip to Pineville as she picked up a log, and thinking about Mark Murray, the son of her father's best friend, her cheeks blushed. At twenty, he was already a man, and when Mark smiled at her, she felt warm all over. Sometimes, she was confused by all the strange new feelings rising to the surface when she wondered what it would be like to kiss him or have his arms around her. It was all a mystery and a little frightening, this knowledge that some day she would be married and living with a man. Although Adelaide, the oldest of the girls, was still single, Josephine and Mary were already married. Josephine had married only three months before and was living up north in Caldwell County with her husband's parents. He was away fighting in the war. Florence smiled as she remembered how handsome her brother-in-law had looked in his pretty blue soldier's uniform. Mary already had her own family over in Fort Smith, where her husband worked in his father's mercantile store. So, Florence stood there looking toward the woods where her brother Newton had gone to hunt. Just as she realized that her daydreaming, her dawdling, as mother would have said, was keeping her too long, someone slapped her hard on the back, and she stumbled into the pile of firewood. Straightening up, Florence was confused by the painful blow and clap of thunder. Looking down, she noticed a pretty red flower growing on the front of her coat. She smiled and touched it. Why, it's wet, she thought and fell backwards onto the ground. Florence continued to smile as she stared into the morning sun. It felt good and warmed her face, but it was bright, so bright her eyes couldn't focus. It seemed she could hear the faint sounds of loud drums and shouts of men. We having a parade at Honey Creek?

"Mama."

Newton, deep in the woods and already stalking a white tail heard the single rifle shot ring out and then more shooting and thunder of galloping horses.

"Bushwhackers!" Newton said to himself with alarm and turned back toward the house.

He had taken only a few steps when the low pitch whirl of beating hummingbird wings buzzed by. Simultaneously, there was a loud report, and bark flew from the tree in front of him. Not hummingbirds, it's January, he thought in panic and threw himself behind a fallen tree.

"Think I got him Abe," came the high pitched voice of an excited youngster.

Newton was on his back and gripped the rifle so tightly his knuckles were white. Raw fear choked him. His breathing was heavy and labored. He couldn't think straight and knew he had to think. He began to make a conscious effort to clear his mind as the words of his aunt Judith's Cherokee brother, Marshall, came to him. "Do not let fear overcome you. If you do, you die. The warrior can turn fear to his advantage, so use it to sharpen your mind. When your mind is clear, you can make decisions to stay alive. Then the fear becomes your weapon to defeat the enemy." Newton closed his eyes and thought hard about his uncle Marshall and the long, quiet conversations shared over the glow of campfires. His eyes focused on one red leaf that hadn't yet fallen, and his breathing began to slow. He concentrated on what he already knew about this unexpected enemy. There were two. The youngster gave that away when he called out the other's name. The boy was probably inexperienced, or he wouldn't have given away his position. The Abe fellow probably was experienced, because he didn't answer the boy and was most likely distancing himself as far as possible from his partner as he looked for Newton. This Abe fellow would be his greatest danger.

Newton glanced to his right. The ground fell off rapidly behind the log, and there was thick brush a few feet away. He took a deep breath, rolled down the slope and crawled into the cover. Making himself as small as possible, he thought of the final weapon the enemy had given him. The boy's voice had come from the left, and he wasn't too far away. He would concentrate on him first. Again, he thought like his Uncle Marshall taught him. What would I do if I were Abe? Of course, circle around. I've got to make fast work of the boy, then change my location quickly. Newton had his rifle leveled toward brush two hundred feet from his position, but his eyes swept from left to right.

"Abe, Abe, you see that Newt? Did I get 'em?" There was panic in the boy's voice, but no answer came back.

Another mistake, Newton thought, for now he knew his adversary was in the brush where he had his rifle leveled. He strained his eyes to try and discern a figure, but could see no one. Suddenly, he saw a small movement beneath the foliage, and something wasn't quite right.

There was black where there should only be the color of yellow and brown leaves. Boots, Newton thought. Carefully, he raised and aimed his rifle in a straight line four feet above the boots. As he carefully began to squeeze the trigger, he was overcome with doubt. Newton had never killed a man. Hearing more gun shots and shouts from the direction of his home, he steeled himself and took careful aim at what should be the boy's chest. The recoil of the old muzzle loader slammed against his shoulder, and he heard a sharp grunt—then silence. He had no time to wonder if he hit his mark. He had to get away from his position that was now exposed by black powder smoke and noise of the shot. Quickly, he began crawling toward his adversary. He couldn't think about a chance the boy might still be living and dangerous. Get away now, worry about that later. Just as he reached another fallen log there came the report of a rifle, and a shot tore up ground where he had been less than two seconds before. The sound did come from behind him where he guessed the other enemy might be. He kept crawling and reached the boy's location. Newton glanced at the bushwhacker's face as he quickly began reloading his rifle. Just a boy, Newton thought, no more than sixteen. His eyes were open, and there was a look of surprise on the young face. Blood was pooling beneath the body, and Newton noticed an entry wound just above the sternum. He swallowed bile and sorrow rising in his throat and hardened himself. His rifle loaded and ready, he began to crawl away toward the north, but paused to take a second look at the body and noticed the boy carried a revolver, a 1860 Colt army 44 caliber. Retrieving the weapon, he stuck it in his own belt. Then, with shock, he noticed a blue Union cap askew on the bushwhacker's head. We're neutral and haven't supported the Rebs, he thought and hurried out of harm's way to find a new hiding place. Five minutes later he heard the snorting of horses. Crawling closer to the sound, he discovered two horses tethered to a tree. As Newton looked around for cover, more shots rang out from the direction of his home, and cold fear gripped his heart. He had to get this over and protect his family. They were in danger, and he was the oldest. Got to find this other bushwhacker, or let him find me and get home fast. Again, the sour taste of acid rose in his throat, and he wondered what this band of cutthroats was doing to his family and why. It was true the MacEvers were trying to stay out of the conflict, but the family followed the advice of both father and their oldest brother. They were not taking sides and were certainly no threat to the Union. Newton had even negotiated the sale of twenty of their best horses to the Union army only a month ago.

At the house, a firebrand came crashing through the front window. Jasper, Newton's younger brother, his father's old Kentucky rifle in his hands, stomped it out. Mother Barthenia, and sisters Bertie and Adelaide, huddled behind the overturned kitchen table as he told them. Another firebrand came through the broken window, but this time Bertie came forward, picked the torch up, and doused it in a bucket of water by the hearth.

"Get back!" Jasper shouted at the baby of the family.

"Jasper, I can help too. I'm not a child anymore. I'm sixteen and full grown. You just shoot those murderers. Newton will be here quick when he hears all this commotion."

Jasper knew better than argue with his youngest sister. She had a lot of father in her. Bertie was ramrod straight and already taking charge of Adelaide. Though the oldest sibling, Adelaide had always been fragile, withdrawn, and prone to deep, dark spells of melancholy. He nodded at Bertie, cocked back the hammer of his rifle, and prepared to find another target.

Suddenly, the door crashed open, and a dark figure came rushing in with a revolver. Jasper fired point blank into the man's face, and the intruder fell backward over the threshold. He frantically began reloading, but it was too late. There was another figure in the doorway, and this one fired first. Jasper staggered backward and fell. He saw the flash, heard the simultaneous roar, and was confused. Why can't I get up? From far away he could hear his mother and sisters calling his name. There were three faces over him.

"Jasper, speak to me," Mother was crying. "Please, darling, please, please don't go. Not another of my babies. Stay with us."

Adelaide and Bertie are crying. Why are they crying? Jasper wondered. Just help me get up, and I'll be all right. I promise, don't worry, help me.

"Mother."

Embracing her son's lifeless body, Barthenia turned her head upwards, and a terrible cry of anguish and pain reverberated in this home Burton had built for her so many years ago. The animal sound of her loss even affected two of the bushwhackers who were now in the room with their captain. They flinched as this terrible cry hit them like a fist, and they thought of their own families living in this killing field called Missouri. Their captain, however, seemed unaffected and pulled her roughly from Jasper's body.

"Where's Burton's gold hid? I know it's here. Burton wouldn't trust that cracker box bank in Pineville. You can live to grieve later if we have the money."

Barthenia looked up and was shocked to see who was leading this band of murderers. "Amos Quigley. What have you done? Why? Why? You did business with my Burton and broke bread in our home. This is Satan's business, and you'll burn in hell."

"Capt'n, watch it!"

Quigley looked up to see Bertie rushing at him with a fireplace poker. She swung the poker at his head with all her might. Quigley dodged, and the blow glanced off his shoulder. Grunting with pain, the leader struck Bertie with a closed fist. She staggered and fell to the floor. He walked toward her intent on doing more harm with the poker.

"Stop it! In the name of God, stop it. She's only sixteen, just a child. Have you no mercy left? Haven't you killed enough this day?" Barthenia cried out.

Adelaide walked toward the captain with a strange smile on her face. She looked up into his eyes and spat. The retaliation came— immediately—cold—merciless. He swung the poker he had taken from Bertie. Adelaide went down hard without a sound, and blood ran from a deep scalp wound on the side of her head.

"Get these harlots out of here and strip their clothes. The men can take their pleasure with 'em while we burn this place to the ground. Old Burton always thought his girls too good for honest men like me. Even offered to marry that Mary. Turned me down. Too good, these high and mighty MacEver women. Now, we'll see how high and mighty they be."

"No," Barthenia shrieked. "The money's under the loose brick at the hearth. Please, Amos. The girls done suffered enough. Take the money. There's two thousand dollars in good Union gold and silver coins. Don't kill any more of my babies, please."

Quigley smiled as Barthenia went to the hearth and returned with two leather pouches, heavy with the weight of gold and silver coins. It was a smile of triumph. He felt the heft of the bags, grinned wickedly, then turned and tossed them to one of the men behind him.

"Put them in your saddle bag. We go back with more than we expected. Good horses and gold."

"You won't torch my home now, will you, Amos? Please, Amos, don't shame the girls. Leave us be to bury my children and grieve in peace," Barthenia pleaded.

"Maybe not. Two of my men be takin' care of Newt, but where's the youngest boy?"

"Worth? He died of fever last year. He's buried next to Burton," Barthenia answered and ran past Quigley. Outside, she saw her girls naked on the ground and screamed. It was a long scream of terror, the scream of a suffering animal surrounded by predators. Two of Quigley's men were on top of the girls. Both had dropped their pants and were raping her daughters, grunting like two hogs. Adelaide lay silently, her eyes staring vacantly toward the sky. Bertie was still fighting and writhing beneath her attacker.

Bertie spit in the ugly man's face and screamed, "You smell and look like a dung heap, you son-of-a-bitch!"

The man snarled and slapped her into submission. Bertie reached out, grabbed Adelaide's limp hand and held it tightly. She was overwhelmed by the man's stench of sweat and filth but made no more resistance. Bertie turned her head to look at Adelaide, and her eyes filled with tears of pain, humiliation, and sorrow for Addie. They ran across her face and pooled on the cold ground. Finally, she closed her eyes tightly to try and close out the horror of the violation—a violation born more of brutality than sexuality. She opened them again when her sister moaned and said no. The leering man on top of Adelaide had almost black teeth and was trying to kiss her. Addie turned her head toward Bertie. Her face was smeared with tobacco juice, and her own tears mixed with Bertie's.

Barthenia screamed again and threw herself on the back of Addie's attacker. She raked the man's face with her finger nails, and he howled in pain. Quigley grabbed Barthenia by the hair and dragged her off his man. She tried to rise, but the captain shoved her back to the ground with his boot.

"Get up again, and I'll shoot the girls, you old whore!"

Barthenia looked up at Quigley's face. She could see no human compassion, only hatred and triumph. She looked toward the other men. They had backed away, and she saw shame in their eyes but knew they wouldn't help. Quigley leaned down, slapped her, and forced the mother to watch the rape of her girls. When she did so, he backed away and laughed.

In the woods, Newton heard the anguished cry of his mother echo through the trees and made his decision. Squatting low, he ran toward the horses and mounted one. Thinking a moment, he removed the pistol from his belt, checked the cylinders, and decided he was ready. Holding both his rifle and reins of the horse in one hand, he gambled and charged forward in the general area he thought the other bushwhacker might be. He made all the noise he could, hoping for the other man to stand up and take a shot. Within a hundred feet, Abe did like Newton hoped and stood up with his rifle leveled. Newton hunkered down behind the horse's bobbing head and fired the pistol twice to distract the shooter. He missed, but so did his adversary. Newton heard the bullet whisper by his ear. Without hesitation, he reined in and jumped off the horse. Down on one knee, he aimed his pistol at the man's chest and fired twice. The stalker went down groaning. He was still alive but dying.

"Who you riding with?" Newton demanded with his pistol leveled at the man's face.

"Quigley's Rangers," the man gasped. "And he's gonna hang—" Abe never finished his sentence.

"Quigley?" Newton knew this name and was puzzled. He removed Abe's pistol and stuck it in his belt, then walked his horse to the edge of the woods to look down at his home on Cowskin Prairie. The barn was already an inferno, and four men were driving the horses north away from the house. Their cattle and pigs, obviously slaughtered, lay on the ground, and smoke was just beginning to drift out of his home's windows. Then he saw his mother and sisters. His mother was prone, beating the ground with her fists. The girls were naked and two men were on top of them. One stood up and began pulling up his pants. Other men seemed to be backing away from the scene as if they wanted no part of this ugliness. He counted a total of six and noticed the man standing a few feet from his mother. He was tall and had long, red hair. Quigley, Newton thought. The long, flowing, red mane was the man's signature of vanity.

"I'm sending you to hell," Newton muttered between clinched teeth.

He got down on one knee and aimed his rifle. It shouldn't be a difficult shot, he thought to himself, a hundred yards at the most and no breeze. He took a deep breath, aimed, let out half the air, and slowly squeezed the trigger. He looked up from the recoil just as Quigley staggered and fell. Jamming the rifle into a rolled blanket tied to the back of the saddle, he rode hard toward home yelling and firing the revolver.

The two men who had been in the house with Quigley were the first to mount. One looked at the others and said, "We want nothing more of this. The rest of you can do what you want, but hear this. If I was in that fella's place, riding down on men who were murdering my family, you wouldn't want to face me. We're gone."

The two men raced north after the four who had driven off the horses. They didn't look back, and the others followed with Quigley's horse in tow. The only man left was the one trying to do up his pants. He had his hands full as he fumbled with his trousers and the reins of his skittish horse. Unfortunately for him, he was too slow. Newton reined his horse in not twenty feet away and walked toward him with deadly intent on his face. There was fear in the man's eyes as he dropped the reins and groped for his weapon. It was too little, too late, as Newton raised the pistol and fired. The man's genitals exploded into pulp, and he screamed. Newton fired again, but the hammer struck an empty chamber with a click. He pulled the other pistol and fired again. He fired, and fired, and fired.

"Newton, son, please. He's dead. You can't kill him no more," Barthenia pleaded.

Newton turned toward his mother. She was trying to cover her daughters' shame as tears of anguish ran down her cheeks. Bertie had her arms around Adelaide. There was a quiet look of resolve on his baby sister's tear stained face, but Adelaide had the look of a wounded bird.

"Son, see if you can save some blankets, and bring Jasper's body out. We got to bury him and Florence decent."

Newton grunted and ran into the house. In the bedroom, he found his mother's chest and took out five blankets. He also saw the coats and brought them outside, then went back and picked up Jasper. He cradled his brother in his arms, the one he loved to tease so much, and carried him outside. He gently placed him beside Florence. Tenderly, he straightened both bodies and folded their hands. Tears streamed down his cheeks and dropped on the faces of the boy and girl he loved and failed to protect. Leaning down, he kissed each on the forehead and closed their eyes for the last time. Still on his knees, he bent over, and great sobs racked his body. Little more than an hour had passed, and now a brother and sister lay dead. His home was destroyed, his two remaining sisters had been shamed and beaten, and Newton? He had killed four men. He thought of his youth and wondered. Am I the same person who choked up when I shot my first deer? He didn't notice Bertie standing by his side.

"Newton," Bertie said softly as she knelt beside him and put her arms around this big brother, her protector, and gave him comfort. Bertie held on for a long time, for she knew. She knew from this day forward they would never be the same.

"What happened in the woods? We thought you'd never come back," she said.

Newton raised up to look at his sister and searched her eyes, blue eyes that matched his own. She had changed, and eyes that reflected a determined resolve looked back into his. Bertie had always been the most mature acting of his sisters, but now there was something different. It wasn't hardness, but her childlike wonder and softness were gone, and he also understood as Bertie did, innocence lay buried in the ashes of their home.

"They sent two men after me. I was lucky. The first to find me shot and missed. I killed him and the other one too. Soon as the killing was over, I came on one of their horses."

Bertie reached out and stroked her brother's face. "Newton, don't blame yourself for what happened. You couldn't help us with two men trying to kill you. The four of us are alive, and let's be thankful for what we have left of the family. We'll go on."

Newton nodded, admiration building in him for this young girl, his baby sister, who was suddenly a woman. "We need to bury Florence and Jasper, then we can make our way to Pineville. Father's friend, J.P. Murray, and his family will help us."

Bertie thought a moment and answered., "We can be at Aunt Judith's place in Indian Territory within two hours. We'll take Florence and Jasper with us to bury them on their land. Our kin will understand, and Aunt Judith will know what to do about Adelaide. I don't think those bushwhackers will cross the border, but they might get their gumption up and come back here."

"You're right, Bertie. We need to get."

They both got up and walked over to their sister and mother. Barthenia had gotten Adelaide dressed, but his sister starred vacantly into space. Her eyes were filled with fear, and the sound coming from her parched lips sounded like the mewing of a kitten. The wound in her head had stopped bleeding, and the bright red blood was now turning the color of dark rust as it clotted. If there was anything in the house to treat her with, it was too late. The home Burton had worked so hard to provide for his family was in flames.

Newton knelt in front of Adelaide and placed a kiss on her forehead. She scarcely seemed to recognize him. He turned to Barthenia and said, "Mother, we're going to Aunt Judith's. It's closer than Pineville, and she can help Adelaide."

His mother nodded. "You think that horse you took will pull the wagon?"

Newton said, "We'll find out."

While Barthenia tried to comfort Adelaide, Bertie and Newton hitched the horse to the wagon and got things ready. Newton put the saddles and horse blankets in the wagon and arranged blankets as a pallet for Adelaide. He positioned one saddle as a pillow. Florence and Jasper were wrapped in blankets and placed in the back.

"Good fortune with the horse, Bertie. Probably came off someone's farm, and he's pulled wagons before. Think you can handle him?" Newton asked as they pulled away from their home headed in the opposite direction the bushwhackers fled. Two tethered Union horses followed.

Bertie looked at him with a cool smile. "Did I ever have problems with a horse and wagon before? What you got in mind?"

"I'm going back for the other horse. You keep going, and I'll catch up. You won't be gone more than a mile before I'm back."

Bertie nodded, shook the reins sharply, and shouted, "Heaahh." They were on their way as Newton sprinted across the field toward the woods. She never looked back and would never return to this place where childhood and trust died.

Within ten minutes, Newton found the other horse. Then he did what he really came for. He draped the bodies of the two partisans he killed over the horse's back and took them back to the house. Once there, he cut the men loose and let them fall to the ground. Then he walked over to the fence and tore off a long horizontal board. Using his knife, he scratched these words. "We murdered Burton's family. This be our fate from Newton MacEver" He lay the board across the chests of the men, and rode out to his father's grave. He quickly paid his respects and dug behind the head stone with his knife. Only a few inches down, he found the tin box with a leather pouch. The pouch held more than five hundred dollars in gold coins that was saved mostly from the inheritance grandfather James had left him. Newton had never spent it and preferred keeping it here instead of the house.

Mounting the horse and taking a last look at this land he knew so well, he whipped his mount into a fast gallop after his family. He would never return.

True to his word, Newton caught up with the wagon shortly and waved Bertie to a stop. "Want me to take over?" He asked, after tying his horse to the back of the wagon.

"I'm doing just fine, as you can see," Bertie answered.

They rode on in silence for several minutes, each with their own thoughts about what the future would bring. They were worried about Adelaide and their mother. Mother seemed just a little less strong than she had been. She still wasn't over losing Worth, and now more tragedy had been inflicted on her children. Worth had died only ten months before, and Barthenia spent a lot of time at the grave site grieving for her favorite. And now, they just weren't sure. At the present, mother was occupied trying to comfort Adelaide and was still in shock, but later how would she cope?

The wagon lumbered down the narrow road into Indian Territory the family knew so well. They were in heavy forest now, a gift from the softer outer fringe of the Ozarks, spreading north from Arkansas. Tall, stately, green pine rose all around them, blocking what little warmth the sun still had in midwinter, as they rode through nature's tunnel of shade. The pine trees' companions, hardwoods with bare and naked limbs, looked inadequate next to the green foliage of the evergreen trees. Their glory lay scattered beneath the wheels of the wagon in a carpet of yellow, gold, and red.

After a few minutes of riding in silence, Bertie said, "Soon as we get there, I've got to write Pleas." He'll know what to do."

"Pleasant's in the Cherokee capital at Tahlequah, selling his cattle," Newton said. "He left last week."

"Well, I'll ask one of Aunt Judith's boys to take a letter to him."

Newton only nodded. He thought of Pleasant and smiled at the way Bertie pronounced his nickname—Please. She was right, Pleasant would know what to do. At twenty-eight, he was six years older than Newton, and there was something about Pleasant hard to define. There was a way about him, that was sure, and people were attracted to him. He was smart and had experiences behind him Newton knew he would never have. Pleas had been to the gold fields of California, waded in the great Pacific Ocean, and even ridden with the wild Arapaho of the great Rockies. Why, he saw the great Salty Lake and those strange people, the Mormons. His half brother was an enigma to him. There were things not talked about in the family, like why did their grandfather

James raise him instead of Burton and Barthenia? No one ever talked about who his mother was. It was a closed subject. But, there were good times at Honey Creek when Pleasant returned from California and stayed. There were warm memories of the family sitting in front of the fireplace listening to Pleasant tell of his adventures in the west. Newton was glad for those years he got to know Pleasant and see his father reunited with his son. At first, the father-son relationship seemed strained, but then they began to go for long walks and often went hunting together. Now, Pleasant was working the cattle business in Missouri and Indian Territory. He went to Georgia last year and brought back a bride. She was not only a beautiful woman but sweet and kind, and the whole family took to her. Newton sighed. He was glad Pleasant and his father reunited and obviously learned to love one another, but sometimes he was filled with great sadness for Burton when he thought of the pain he must have carried for years not seeing his son grow up. The reasons were a mystery and probably always would be. Bertie was right, Pleasant would know what to do. It seemed he always made the right decision, and Newton trusted his brother's advice. Everyone who knew Pleasant instinctively deferred to his judgment, and it was part of Pleasant's character, Newton surmised. He was always calm in a crisis, and there was never a hint of arrogance when Pleasant spoke, even when arguing. He only calmly and cooly laid out facts for his argument in terms anyone could understand. Yes, Newton thought again, there's something about my brother.

"Penny for your thoughts," Bertie said.

Newton woke from his daydreaming. "Nothing, Bertie, I'm okay." The tone of voice was flat.

Bertie looked at Newton's face. A hardness seemed to be taking over her brother, and she was worried. Bertie didn't want to see this young man she loved so much become like the men who attacked them. They all had dead men's eyes.

"We're almost there," Bertie said. "Aunt Judith will welcome us like she always has."

"I know she will. Another twenty minutes, and we'll cross Honey Creek again to see the house."

Chapter Two
Cherokees

"Mama, Mama, our cousins are here from Cowskin Prairie," little Frances shouted excitedly as she recognized Newton and Bertie in the wagon lumbering over the rise toward their home. Within seconds, Judith and the remaining children were on the porch waving hellos as Bertie reined in the horse and stopped the wagon. The children, in their excitement, hadn't yet noticed that something was wrong. Judith knew. She woke in the night and couldn't fall back to sleep. She had dreamed of Burton's family. Her sister-in-law's namesake, Elizabeth Barthenia, Judith's twelve year old, had run a fever the evening before and cried out Bertie's name. Judith had gone through the same revealing experiences a day before the beginning of the terrible march on the Trail of Tears, and before her husband went out into the awful blizzard two years back and died of pneumonia. Years before, when first arriving in the new Cherokee lands, she wasn't surprised when the body of John Ridge, son of Chief Major Ridge, was brought to Ambrose and Judith to prepare for burial. And today? Only one hour ago, a neighbor stopped by and mentioned he heard gun shots while hunting farther up stream on Honey Creek, which only confirmed what she already knew. So, as always, Judith knew. She knew tragedy and grief were parts of life. The blood of Cherokee ancestors coursing through her veins told her about life and the uncertainty of happiness but the certainty of human frailty and mortality. Now her big heart and strong arms were ready to embrace this part of her family. She would keep them safe. She would bind up their wounds, and bury their dead. Judith didn't need to be told who was wrapped in the blankets. She had seen the raven flying toward Burton's place. The matriarch stepped down from the porch as her children were just beginning to realize something was wrong. The sounds of delight and laughter were gone. They were now somber.

"Aunt Judith," Bertie cried as she ran to her aunt's embrace. Suddenly, she was not so able and now needed this strong woman's arms and comfort. She wept into her Aunt's bosom and finally released some pain through tears. Judith hugged and kissed her, and then she looked closely at the swollen, ugly bruises on the side of her face. She also checked Addie's wound.

Judith said, "Eliza, take Bertie in the house and get a poultice for her face. Swelling's bad. Elizabeth, help Newton. Mary Ann, help your cousin Adelaide into the house. Get her by the fire, and heat water to clean the cut." In a quieter tone, she told David to ride for the neighbor's home and tell him a carpenter was needed for building two coffins.

"Barthenia," Judith said softly as she faced her sister-in-law. "Bless your heart." Then she took Barthenia in her arms and held on for a long time. Barthenia wept. Judith wept also. They both wept great, heaving, sobs of grief for what this day had brought to Burton's children and Judith's nephews and nieces. It was shared grief perhaps only mothers can fully understand.

Afterwards, with one arm around Barthenia, Judith guided her sister-in-law into the warmth of her home. She and the girls went to work getting their cousins comfortable and warm. After a few minutes, Judith went back outside to see Newton.

"Hello, Aunt Judith," Newton said as he hugged his aunt. "It's been a terrible day at our end of Honey Creek."

Judith hugged Newton, then stood back and smiled at this nephew who had the same fair good looks of her late husband, Ambrose. He had Burton's blue eyes and sandy blonde hair, but was taller. His face had a lean, chiseled look, and she thought him wiry, while his father had been rather stocky. Like his father, Newton had a sprinkle of freckles across the bridge of his nose. She spoke to him gently with assurances she would take care of all the arrangements. David was already riding to spread the news and meet her sons, who were on their way. Their neighbors, the Becks, would be coming to make caskets, and a preacher from the Moravian Mission would be here for the service. One of the Beck boys would take a note from Bertie to Pleasant on the Tahlequah road. Her nephew and his family need not worry about the details for tomorrow. When she finished, Judith helped Elizabeth and Newton carry Florence and Jasper into the shed at the side of the house. It had a stone floor and was clean. They would be safe until her brother Marshall arrived to help her clean and dress the bodies.

As they closed the door of the shed, Judith turned and embraced her nephew again. "Know your Cherokee family's love, Newton."

Newton choked back some tears. How right Bertie had been. Judith and her family had opened their hearts to them. He watched his aunt and cousin walk back to the house and began the chore of putting the horses away. As he did, his motions were mechanical. There was no keeping the face of the youngster he shot out of his thoughts, and he couldn't forget the utter look of surprise on the boy's face with sightless eyes staring into his own. Some place, probably in a few days, on some farm in Missouri, the boy's mother would scream the same terrible cry of anguish his own mother had. These thoughts, and his own grief at what happened to his family were all meshing with the amazement and guilt about how easily he had killed. In his mind, he could hear the sounds of Barthenia's wooden spoon whipping a batter of corn bread. That's what it felt like to him. Someone was whipping all the ingredients of his nightmare together, and he was afraid it would haunt him for the rest of his life. Finally, he shook his head and tried to make it stop.

"I've got to go on," he murmured. "Mother and the girls need me. Can't let them down again."

Inside his aunt's barn, he hung the saddles, blankets, and saddle bags over a railing. He also had the four Union army issue sidearms with holsters and belts taken from the dead partisans. They were all Colt 44 caliber powder and ball. Looking in the packs on each belt, he found paraffin, percussion caps, lead balls, powder flasks, and extra cylinders. Newton wasn't sure what to do with the weapons. Suddenly, he was tired and didn't want to think about guns anymore. He stuffed them in the saddle bags and sat down. Leaning against the barn wall, he held his throbbing head in his hands and went through the night mare of the day over and over. It was over an hour later that he finally stood up and walked out of the barn.

"Will you be Newton MacEver?"

The loud question startled Newton as he shut the barn doors. Looking up, he saw two men sitting in a wagon and watching him carefully.

"Yes, sir, I'm Newton," he said, walking toward the wagon and now wondering if he had made the right decision to hide the weapons. He also regretted giving in to the impulse of leaving behind his message. Maybe the Union guerillas were already looking for him.

One of the men climbed down and came forward with his hand out. "The name's Franklin, Franklin Beck. This here's my boy, Benjamin. Your aunt sent for us to build coffins. We heard what happened. Sorry to hear. It's hard times, very hard times. We're sorry, uh, well, we're sorry about your family," Franklin stammered.

Newton took the man's hand with relief in his heart. With dark looks and high cheek bones that matched his aunt's, Newton knew he was Cherokee. He grew up around men like this one and had their sons as playmates. All his life he heard about the horrors of the trek west when these original Americans were forced from their homes in old Cherokee Nation and always marveled at the strength of these proud people. He knew there were good reasons why the Cherokees called that terrible forced march where thousands died, the Trail of Tears.

"Thank you, Mr. Beck," Newton replied as he shook hands. "Appreciate you doing this, but what would I owe you for the job?"

The somber man stood back and held his hand up. "No. Don't you worry none bout that. We done it for your uncle, and we'll do it for his kin. No charge. You go on and take care of your family."

Newton thanked the two men again and walked toward the house. He reached the step just as Aunt Judith and her brother Marshall walked out the door. Judith was carrying fresh, clean, and ironed clothing for his brother and sister. Marshall carried a pail of steaming hot water, and two towels hung over his shoulder. Newton knew the purpose of everything. They were on their way to cleanse and dress the bodies. Strung over his shoulder, hanging from a leather thong, Marshall also carried his medicine bag. Newton knew most of the Cherokee were at least nominal Christians, but they also carried the old ways, the comfortable ways, the proven ways. Newton was familiar with them and had no objections. He had learned to respect the traditions of his Cherokee family.

"Uncle Marshall, To hi tsu?" Newton asked with real pleasure. "I didn't know you were here."

"Os da, fine. Wa do, Nephew," Uncle Marshall said. He put down his burden and smiled broadly at this nephew who had walked by his side so many times. Newton became his favorite of Burton's boys when still a small child. He once climbed upon his lap, and with the innocence of a four-year-old, looked at him soberly and asked, "Can I see your scalps?" Marshall had laughed long and hard and still smiled thinking of it. He took Newton's hand in both of his, then looked at his nephew carefully, taking full measure of the boy who had become a man. He placed his hands on Newton's shoulders and spoke. "I know what happened. I know what you did. Listen, Nephew. I know what you had to do. Don't let it rest heavy on your shoulders. Later, we'll talk, but now, Sister and me got a job, and we do it with our hearts. Go in the house and comfort your mother and sisters. They need you."

Newton nodded. "Wa do, thank you, Uncle."

He hadn't missed the emphasis his uncle used on the words, "had to do." Inside, he noticed his cousins were spooning out stew to his mother and younger sister. It smelled delicious, but he went to the bedroom and checked on Adelaide first. She rested against pillows while Elizabeth fed her broth. It was obvious she had been bathed and had a change of clothes. There was a large poultice over the wound, held in place by bandages wrapped around her head. Taking a seat on the edge of the bed, he held his sister's hand while Elizabeth continued to feed her. Newton's heart was fearful for this woman who was five years his senior. Her eyes were full of fear even when she glanced his way. Newton knew she wasn't afraid of him, but he wondered if fear would become the overwhelming emotion of her life. Adelaide was a fragile piece of porcelain, and with only a slip, she would shatter. He squeezed her hand.

"How's the soup, Adelaide?" He asked. "It smells good, and I'm getting hungry too."

"Yes, try some," Adelaide whispered weakly as she turned her head toward him.

There were few words and not much expression, but Newton felt better hearing her say even that much. At least the gut wrenching mewing sounds were gone.

"Mama gave her hot tea with herbs for the pain. Her head hurt real awful," Elizabeth said.

Newton kissed his sister on the cheek and told her, "I'm hungry, Adelaide. I'll be back to talk later. You look better." She nodded, but said nothing. Newton squeezed her hand one more time and joined the family to eat.

"Want some venison stew and cornbread?" little Frances asked with a grin. Her wide brown eyes, so full of curiosity and childish trust, had always warmed Newton. Though sobered by the terrible news, it was hard for Frances to hide her excitement at having company.

"I sure do, Frances. Did you make it?" he asked.

"No, but I helped Mama mix the cornbread," she answered and filled a bowl.

Newton attacked the stew as Frances placed a large piece of cornbread next to his bowl, then sat opposite him and leaned forward with her chin resting in her hands. It was fun with Newton in the house. He always teased her and usually had a little surprise when they visited. She hoped he liked the cornbread and waited for him to take a bite.

Newton noticed the anticipation on his youngest cousin's face. He put his spoon down and with exaggerated formality picked up the cornbread and took a large bite. He chewed slowly and rolled his eyes with one hand over his heart. Frances started to squirm and giggle. Taking another large bite, he began to moan with pleasure as he chewed.

"It's too good for me! I think I done died and gone to heaven. I never knew corn bread could be this good. Why, Frances, my cousin, is just about the best cook in the world," Newton exclaimed to her delight. She squealed, clapped her hands, then jumped out of the chair and ran to him.

Newton picked his cousin up and held her tight as she squeezed his neck. "Goodness, Frances, you're getting more beautiful. Have you got a beau yet? Times a-wasting. All the good ones will get away if you dawdle very long."

"You're silly, Newton. I love you best," Frances said and kissed him on the cheek with an exaggerated smack.

"You're both silly," Elizabeth said. "Newton, put her down and finish eating. The baby's spoilt enough."

Newton put her down and noticed both Bertie and his mother smiling. He felt better and winked at Frances, who giggled appreciatively.

Barthenia stood and said, "Thank you, girls. The food was good, but I'm going in and lie with Adelaide for a while. I'm very tired."

Newton finished his meal while visiting with his cousins. They caught him up on the latest events. "So, Thomas, has been elected lieutenant in his company. When did that happen?" he asked.

"Month ago," Eliza answered. "Even though he's the youngest, the men in his company have confidence in him. We're proud, and Papa would be too."

"He's smart," Newton said, "and he'll make a good officer." He turned his head toward the front door. Horsemen were riding up.

"They're back!" Frances said with excitement and ran for the door to greet her big brothers. "They're here. They're here."

Newton and Bertie followed the girls to the front door to greet their cousins. On the porch, they noticed David was with them. Thomas was the first one to dismount and walked quickly to Newton and Bertie as the others followed. His face was solemn.

"David told us what happened," Thomas said, as he took Bertie in his arms and held her a long moment. "What can we do?"

Bertie wiped away tears and replied, "Just be here, that's all you can do, Cousin. We thank you all for giving us refuge this terrible day."

Thomas turned and took Newton's hand as the other boys crowded around, hugging Bertie and giving her and Newton condolences and assurances that the entire family was here for them for as long as they were needed.

Inside, the boys went into the bedroom quietly to see about Adelaide and Barthenia. Both the women obviously needed rest, so they soon returned and gathered around the table with Newton and Bertie.

"Newton, if you feel up to it, fill in the details for us," Thomas said.

Newton looked at his cousins, who seemed different in a way—older he thought, much older than they actually were. When his family last visited Aunt Judith, the brothers had already gone off to war. He thought they looked rather dashing in their homespun uniforms, but there was a change about them. Albert was the oldest at twenty-three. Newton smiled. He still had a devil-may-care carriage about him. John was the quiet one, always thinking and measuring his words carefully. He was a lover of books and probably the smartest. Thomas Jefferson favored Ambrose the most and was the tallest and heaviest. With broad shoulders and a muscular build, he could intimidate others by his presence. There was a certain assurance in his attitude and deportment.

Newton started his story from the beginning of this awful day, this day that began in the early morning without a care, a morning that now seemed so long ago. Everyone listened without questions. His cousins seemed to know it was important to let him finish his story without interruption. He did just that and gave them the ugliness of that morning of horror on the Missouri side of Honey Creek. When he was finished, Bertie got up with tears in her eyes and joined the women in the other room with Barthenia and Adelaide. Thomas was the first to speak.

"Cousin, you did a hard and necessary job today. If you hadn't acted with courage, your mother and sisters wouldn't be here with you. Take comfort from that. All of us would have tried to do the same," Thomas said.

"Wish we'd been with you, Cousin. We'd caught the rest and hung 'em," Albert, the impulsive one, blurted.

"Newton, I'm worried," Thomas continued. "You shouldn't have left the message. You know Amos Quigley has brothers riding with his bunch, and he's a saint compared with those two. This could bring you trouble later."

Newton nodded his understanding and said, "I know. I appreciate what's been done by your family already. Don't know why I left the message. It was impulse, and I was thoughtless."

John leaned forward and said quietly, "Newton, think on this hard. Barthenia said something about going to Pineville. I don't think that's a good idea now. You're safe here. Right now, none of the Union partisans will be coming. Some tried a while back and Frye's Battalion chased them halfway across Missouri."

"Yep, stay right here. Nobody be bothering you here," Albert offered. "Stay long as you want."

John pulled on his chin and leaned forward again. "Newton, we know how Burton and his family felt about staying out of the war, but think on this. It may be too late to try and be neutral. It's not working for Missouri. They wanted to, but Lincoln sent troops to occupy the state, and the killing is just as bad in Missouri as the rest of the country, maybe worse. Could be it's too late to sit on the fence. Maybe it's just too late. You and Pleasant might have to make a decision to fight on one side or the other."

Albert spoke up with a laugh. "Yeah, Newton, join up with the Cherokee Mounted Rifles. Hey, think about it. You'd get to salute your cousin here."

John grinned, and in mock despair said, "It's a shame how Thomas lords it over his elder brothers. You notice how much bigger his head is?"

"Yours will be bigger from the lumps I give you tonight," Thomas retorted with a broad smile.

37

"See how he is. What he really wants is for us to bow down low every time he struts by. Wants us to keep his boots polished," Albert said, and all four laughed.

Newton joined in the banter. It was good medicine to be around his cousins and laugh with them. He also knew he had to give serious thought to the advice they gave—very serious thought.

"I'll speak on these things with Pleasant. He'll know what to do. He always does," Newton finally said.

"Do, Newton. Your brother's smart and has good judgment. He could be here before dark. The messenger's probably found him by now."

Chapter Three
Pleasant

Ten miles down the Tahlequah road, Pleasant MacEver and Frances, his wife, rode toward Honey Creek. It had been a good business trip, and they were both pleased with the week's work.

"We'll spend a day or two at Honey Creek and then head for home," Pleasant said as they rode side by side.

"Good, let's do," Frances answered. "We didn't have time for a proper visit with your aunt and cousins last week. I do love Judith. She's such a strong woman."

Pleasant grinned broadly at his bride. "Stubborn too. Seems I know another woman that's 'strong' as you say."

"Thank the Lord for your good fortune," Frances retorted, smiling with a raised eyebrow and sideways glance. "I could have married Jonathan Vincent Williams II. Bet I would be riding in a closed carriage warmed by hot bricks instead of dressed like a man on horseback. Think on that, Pleasant MacEver."

Pleasant tilted his head back and laughed. "You'd be bored to death living on a plantation and being waited on by servants. Besides, old Jonathan never read a book in his life or ventured out of Georgia."

"You might be surprised what a genteel woman such as I might get used to, and now, 'Ride, boldly ride, The shade replied—If you seek for Eldorado!'" With that, Frances applied the quirt and trotted ahead of him. She loved this play they often engaged in.

"Poe! And the poem's name is obvious," Pleasant shouted, then nudged his horse into a faster pace to catch her. 'Love me with thine hand stretched out, Freely—open-minded.'"

"Easy. 'Love me with thy loitering foot,—Hearing one behind it.' Browning, " *A Man's Requirement*." Then she turned her face with wide, green eyes embracing his, and said, "Oh, I do love you, Pleasant MacEver. My behind may be tired and saddle-sore from this mount, but I do love you so much."

"And I, you," he replied. "Don't protest about your horse too much. We both know who sits a horse like a master. You're the only woman I knew back in Georgia who could jump a fence riding side-saddle without losing her hat or decorum, and the only one to love books as I."

Frances gave him a radiant smile and leaned over to touch his hand. Pleasant was proud of this beautiful woman who rode by his side. Her carriage was straight, and she looked elegant even in the men's clothing she wore—heavy, wool, butterscotch colored trousers and a padded deer skin coat over a thick wool sweater. Long auburn hair sprayed out from beneath the floppy, brown hat, and a red scarf was tied around it and knotted under her chin. It crushed the brim against her ears, but there was no hiding the beauty of the peaches and cream complexion of a finely sculptured oval face. As he reached up to twist on his blonde mustache, he knew he was a fortunate man indeed. Frances had known when she agreed to marry him they would be leaving the comfort of her beautiful home in Georgia for the unknown wilds of Missouri and Indian Territory, but she adjusted to the hard edge of frontier life with aplomb and grit. Like her husband, Frances relished the adventure and challenge of building a new life in this raw and yet untamed land. It excited her.

"We're into the woods now," Frances said. "I'll be glad for spring. The bare limbs of winter always make me a little sad and anxious for green again."

"Me too. Look, another rider coming." Pleasant patted his coat and took comfort knowing his pistol was beneath it. He undid one button so his weapon was within easy reach. The roads were not patrolled, and brigands were not unknown. He glanced over and noticed Frances had done the same thing. She was not unfamiliar with firearms.

The rider continued his approach at a fast trot. Soon, he was upon them.

"It's one of the Beck boys," Pleasant said. "Wonder where he's going."

The rider stopped in front of them. He looked tired and worried with a solemn expression on his dark face.

"Where you off to, Abraham?" Pleasant asked.

"On my way to Tahlequah, looking for you. I bring bad news and a letter from your sister Bertie. Something terrible has happened on Burton's side of Honey Creek. Your family needs you." He handed Pleasant the note from Bertie.

"Read it," Frances urged Pleasant with anxiety in her voice.

He read the short letter aloud. "My dearest brother Pleas, Please come to us quickly. Aunt Judith and our cousins have given us refuge. We need you something terrible. Union men attacked our home and burned everything. Our dear, sweet, brother Jasper and sweet, sweet, sister Florence were killed by a band of murderers in blue. They didn't care we had not taken up arms against the Union. They only wanted to murder, burn, steal, and do other unmentionable things to us. Our home and fortune are no more. Please come quick. We bury our beloved brother and sister tomorrow. Your loving sister, Bertie."

"Oh, Lord, no!" Frances exclaimed. "Not dear Jasper. Not that bright flower of sweetness, Florence. What evil creatures could do such terrible things?" Tears welled up in her eyes and flowed.

Pleasant was in shock and asked, "Do you know who led this band of cutthroats, Abraham?"

Abraham answered, "Newton said it was Quigley's Rangers that done it, and he kilt Quigley and three more."

"Amos Quigley." Pleasant repeated the name with distaste in his voice. "Father and Uncle Ambrose did business with him once, but told me he was a thief who couldn't be trusted. He and his brothers are a sorry lot, but this—"

"If we ride hard, we'll be there before dark, Pleasant," Frances said, wiping her eyes. Suddenly, a numbing pain gripped her heart, and her breath was short. She needed the frigid wind in her face to unclench the cold fingers clutching her heart.

Pleasant carefully folded the letter and stuck it in his pocket. There was a flinty, hard look in his eyes. He turned to Frances and choked back tears of his own as he saw hers.

"We ride!" He yelled, kicking his horse hard, and the trio galloped fast toward Honey Creek.

At Honey Creek, Newton and his cousins spent the late afternoon digging the graves for Florence and Jasper. It had been hard painful work, but necessary work. Just after dark, they finished, and the exhausted cousins walked into the house to eat and rest. On the table were more beans, collard greens, cornbread, and stew. Judith and the girls were scurrying around the kitchen getting plates and cups ready. Coffee was boiling in the large pot hanging over the open fire place, and its rich aroma filled the room.

"I'm hungry as—" Albert started to say and then stopped. His face was wary. "Two horses coming fast."

The rest turned toward the door. Thomas took down the rifle from its pegs and went to the porch. Newton and the others followed.

Two riders stopped at the porch. In the faint glow from the front windows, the men could see the horses had been ridden hard. Their chests labored with heavy breathing, and steam rose from lathered sides and mouths.

"Well, Thomas, will you shoot your cousin?" came a loud voice.

"Pleasant!" Newton shouted with pleasure. "Oh, God, Brother. I'm glad you're here at last."

Suddenly, Pleasant and Frances were on the porch hugging Newton and their cousins in warm embraces. Inside the house, John shouted, "Hey, everybody, Pleasant and Frances are here."

Bertie and Barthenia came racing out of the bedroom. They both were already crying again. Judith held back her girls momentarily.

Frances simply said, "Dear Mother Barthenia, we grieve for you." Then she embraced her for a long moment, each shedding tears.

Pleasant took Bertie in his arms. He kissed her forehead, and let her cry into his shoulder as she sobbed. Hearing her pain, his own eyes filled with tears as they held on to each other. He took her face in his hands and kissed the tears away as she wiped his. When he released her, he shook Newton's hand, stood back for just a moment and then embraced his brother, who was choking back tears himself. Then in a flood of catharsis, the entire family was in a tight group, embracing and trying to comfort each other.

"Take those coats off and sit," Judith interrupted . "Eliza, you and Elizabeth get some warm water, towels, and soap for these two to clean with before supper. Boys, those horses be lathered up. Get the poor creatures inside the barn for tonight. Wipe 'em down and put blankets over their backs. You know what to do with lathered horses when it's cold. You can eat when that job's done."

"Okay, Ma," Thomas said, walking outside with a lantern. His two brothers followed. They knew better than argue. She was right.

"Where's Adelaide?" Frances asked.

Barthenia led them to the bedroom where Adelaide rested. She had been napping but was now awake from the commotion. Frances and Pleasant took seats on opposite sides of her bed and leaned over to kiss her.

"Pleasant and Frances are here, Adelaide," Barthenia said. "They rode a long way to see you. You know them, don't you?"

"Yes, I know my brother and his wife," she said softly. Then suddenly, she cried out anew in anguish and pain. "Pleasant, Frances, why did those men do this to us? Why, sweet Jesus, tell me why? Jasper was good and gentle. Florence was the sweetest person in the world. They both were true to our faith. Has God abandoned us?"

The cry torn from inside of Adelaide's soul was almost more than Pleasant could bear, but he took his sister, this sister he didn't grow up with, but loved dearly, into his arms and stroked her face as she continued her pitiful weeping. Frances could not stop her own tears and she wept along with Barthenia, who was being torn apart watching her oldest child in such torment. After a few minutes, Adelaide's cries began to lessen, and she became calm as both Frances and Pleasant

43

held and comforted her. Barthenia stepped forward and wiped Adelaide's face gently with a damp rag.

"Adelaide, Aunt Judith's made beans and collard greens for us," Barthenia said. "Would you like some instead of broth?"

Adelaide nodded and whispered hoarsely, "Yes."

Frances spoke. "We're going to the other room and eat too, Adelaide. We'll talk later."

"I'll bring you some supper," Barthenia said.

As they gathered in the main room, Judith said, "Pleasant, there's soap, hot water and towels on the dresser in the far bedroom for you and Frances, if you want to clean up before supper. You'll be sleeping there tonight."

"Thank you, Aunt Judith," Pleasant and Frances answered and followed her instructions.

Newton was already beginning his meal with the girls. Little Frances watched him with a big grin as she ate her own meal.

"Started without us, we see," Albert blurted out and gave Newton a slap on the back, causing him to cough up a bite of cornbread.

"Albert, mind your manners," Judith scolded, wagging the ladle at him.

"Ha, ha," Newton said with a smirk for his cousin.

"Where's Pleasant and Frances?" John asked. "They tired of our company already?"

"No, just yours," Albert teased. "So tired of the five minutes they had to look at your ugly face they walked back to Tahlequah."

Newton smiled. He knew his cousins were trying to keep the conversation light for his and Bertie's sake. It did help, and he appreciated the effort. As the men took their places and began eating, Frances and Pleasant joined them. The meal went on with pleasant talk, interrupted with awkward moments, and punctuated with silent sorrow. When the meal was over, the women cleaned up as the men lingered over coffee. Frances came back to the table after helping the girls and took her seat by Pleasant.

"Newton, I know you've had to tell your story once today, but if you don't mind, tell me what happened in your own words."

Newton took a deep breath. It was the second time he had told the story, and he hoped it would be the last. Once again, he started from the beginning and gave the painful details. He knew his brother needed to hear it, and he respected Pleasant's advice. As before, no one interrupted, and there was only an occasional cough or clearing of throat. Once, Frances gasped and clutched her throat as she reached out to clasp Bertie's hand. When Newton was finished, there was silence for a long while until his brother spoke.

"Newton, it was unwise to leave a message with your name," Pleasant said. There was real concern in his voice. "If the rangers go back for the bodies, it will mean trouble."

Newton nodded. "I know. Our cousins told me the same thing. I was stupid to do it. So, what should I do now?"

"First of all, stay here in Indian Territory for now. When the time comes, I'll take our women folk to Pineville. You're right, J.P. will be willing to help, and Pineville should be a safe place, but for now, you stay out of Missouri."

"Maybe we should check and see if the bodies are still where Newton left them," Thomas suggested. "If so, we can bury them in the woods."

"Good idea," Pleasant responded. "We can go tomorrow or the next day."

Thomas took another sip of coffee, looked across the table at Pleasant and said, "Pleasant, we told Newton something we think you should consider too. The time for sitting on the fence might be over. All of you have done your best to stay out of this war, but look what's happened."

Pleasant nodded. "I understand and your points are something to think on. I've already been thinking on it. I've always thought it made sense for the Cherokee nation to join with the Confederacy and wasn't surprised when it happened. After all, wasn't it the Union that broke so many promises and drove a proud people from their ancestral home? Wasn't it the Union that caused the death and suffering of so many on that awful march west? But, I've also thought the country would be better staying united, but now, I don't know. It's probably time to consider which side to join and take part. Newton and I need to think hard on this subject, and we will. The Union committed a terrible crime on my family, and I don't know if I can forgive. We've got family and friends fighting for the Confederate cause, not only here, but back in Missouri and Georgia also. I lean to the South, but first things first. Tomorrow, we bury our dead. Second, we need to find if those Union bodies and Newton's message are still at Cowskin Prairie. When we find out, we can decide what to do. It's been a long day, and I vote we go to bed."

The others nodded their agreement. It had been a long day. It had been a bad day, and tomorrow would be another long, hard day. In the darkness, family members slept, some the dreamless sleep of physical exhaustion and others the sleep of nightmares.

Chapter Four
Requiem

Morning came for Newton. His sleep had been fitful and filled with the horrors of yesterday. The face of the young boy he killed haunted him, and a snarling, laughing Amos Quigley moved in and out of his dreams. He awoke with the brightness of sunlight filtering through the window onto his face. Rising from his pallet in the front room, Newton tried to wipe the sleep from his eyes.

"Good morning, Cousin," Thomas said, grinning over the rim of his coffee cup. "Better join us. Biscuits are almost gone."

Newton turned around to see the entire family sitting at the dining table quietly eating.

His mother smiled. "We didn't want to wake you. I came in and checked on you twice last night. You kept calling out, and I knew you were having a bad time."

"Thanks, Ma," Newton said and joined the family with a sheepish grin on his face.

Little Frances jumped up and ran to fill a plate with biscuits, eggs, and peach preserves for Newton. After kissing Frances on her cheek when she served him, he began his breakfast.

"How's Adelaide?" Newton asked.

"She's a little better," Judith replied. "She ate most of her breakfast and isn't as dizzy. Her head hasn't bled any more and the pain isn't as bad. She needs to get up and move about this morning. It'll be good for her. Make her stronger, believe me."

Newton nodded and looked around the table. Conversation was on trivial things, and it was obvious everyone was straining to keep the talk as light as possible, but sorrow was heavy in the air. He noticed Frances was dressed in a dark brown dress, probably borrowed from one of the girls, he assumed. All the girls had on dark mourning dresses, and his mother and Aunt Judith wore black. Barthenia's dress looked a little loose on her, and he assumed it was borrowed from his Aunt Judith.

Newton spoke as he finished breakfast. "Thomas, I have something to show you and your brothers in the barn when we finish our coffee. You too, Pleasant."

The others nodded, and when the girls began clearing the table, the boys followed Newton to the barn. He showed them the weapons and saddles he had taken from the Union soldiers.

"44 Colt, U.S. army issue," Thomas said as he looked at one of the heavy revolvers with admiration. "Good weapon. Stop a horse."

"Well, I've been wondering if my cousins have any use for them. Not sure I want one."

Thomas looked up and said, "I carry the Navy Colt 45, thanks to old Stand Watie and the Confederacy. All Stand's officers carry one," he added with a teasing smile at his brothers. "Poor John and Albert are privates."

Pleasant said with a smile, "Let's correct the situation. Newton, give Albert and John one each. You keep one for yourself." He paused, and in measured words said, "Brother, don't assume you won't need a side arm for protection. If you want, I'll take the other."

"Well, then it's settled, and my problem's solved," Newton responded. "I'll keep one for myself."

"By the way," Thomas said, "Newton, you and Pleasant are to help Adelaide take a little walk. Mama thinks it would be good for your family to be gone while we bring in Florence and Jasper. Lots of folks will be here to pay respects to them when you get back."

Pleasant and Newton nodded and walked back to the house. Inside, Judith was waiting with a change of clothes for each of them.

"Boys, I think these things will fit you. Why don't you wash up and change? By then, Adelaide will be ready for a walk. There's sunshine, and we're in for a warming spell. Be good for all of you to walk."

In the boys' bedroom, Newton laid out his change of clothes. There were brown wool trousers and coat. A beige shirt with black string tie hung on a chair. Whether from a neighbor or one of Judith's sons, he wasn't sure. What he did know was his aunt's resourcefulness amazed him. She had seen and survived a lot he decided, and those kinds of experiences either toughens a person or destroys her. Aunt Judith was a survivor, but through it all, life hadn't put a sharp edge on her humanity.

Newton quickly cleaned up with the soap and water left for him and changed clothes. Albert's razor and shaving mug were by the wash bowl, and after stropping the razor on a wide leather belt, he shaved the stubble from his face. Newton looked carefully at his mustache, and it hadn't gotten any better. He envied Pleasant's luxuriant mustache while he despaired at his own. Sighing, he lathered the mustache and scraped it off also. He turned around to put on his boots, but they were gone. Walking to the front room, he saw his little cousin Frances in the corner bent over at some task.

"Frances, what are you doing?" he asked.

"No! You can't see. Newton, please don't look yet. I got a surprise for you."

"Okay, I'll turn my back and won't look," Newton said, smiling to himself. Now he knew where his boots were.

"Turn around, turn around, see what I found," Frances said proudly.

Newton turned, and Frances looked up at him with a grin to melt hearts. She proudly held his boots up for inspection. They were cleaned of yesterday's grime. He knelt on one knee, held his cousin tightly, and then kissed her forehead.

"Frances, thank you. They're beautiful. My goodness, you're talented, but we do have to find you a husband quick. You'll be an old maid soon."

"No, I won't," Frances said. "You're teasing again. Can I go walkin' with my cousins? Please. Mama says I have to ask you first."

Newton stood up and looked down on the face of purity and was reminded where the last of his own youth was buried. He prayed his cousin's childhood would not end early.

"Of course, Frances, I wouldn't want to walk without you."

"We're ready," Barthenia said, as she and Bertie guided Adelaide out of the bedroom.

All three ladies were dressed in solemn, dark clothes, but Adelaide did have a splash of blue at her throat. It was a pretty medallion Eliza had given her to wear and was held by a black, velvet band. She also wore a black knitted scarf around her head which covered the awkward looking bandage. Addie seemed to be steady on her feet, and Newton was encouraged.

"Okay, Frances and I are ready. She'll make sure we don't get lost," Newton said.

The family left the house and walked down a tree lined walking path that led toward the creek. As they disappeared into the woods, Ambrose's sons walked into the house.

"Okay, bring our dear ones in now," Judith said. People will be arriving any time. Let's get those sweet souls ready for company. Everything prepared at the graves?"

"Yes, Ma," John answered. "We're ready."

Thomas spoke. "By the way, Ma, the three Deerhead boys will be here in uniform soon. I sent David this morning to ask them for help with the burying. We'll all be in our uniforms to carry Jasper and Florence to their graves."

Judith looked up from the pile of dried flowers she had been pouring from different jars. "That's good, Son, a good idea. There's dignity in it. Did David find the preacher? Where did that boy get to anyway?"

"He's in the barn practicing on his flute. The preacher will be here soon," Thomas said, as he and his brothers walked outside to bring Jasper and Florence in for the viewing.

"Ma, Uncle Marshall's here with his family," Albert called as he stepped off the porch.

As Albert, John, and Thomas went about their job at the house, their cousins had reached Honey Creek and rested on several large rocks by its bank.

"Adelaide, do you feel better?" Pleasant asked.

"Yes," Adelaide answered. "My head still hurts, but it's okay if I don't have to move or turn quickly. I'm still a little dizzy. Honey Creek looks wider than at home, doesn't it?"

"Yes, it's wider here," Newton answered.

Newton watched his sister carefully as he held little Frances' hand. Addie was sitting between his mother and his brother's wife on one of the rocks. Bertie sat apart, staring into the water, nurturing her own thoughts. Aunt Judith was right. The walking was doing Adelaide good. There was a little color back in her cheeks, and her voice was stronger. But the fear, the fear was still in her eyes, and he wondered if it might always be there.

Pleasant seemed deep in thought as he teased his mustache. He looked at Newton suddenly and asked, "I wonder why J.P. didn't come during the raid. The trading post isn't far from home. He must have heard the shooting and seen the fire. Did the partisans attack his place?"

"No, they left it alone," Newton answered. "J.P. was in Pineville taking care of his new store. He's hiring a man to run the trading post at Honey Springs."

Pleasant nodded. "Our father always said J.P. Murray had a good business head. He'll be rich some day. Yes, sir, he's a good business man, and was always a good friend. He'll help us when we get to Pineville."

"Newton, are you still writing poems?" Frances asked.

Newton blushed and answered, "Oh, I still write sometimes, but they're all gone—burned with the house. I'm afraid the books you gave me are too. Poe and Hawthorne are ashes now, along with my father's journal, his Bible, and my other books. The only thing I had time to pull from the house were coats and blankets."

"Oh, Newton, I'm sorry, but there will be other books, and you must keep reading and writing."

Newton nodded as Pleasant spoke up. "I think it's time to get back.

51

There'll be people there by now to say their last good-byes."

The family rose from their resting places and walked back to finish the unpleasant part of the day, a final farewell to their brother and sister. Newton carried Frances piggy back.

There were already some buggies in front of the house, and Newton noticed his cousins on the front porch with three full blood Cherokees. The Cherokees wore the same style uniform as his cousins, and Newton correctly assumed they were also part of the Cherokee Mounted Rifles. The cavalry-men were all carefully brushing and grooming their uniforms. As the women went inside, Pleasant and Newton stopped to chat.

"Boys, this is Pleasant and Newton, our cousins. It's their brother and sister we'll be burying today," Thomas said.

There were polite murmurs of condolences among the men as Pleasant and Newton shook hands and thanked the soldiers for their help. As they visited, Newton thought I was right, my cousins do look dashing in their calvary uniforms. After a short conversation, awkwardness crept into the men's talk. The two brothers made polite excuses and walked into the house.

Inside, the two coffins were resting on the makeshift table in the front room's southwestern corner. A black cloth covered the table beneath the coffins. Barthenia, Bertie, Adelaide, and Frances were sitting in chairs arranged around the caskets. Aunt Judith and three other women stood behind them offering words of comfort. All the women dabbed at their eyes with handkerchiefs as Newton and Pleasant walked forward to view their brother and sister. A faint smell of lilac and pine greeted them. Aunt Judith had sprinkled dried flowers over Jasper and Florence. Pine cones lay next to them. To Newton, Jasper and Florence looked natural and slept the sleep of angelic children. The bodies had been cleansed and the hair groomed. He noticed the right hand of each was clasped into a fist, and he knew each held seven kernels of Indian corn, the Cherokee magic number. The casket lids were standing upright against the wall, and attached to the top of each were three colorful ears of dried Indian corn. He turned and noticed the large dining table was laden with food brought by neighbors and kin. There were loaves of fresh baked bread, jars of preserved vegetables, fruit, cheeses, sausages, and beans. There would be more than enough food for the guests and mourners.

"Newton," someone from behind said softly. Newton turned and saw his father's brothers, Albert and Larkin. They both looked sad. Their families were crowding in behind them.

"Uncle Larkin, Uncle Albert, thank you for being here," Newton said. Then he continued. "Mother, look who's here, father's brothers have come."

His uncles and cousins crowded around the family and there were hugs and encouraging words. Newton was gratified to see so many people who obviously cared about his family. He noticed one stranger dressed in black. He was holding a Bible and talking in whispers to his mother and sisters. He realized that it must be the preacher. Two hours passed, and people continued to come in. Most of them stayed to wait for the funeral service, and a few left their condolences, gifts of food, and parted. Just as he decided to walk outside for a spell, there was a commotion on the porch.

"De-ga-ta-ga," he heard someone shout. Stand Watie, Newton thought to himself as he recognized the chief's Cherokee name.

Stand Watie walked through the door. The man had a dignified carriage about him, and he was dressed in a black suit. His dark eyes darted around the room and missed nothing. Graying hair, which hung to his shoulders, betrayed his age, but the square jaw and high cheekbones of his ruggedly handsome face embodied confidence. He was a man who commanded respect by his very presence, and others deferred to him. Stand had already become a legend among his people and with many of the white settlers across the border. He had escaped being murdered during the Massacre of '39, when members of a Cherokee secret society, who had sworn revenge on those chiefs who signed the Treaty of New Echota, murdered Chief Major Ridge, his son John, and Chief Elias Bourdinot, Stand's brother. They missed Stand, but assassinated his other brother Thomas in 1845. The treaty gave up the Cherokee lands in Georgia for land in the new Indian Territory in the west plus fifteen million dollars, but Andrew Jackson ignored the provision that called for ratification by a full vote of the Cherokee people and forced the Cherokees onto the Trail of Tears in spite of a Supreme Court decision that went against him. Newton knew this man had gone through many ordeals, had accomplished much, and had also been a friend and Masonic lodge brother to his father.

"De-ga-ta-ga," Newton said as he walked forward to welcome a legend. "Tsi-lu-gi, welcome." Newton knew this man's Cherokee name meant "Stands Tall," and he did, physically and by reputation.

Stand smiled as he recognized his old friend's son and shook Newton's hand firmly and warmly. "Your sorrow is my sorrow, Newton MacEver. Whatever my people can do, we will do. Where is your mother?"

"Wa do," Newton answered and pointed to the circle of ladies. Then he walked outside to visit with his cousins. He smiled as he noticed all the troopers were seeing if there was anything amiss with their uniforms.

John seemed the most nervous. "You sure I'm okay, Thomas?" he asked. "Old Stand was sure giving me the eye."

His brother laughed and said, "Don't worry. You probably won't get more than ten days in the stockade for that smudge on your coat."

"Smudge! What smudge? I don't see a smudge," John said with panic in his voice. Then he noticed the grins and shook his head.

Thomas and Albert were smoking their pipes and enjoying the pleasantly mild winter weather. It was a nice reprieve from the bitter cold of December and beginning of January. Newton sat on the porch step and was soon joined by Pleasant.

"Everyone seems to be here," Pleasant said as he lit his own pipe. "I didn't realize such a crowd would show up."

"Burton's family is well known on this side of Honey Creek," Thomas offered. "Besides, this is a large family with the children of four brothers. Lots of kin."

Pleasant nodded. "You're right, Thomas, and this side of Honey Creek's growing faster than the Missouri side. I think the settlement here will be a nice size town soon, a real nice size town."

"Too many people already," their Uncle Albert said as he stepped onto the porch. "I've been thinking of moving north to Kansas when this war's over."

"Uncle Albert, you've heard the story," Newton said. "What do you think I should do? Doesn't look like I'll be going to Pineville with the family."

Albert pulled on his chin and thought a moment. "Gone to Texas," he said, quoting the old refrain of pioneers who left their homes and moved to the new land when it was still a republic. "Of course, you've got family close by, and you can stay on here."

John looked up quickly and said, "Maybe we could start rumors that Newton did head for Texas."

"That's an idea too," Thomas said. "But, let's wait and see what we find on the other side. Maybe the partisans haven't been back yet. We'll see this afternoon or tomorrow."

"Don't wait til tomorrow," Uncle Albert said. As he spoke, the circuit preacher walked outside.

"Gentlemen, it's time," he announced.

The men stood up, knocked the fire from their pipes and prepared for the hardest part of the day. Others drifted out, and they all followed the preacher toward the burial site except for the Cherokee honor guard and Uncle Marshall. The large crowd stood around the open graves, waiting for the service to begin. Newton and Pleasant stood in front with their mother and sisters. The sound of hammers rang from the house. Those still inside were nailing the coffin lids on. After a few minutes, the soldiers carried Florence's coffin out, three on each side. Uncle Marshall walked behind offering a Cherokee mourning chant. At the open grave, the soldiers gently placed the casket on two boards positioned over the final resting place for Florence. As the boards were removed, they used ropes to carefully lower the coffin into darkness. Dropping the ropes over the casket, they saluted smartly and turned back to the house, marching in a slow cadence as they returned for the other casket. They soon returned and went through the same routine with Jasper. When the job was over, the men moved to join the other mourners. The preacher walked forward with his Bible and prepared for the short eulogy.

"Brothers and sisters," he began.

Newton had difficulty concentrating on the sermon. It was from a man not acquainted with his family, but he did his best with the information gotten from Barthenia and others. There were parts that were eloquent, and Newton wasn't critical but found it hard to listen. He glanced at his family. Barthenia and the girls were holding their composure and dabbed at their eyes with handkerchiefs. He was glad when the preacher finished, and they all recited the 23rd psalm together. With the last words said, his cousin David stepped forward with his Cherokee flute that was made from the tibia of a deer. It was a delicate looking instrument and well suited for David. As David began, and the melancholy music floated through the air, Newton choked. He recognized the tune. It was *Ashokan Farewell*, a sad refrain popular on both sides in this war and played around the campfires by homesick soldiers. Tears rolled down Newton's face, and he wept without shame as the mournful tune pierced his heart. It was an appropriate requiem for his brother and sister. David played not only with skill, but with feeling from the heart. This youngest of Judith's boys had large, sad, brown eyes set expressively in a softly sculptured triangular face, a face that mirrored his sensitivity. Newton hoped the war would be over before this tender hearted young man was old enough to be drawn into its malevolent disregard for human life. He prayed for that, but within two years David would ride with Stand Watie and his older brothers. When the music was over, the girls went forward to hug David. By that time, he was shedding his own tears.

In the last gesture of goodby, Newton stepped forward and spaded dirt into the graves. Each member of the family also added a handful of earth. The rites were over, and they knelt before the graves of their two loved ones. They held each other, weeping tears of remorse and sadness, a sadness Newton never knew was possible to feel, sadness that brought pain to his chest, sadness he feared would never leave his family. The rest of the crowd began to walk back to the house, and there were gentle touches and murmurs of condolences for the family members. But for now, they would be left alone to bid their private farewells. As they held each other, Frances looked up to see little Frances standing a short distance away. She was weeping, and it was obvious the child was now beginning to understand the significance and finality of today's sorrow. Barthenia noticed also and motioned Frances to come forward. She did, and they embraced Judith's youngest, each holding her for a moment as they took time to kiss away the tears. In her hand, she held a jar of dried flowers and asked if she could leave her good-by offering.

"Of course you can," Barthenia said. She and Newton helped her sprinkle flowers over the coffins.

"Good-by, Jasper. Good-by, Florence," Frances said. "Did they hear me, Newton?"

"Yes, Frances, they heard you from heaven," Newton said, almost choking on the pain in his chest. He picked his little cousin up, and the family followed them back to the house. As they walked, Newton held onto Frances tightly, again praying that childhood would not end early for this guileless child. However, within a year, childhood would end with the arrival of Union troops accompanied by Pin Cherokees searching for her brothers and Stand Watie. The Cherokee Mounted Rifles would be away fighting and not able to protect Honey Creek. The family entered the house without looking back. This hardest part of the day was over. Visiting and breaking bread with their family and other mourners would help them begin the healing. Conversation and the need to be courteous to guests in their aunt's home would occupy their minds. Later, as others slept, there would be time, time for solitary grief and pain over the loss of Florence and Jasper.

Chapter Five
Cowskin Prairie

The following morning Newton awoke to the rich aroma of coffee and bustle of his family moving about the kitchen. He mumbled good morning to Thomas and John, then hurried outside into the bitter cold of the early morning. Honey Creek had a thick white frosting from an overnight hard freeze, and fog kept the dim sun's warmth at a distance as he hurried toward the outhouse to take care of the first of his morning rituals. Inside, steam rose as he relieved himself, and the inside of the tiny building had its own fog. He grimaced through chattering teeth as he tried to hurry his uncooperative bladder. When it was finally over, Newton sprinted back to warmth.

"Frances poured your coffee already, Newton," Thomas said as he grinned at his shivering cousin.

"Thanks, Frances," I'll be right out. Newton walked to the boys' bedroom and found the porcelain bowl already filled with clean, warm water. He was hungry and finished the second part of his morning ritual quickly—a quick wash and shave.

"Awake yet?" Albert asked with a grin as Newton took a seat at the dining table.

"Ask me after coffee," Newton answered and cupped his hands around the warmth of the coffee cup.

A few minutes later, all the family members were eating and chatting at the table. As the conversation drifted around him, Newton suddenly realized someone was missing.

"Where's Pleasant?" he asked.

"Gone," Thomas answered. "Left early. He and Uncle Marshall are checking things out at your place."

A few miles away, Pleasant and his uncle rode onto Burton's ruined homestead. The house was burned to the ground, all gray ashes now, intermingled with parts of ruined furniture and black, charred ceiling beams. Barthenia's prized china hutch, brought all the way from St. Louis, was barely recognizable. The white limestone chimney, smudged with soot, stood like a silent sentinel, waiting, but waiting for what, justice? The ugly scene of his family's burned out home was a kick in Pleasant's gut, and he dismounted breathing hard. He got down on one knee and was shocked at how hard it hit him to see the ruins of the MacEver home, the fine house Burton worked so hard for twenty years to provide for his family. The first crude log cabin had been expanded over the years, and the entire outside of the home framed and covered with clapboard siding and painted. The result was a fine-looking home that equaled any house of a moderately well off family in the city. He knew Barthenia came from a well to do family, and Burton had worked hard to furnish this dwelling with some of the fine things she had grown up with. The plank flooring had also been brought from St. Louis but was now ashes. Barthenia wasn't especially materialistic and certainly not grasping or pretentious, but like other women of the frontier, she treasured the nice things her family did have, and had lived in that early, crude, three room log cabin with a dirt floor for years without complaint

"Gone, Marshall, all gone. My father's life work gone with nothing but the acrid smell of charred wood left and two of his children murdered. Why, Lord, why?" Now, anger and bitterness rose in his voice.

"Sometimes there are no answers, Pleasant, but look."

Pleasant stood up to see what Marshall was pointing to—blood, lots of blood. Dark red stains discolored the frost covered grass and ground, and impressions of bodies were also still there.

Marshall got down on one knee to see closer. "Many hoof prints. A dozen men on horses were here, and there are fresh wagon tracks heading north. The bodies were moved not more than an hour ago, maybe less," he observed.

"Do you see the plank Newton left the message on?" Pleasant asked as he looked around the ruins.

"No, and this isn't good, Pleasant. Not good at all. These were Quigley's men, I think."

Both men mounted their horses as Pleasant said, "I'm paying respects to father, then we'll ride over to the trading post and see if J.P. is back from Pineville yet. If he's not, we need to leave word of what happened here before heading back to Aunt Judith's."

At his father's grave, Newton took his hat off and thought for several moments. He wished his father could still give him counsel.

"Father, part of my heart is glad you were not here to see the terrible crimes committed here in the name of the Union. The other part wishes you were here to give me counsel. I wanted no part of this war myself, but now I will. I'll take the Confederate side, but it will be with an honorable regular unit. I imagine Newton will join me. I promise you this. I will watch over Newton and keep him safe. Father, if you can hear me, pray for me, pray for us all in these bloody days."

Pleasant mounted again and rode to Marshall, who had stayed a respectful distance away. They both turned their horses toward the little hamlet that was growing up around J. P.'s trading post only a half mile on the other side of the wooded hill where Newton had killed the partisans. Suddenly, Marshall brought his horse to a halt and stuck his arm out to stop Pleasant.

"Two riders coming fast," Marshall said with alarm.

Pleasant was amazed that Marshall could hear the horses. He heard nothing but the quietness of ruin and desolation. But, within seconds he saw riders coming over a slight rise not a hundred yards away. He could see they had piecemeal Union uniforms. Partisans, he thought.

"Marshall, I'll do the talking. Use your first name, John. I'm Pleasant McCaw, if they approach us. We'll just have to wait and see what they want."

"Look, another rider behind them," Marshall said. "I think we should just keep riding slowly toward them."

The first two riders bore down on them fast and a few feet away reined in their horses hard. The third rider held back holding a rifle over his knees. Having never met Amos Quigley's brothers, Pleasant wasn't sure, but guessed these men with their dirty, matted, red hair were the notorious twosome. Even before the war they had reputations as brutes. Knowing he and Marshall were in danger, his quick mind ran through the possibilities. It took him only a split second to know there was only one way to survive—by his wits.

"What you boys doin' here?" the largest brother snarled. He had his revolver drawn and the other man had a hand on the butt of his weapon. "Murder been done here, and we don't want nobody snooping."

Pleasant put on his best disarming grin and dismounted. Slowly he walked toward the brothers with his hands held up, palms towards the men.

"You gave us a start, Mister. We thought you were Confederate Bushwhackers coming back to finish the job here. We mean no harm. The name's Pleasant McCaw and this is my trading partner, John Cochran. We come from Fort Gibson, and we're on our way to the trading post over yonder. We need some supplies before headin' for St. Louis. Those blue uniforms are a comfort to our eyes, yes, sir, a real comfort. We thought it was all over for us."

The brother with the gun was disarmed by Pleasant's boyish grin and demeanor. He wasn't the first or the last to be so disarmed. He holstered his gun.

"The name's Quigley, Jonah Quigley, and this be my brother, Joshua. Our oldest brother was murdered here by a MacEver, name of Newt. Know of him? Our brother was the captain of our unit."

Pleasant removed his hat. "No, sir, I don't know anyone who goes by Newt MacEver. Sorry to hear about your brother. It's a terrible thing to happen, yes, a terrible thing what the bushwhackers are doin' in these parts. Was he a bushwhacker?"

"No, just a cowardly murderer, and he'll hang when we find him," the brother Joshua barked as he spat a long stream of ugly, brown tobacco juice on the ground. Pleasant noticed he didn't bother wiping his beard. Like his brother, the man had a hard, flinty look in his freckled face, and the washed out, pale, gray eyes were dead, Pleasant thought. Soulless eyes, Frances would have said.

"Hope you find him soon," Pleasant said. "That's a hanging I'd like to see. Killing brave soldiers fighting to save the Union. Yes, sir, hanging's too good for murderers like him." Pleasant looked down and shook his head.

"Amen to that," the first brother said and spat his own stream of tobacco juice. Again, Pleasant noticed there were some leftovers on this brother's beard also. Must run in the family, he thought to himself. Pleasant had a distaste for unkempt people, but he only smiled up at the men and twisted his mustache.

"Tell you what," Quigley continued. "You boys go bout your business, but stay away from here. We'll be keepin' an eye on this place in case any MacEvers show up."

Pleasant put his hat back on, mounted up, and with a salute to the brothers, he and Marshall rode off toward the trading post. They rode slowly and didn't turn around to see if they were being watched. They were. The Quigleys stared after them with suspicious eyes.

"Men living on hate, men without souls," Marshall observed after they were a good distance away. "Newton is in danger."

"You're right, Marshall, he mustn't return to Missouri. Too dangerous. In a couple of days I'll take the women to Pineville, but my brother must remain in Indian Territory for now. What do you think of Uncle Albert's idea that he go to Texas? Does it have merit?"

Marshall thought for a long moment. "Texas. Newton's destiny may be in Texas, but I don't think now is the time. If you do join up with Parsons' Confederate Brigade, you'll both be fighting a war in Arkansas and Louisiana. It seems strange, but for now, Newton may be safer fighting a war than being on the scout by himself. Those are my thoughts. It's for you and Newton to decide."

"The sun's warming up finally, and the sky's clearing," Pleasant observed. We're in for another pleasant day, if Pleasant does say so." He laughed at his own playfulness, and Marshall grinned, then shook his head in mock despair.

"Cherokee never understand white man. Strange. Their ways a mystery. Only Great Spirit can unlock such mystery. Poor Indians cannot," Marshall said with laconic teasing as he spoke with an affected Cherokee accent. "We must learn your ways. Teach me your wisdom, White Brother."

Pleasant laughed out loud as he always did when Marshall played this game. He had known his Aunt's brother for many years and was already aware that Marshall had a good education, and like his sister, was well read. They both spoke and read English fluently.

"Hey, Marshall, there we are."

The small hamlet lay before them. Smoke rose from several chimneys, and in the distance, came the familiar sounds of a blacksmith at work already. The trading post J.P. and his father started years ago had grown into a general store with four large rooms of merchandise. The post office and school Burton built had been enlarged, and now there was also a gristmill not far from the small lumbermill. Smoke curled from the chimneys of several homes.

"Look," Pleasant said, "someone's building another house, and there's already half a dozen families living here full time. The place is growing."

"Yeah, you're right. Burton and J.P. picked a good location when they came here. Why do you suppose Burton sold the business to J.P.?"

Pleasant thought a moment. "You know, Marshall, my father did well in the trading business with his brothers and at the trading post too. Built a fine home for his family and put away a good sum of money, but I think his heart was never in business dealings completely. Deep in his soul, he was always a farmer and a good one, just as his father was back at Spring Place, Georgia. So, I think that's the reason. He just wanted to be a farmer and work the land."

Marshall nodded. "Back to his roots. Men often return to their roots, and it's a good thing to work the land, a good thing. Mother Earth needs men who understand her."

They both dismounted in front of the trading post and tied the reins of their horses to the hitching rail. Pleasant turned around, looked the little hamlet over and smiled, teasing his moustache as he did.

"Yes, sir, Marshall, this place will soon be a nice sized town. Bet they name it Murrayville." Neither could know that in a few years, Burton's Honey Springs would become Southwest City.

"Pleas, Marshall," J.P. shouted as they walked in. He came forward with concern on his face. "In God's name, what happened at Burton's place? I got back yesterday and saw the ruins."

"Terrible news, J.P., I bring terrible news," Pleasant said as he shook the hand of his father's old friend.

J.P. nodded his head solemnly. "Come, both of you have a seat at the table in the corner, and we can talk over some hot coffee and biscuits. It'll take the chill off."

"Are you startin' a restaurant, J.P.?" Marshall asked as he took a seat. He noticed several new tables in this part of the store and the beginning of a partition going up.

"Yep, thought I'd see how it went here, and if it does well, I'll build a separate building. We'll also have a bigger school soon. The little log school Burton built years ago is too small. Now, tell me what happened, and I'll tell you what two soldiers said earlier this morning."

Pleasant took a deep breath and began the story as Newton had told him. He went through from beginning to end, the attack on Burton's home, Newton's fight in the woods with two of the partisans as Burton's home and family were attacked by the others. He related the horrors visited upon Florence, Jasper, and their two sisters. He told it all, and as he did, Pleasant prayed he would never have to dredge up this painful story again.

"Oh, no, not Jasper, not sweet, beautiful Florence," J.P. said with a moan of sorrow. He shook his head in disbelief and continued. "Mark will take this news hard. You know he and Florence were sweet on each other. The boy would mope around like a puppy dog between your family's visits to Pineville. In another year or two when Florence came of age, well—" His voice broke off.

"The family's with Judith," Marshall said. "Adelaide's wound will heal. They're all in good hands with my sister for now."

"I know they are, Marshall," J.P. said. "Judith and all her children are good people. I bet the boys looked handsome in their uniforms at the funeral. Lord, Pleas, I'm so sorry we weren't there for you and your family. If I'd only known. My oldest and best friend's family driven off their land. What can I do to help?"

"There is something you can do, but first tell us about the soldiers this morning."

"Oh, yes, I almost forgot. They were the Quigley brothers. They said Newton had murdered their brother and other Union men. Listen, Pleasant, I know Newton's no murderer, and others here already told me enough to know there was some kind of raid on Burton's place. The Quigley's and their reputation, I know too. Why the Union would put a sorry brute like Amos Quigley in charge of a troop of soldiers is beyond me. I knew these things, but kept my mouth shut and let those sorry pieces of scum talk."

"Did they say anything else about Newton?" Pleasant asked.

"Said they had proof he was a murderer, and there would be a reward. That's when I thought of something. Maybe this was wrong, but you decide. Told them the rumor around here was he ran off to Texas. What do you think? Did I do right?"

Marshall and Pleasant nodded and smiled. "You did right, J.P., you did right," Pleasant said with a chuckle and told their friend about the discussion with Burton's brother.

"Well," J.P. said with relief in his voice. "That's a weight off my shoulder. The rumor will be spread around Pineville also. Look, you know I'm staying neutral just the way Burton wanted, but General Price is a good man and his Missouri 16th Confederate Infantry is formed up just across the border in Arkansas. I know Parsons personally, just as Burton did. Pleasant, you've taken his measure also. His brigade is part of Price's army. If my son was to take the Confederate side, Parsons' Brigade would be the one I'd tell him to join. You said there was something else I could do. Tell me, and it'll be done."

Pleasant took a deep breath of relief and said, "Thanks, J.P. I told mother and Newton we could depend on father's friend. I'm taking Barthenia, Adelaide, and Bertie to Pineville. I think they would be safe among friends and family. Of course, they're welcomed to stay with Aunt Judith also, but Pineville is already their second home, and they would be comfortable. Could you help get them settled? I'm bringing Frances also."

J.P. smiled, took another sip of coffee, and said, "That's the easiest thing you could have asked me. The answer is yes. Besides our new home and store, I've built three cottages for renters. A fourth will be finished shortly. You bring those sweet ladies to Pineville. We have plenty of room for them, and if it's their pleasure, they can live in the new cottage when it's done. Don't worry about rent. Consider it done. Bring them right away. Now, relax and try these biscuits with some of Bertha's fruit preserves. She's a good cook and wife of our miller." He laughed. "Don't worry, Pleas, the barber uses the other room. I know what refined stomachs you Georgia boys have."

Both Marshall and Pleasant laughed and bit into the hot biscuits. Suddenly, they both realized they were hungry, and some of the tension began to drain from their bodies beneath the warm umbrella of J. P.'s hospitality.

"Good, J.P. You have a good cook. Got a lot of work for her?" Marshall asked.

"Well, no, not yet. I just call her over when she's needed, but as more people move in, I think she'll have a full time job. Had half a dozen customers for breakfast earlier. You have to be patient in the business world. Someday soon, I hope to have a full time restaurant and someone here to run my business, so I can spend most of my time in Pineville. Gettin' too old for all this running back and forth," J.P. said with a laugh. "Have some more, boys. By the way, Pleasant, do you think Adelaide will recover?"

"In her body, she will. You'll be seeing us in Pineville within two days. She'll be ready to travel by then. In her mind, I don't know. You know Adelaide's always been kind of timid like and well, uh, fragile, I guess. Right now, in her eyes, she worries me. It's hard to explain. I remember once running across a fawn with a broken leg and the frightful look in that poor creature's eyes." Pleasant paused. He was choking up. "Never mind, she'll heal and get better in Pineville. Yes, Pineville will be the cure."

J.P. and Marshall nodded solemnly and both hoped in their hearts that Pleasant was correct. Adelaide would heal inside. After another cup of coffee, Marshall and Pleasant decided it was time to head back. Outside, they bade their farewells to Burton's friend and turned the horses toward Honey Creek.

"We'll expect you in two days," J.P. shouted, and the men turned to wave good-by.

The ride back by a different, if slower route, was uneventful and three hours later they rode up to Judith's home. Newton and the boys were on the front porch talking while Albert and Thomas smoked their pipes. Marshall bid Pleasant good-by. Pleasant thanked him and took his own horse to the barn. A few minutes later, he joined his cousins on the front porch.

"So, what did you learn?" Newton asked as Pleasant turned a pail over for a seat.

Pleasant sat and told the story of the run in with the Quigley brothers, everything J.P. had told them, and the danger for Newton.

"They called Newton a murderer!" Albert shouted with righteous indignation as he stood up. "I know the cure for those Quigleys. Thomas, let's get leave from Stand, find those sorry pieces of pig dung and hang 'em. I bet Stand goes too. He knows Newton ain't no murderer."

"Calm down," Thomas said. "No, we can't take leave to go on a family man hunt, and we're due back in camp day after tomorrow."

"Well, we should," Albert muttered to himself, as he clamped down on his pipe stem in frustration and anger, almost biting it in half.

Newton was quiet for a moment, rocking silently, thinking of the past two days and the news his brother brought back. He was quickly making up his mind about what to do.

"Pleasant, I've decided it best to join up with Parsons' Brigade, even if you don't. I can't just stay around here. I need to have some purpose and do something. I'll go mad without purpose, thinking only of what happened to our family, feeling like a eunuch, unable to go back to Missouri and fight this battle with Quigley's brothers or unable to find the others who hurt my family and have justice." He paused and choked back the anger rising in his throat. "Do you understand?"

Pleasant cocked his head and looked intently at Newton. "Yes, Brother, I understand. I've already made the decision to join also."

Albert had a look of puzzlement on his face as he turned to Thomas and whispered, "What's a eunuch?"

Thomas rolled his eyes and shook his head. "Shhh. Never mind. Newton reads a lot."

Pleasant spoke above the whispers. "In two days, I'm taking the women to J.P.'s home in Pineville while you stay here. When there, I'll contact a recruiter and make the arrangements. I might just have you meet me in Arkansas, but where ever it is, Bertie will write when and where to meet. By the way, you'll be introduced as James MacEver, not Newton. Get used to your new name."

Newton nodded. "I agree and understand." He rose from the rocker and stood. "Think I'll go for a walk. Been sitting around too much." He walked off the porch into the woods.

Pleasant watched his brother and remembered his own words at father's grave site. He was worried. All the family watched Newton with concern as he disappeared into the forest.

"Pleasant, he's going to be fine," Thomas said. Taking another draw on his pipe, he continued. "Newton's mind is full. It's full of the horror done on his family and the horror of realizing how easy it is to kill. He needs some time to sort things out. Newton thinks deeply on things, but he's strong, and he's a good, honest man. Unlike many men, he's also honest with himself. Men who are honest with themselves are often cut the deepest by things like this, but his strength will pull him through. For now, he just needs time alone. That's all. Don't worry."

Pleasant nodded in agreement. "You're right. I know Newton, and he'll be okay when he sorts things out in his mind." Then he stood up and turned to Albert. "After meeting those delightful brothers this morning, I do believe hunting down those 'pig dungs' with you and hanging them would perk me up. Yes, sir, Albert, perk me up a lot." He grinned as he spoke, giving his moustache a flamboyant twist. "And, Albert, a eunuch is one without his privates. Perhaps you and I could arrange that for the brothers Dung also."

The cousins laughed together, Albert so hard, he began to choke. It was good to laugh, to laugh hard, to laugh together, to feel the tension of these three days loosen just a bit and begin the healing just a bit. It was a good start for them all.

Chapter Six
Refuge

Two days later, Judith's older sons returned to their regiment's encampment in Arkansas. On their way, they escorted Pleasant and the rest of his family. Pleasant rode horseback beside his cousins, while Frances rode in the wagon with his sisters and stepmother. She and Bertie took turns at the reins.

"Think I'll get rid of the wagon and find a buggy when we get to Pineville," Pleasant said as he rode beside his uniformed cousins.

"Good idea," Thomas said. "You'll find something. Got money for one?"

Pleasant smiled. "Oh, yeah, we had a good trip to Tahlequa, plus I keep money at the Pineville bank. Newton gave me a hundred dollars in gold for the girls. I'll add some to what he gave me and open an account for Barthenia and the girls. They'll need some things."

Albert laughed and said, "You know how Burton felt about banks. Pleas, better watch it, he might return to haunt you. Feel the same way myself."

"I know, but look what happened. Times are changing boys. We have to adjust to a changing world. It's change with it or be left behind. Banks are a good idea, better save your money in a bank too."

"What money?" John asked with a chortle. "Every time Stand pays us, Albert loses it gambling around the campfire the same night. If mother ever finds out he's been gambling, she'll take a switch to him. Look. There's the north road going to Pineville. Time to stop and eat the lunch mother packed for us. Tell Bertie to pull into that little glen, and we'll have us a picnic before parting."

The snacks were unpacked and passed around to the hungry family members. There were biscuits layered with peach preserves, some cheese, and pickled eggs. After stretching their legs, the women ate in the wagon while the men sat in a circle on the grass.

"John," Albert asked, "You wouldn't tell Mama bout my gambling, would you?"

"Tempting, very tempting, Albert. It'd be fun watching Mama switch you again. Might do you a wealth of good. Yes, sir, a wealth of good." Then he dodged the fist Albert aimed at his shoulder.

"Now, boys, play nice," Pleasant said as he passed the tin cup and water jug around. "And Albert, stop punching on your brother, or I'll have to talk to your mama also. Shame on you. Now eat your biscuit and be good."

Albert mumbled something through a mouth full of biscuit, but no one understood what he was trying to say.

"Can't believe how nice the weather has been the past couple of days," Frances said

"It'll change. Something's in the air, something's brewing up to bring a change. Winter's not over yet," John answered.

"That's not all that's brewing," Thomas said with a serious note to his voice. "Lots of things are in the air this winter."

"What's that?" Pleasant asked.

"A large Union army has moved south out of St. Louis. There's talk their purpose is to secure southern Missouri under Union control and then drive our forces out of Arkansas." He took another puff on his pipe and continued. "Sterling Price and McCollouch are moving forces west here in northern Arkansas to join up under General Van Dorn. So, there's a big battle shaping up, and rumor has it Stand will attach our boys to the same group."

"That means Parsons' Brigade will be coming too, doesn't it?" Pleasant asked.

"Most likely," Thomas answered. "You might run into Union patrols on the way to Pineville, but that's just a guess." Then he knocked the fire from his pipe and stood up. "Brothers, it's time to move out. We've got to be in camp before sundown."

There were hugs and tearful good-byes, then the families went their separate ways, Judith's sons into the certainty of eventual combat and Pleasant's family into the unknown between the Arkansas border and Pineville. They rode on for an hour and only met one group of civilians in a buggy, who nodded and smiled. The men tipped their hats as they passed.

"Pleas, do you think Thomas is right, will, will we see—?" Adelaide tried to ask but her voice choked with fear as Frances put her arm around her.

Pleasant looked at his sister and saw that soul crunching look of a wounded animal in her eyes again. "Don't worry, Adelaide. Thomas was speaking of regular Union patrols, not partisans. If we do see them, we'll not be harmed. They may question us, but that's all."

He looked over at Bertie, who had the reins under tight control with her gloved hands and could tell she was worried also, which gave him some doubt about the wisdom of his choice. However, the decision was already made, and in another hour or so, they would be safe. He patted his coat to reassure himself his gun was still in place. It was, just as it was a few minutes ago. The U. S. issue revolver Newton gave him was hidden safely in the wagon.

"Let's sing a song," Frances said suddenly. "Come on, Adelaide, I've heard you sing so many times at church. You have a wonderful voice."

"Oh, yes," Barthenia added, "let's do sing. You pick the songs, Adelaide, and we'll follow along."

Adelaide's dark blue eyes brightened, she looked up, and her beautiful soprano voice rang out through the trees with the words of "Amazing Grace". As the words of the old spiritual floated around him, Pleasant remembered Adelaide's gift. He had heard it many times before, both in the little Methodist church in Pineville and at his father's home. He often thought it a shame Adelaide wasn't sent back east to study music. The others joined in, and suddenly they had an outdoor choir to accompany them. The next song Adelaide started was "When Johnny Comes Marching Home", and with that robust song, Pleasant joined in with gusto and animation. "Hurrah, hurrah," his voice rang out as he slapped his hat against his leg. Soon, they were laughing and enjoying themselves. Pleasant felt relieved and better about the trip. Tension was released as their combined voices floated above the trees toward the clear, azure sky, broken by only a few gray clouds. There was a pause in the singing, and then Adelaide's voice again broke the silence with the words of "Danny Boy". No one else joined in. They were too enraptured listening to Adelaide's clear, beautiful voice interpret this old, soulful, Irish ballad. Just as good poetry could, this song stimulated Pleasant's imagination, and he was an Irish immigrant, pining for his family so far away across the wide Atlantic.

"Pleas, horses coming fast! " Bertie interrupted with alarm. From her tone of voice, Pleasant knew his sister was frightened.

Pleasant stood in his stirrups and peered ahead. From around a far bend in the road, he saw them, Union Cavalry coming fast. He motioned for Bertie to pull the wagon over to the edge of the road and stop. He was calm and turned to smile at the women, but his heart was beating faster as he tried to reassure the women. Might be harder to reassure me, he thought with a tight smile. He loved these women, and their safety was a responsibility he didn't take lightly.

"They're regular Union troops, not partisans. These will be honorable men. Don't worry," he told them and urged his horse forward of the wagon. "They may want to ask a few questions is all."

They waited with anxiety as the galloping cavalry men bore down on them, stirring up billowing clouds of red dust as they came, dust that almost obscured their blue uniforms with the pants legs tucked into high black boots. Yes, regular army, Pleasant thought to himself with relief as the column of troopers came to a halt in front of the family. He counted fourteen, plus the young captain, who gave the ladies a salute and studied Pleasant with earnest intensity. He was a dashing young officer with the brim of one side of his dark, blue hat pinned against the crown, and it was worn at a rakish angle. It took only a second for Pleasant to decide he had but one option. If questioned, tell the truth with little detail as possible.

Pleasant leaned forward, smiled, and said, "The name's Pleasant MacEver. My friends call me Pleas. What can I do for you, Captain?" Pleasant held his hand out as he talked.

The young man nodded, took his glove off and shook Pleasant's hand. "Captain McCulley, at your service, Mr. MacEver. May I ask where you and your friends are going?"

"Pineville, Captain. We're on our way to Pineville, and these ladies are my family." Pleasant turned and pointed. "My sister Bertie, my wife Frances, my stepmother Barthenia, and my sister, Adelaide."

"I see," the captain said. Then suddenly, Adelaide was in tears and moaning frightfully. The captain was taken aback and a little flicker of suspicion passed over his face. "What's wrong with your sister?" He urged his horse a little closer to the wagon, and Adelaide began to make the pitiful mewing sounds Newton had told Pleasant about.

"Her head's bandaged. Why? Both your sisters have bandages. What's going on here?" Suddenly the Captain was full of questions.

"Can we talk alone, Captain? The ladies have been through a lot, and I'll explain," Pleasant said and rode to the other side of the road. The captain followed, but Pleasant knew he was suspicious.

"Mr. MacEver, I'll listen," the captain said guiding his horse next to Pleasant's, "but understand this. We're patrolling for spies and Confederate recruiters. We've found two spies in the past week, and we hang spies."

"Captain, my family's home was burned to the ground, their savings stolen, and one other sister and a brother murdered. These two sisters were ravaged, shamed, and beaten by Union partisans."

So, once again, Pleasant went through the brutal details of his family's ordeal, and once again, he hoped this would be the last time. The captain listened intently as Pleasant talked. At times, the young officer would look over his shoulder at the ladies and shake his head.

74

Pleasant could tell the man was appalled by the story. He finally finished and watched the young soldier's face carefully. Pleasant could only hope the man not only believed him but was also honorable.

"Can you understand my concern?" Pleasant asked when finished.

Captain McCulley looked back at the women again and shook his head. "Unbelievable this is happening to civilians. I'm sorry, but you have to understand we need to be careful. There are women spies also, on both sides, I might add. I don't know—" His voice trailed off as he shook his head.

"We're not spies, Captain. In fact, none of us have taken sides with the Confederacy."

Pleasant knew the young officer was puzzled and turning this new information over in his head as he tried to make a decision on what to do about an unfamiliar and perplexing problem. He would probably rather lead a charge against the enemy than have us in his hands, Pleasant thought.

Finally, after his internal debate was finished, the captain said, "Look, follow us back toward Pineville. We'll be going past our camp twenty minutes from here, and from there, you can make your own way to town. No, I don't believe you and your family are spies."

Pleasant went back to the wagon to reassure the women. Adelaide began to calm down as Barthenia and Frances held her. Half the troop rode ahead of them and half behind as they once again headed north.

"The dust is awful," Bertie cried out to Pleasant. "It's choking us."

"Pour some water over handkerchiefs or scarfs and tie them round your faces," Pleasant called back. The women complied. It is choking, Pleasant thought to himself. Be glad when this escort is over. Don't really need such favors.

Twenty minutes later, Pleasant was shocked. A hundred yards from the road, a large Union encampment spread to the east, taking up all the plain and pushing into the woods. Row after row of neatly arranged gray tents spread before him. Black smoke from cooking fires rose over the camp, and there was a bustle of activity, soldiers marching to drill and wagons of supplies arriving from the intersecting road that went eastward. Just as the troopers rode off the road and toward the camp, the captain turned back for a moment and waved them on, but an older man rode over to the captain and pointed at them, apparently asking what was going on. He could see the captain was explaining the situation as he gestured occasionally back at Pleasant and the women. The other man was older and a major. Newton's brother didn't like the looks of things. Finally, both men rode back to Pleasant and his family.

"Mr. MacEver, this is Major Ferris. He says you have to come with us."

"Why?" Pleasant asked with a smile on his face.

"Why? Because that's an order, Mister," the major yelled in a high-pitched voice and spurred his horse to move close to Pleasant. "Your story sounds suspicious to me, and we're taking you to see General Curtis. This miserable state's full of Confederate lovers, and I don't like your attitude. Get moving!"

Pleasant took the man's measure. From his accent, he guessed New England or thereabouts would be his home, and he had an arrogant attitude about him. Full of himself, he thought, and with his authority, that makes him dangerous. Adelaide began to moan again. He looked back at her. She was terrified, her eyes now wide, and the pitiful look of a wounded fawn was back. He was beside himself with alarm.

"What's wrong with the gal?" the major asked without any concern in his voice.

"I think the captain probably explained things," Pleasant answered with anger rising in his voice. "The gal, as you say, is my sister, and her name's Miss MacEver to you."

"Got a real bad attitude, don't you, Reb? Got a weapon to go with it?"

"Of course. Wouldn't you carry one on the open road?" Pleasant replied, barely able to keep his contempt from showing. "And, I'm not a Reb."

"Hand it over!" the major demanded, pulling his own weapon out and pointing it at Pleasant's head.

Pleasant did as he was told, almost choking on his anger and contempt for this little man, this pompous, arrogant, little martinet. A man badly in need of a good thrashing, he thought, handing his pistol to the major.

The major looked at Pleasant's pistol carefully and said, "Huh, Remington derringer. Haven't seen one of these in awhile." Then he turned and ordered curtly, "Follow us."

The captain glanced back at the family as they followed behind the two Union men. Pleasant could tell the young man was embarrassed by his superior's behavior and would rather be somewhere else. The two men seemed to be in a heated argument, but Pleasant couldn't make out their words. Even with Frances and Barthenia holding Adelaide, she was still moaning. How much, Lord, how much more of this can she endure? He prayed silently as he strained to distinguish the words of the two men riding ahead. As they rode into the center of the bustling camp, it was obvious to him this was an encampment of thousands of soldiers, made up of cavalry, artillery, and infantry. He remembered Thomas's words about a battle brewing.

"But Major, I don't think—," the captain tried to say, but was cut off.

"Captain, don't forget, you almost let these people go. I know this MacEver fella's a Confederate recruiter and no telling what the gals got hid 'neath those bandages and dresses." His face was flushed with anger at having a subordinate argue with him.

"You're wrong, Sir, and with all due respect, surely you won't have those poor women searched. They've been through enough. For the sake of God, can't—" Once again he was cut off as the major bumped his mount against his. Now, the major's face was almost purple with rage.

"Enough insubordination! There'll be a court-martial for aiding the enemy. Yes, by God, I could see you in prison and those rebels hung!" Major Ferris seemed almost out of control, his voice strident and loud.

This, Pleasant could hear plainly. He was in awe that the captain didn't jerk this arrogant little pop-in-jay off the horse and beat him within an inch of his life. He turned again to check the women. Of course, they also heard, and it wasn't helping matters. His wife and stepmother were still trying to calm Adelaide, and Bertie had a hard, hostile look in her eyes. Up ahead, there was a clearing in the center of camp with two large tents. The stars and stripes and regimental flags hung limply in the still air. Too make things worse for the ladies, there were now soldiers gathering around to gawk at the appearance of women in their camp.

"Get your people out of the wagon!" the major barked as he walked into the headquarter's tent.

Pleasant gathered the family around him. Barthenia, Frances, and Bertie stood huddled protectively around Adelaide.

"Mr. MacEver, ladies, please accept my apologies for the major's behavior. I'm staying here, and I promise no harm will come to you," Captain McCulley said. "Trust me, the general's a reasonable man. You'll be allowed to tell your story, and he'll listen."

"Thank you, Captain," Pleasant said, "but could you do something about these men. Look what it's doing to my sister."

The captain nodded with understanding and walked to the crowd of soldiers gawking at the ladies. "On with you now. You men get back to your details before you're put on report. Move along." His voice was firm with authority and the men quickly dispersed.

Inside the tent, the doctor cleaned a cut on the general's arm as the major told him about the "spies" he just captured.

"Sir, you've been wounded," the major said with just the right amount of concern in his voice after finishing his version of the story.

"No, Major, there's been no battle lately I'm aware of. I tripped and scraped my arm on the edge of the table." As the doctor wrapped his arm, the general digested the major's story. Why did this martinet have to be my wife's nephew, he thought to himself? He's been nothing but a nuisance since becoming my aide at the beginning of this campaign. Both officers and enlisted men despise him, and the only reason no one has shot him is because I haven't put him in command of soldiers. Maybe I should, he mused.

"Well, General, what shall I do?"

The general gave serious thought about telling him what to do, but instead stood and said, "Let's take a look at these dangerous people, and see what Captain McCulley has to say."

Outside, the general saw the tight group of civilians, noticed the terrified Adelaide being held by three women, and a young man with anger and worry on his face. Captain McCulley stood to the side with a look of consternation. The young captain saluted sharply when his eyes met the general's. It didn't take long for the general to make a decision.

"Major Ferris," the general said. "Why don't you check at the Quarter Master Depot, see if that load of blankets arrived, and make sure they get distributed right away."

The major's face darkened, and there was no hiding his anger, but he saluted, mounted his horse, and rode away. Watching his aide disappear, General Curtis sighed, shook his head and motioned for Captain McCulley to approach. The captain told Pleasant's story. Pleasant observed it all and watched the general intently. He noted the general was middle aged with a receding hairline. Bushy sideburns and thinning hair, once brown, was quickly graying. The ruggedly handsome face was lined, and his deep-set brown eyes looked tired. *The general looks like a man carrying the weight of command heavily,* Pleasant thought. *I only hope he's also a man of conscience and character.* At one point, the general shook his head and rolled his eyes. Then he looked inside the tent and called his personal physician to come outside. When the doctor appeared, he motioned him toward the ladies and asked Pleasant to come forward.

"Mr. MacEver, I'm General Curtis. Accept my apologies for this incident. Captain McCulley's told me the story. Would you see if you can coax the ladies inside with the doctor? He'll look at your sisters' wounds and take care of them. He's a good man."

"Thank you, General. I would be most grateful," Pleasant said and took the general's hand. The grip was warm and strong.

Inside the tent, an orderly brought warm water, soap, and towels for the ladies. The general personally poured hot tea for the women, and after a few minutes, even Adelaide had relaxed under their host's courtly manners and hospitality. Finally, the doctor sat his own tea cup down and took Adelaide's bandage off.

"Who dressed your wound young lady?" the doctor asked kindly.

"My Aunt Judith over in Indian Territory," Adelaide answered softly.

"You can tell your Aunt Judith for me she did a good job. I'll just clean it a little and put on a fresh bandage." After dressing the wound, the doctor poured some white powder into her tea. "This will help with the throbbing. I think in a few days the wound will heal nicely."

"And you must be Bertie, let's see what you have," the doctor continued as he moved to her side.

As the doctor went about his job with the women, the general walked outside with Pleasant and Captain McCulley.

"Do you know which partisan group was responsible, Mr. MacEver?" the general asked.

"My brother told me it was Quigley's Rangers," Pleasant answered.

The general nodded knowingly. "Heard of 'em. Look, Mr. MacEver, I've been in Missouri long enough to know the bloody record of these partisans. Bloody on both sides, I might add. Frankly, it seems many of them aren't much better than murderers and thieves." With a deep breath and heavy sigh, he continued. "If I had my wishes, most of them would be locked up, and we'd fight this war without them, but it's not a perfect world, the war is a bloody affair, and we take help where we can find it. However, what happened to your family is unforgivable, and your brother shouldn't have to be hiding in, Texas, did you say?"

"Yes, sir, he's gone to Texas."

The general smiled. "Of course he did. I hope he gets there safely." Then he turned to the captain. "Captain, I want you to take four men and escort this family to Pineville." Then he laughed. "Oh, ride behind them this time."

Within thirty minutes, the family pulled away from the general's tent with an armed escort of five men following.

"Well, Doctor, what do you think?" the general asked, taking a long puff off his cigar. "Think the MacEver brothers will be fighting with us or against us?"

The doctor watched the wagon grow smaller for a few seconds and then replied with a grin, "Which side would you fight for if your family had suffered these horrendous things? By the way, I know the Quigley family. Grew up in the same county they did. Amos Quigley got what he deserved. Hope it was a belly shot and he had a painful death. Sure you didn't make a mistake by sending them on their way?"

"Don't believe so. Besides, what could they tell? I can guarantee Sterling Price already knows we're here, and it won't be long til this army is fighting Sterling's Home Guard and other Confederate troops out of Arkansas and Louisiana. We've got to face the enemy in this part of the state and have a decisive victory to secure all of Missouri for the Union. A bloody day is coming soon, very soon. Oh, by the way, ever heard of this MacEver family?" the general asked.

"Just heard of them, that's all. Didn't know them personal, but I heard tell of Burton and Ambrose MacEver. They did a lot of trading and were well know even up in Newton County where I came from. I'll say this. Hope they do stay with our side. From what Pleasant told us, his brother must be one hell of a warrior."

The general nodded in agreement and jabbed his cigar at the wagon. "And that young man is very intelligent and thoughtful. I like his bearing and the way he carries himself. Which ever side he takes, he'll probably be in command of men, and he'll make a good field officer. Too bad he'll probably be fighting on the other side. We need good field officers, Samuel. Damn, we need good officers. And then there's my wife's nephew. I love her dearly, but he's become a burden, and with his political connections, he'll probably be a general someday, and I'll end up as his orderly. Damn this bloody war to hell. Damn the day I went to West Point. Soon, I'll be sending boys to their deaths. God help me. God help all of us. God forgive us all. Speaking of hell, I've got to get more cavalry patrols out. McCulley will be busy tomorrow."

"General, listen to your doctor's orders. You need a glass of good brandy. Come back inside with me. I just happen to have a bottle in my medicine bag. That is, if you're willing to take some medical advice and also willing to share one of those cigars."

The general grinned. "I just might have one or two left. My heavens, I do appreciate the expert advice of this army's best surgeon." He put his arm around the doctor's shoulder and they both went inside. "Don't forget to save some brandy for tomorrow. The sergeant major from the supply depot will be wanting my hide for sending Ferris to him this afternoon. Even a general doesn't relish facing the wrath of a crusty, old, Irish sergeant major."

The two sentries standing by the entrance of the tent grinned as they snapped to attention and saluted when the two men entered laughing.

They also knew Major Ferris well, quite well indeed.

On the road to Pineville, Captain McCulley urged his horse ahead and rode beside the wagon. "Where did you learn to handle a horse and wagon so good, Miss Bertie?" he asked.

Bertie turned her face to his and said, "From Newton, my brother," she answered "I like horses, and I'm a good rider too. We raised horses, so I've been around them all my life. Where you from, Captain?" She smiled again and blushed. She thought this young man was handsome with his boyish face and kind hazel eyes. Besides, he had shown kindness toward all of them.

"Illinois. The army brought me to Missouri, so it's my first time here." Even with the bandage covering one side of her face, there was no hiding Bertie's beauty, he thought. He loved her wide, open, blue eyes and the deep dimples that appeared when she smiled. He was also drawn to her strong character and the open straightforward look in her face. He was enraged when first seeing her bruised face and felt protective for both Bertie and her sister. At the time, he wanted to wrap his arms around both of them.

"Illinois. My sister's husband is in Illinois with the army. That's where his parents are from," Bertie said. "Do you miss home, Captain?"

"Sometimes I get a little homesick, but mostly there's not time to think about it." Then, he grinned and continued. "But now and then you meet someone who takes your mind off home. There's no need to be formal. My name's John."

Bertie blushed again and thought, why, he's flirting with me, and here I am all dirty and bandaged. She had little experience with boys except teasing when she was younger, and suddenly she liked being flirted with by a handsome young man. She liked it very much indeed.

"So, tell us, Captain, do you like being in the army?" Barthenia asked, with just a hint of a mother's protectiveness in her voice. "My daughter's a very mature young lady to be only sixteen, don't you think?"

The Captain was taken aback a little, but replied, "Why, yes Ma'am, I do like the army. I intend to make it my career, and yes, your daughter is very mature and very pretty too. In fact, all the MacEver ladies are very pretty indeed, if you don't mind me saying so." With that, he tipped his hat to the ladies and moved ahead to ride with Pleasant.

Frances leaned into Barthenia, patted her on the shoulder and laughed softly. Adelaide even managed a grin over the little flirtation attempt by the young man. She liked him also. Bertie flushed a deep red and could only think, oh, Mother. Then she grinned. She hadn't known it could be so nice having the attention of a handsome, young man. Now she understood what Florence meant when talking of the "warm feelings" she had around Mark Murray. She was also disappointed that the Captain had given up so quickly.

"We don't mind you saying so at all," Frances shouted as the Captain moved ahead.

The young man turned, grinned broadly, then with a flourish, took his hat off and bowed from the waist.

"We should be seeing the town in ten minutes or so," Captain McCulley said to Pleasant. "I've enjoyed meeting your family. I'm glad our paths crossed this day."

"I do believe my wife and sisters are glad for the crossing also," Pleasant said with a big smile. "They are a bouquet of beautiful red roses, I must admit."

The captain turned to Pleasant with a big grin and said, "Yes, indeed, Mr. MacEver, you're a fortunate man. I envy you and whoever meets your sister when she's of age. I thought for sure she was eighteen or better. Oh, well, it's my misfortune."

Pleasant chuckled and stuck his hand out to shake the captain's. "Well, John, it may be a long war, and she'll be in Pineville. Call me Pleas. All my friends do."

John pumped Pleasant's hand firmly and with warmth. Then he returned Pleasant's pistol and said, "Yes, by thunder, it may be a long war, and no one can know when our paths may cross again, Pleas. Let's pray it's not on opposite sides of a battle field."

"Amen to that, John. Let's pray not. Well, there's Pineville."

They stopped just outside of the town's limits to part and say good-by. Captain McCulley dismounted and walked to the wagon to say farewell to the ladies. As he said good-by, he removed his hat and kissed the hand of each. Even Adelaide enjoyed this small display of old fashioned, courtly charm. They all waved as he joined his men, and with a last wave of good-by with his hat, he rode back to his destiny. Within two months, he would fall at the battle of Pea Ridge as his cavalry company met the Cherokee Mounted Rifles on the border of Missouri and Arkansas. The family moved toward the Murray home and final sanctuary.

"Oh, I like that young man," Barthenia said. "Did you like him, Bertie? He seemed taken by you."

"Oh, Mama," was all she said. With grin on her face, she thought oh, yes, I liked him very much.

The Murray family was watching from the window as the MacEvers pulled up in front of their impressive new home. They were on the front porch quickly to welcome this family who had lost so much since last seeing them only two weeks before.

"Come in, come in," J.P. and his wife Cynthia said. They embraced each one and guided them all inside.

"Marcus, you and George see to the horses. It'll be dark soon," Cynthia told her oldest sons. "They're all tired now and will want to clean up. We'll eat when you finish."

"How was the trip," J.P. asked Pleasant as he showed him to the parlor.

Pleasant went through the entire trip again for J.P.'s sake. He left out no details about the incident at the Union encampment and the major's behavior. J.P. laughed heartily when hearing about the general's attitude toward his nephew and the courtesy extended by General Curtis and the young captain. Cynthia was busy with the women. She took them to the bathing room to help with their baths. Later, when everyone had cleaned up, they talked more over the meal Cynthia had prepared.

"I believe Newton will be just fine with Judith and her family," J.P. offered.

"Of course he will," Frances said. "Newton loves Judith and her family. He'll be a big help to her while the boys are away."

"Frances is right," Pleasant said. "By the way, J.P., when the ladies are settled, I'll be looking for a recruiter from Parsons' Brigade."

"You and Newton have made your decision. I'll help with that, and you won't have to worry about the women. Tomorrow, we'll show them the cottage I told you about. Looks like it'll be finished by next week. There's room for all four, and it'll be furnished nicely too. You'll see."

"I'm taking the ladies shopping for clothes tomorrow," Cynthia said. "And don't worry about money."

Pleasant held up his hand. "Please, Cynthia, you're too kind. Newton gave me some money for his mother and sisters, and I have funds in the bank here. We'll pay for the clothes."

"All right then, but it's our store, so you'll get a big cut from the regular price."

"Thank you, Cynthia," Barthenia interrupted. "You and J.P. have done so much already, taking us in like this."

"Oh, Barthenia. We only do what you would have done and what your faith and mine teaches." Then she smiled broadly and tried to lighten up the dinner table conversation. "Besides, the church members will probably take up a collection for me now that I'll have the MacEver women in church every Sunday to liven up our poor little choir."

As J.P.'s other five children visited politely, Marcus seemed lost in his own thoughts and only picked at his food. He had been shocked and grieved deeply on hearing about Florence's death. He had loved her and was prepared to ask Newton for her hand.

Pleasant noticed and understood. "Marcus, would you help me find a good buggy? That old wagon has to go. Know anyone looking for one?"

Marcus perked up a bit. "Sure, Pleas. I'd like to help. I'm running the lumbermill for father now, and we could use another wagon. Oh, want to go hunting while you're here?"

"Good idea, Mark," Pleasant said with a broad smile, "but let's go north for our hunting. There's a little too much activity south of here. I'd hate to have that Major Ferris arrest me for attacking the Union army when he hears the gunshots. Probably hang me on the spot."

"Oh, girls," Cynthia said smiling. "It's going to be wonderful having a house full of book lovers. J.P. nods off when I start talking about the latest book I've read. Oh, come and see the additions in the library while the men talk about hunting and business."

The women left the dining room, and J.P. leaned closer to Pleasant. He said, "I've met a couple of recruiters who show up in the area from time to time looking for volunteers. I'll introduce you the next time one of them is here."

"Thanks, J.P. That's most helpful, but for now, I need to look after my family. When the ladies are settled, I'll be ready to join up. We'll need to get word to Newton also."

"We can still get mail to Indian Territory. Authorities haven't tried to stop either mail or trading across the borders," J.P. said.

"Pleas, are you sure Newton's gonna be safe?" Marcus asked. "There's a rumor the Union is going to invade Indian Territory from Kansas."

"Haven't heard that, but Newton knows how to be careful. Right now he's safe, but I'll be glad when we're both in Arkansas with Parsons' people. Until then, let's pray he stays out of harm's way."

"Amen to that," J.P. responded. "Newton will be in our prayers."

Chapter Seven
The Hunters, March 1862

At the MacEver family's ruined home, two men talked about Newton. They were full of hate and held a fanatical thirst for vengeance. Thoughts of retribution consumed their very being to the point they no longer considered taking part in the war important. Like a malignant tumor, this rage of enmity had eaten their souls to its core, destroying even reason. Both men were in disheveled civilian clothes, and the trademark bright red hair had the same unkempt look Pleasant observed two months earlier.

"You think that Newt fella's really in Texas?" Joshua asked his brother.

"Not sure," Jonah answered. "Maybe so, maybe not. Could be in Indian Territory with his breed kin. We learned some things by hangin' around Pineville. Could be we can learn more over in Indian Territory."

"Yep," Joshua replied. "Found out that Pleasant fella was a MacEver after all. His sisters and mother are with him. Too bad we didn't shoot that grinnin' snake when we had a chance."

"Maybe. Don't know if that woulda got us any closer to Newt though. If that cowardly Jay Hawker, Colonel Wiggings, woulda done like we told and raided Indian Territory, we might have had him.

Pleasant and the MacEver women can wait till later. For now, finding Newt MacEver is our main job. At least we got a description of him from the blacksmith at Honey Springs. To think our brother once looked up to the Jay Hawkers."

"Yeah, but all Wiggins said was he didn't approve of what Amos did. He can rot in hell! His hands ain't clean either. That soured me on fightin' this war." With that off his chest, Joshua spit a long stream of tobacco juice.

"Me, too," Jonah replied with both his opinion and tobacco juice. "But it's wastin' time guarding this place any more. That Pleasant remembers what we said, so no MacEvers will be comin' here. We'll spend time around Pineville and the Honey Springs settlement kind of quiet like and see what we learn. We'll head over to Indian Territory later this summer when we know more. For now, Honey Springs and Pineville be the places to watch. After we take care of Newt, we're gonna have us a talk with his brother."

"You gonna shoot em, Jonah? How bout them MacEver wemmen?" Joshua asked with a cackle.

"Maybe I'll just cut his lying tongue out. Don't know yet. Kinda sweet on that little Bertie gal, ain't you? Glad the store clerk pointed the sisters out to us. They ain't bad to look at. Don't forget, Pleasant knows what we look like. Think we better cut our hair and keep covered when we go back."

"Yeah, shave too. We'll find Newt," Joshua said. "And like Amos done told us, be patient like, sometimes you gotta be patient when killing's gotta be done, real patient."

"Yeah, and this is a killing that needs to be done real bad like. We'll do it too. If it takes the rest of my life, Newton MacEver will die at my hands."

The brothers were silent for a long while, each lost in his own thoughts—malevolent, consuming, and soul destroying thoughts having nothing to do with justice. Joshua, mentally the slower of the two, began to chew silently on a wad of an idea. It took a while to gel in his head, but finally he thought he could contribute something positive. He was quite aware others thought him dull and not as smart as his brothers. And in the past, more than one unfortunate who questioned his intelligence had been the target of his uncontrollable temper, paying with broken bones—on one occasion, with a life.

"Jonah, how do people in Pineville get mail to Indian Territory?"

Johah gave his brother a puzzled look. "I suppose with someone taking trade goods or happens to be goin' that-a-way. Have to ask the postmaster for sure. Why?"

Joshua grinned, showing ugly, stained teeth. "Suppose those MacEver gals ever write their brother?"

Jonah stared at his brother blankly for a minute. Then he returned his own flawed smile and said, "Bet they do. By Gawd, you got something Joshua. We just might get to read a letter from Pineville before it reaches Newt or his kin. If we do, we'll know for sure where he is. You're on to something."

They both began to laugh, it was ugly laughter, obscene laughter, and it rang over the ruins of the burned out home like the insulting cries of buzzards heard by a white tail doe as she watched her dying fawn being torn apart.

Chapter Eight
Indian Territory, March 1862

Newton stood in the middle of the freshly plowed field. He had a "good tired," his father would have said, and by tomorrow, he and David would be sowing. He breathed deeply of the freshly plowed earth, inhaling the pungent aroma of damp soil. In his mind, it was a perfect day, almost spring after a long winter that brought a final blast of wind, freezing temperatures, and sleet the first week of March. Now, scattered clouds muted the glare of the overhead sun, and the sky was a vivid blue, holding the promise of spring rites. This week, David and I will be planting, he mused with a smile. As he surveyed his work, he thought of his father and learning to work the land from him. Good memories from a good man, Newton recollected. Learning to farm and work with the order and disorder of nature was hard, but learning to plow straight rows with a mule who had his own mind was even harder. His father worked in the trading business with Ambrose and did well, but in the end, sold his business interests and returned to farming, his first love. Even grandfather James had a trading business, but most of his life was spent farming the large spread back in Georgia, the site of Newton's own birth. He remembered and became lost in thought— Georgia. Burton had brought his family to Missouri when Newton was only five, so his memories were dim except for 1850. That year, Burton took his family back to Georgia for the reading of his father's will and to comfort his mother. His uncles were there and so was Pleasant. Newton was only nine at the time, but Pleasant was sixteen and almost grown. It was the first time Newton had memories of Pleasant. They both hit it off immediately in spite of their age difference. A few years later, Pleasant would come to visit before his adventures in the Rockies and California with three friends. He stopped again on his way back and stayed. He had been in Missouri ever since, except for a brief sojourn in Georgia to woo and wed the beautiful Frances Cleveland.

"Newton, Newton," little Frances cried, waving a letter. "Mail from Pineville. Mama just brought it from town."

Newton looked up from his revery to see Frances running toward him as he wiped the sweat band of his floppy hat with a bandana. She bounded over the furrowed ground like a nimble fawn, laughing as she ran toward him and waving the letter with excitement. He smiled.

"Guess who it's from," Frances said, hiding the letter behind her back. She giggled as she played her game.

"Me don't know. Me don't know nobody who can write." Newton said. "Me can't read anyhow."

"Yes, you can, please guess," she pleaded.

Newton smiled down at her and said, "All right, I'll guess on the way back to the porch. Is it from Abraham Lincoln or Jeff Davis?"

"No, Silly. They wouldn't write to anyone at Honey Creek."

"Why, they might. I bet they need my advice. My brother?"

"No, not Pleas. Guess again," she said, as Newton picked his cousin up and carried her the rest of the way.

"Hummm, this is hard. I know. It's from Adelaide."

"You're getting closer," Frances said.

Newton sat his cousin down on the porch step and took a seat next to her. "I give up, Frances. I just can't think of anyone else who might write a letter to me."

Frances held the letter in front of her and pointed at the name on the return address. "B-E-R-T-I-E. It says Bertie." She smiled broadly. "See, I read the name. Can I open it for you?"

"Of course you can, and after I read it, you can get me a drink of water."

She carefully opened the envelope and removed the letter, then solemnly handed it to Newton. He took the letter and read it aloud for her. The letter was full of news from Pineville and his family's love for him. Bertie also expressed concern about her cousins. There had been news that Stand Watie's command had been part of a bloody battle at Pea Ridge, Arkansas. Frances hung on to every word as he read. Bertie also said Pleasant was busy trying to raise an entire company of men for Parson's Brigade.

Frances clapped her hands when he finished. "Thank you, Newton. Oops, I mean James," she said as she laughed and covered her mouth. "I forgot. You have to give me a kiss. Bertie says so." With that, there were more giggles.

Newton smiled and put his arm around Frances, then kissed her on the cheek with exaggerated smacking sounds. He said, "Oh, it's nothing to worry about when we're alone, but where's my water?"

"Oh, no, not again. I forgot," she said and ran to the well.

Newton watched Frances struggling at the well to pull up a bucket of water. After several tries, she finally raised a partially filled bucket and carefully placed it on the lip of the well's masonry wall, then dipped the drinking gourd into the cool, clear water. When the gourd was full to the brim, she walked cautiously back to him, holding the vessel gingerly in her small hands. Each time a step brought a slosh of water over the gourd's brim, she would stop and look at Newton with a pained expression. Watching her, his heart ached, and he suddenly had a deep longing to have a family of his own with a daughter like this precious child.

"She adores you," Judith said as she stepped from the house onto the porch. "She simply adores you. When you leave, she'll mourn, and I dread that day."

"And I her, Aunt Judith. Just now, I had a sudden great longing in my heart to have my own family with a little girl like Frances. It makes me sad sometimes, and I don't know why I feel sad. Maybe it's because I don't know when that day will come or if it ever will."

"You'll have your own family, Nephew. This I know, but not until the war is over, and it will be. All wars finally end."

"Oh, here's Bertie's letter," Newton said, "if you'd like to read it."

"Oh, yes, I want to read Bertie's letter. She always has news and just reading her
beautiful handwriting's a pleasure. Wa do. I'll read it inside."

"There, I made it," Frances said, holding the gourd out to Newton. "I didn't spill much, did I?"

Newton took the half empty gourd and said, "Nope, you sure didn't." Then he raised it to his mouth and drank it all in one long gulp. "Ahhhh, Frances. Good job. Don't know if I could go on if you weren't here to help me. Thank you."

"You're welcome," she piped. "I like helping you, Newton. It's fun." She grinned broadly as she rocked back and forth on her heels with hands clasped behind her.

Newton wiped his mouth and then impulsively picked his cousin up, sat her on his lap, and held on tightly. "I love you, Frances. I love you the most, yes, I do."

When the hug was over, Frances held Newton's face in her hands and looked long and intently into his eyes. "Mama says you have to go soon. I want you to stay here forever. Why do you have to leave? Everybody always leaves here. It makes me sad." Two large tears slid down her cheek and dropped on Newton's hand.

He choked back his own and said hoarsely, "I have to help my brother do important business in Arkansas, but it's not so far away, and it won't take forever. I'll be back, and I promise to write when I'm gone. And after I return, maybe I'll find a Cherokee lady who doesn't think I'm too ugly. I could live here in the Cherokee Nation."

Frances clapped her hands together, put her nose to Newton's and said, "Amanda Beck's real pretty and she's eighteen already. How 'bout her?"

"Yes, she is. She's very pretty, but I think your brother John is sweet on Amanda. He might not like me marrying her."

"Oh, I forgot. Will you really write to me? Nobody ever wrote me a letter. I can read, and I can write too. Papa taught me all my letters before he went away. I miss Papa. He used to hold me the way you do. Can people write letters from heaven?"

"I promise to write, and I know you can read. Your mama tells me how smart you are in school." Newton paused. Frances's eyes were solemn. "Yes, Frances, I think people we love do write us from heaven but not on paper. They write their words in our hearts."

"Do people out of heaven write on our hearts too?" She was still looking into his eyes intently with her head tilted to one side.

Newton thought for a moment. "Sometimes they do. You've written on my heart, and I know what it says."

"What?"

"It says I love you forever, and you're my forever friend."

"Forever! Yes, Newton. That's right. Forever and ever." She squeezed his neck again.

"Now scat back in the house, and help your mama with the chores," he told her. "I've got work to finish. We're late with the planting after waiting out the last cold spell."

"I'll bring you and David something to eat when Mama fixes it," she said and ran into the house.

As Newton walked back to the field, he saw David putting away the mule and plow. He felt good about their progress. They were a little late, but not too late for good crops on Honey Creek, not too late at all. He began to whistle as he walked across the field. He'd have to write and tell Bertie the good news that her three cousins survived the battle.

Chapter Nine
The Hanging

Spring turned to summer, and on the last day of July, after getting all the hay in, Newton became apprehensive. There had been no word from Pineville for three weeks, and he normally had letters twice a month from Bertie. He thought of these things one hot, sultry day as he rested in the shade of the porch and talked with David and Marshall about the farm's progress.

"What's wrong, Newton? You look worried," David asked.

"I am. Haven't heard from Bertie, and I should have. It's about time to find Parsons' Brigade in Arkansas, and Pleasant should have let me know by now. I've got a bad feeling. something is wrong. Don't know why, just a bad feeling in my gut, and I need to be prepared. Don't even know what I should take with me."

"Got a suggestion for you," Marshall offered. "I've heard about the shortage of supplies for Confederate troops in Arkansas. Pay a visit to our trading post. Get some sturdy trousers, shirts, and heavy shoes or boots. If I were in your place, I'd give up your father's flintlock, and buy a new Springfield. The trading post has some in stock. I keep hearing rumors some of the Confederate soldiers have to wait for hand-me-downs if they enlist without their own weapons. Anyway, get what you need now, so you'll be ready when word does come."

"You're right, Uncle Marshall. Think I'll go today. I promised Frances some hard candy anyway. Want to go along?"

"Come to think of it, sure. I could use a couple of things. David?"

"Yeah, haven't been in a month. I'll tell Ma and the girls. Let's all go."

Two hours later, they were at the trading post in Honey Creek's growing hamlet. Newton and Marshall rode on horseback, and David and his sisters followed in the buggy. Inside the store, Newton quickly found tinned beef, utensils, clothes, and another blanket to take with him, but lingered over purchasing the Springfield rifle and accessories. It fired a Minie ball, using a percussion cap, and this was something Newton wasn't familiar with. Invented by a Frenchman, the bullet shaped Minie ball wasn't a ball at all, but American soldiers had named it after the inventor with a bastardized version of his name. The bullet shaped 58 caliber Minie ball came in a paper cartridge with powder and was fast to load. When fired, the lead projectile expanded to fill the grooves of the rifled barrel, giving it accuracy over three hundred yards. The sales clerk explained in detail cleaning, loading, firing, and maintenance procedures. Newton was experienced with rifles and absorbed the information quickly. As Newton and Marshall visited with the clerk about the Springfield, David helped his sisters pick out material for new dresses and got a hat for himself. No one was in a hurry. It was pleasant socialization for the family to go shopping in town. Newton had bought Frances some hard candy and her right cheek bulged from a piece as she sucked the wonderful, sweet flavor. She also enjoyed looking at the beautiful material laid out in neat stacks on the counter tops.

"From Connecticut," the clerk said to Mary. "Their mills are famous for turning out durable cloth. Just look at these choices, Ladies. Blue, green, red, brown, yellow, gray, and butternut. Over here, we've got some beautiful plaids and prints also."

The girls began to drape different bolts of cloth across each other to test the colors, and there was laughter as they teased Frances about the scarlet cloth she wanted. Newton could hear the banter coming from his cousins and smiled. It was obvious the girls were having a good time on the shopping spree. Over his aunt's protest, he had agreed to buy each member of the family something today. David had his hat. and the girls would have their material. It pleased Newton to buy these things for his cousins, and he also gave instructions to buy something pretty for their mother. He had the money, and besides, Newton had been thrilled with the leather belt and holster David made for his Colt revolver. It was patterned after the army holster and belt it originally came with, but David used deer leather and added some Cherokee flourish. Newton thought it a work of art and was touched deeply by his cousin's gift.

As the family enjoyed their day of shopping, two men talked over their lunch of boiled eggs and cornbread on the far side of the store. This was the darker corner of the trading post, and the family hadn't noticed these two men absorbed in their own conversation.

"The letter didn't say whether Newt was in Texas or here," Joshua said.

"No, but it was coming here. Must mean he's here," Jonah responded. "Don't see no other choice."

"Maybe, but if it be going to Texas, this would be the best way. Just go south from here, I'd think. Besides, that clerk feller said he heard Newt went to Texas."

"I don't trust nobody, Joshua, no more, specially no breed. Everybody says he's gone to Texas. I'm beginning to figger that's the plan. Make us think Texas is where he's laid up, then keep his sorry hide hid away someplace round here. Another thing, you shot the mailman before I could ask all my questions. Might have told us where the letter was going."

Joshua was defensive. "Got the letter and more out of him. Had good Union gold from Murray to pay this store owner for hides. Yeah, I liked killin' him. Didn't like his uppity attitude. Thought he be better than us. Now he's just deader than us." Then he began to laugh at his own wit, almost choking on the boiled egg he had stuffed in his mouth. After spewing half the egg on the table and washing down the rest with a gulp of beer, he noticed his brother was staring toward the counter where two men were looking at rifles.

"Whatcha lookin' at, Jonah?"

"The Injun. Don't that fella look familiar? Remember the Cherokee that Pleasant had with him?"

Joshua looked carefully at Marshall. "All Injuns look the same to me. What does it matter? Dresses kinda fancy don't he though? Bet he's uppity too. Can't bear a Injun who thinks he's good as white folk. Too bad we're here. If we was in Missouri, I'd shoot him."

Jonah sighed. "Here's why it matters." Sometimes Joshua's slowness riled him, and he patiently explained. "He was with Pleasant MacEver at Honey Springs on Cowskin Prairie. Remember? Then later, we find out Pleasant's a brother of Newt, so this Injun might know where he's hiding, that's all."

"Oh, see what you mean," Joshua said and stared hard at the two men. "Gawd, Jonah, what if that's Newt he's with?"

"We wouldn't be so lucky, besides this fella doesn't look right. No mustache and he ain't extra tall."

Joshua took his hat off and scratched his head. He wanted badly to say something smart after looking dumb again. His dull eyes glimmered a bit, and he said, "Brother, what if the description was a lie too?"

Jonah looked at his brother and smiled. "Possible brother, possible. If this is Newt or if we find him someplace else here, remember just where we are. I don't wanna be hung by Cherokees, and that's gonna happen if we ain't careful. This ain't Missouri, and we're surrounded by his breed kin. We get caught, we hang before sundown."

At the counter, the brothers had not gone unnoticed by Marshall's watchful eyes. He had watched the men obliquely since he saw them when first entering the store. The clerk waiting on them was Henry, his nephew by marriage. He already told them these two had asked if he knew a Newt MacEver. His response had been no, but heard he passed through on his way to Texas. Newton and Marshall were quite aware of the men but went on with the business of shopping, giving no indication of acknowledging their presence. Marshall's alarm went off when one of them took his hat off and scratched his head. The red hair, though short now, made Marshall realize why he thought the two men looked familiar. He kept the appearance of still being interested in the guns as he smiled and spoke in muted tones.

"Newton, I'm sure now they're the Quigleys. Henry, walk over and tell David to get the goods and girls to the buggy and go home quickly without showing alarm. He's to take Newton's other supplies also. We'll stay here at the gun counter and settle up in a few minutes."

As Henry walked slowly to the dry goods section, Newton and Marshall began to talk about the quality of the Springfield. Newton hoisted the weapon to his shoulder and aimed down the barrel to give the appearance of taking its measure. He slowly swung in a circle, and half way through his turn, the Quigley's came in sight. They both stiffened for a second as Newton paused just a second to give them a good look over. After finishing the circle, he placed the rifle back on the counter with a smile.

"Good feel, Marshall. Take a try," he said. Then he called loudly across the store, "I'll take it Henry."

"Good choice, James. I'll be there soon as I get these ladies' things to their buggy."

"Called him James," Joshua whispered to his brother in the corner. "Look at that though, the Injun's taken care of the breeds before the white man. What's this country coming to?"

"Yeah, well, I don't know. Guess it's their country. Why it's called Indian Territory. We'll bide our time. When he leaves, we'll follow. I got a gut feelin' something's wrong."

Outside, the family was ready to leave when Frances cried out, "I forgot," and ran to the door before anyone could stop her. At the store's entrance, she called loudly, "Thank you, Newton."

Newton and Marshall stiffened, but neither turned. Henry was quick enough to yell back, "You're welcome, Frances."

The two Quigley's froze and looked at the clerk, Newton, and Marshall with cold suspicious eyes.

"Whacha think, Jonah?"

"Damn, Joshua, I ain't sure. He don't look like what we was told, and the clerk called him James. Don't know what to think now. But I swear, the clerk was called Henry, and I got a raw feelin' in my gut that little breed girl was talkin' to this James fella. Don't let on anything's wrong. We'll follow when they leave. If we find him off some place alone, and he's not Newt, well, he's got money on him and a new rifle."

Joshua only nodded his head solemnly and marveled about how smart his brother was. Yes, sir, his brother was always thinking real deep like, he thought to himself.

A few minutes later, Newton and Marshall were standing by their horses and talking in front of the trading post. As Newton put things in his saddle bag, they spoke about their plan and kept a watch on the door. He stuck his new rifle in the leather sheath attached to the saddle.

"I'm riding east through town on the main road to Missouri," Newton said. "That'll keep them away from Aunt Judith's place. Do you know where the little creek flows across the low point in the road?"

Marshall nodded. "I know it."

"There's a game path to the right as you cross the creek. It follows the stream. If they're following me, I'll head up the creek and wait under cover. There's a cave a ways up the creek with a large outcrop of limestone above. That's where I'll wait."

Marshall nodded again. "Good. Let's ride slow and see what they do. If they follow us, we'll say good-by at the blacksmith shop. I'll go in and visit with John. If they follow you, I'll follow them."

They mounted their horses and slowly rode toward the Missouri border. Inside the dim light of the trading post, the Quigley brothers watched carefully and then walked outside as Newton and Marshall rode off.

"Let's go get 'em," Joshua said.

"Hold your horses. Let 'em get a ways up the road. We got time. We'll see if they stick together. Not really interested in the Cherokee. We don't know, he might be a relative of old Stand Watie. I sure don't want him chasing us. Remember what Amos said—patience."

The men mounted and followed their prey slowly.

"They following us?" Newton asked a few yards up the road as they approached the blacksmith shop.

"Oh, yeah, they're following," Marshall answered without looking back.

The two relatives stopped in front of the blacksmith's shop and made a point of shaking hands to say good-by. Marshall tethered his horse outside his brother-in-law's shop and waved to Newton. Out of the corner of his eye, he could see the Quigleys. Marshall walked inside and told John what was going on.

"They just rode by," John said.

"Thought they would. Newton's going to turn up the trail where the creek crosses the low point in the road. Know where it is?"

"Know it well. Want me to follow along?"

"Yeah, but I don't have a gun on me."

John nodded, turned and went to his office. He returned with a rifle. "Loaded and ready to use. My compliments." John stuck a revolver in his belt.

Marshall thanked him and tested the rifle's feel. "Let's walk outside and stretch," he said with a grin.

The Quigley brothers were just turning the bend in the road where it left the Honey Creek settlement and were soon out of sight. Marshall and his brother-in-law mounted and followed.

Up ahead, Newton was approaching the creek bed where he intended to turn off. Slowing, he strained to hear something behind him. He didn't want to look back and become obvious but wanted the brothers to see him turn off the main road. There was the distant snorting of a horse, and he continued. At the creek bed he turned up the game trail. When he was sure there was enough cover from the trees and brush, he kicked his horse into a run. He wanted to be in cover before the hunters caught up with him. A few minutes later, he waited patiently behind the outcrop of limestone above the cave. He waited with his new rifle ready, and once again he waited to kill. Confused thoughts were churning in his mind, a combination of apprehension and doubt.

As Newton carried on his internal skirmish, Marshall and John were talking to the local Cherokee constable who had recognized them as they passed by his office. The constable wanted to ask John about shoeing his horse and had ridden hard to catch up.

"You say these men mean to kill Newton?" Constable Ridge asked. The Constable was a cousin to the primary chief, John Ridge.

"That's right, Abraham," Marshall answered. "Their brother was the one Newton killed defending his family. They have murder in their hearts. These are evil men."

The constable nodded. He already knew the story, just as he had known Burton MacEver and his family for years. "Newton's a good man. I'll help. Rather not have a killing, but I sure ain't opposed to locking these two brothers up til Newton's safely gone to Arkansas."

"That's another worry. Newton expected to hear from Pineville two weeks ago about when to leave. Been no mail," Marshall said.

The constable rubbed his chin. "No one's had mail from Pineville. Got a notice two days ago from the McDonald County sheriff. A mail courier was found murdered just the other side of the border. He was carrying gold too. Murray sent him with both the mail and gold for our trading post. Let's not waste more time talking. Know the spot you're talking bout. I've waited behind those same rocks for a deer to pass by many times. Follow me. I know another way."

As he waited behind the rocks, Newton wasn't sure what he was prepared to do. The idea of just shooting the men bothered him. It was different a few months ago. During the raid on his home, he was defending himself and his family. This wasn't the same thing. He was convinced these two men wanted him dead, but he had no proof. He couldn't know for certain what was in their hearts, and the nightmares about the other shootings still troubled his sleep. He looked around him. The forest of green pine, cottonwood, and white oak was still and the air heavy and hot. No breeze brought cool relief as a bead of sweat dropped from his nose onto the gun metal gray of his rifle. He quickly dabbed it off with his shirt sleeve. To his left, a brown squirrel stood on his hind legs and watched him intently. Then it began the rapid chirping that sounded like scolding to Newton. Must be sitting on his favorite gathering ground he thought with a smile. He was beginning to worry a bit. The brothers hadn't appeared yet. He looked around but could see neither movement or other signs of men. The sky above was cloudless now, and the blue seemed a little washed out as the sun beat down without mercy. It was directly overhead, and the surrounding trees gave no shade to his spot. Hearing the song of a cardinal, he looked up to watch the bird preening his bright red coat. He wiped more sweat from his face with the back of his sleeve and watched the path again. Where are they? Then, with a glimmer of hope, he thought perhaps these men weren't the Quigley brothers after all. At that instant, he felt cold metal against his neck and the bone chilling sound of a hammer being cocked back into firing position.

"Don't move, Newton MacEver, and drop the rifle," Jonah Quigley said in a stone cold voice. "Now turn round, slow like."

Newton did as he was told and was immediately knocked to the ground by a heavy blow to the side of his head. For good measure, Joshua Quigley gave him a couple of kicks in the stomach.

"Enough," Jonah barked as he reached down and grabbed Newton's revolver from his belt. "Stand up and face justice you thieving murderer."

Newton stood and faced his hunters. Jonah only had hatred, cold murderous hatred, in his face, but Joshua seemed beside himself with glee and was almost dancing.

"Gotcha, Newt," Joshua said with a cackle. "We gotcha, by God, and now you're gonna pay. Thought we wuz dumb, didn't you? Thought we'd just ride into your trap. Not so smart after all. This be the place we slept last night. Saw you trottin' along slow like thinkin' we'd just go the same way you did. My brother, he's smart. Yes, sir. You was gonna bushwhack us like you did Amos." With that, he slapped Newton hard across the face twice, then spit a steam of dirty, brown tobacco juice in his face.

Jonah was looking at the revolver he took from Newton. "You stole this from Amos, didn't you, Newt?" His voice was cold and flat, the face still a mask of hatred.

Newton wiped the spittle from his face and said evenly, "My name's James, not Newt. I never heard the name before.

Joshua spit again and slapped again. Newton knew he was helpless at the moment and only stared hard at the two men. If he lived, he would remember. But now, he could only assume he would not live.

"Let's shoot em, and take his horse and things back to Missouri," Joshua said, cackling a hideous laugh. "I'll pay a visit to that little Bertie gal."

Newton's blood ran cold, and his face reflected contempt.

"Joshua, get that length of rope from your saddle bag," Jonah said flatly.

Joshua's eyes lit up with glee as he ran to his horse and fetched the rope. Newton thought the second brother was so excited and happy, he might collapse and have a fit.

"We're gonna do this slow, real slow," Jonah said evenly as he knotted the rope tightly around Newton's neck and then tied his hands behind him. Unlike his brother, he still revealed no real emotion.

"Let's put him on his horse," Joshua suggested.

"No. The two of us gonna hang him. That's justice. Throw the rope over that big limb. Then we'll pull him up slow like till his feet be dangling. I wanna see his sorry face turn purple. Might as well tell us. You be Newt MacEver that kilt our brother."

Newton looked at them coldly and answered. "The name is Newton John MacEver, son of Burton MacEver, and your brother died because he murdered my brother and sister. Yes, I killed him and I'm glad I did."

For the first time, Joshua showed real emotion, and then both brothers wrapped their hands around the rope and pulled. Newton was lifted off the ground and the results were immediate. There was no air, and his head felt like it was ready to explode. He couldn't even attempt to gasp for air. Within seconds his oxygen starved brain was becoming confused and he wanted to say something but couldn't. He only had an animal instinct to breathe fresh air and cool his burning brain. Spasms kicked his legs and feet into a dance of death.

"Drop the rope! It's the law," someone yelled. The brothers didn't, and a rifle shot rang out. Joshua went down crying out in pain as he clutched at his shoulder. Jonah dropped the rope and in a split second was on his horse. He disappeared into the woods headed for Missouri, only a mile away. Jonah left his beloved brother writhing in the dirt. Constable Ridge, John, and Marshall were at the fallen Newton's side within seconds. They cut the rope from his neck and hands. Marshall pulled his nephew into a sitting position and gave him two hard slaps on the back. Newton gasped and took in a deep breath. In a few minutes he was standing, dazed and bruised, but alive and breathing.

Newton shook his head and looked over at Joshua Quigley. He was still on the ground, moaning and cursing. The constable had already removed the man's weapon and was now searching through his saddle bags.

"My, my. Look what I found," Ridge said. "It's the letter bag from Pineville. Let's see what we got. Newton, here's the letter from your sister. Don't see no harm you reading it. It's already been opened. I'll need it back though."

Newton read the letter carefully and returned it. He kept the map that was included, and the constable made no protest. Newton knew the mail would be turned over to the McDonald County sheriff as evidence and so would Quigley.

"Somebody help me," Joshua whined.

The constable gave him a kick in the ribs and said, "Shut up. Lucky I didn't kill you. You'll be in my jail till the Pineville sheriff gets here to take you back to Missouri. You and your brother left the courier with a widow and five younguns. Ought to hang you with your own rope, but I'll let the boys over in Missouri do that. They'll find your brother too. Why, you can share the same gallows. Stop whining, the doctor will see you in jail."

"How bout Newt? He kilt our brother. That's why we was hangin' him."

"Newt! Why, this is James MacEver. There's no Newt MacEver in Indian Territory. He lit out for Texas months ago."

Within an hour, Joshua Quigley was in the local jail waiting for the McDonald County sheriff, and Newton was home with his cousins. It had been a long day, and Newton needed to get things ready to leave by morning.

"I'm to meet Pleasant at Caddo Creek, Arkansas, where Price's army is camped. He's already enlisted both of us in Company H of Parsons' Brigade. Seems he recruited this entire company of men for General Parsons. My, but Pleasant's been busy." Newton shook his head and chuckled. "Probably be general before I get there. I'm to meet him by August 5th. That's next week, Aunt Judith. If I leave tomorrow, I'll still be late, but it can't be helped. It's a long ride."

"Do you know where this camp is?" Aunt Judith asked.

"He drew me a map. It's near a town called Arkadelphia. Don't worry,

I'll find it. It'll be an adventure being on the road by myself. I've got to write Bertie, explain what happened, and tell her I'm on my way."

"Good, I'll post it tomorrow. You write the letter, and David will get your things ready."

Thank you again for the presents to all of us, Newton. You shouldn't have, but," she added with a grin, "I'm glad you did. You're a sweet man." Then she hugged her favorite nephew. "David is thrilled to have your old rifle. Hope the boy don't shoot his big toe off."

Newton laughed. "Don't worry, Aunt Judith. He won't."

Newton wrote his letter, telling Bertie all that happened this day. He thought she would at least be glad to hear one Quigley was in jail for murdering the mail courier. He didn't go into a lot of detail about the attempted hanging, but assured her he was safe and would be leaving for Arkansas in the morning. He did warn her that Jonah Quigley was on the loose and had watched his family in Pineville. He ended the letter by observing it might be ironic if Jonah were the one fleeing to Texas instead of himself.

"What do you think, Newton?" David asked.

Newton walked to the table and was impressed. The two blankets were tightly rolled and tied with rawhide. The saddle bags were full of his food supplies except for the fruit. His clothes had been folded neatly and rolled into a water proof canvas square that could double as a small tent in case of rain. His revolver and rifle had been cleaned and loaded. The pouch for his rifle's accessories had been attached to the belt and holster. Everything was in place.

"Thanks, David. Wonderful job. I really appreciate what you've done."

"It was fun, Newton, and thanks again for the rifle. I'm anxious to go hunting with it."

"I helped too, Newton," Frances said.

"I know you did," Newton said, and picked his cousin up to hug her. "Now you can help us put everything in the corner by the door. Your mama and the girls will have supper ready soon. Uncle Marshall and his family are coming too."

Supper that evening was bountiful to say the least, Newton thought.

After the meal was over, Newton and Marshall went to the porch and visited. They talked of many things, but mostly Newton listened. His uncle reminisced about the old days and his service as a scout with Bishop's Rangers in Georgia, where he met Ambrose and Burton. Then he talked of family.

"Newton, you're loved by many people. Remember them while you're away. Keep them and their love in your heart, and it will help keep the horror of war from building a nest. If not, you can become hard and soulless like the Quigleys and many more consumed by this war. When you dwell on hatred and bitterness, you feed them, and then you lose the battle and lose your soul. Do you know what I'm trying to say?"

"Yes, Uncle Marshall, and no, I don't want to become like the men who murdered my brother and sister. Since I was a child, I've learned many things from you. Your advice about overcoming fear helped save me in the woods against the two partisans who were trying to kill me. Thank you for your wisdom. Thank you for becoming my teacher and friend. I'll carry all those gifts from you in my heart for the rest of my life."

"I know you will. You've become a good man, and you'll grow into a wise one also. Remember this always. You carry your Cherokee family's love and prayers. And like all our other sons away fighting this war, on both sides, I might add, you'll be remembered in the prayers of the Cherokee lodge meetings every month."

Marshall stood up just as his wife and family walked out the door. It was time to leave, time to part, and time to say good-by. It was difficult for Newton to bid farewell, and tomorrow's parting would be hard also.

Late in the evening, Newton noticed Aunt Judith and his cousins scurrying back and forth with water to the porch. He was curious and walked outside. The family was pouring water into the large metal tub used for bathing when weather permitted. Hot water was also being added to the bath water.

"Tonight, you take a proper bath, Newton," Judith announced.

"Aunt Judith, that's too much work. I can do my usual cleaning with a wash rag."

"No, and don't argue. There's no telling when you'll ever get a chance for a proper bath again. So get ready. David, bring towels, the long brush, and soap for Newton."

"All right, Aunt Judith. Thank you." Newton was touched and knew there was no arguing with his aunt.

Soon, Newton was in the tub of hot water, soaking away the day's grime, the day's tiredness, the day's fear and stress. He was glad Aunt Judith ignored his feeble protest. Clean clothes were already laid out, and he would start his trip with a pair of his new gray trousers and shirt. Aunt Judith was already washing his dirty clothes, and they would be dried, ironed, and packed by morning. Yes, Newton thought to himself, it is better to remember kindness and love rather than the bitterness and hurt he had felt so much of. The entire family was exhausted by bedtime, and Newton's sleep was restful and not haunted. The next morning, Judith insisted they have a good breakfast together before leaving.

"More biscuits, Newton?" Frances asked with a big grin.

"Well, maybe just one more."

"Good." Then she broke open the steaming biscuit and spread a large dollop of peach preserves on each half. "Did you like the scrambled eggs. I stirred in the bacon bits."

"That's why they're so good. I should have known. My cousin, the world famous cook, helped."

Soon, Newton was finishing his last cup of coffee. He lingered as long as possible, then stood to say good-by. Aunt Judith had already wrapped some biscuit and bacon sandwiches for his lunch.

"It's time," he said. "I have to go."

Tethered to a porch post, his horse waited patiently. Newton shook his head and marveled at David's early morning hard work. The blankets, clothes, boots, eating kit, and even his heavy Cherokee coat were neatly rolled in a gum blanket behind the saddle. This rubber coated cloth sheet could also be a rain cover, and was Uncle Marshall's parting gift. He would need it. Behind the saddle on each side hung a large canteen of water. The saddle bags were bulging, and his sack of apples hung from the saddle horn.

"Rifle's in place too, New—uh James. You're ready to go, Cousin."

"Thank you, David," he said, then turned to hug his aunt and cousins. There were tears naturally. He had become even closer to his Cherokee family the past months. Frances stood expectantly with her hands behind her. He knelt on one knee in front of her, and she held out a bouquet of wild flowers, a red, yellow, and white bouquet of love. She began to sob and tears flowed as her chest heaved. He held her close, this child he would think of often in the coming years, then kissed away the tears.

"Frances, thank you. Here, put the bouquet in my shirt pocket, and I'll proudly wear it all the way to Arkansas. There won't be any other men with a bouquet from a beautiful girl. They'll all be so jealous." She arranged the flowers carefully, and the sobs began to calm as she concentrated.

"Will you still write me a real letter?" she asked.

"It's my promise. I'll write. Remember, I still have your message on my heart and your heart has my message." Finally, Newton could handle it no more. He kissed Frances and held her tightly. Then he embraced the other girls and Aunt Judith one more time, who was now shedding tears of her own. David held the reins of his horse and waited sadly. Newton shook hands with his cousin, slapped him on the back, said thanks, and mounted.

"Go with God," Judith shouted as he turned his horse toward Fort Wayne and southward. Turning, he waved his hat a final time and saw Frances in the road crying. She ran after him. Newton choked back a sob and kicked the horse into a gallop. A mile away, he slowed the horse down to a walk and concentrated on the many happy memories of Honey Creek.

"I'm coming, fellow Missourians. I'm James McEver, and we'll drive those Yanks out of Missouri." Then he laughed out loud at himself and his solitary bravado. "Well, we'll see," he continued and began to whistle *Dixie* as he rode toward the unknown horror of war.

As the day wore on, he thought about the Quigley brothers and wondered of their fate. He would find out later in one of Bertie's letters that Joshua was tried and convicted of murder in Pineville. A month after his trial, he was hanged on a gallows specially built for him in front of the jail. Witnesses said he went crying and begging for his life and had to be dragged to his fate. Bertie was the only MacEver present. J.P. was with her, and said there was no look of pleasure in her face, only a grim resolve. As soon as the trap door tripped, she turned and walked purposefully back home. Later, she said there was nothing to celebrate but thought it was simply justice done. The mail courier's wife and children were her friends, and the widow was left destitute, the children fatherless. It was justice, and the hanging was an end to it. No one ever collected the reward money for Jonah. He did flee to Texas where he fed his hatred for Newton, and it festered into a malignant tumor, destroying what little humanity was left in his soul. For now, he was out of the MacEvers' lives. Temporarily, he was out of their lives, but they would be touched by his malevolence again.

Part II
With Parsons' Brigade

Chapter Ten
To See The Elephant

"Everybody says we're gonna see the elephant tomorrow. Think we will, James? We gonna be fightin' them Yanks for sure?"

James MacEver looked at the youngster with a smile. The seventeen year old always made him smile. No matter the situation, the boy was always full of youthful curiosity and enthusiasm. He had attached himself to James only three weeks before when more Missourian volunteers appeared at Parsons' camp at Caddo Creek. Now, December was here, and with little time for preparation, Parsons' Brigade had marched to Prairie Grove in Northwest Arkansas to try and dislodge the Federal Army of the Frontier under General James Blunt. The promise of uniforms and equipment had not materialized, and like most of the Missourians, his companion carried what he brought from home. In his case, it was an old smooth barreled flintlock. There were a few, like James, who had Springfields, and others carried Richmonds, which were Confederate copies of the Union Springfield, but most had inadequate weapons like Henry, including old shotguns. Many were lacking proper winter clothes or sturdy shoes. On the second day out of Caddo Creek camp, Newton had given Henry his spare shoes to wear. The boy's feet were in pitiful condition, and his worn shoes were literally coming apart.

"Yeah, tomorrow we see the elephant. Parsons didn't march us this far just to exercise. Don't worry, there'll be lots of Yanks to fight, and I suspect they'll be ready for us."

"Why they call it seeing the elephant anyhow?"

"Don't likely know. Kinda strange. Just know it means, well, like your first baptism of combat."

"Your brother, Pleas, I mean Captain MacEver, he says you already seen that elephant. What was it like?"

"Not exactly, Henry. It wasn't a real battle." James took a deep breath. He wasn't in the mood to tell the story again. "This is my first real battle too."

"Are you scared? Don't tell nobody, but I'm scared thinking about tomorrow. They'll have cannon won't they? Hope I'm not a coward. Don't want to shame my folks or you."

"You'll do good. Don't worry and scared is okay. It's good to be scared. You should be. Thousands of Yanks will be trying to kill us. Just keep your mind focused on what to do to stay alive, and kill the enemy before he kills you."

"Focused?"

"Oh, just think about what you need to do instead of thinking on your fear. Turn that beef so it can roast some more on the other side. Word came down to prepare food for two days. There's enough for the two of us to carry in our haversacks. When it's done, we'll cut and salt it down. Already get your dried peaches put away?"

"Sure did, James, but I ate some already. You think the battle will last two days?"

"Don't know. Guess it could, or maybe last only a few hours. I don't know, but we gotta be ready. Why don't you fill the canteens while I watch our beef?"

James watched Henry walk toward the creek with the canteens and frowned. He was worried about the boy and wondered about the wisdom of General Hindman. He was taking this army against experienced, well equipped Union forces, and his own troops seemed so ill equipped and trained. Though he and Pleasant had enlisted back in August, many of these men, like Henry, had signed on just three weeks before. He felt they were not prepared. However, he knew morale was high. If nothing else, those men who were part of Parsons' brigade were enthusiastic and ready to do their best. The Missourians trusted Parsons just as they trusted "Old Pap," General Price. But Hindman was in charge of this combined army of soldiers from Missouri, Texas, and Arkansas, and he was an unknown entity as far as the Missourians were concerned, especially among the veterans who had combat experience with Sterling Price, whom they trusted. However, General Price was in New Orleans.

"What you musing about, Brother?"

James looked up with pleasure to see Pleas standing before him with his hands on his hips and smiling broadly.

"Wondering about the wisdom of taking poorly equipped and poorly trained men and boys into a major battle. Worries me, Pleas. Just worries me. That's all, Captain. Know I'm only a private, but still, I worry."

Pleasant squatted next to his brother and said, "Know what you mean. But don't forget, many among us are veterans, and the Texas and Arkansas boys fighting at our side have experience. We'll make ourselves proud, and I've got confidence in this army's ability. Know we're not a pretty site on dress parade, but we'll fight. General Hindman thinks we'll surprise the Yanks, and we can drive them back to Missouri. I know your concern, but we've also got good men like yourself lookin' after our fresh fish."

"Hope he's right. Still some grumbling among the Missourians about losing our horses when we signed on," James continued with a chuckle.

Pleasant laughed. "Yeah, all us Missouri boys were a little naive, weren't we? Thought we'd be riding off to war on our trusty steeds. Guess we should have looked up the meaning of infantry." They both laughed. "Mind if I have a bite of your beef?"

James took his knife and sliced off a piece for his brother. "So, how's this battle shapin' up tomorrow? Know anything us privates don't?"

Pleasant chewed his bite slowly and said, "All of Parsons' Brigade will form up on the left flank. That'll be our responsibility. Hindman wants to hit General Heron's army quickly and decisively. If that can be done, then we march into Missouri and take on General Blunt's Union troops across the border in Missouri."

"What if Blunt joins Herron? Think about it. If I left now, I could be in Pineville within two hours. The Yanks in Missouri are close."

"It would be trouble, but Hindman thinks he's staying put for now. How's your sleep going in the dog tent?"

"Fine. Henry's no problem as a tent partner. He carries his half and I carry the other. Gotten attached to him the past three weeks, but he has a lot to learn. Hope I can keep him alive till he does." He looked at his brother seriously. "How do you feel about leading these men into combat? Does it weigh on you? You recruited this company, and many of them are close friends."

"Yeah. It's not like back at Camp Caddo. This isn't drill, and it's not a game or marching on parade. Yes, I did recruit most of the seventy men in this company. Gotten to know them, care about them. Lord, yes, Brother, tomorrow weighs on me. It weighs on me heavy. I'm untested too. Will I be fit? Will I lead with courage? Will I lead with wisdom enough to keep my men from harm?" Pleasant stood up and looked around the camp. "I don't know."

"You will. The men respect you and have confidence in your decisions. They'll follow and do you proud."

"Ah, but there's the rub," Pleasant said with a slight smile. "Will the boys be glad of their confidence when the battle's over, or will they live to curse the day our paths crossed? Sleep well, Brother. Tomorrow we see the elephant." Pleasant started to walk toward his own tent, then turned and with a grin said, "Cannon to right of them, Cannon to left of them, Cannon in front of them Volleyed and thundered, Stormed at with shot and shell."

"Boldly they rode and well, Into the jaws of Death, Into the mouth of Hell Rode the six hundred—Tennyson," James said with his own grin. "Sleep well yourself, Pleas, sleep well."

"Was that the Captain?" Henry asked as he handed James his full canteen.

"Yeah, he just stopped by to chat. We'll be rising early tomorrow morning. I've already got the beef sliced and salted. Sun's goin' down. Put some more wood on the fire."

Henry and James took seats on logs and looked toward the west. The temperature was dropping fast now as they watched the sun's departing glory slipping beneath the horizon. Streaks of light gray clouds partially obscured the brilliant orange, and smoke in the sky from a thousand camp fires began to deepen the color into dark red. One lonely and stately pine tree in the far distance looked like a knife stabbing into the heart of the dying sun.

"Look, the sun looks almost blood red. Is it a bad sign?" Henry asked.

James noticed too, and it was an eerie sight. "Soldier's sunset," he responded, and in silence they both watched until only a faint glow remained to remind them of the sun's passing.

"Look around," James finally said, "and take comfort. We're not alone."

The boy followed James's gaze, and they both stood and turned in a 360-degree circle to take in the army's encampment. From the height of their position, they were rewarded with a remarkable sight. The glow from thousands of campfires like theirs shimmered over countless Confederate tents. James thought it awe inspiring and comforting.

"I ain't never been part of anything this big," Henry said. "Have you? It's kind of scary to think about."

"No, I haven't. Yeah, it's kind of scary in a way, but take comfort. Just think, all these lights are campfires with soldiers around them, and they'll be at our side come tomorrow. Remember what we see tonight if you feel alone during the battle."

"Yeah, I will. It's gonna be freezing tonight, James. That tent will be cold."

"Don't worry, I know how to take care of it. Get your cup. We'll have some coffee while we get serenaded. Boys in camp will be singing and playing before long. Listen."

The Arkansas and Texas camps were near by, and a male chorus rang out in the distance.

"The Texas boys," Henry said with a laugh as the lyrics of *The Yellow Rose of Texas* floated their way. "I like that song. Makes me think of Emilia back home in McDonald County. Think she's sweet on me a little. She cried when I told her I was joinin' up."

"You sweet on her a little?"

"Yeah," Henry answered, and James could see the blush even by campfire. "Guess I'm sweet on her a lot. We'll both be marrying age when this is over, and we talked about it some. Of course, I ain't had the gumption to ask her pap yet. You sweet on a girl, James?"

"No," he answered. "Not anymore. There used to be a girl in Pineville, I was sweet on. We went to church with her family, and she was a thing of beauty, but the family moved back to Illinois."

The Arkansas boys responded with their own song. It was a sad, sweet song of love, *Lorena*. Henry and James listened intently. It was obvious that the men singing had been together for a while. Their voices blended perfectly, and then one voice took over with the others following softly in the background. It was a rich tenor, and it moved the listeners. Even the chatter of their close neighbors stopped. The soldier's strong voice rose over the others and floated above the tents toward an inky sky illuminated only by distant stars that seemed to mirror the pin points of campfires below. James was disappointed when the song ended, but then a few yards away a group of soldiers from their own company took up with a slow version of *Dixie*. They were accompanied by John McCook and his violin. James already knew this private from St. Louis had studied music and was an accomplished musician. As soon as the singers finished *Dixie*, John continued alone on his violin with *Ashokan Farewell*. Those all around were quiet. James and Henry sipped their coffee and listened also. James always thought there were rare, special, fleeting moments in life that should be savored without interference, then nurtured and stored away to be remembered for a lifetime. He sipped his coffee and looked up at the stars, sharper now that wind had dissipated campfire smoke from the crisp air of winter. He concentrated only on the music and let every strain of the beautiful tune fill his soul. For at this time, in this place, with these comrades and their music, these vivid moments would be with him for the rest of his days. Years later, James would recall this interlude before the horror of battle as one of the most peaceful and pleasurable hours of his life. He would also discover, as other soldiers in other wars discovered, no one but another combat veteran could understand how he could feel this way before battle. No others could grasp the significance of snatching a moment of joy while waiting for carnage to begin again. And tomorrow? Tomorrow would also be remembered, but for different reasons. Those moments, he would spend a lifetime trying to forget, but like the memories he cherished, they would be with him as long as he lived. James closed his eyes and sighed as the music wound down to the ending.

"Really a sad tune," Henry said. "Makes me homesick and kinda blue listening to it. Does it seem sad to you?"

"Yeah," James answered hoarsely, "makes me a little sad too. But, it's beautiful and one of my favorites."

And so the evening went. Other songs rang out, many of them robust and happy tunes, but as December's cold bit deeper, and thoughts turned toward the coming battle, campfires began to dim, and soldiers retreated to their tents. Like all soldiers facing combat have done, they tried to rest as the coming baptism of fire haunted their sleep.

By candlelight inside the tent, James wrote in his new journal as he did every evening when he could. He wrote of his fears and doubts, his young comrade, and how the evening's songs had affected him on this night.

"You're right, James," Henry said. "These hot rocks help. Where'd you learn that trick?"

"Hmmm. Oh, from my Cherokee cousins and uncles." He looked up from his writing. The candle created a light and shadow dance across Henry's face, giving him a ghostly appearance. "Two things to remember. The rocks won't stay hot all night, so the trick is to fall asleep before they go cold. Next, don't turn over and lay your face against one of them while it's hot. Make your eyes water real bad."

"I notice you write a lot in that journal. Do you have your poems in it too?"

"No, not yet, just notes and ideas. I'll be writing poems from these notes one of these days. Let's get some sleep now. Tomorrow will come early." James blew out the candle .

Not far away, other soldiers slept their own haunted sleep. They were soldiers fighting for another cause, soldiers from places like Illinois, Iowa, and Ohio. Dressed in blue, many of them would also see the elephant for the first time on rising. Unknown to James, among those soldiers was his brother-in-law, the husband of his sister Josephine. They would not meet face to face in combat, and James would not know until the end of the war that his sister's husband slept

beneath these same stars and also dreamed of the elephant.

The next day, for reasons not shared with the rank and file, Confederate General Hindman abandoned his original plan to strike the Federal forces aggressively and boldly. Instead, he ordered his men to dig in to take a defensive position, then wait for the Union troops to attack first. If he had kept to his original plan, the battle may have turned out differently. To the Confederate's surprise, General Herron had force marched his troops from Missouri to reinforce General Blunt's Union troops at Prairie Grove and engaged the Confederates even before Blunt got his army into the battle. On the left flank, the Missourians came under heavy artillery fire, as all the Confederates did. They were heavily outnumbered, but they held their positions.

"Get down," James screamed at Henry and pulled the boy off his feet. The noise of the artillery barrage was deafening, and Henry panicked. His eyes were wide with fear, and he was shaking. The earth was being turned inside out all around them. The scream of the incoming shells made James's blood run cold, and each explosion vibrated through his body as he held Henry down and tried to burrow into Mother Earth. Between the noise of explosions could be heard even more horrid sounds—cries of wounded and dying men. Pleasant ran up and down his company's position, urging his men to dig in as deeply as they could.

"Hurry, Henry! Dig as far as you can under the log," James ordered and they both began to try and scoop out at least a partial shield from the missiles of death. Men all up and down the line were doing the same thing. Some even pulled the bodies of dead comrades over themselves.

"Down, keep down! Here comes more!" James shouted again. In the distance, came the rumble of Union cannon again.

Just as they both made themselves small as possible, the terrible screams of incoming shells began again. Some explosions in mid-air brought hail storms of red-hot metal, and ground burst again turned the earth inside out. There were more pitiful cries and moans of pain from the Missourians' ranks.

"I'm hit!" Henry yelled in pain. "God, I'm gonna die! Help me!"

James reached over and grabbed Henry. The back of his head and jacket were covered with blood. The boy's eyes were wild. His whole body shook, and he was beginning to cry. James looked carefully and could find no wound, just blood. Then he looked on the other side of Henry. There was a torn and bloody stump of a leg. Some unfortunate soul had been hit by the last shell and blown asunder. Part of the poor wretch's leg had hit Henry in the back.

"You're okay," James yelled into his ear. "You're not dying. Someone's leg just hit you. That's all."

James ducked again as another shell screamed and exploded close by. Oh, Lord, he thought to himself. A man's leg hit you, that's all, that's all. Can't believe how easy that was to say. A man is blown to kingdom come and...that's all.

After two hours of hell, the artillery barrage subsided. Men all along the line were standing up and getting into firing positions. They knew what was coming next. Soon, Pleasant was running down the line of company H giving last minute instructions and motivation.

"They're coming soon now. Be steady, be true. Wait for my command to fire."

The men strained to see through the gray smoke, strained to see the enemy who had been trying to kill them with artillery The acrid smell of cannon fire was heavy in the hazy air, and they could hear the Yanks coming, but could not see them. Shouted commands came across the clearing and through the scattered trees.

"There! Pleasant shouted and pointed his sword toward the enemy. Ready! Take your aims. Steady, wait for my command."

James was still straining to see, and suddenly he could see them. He made the long blue line to be at two hundred yards distance and advancing at a quick step. Suddenly they stopped. There were two ranks. The first rank knelt on one knee and aimed. He jerked Henry down. Pleasant had already ducked behind the rampart. The first volley did no visible harm, but a couple of men in their company were hit when they rose too fast and received the second volley.

"You learn something from that, Henry?" James asked.

Henry nodded. He understood.

The blue lines continued to march forward and went through the same drill twice more. Then at about a hundred and fifty yards, Pleasant was on the rampart again with his sword pointed at the enemy. All up and down the entire brigade, officers and non-commissioned officers were ready to give the order. James and a thousand other Missourians aimed.

"Fire! Fire! Fire" rang down the line. The volley was deafening and the men were quickly reloading to be ready for the next volley.

"How many did we get?" Henry asked excitedly.

"Don't know, can't see," James said.

"Ready," came the command again. Steady boys. 100 yards. Fire!"

Again, the deafening noise, and then a cloud of thick smoke obscured their targets. The Missourians could see where the Yanks were, but the men in blue were only shadowy figures now, and it was hard to discern individual targets. They aimed again and the order to fire sounded out up and down their lines. It was guess work as to how many yards away the enemy was. Now, there was only a primal emotion to kill or be killed, and pure instinct kept the men firing in the direction of the Yankees. Even the men with shotguns were firing, hoping the enemy was in range of their guns. The command to fire at will came, and the firing had a ragged edge to it. Men were doing their best to pick out individual targets. Others fired blindly, hoping to kill the enemy. Gunfire, smoke, screams, confusion, and terror, James thought to himself. That's what combat is about—confused terror. He knew he was afraid, but strangely gave little thought to it. He just wanted to kill a Yank before a Yank killed him.

"Cease fire," came several voices. Henry kept firing and reloading like a man in a trance. James looked at him closely. Henry's face was blank, the jaw slack, his eyes wide, staring ahead blindly.

"Henry," James said firmly as he shook the boy's shoulder. "Cease fire. The Yanks are pulling back. It's over for now. Relax, Henry. You did good. We all did."

Henry looked at James, and finally his face seemed to relax. He would be fine. "We really whip those Yanks?" he asked.

"Yeah, Henry, we whipped them for now. Rest easy while we can. It's not over yet."

"Men! Get ready," Pleasant commanded. "We'll attack the Union line before they settle into their positions. The whole brigade will advance at the double quick step." He walked back and forth in front of the company's line as he exhorted his company. "Be steady, and we'll drive them back across the border. Make sure your weapons are loaded."

Then, down the line came a noise, a noise that set James's hair on end. It was a high pitch screech, growing in intensity, the sound of a thousand banshees, James remembered later.

"Who—who—ey,! Who—who—ey! Who—who—ey" Yai—yi— yai—yi—y-yo—wo—wo" Suddenly, the noise was deafening, and James joined in with his own cry of the blood curdling rebel yell. He looked up, and Pleasant was standing in front on the company waving his sword in a motion to move ahead.

"Follow me, Boys! Make Missouri proud!" Then Pleasant turned toward the enemy with revolver in one hand and sword in the other.

Still screaming, the men left the ramparts and ran toward the enemy's position three hundred yards ahead. James and Henry were only a few steps behind Pleasant. The other men were fanned out behind their company commander, still yelling at the top of their voices as they charged forward. James figured that if nothing else, maybe they could drive the Yanks mad with all the hollering. Within a hundred and fifty yards of their objective, hornets buzzed overhead, the sounds of hundreds of Minie balls flying toward them—hornets of death searching for targets. Up and down their ragged line, men grunted and fall backwards. The Yanks were beginning to thin their ranks. Within fifty yards of their object, the blue clad soldiers were visible and firing at these wild men charging their position and screaming at the top of their lungs. These raggedly dressed, howling men wearing everything from gray and butternut homespun to farm clothes were apparitions from hell. The Union rifle fire became ragged and seemed undisciplined. Twenty-five yards from the Yankee line, Parsons' Brigade took firing positions and fired into the long blue line. Reload and fire again. Reload and fire again, then the company commanders bellowed the command to charge. The rebel yell started at the same time, and these Missourians engaged the enemy face to face.

"James, I don't have a bayonet!"

"Me neither. Use you rifle like a club when we get in close."

Instantly, the two lines converged, and the cries of men being wounded mixed with the sounds of commands, yells, and curses of men fighting in desperate hand to hand combat. Henry was holding his own, swinging his rifle in wide arcs that caused his adversary to back off. One large, red faced, Irish sergeant charged James with his bayonet. James stepped back and fended the bayonet with his rifle, then with an overhead swing brought the butt down on the man's head. There was a sickening crack, and the sergeant slumped to the ground, blood spewing from the top of his head. Turning quickly, he saw Henry was in trouble. He was still swinging his rifle, but now there were two Yanks after him. Henry continued to back up as he swung. He was sweating profusely, and James could tell he was tiring. He picked up the sergeant's rifle and ran yelling toward Henry's attackers. One man turned to fend off James's attack, but it was too late. He grunted as his own sergeant's bayonet was driven into his stomach. James twisted the bayonet and withdrew the blade. The Union man went down to his knees, holding his stomach. He looked up at James with pain filled eyes and fell forward on his face. The pitiful moans from the man told James it would be a slow death. He turned. Henry was now on the ground with the other Yank. They were attacking each other with teeth, hands, feet—mortal combat at its most primal level. They were two animals trying to stay alive by killing the other. Suddenly, Henry had the enemy's ear between his teeth and was biting hard. The man howled and tried to tear himself away. In doing so, the ear came off in Henry's mouth. There was a look of consternation on Henry's face as he spat the ear out, picked up his rifle, and began beating the man to death. James walked over and shook his shoulders.

"He's dead, Henry. You can't kill him no more. Now throw that old flintlock down and take the sergeant's Springfield. Take his cartridge belt too." Henry seemed dazed but nodded and did as he was told. James picked up another Springfield and removed the bayonet to place on his own rifle.

"Captain! Look out!" Henry yelled.

James turned quickly to see a soldier charging Pleasant's blind side. His brother was preoccupied trying to fend off bayonets from three Union soldiers. His pistol was back in its holster—empty. Before James could react, Henry threw his new rifle like a spear. It hit the soldier in the thigh, and he stumbled to his knee. Henry reacted quickly and grabbed the Springfield, pulling it free, then stabbed the wounded man in the throat. The Yank fell backward and gurgled his life away. James ran to help his brother fight his other two adversaries. Henry soon arrived also, and the two Union men turned and ran from the fight. Up and down the line of Parsons' Brigade, the enemy was beginning to fade from their positions. Some ran in panic, others retreated slowly, firing as they did. The Missourians returned the fire until the Union men were out of range. The ridge was theirs. Now it was time to lick their wounds, care for the wounded, and then they would have to hold what they captured. This was just the beginning, not the end.

"Check your comrades. See who's missing, wounded or dead," Pleasant ordered as he walked back and forth in front of company H.

Men began to walk among the fallen, and the company's count was given to their captain, seven dead, six wounded, and sixteen missing.

"James, you and Henry cover the ground behind us," Pleasant said. "See if any of the missing fell as we charged." Then he took a breath and spoke to all the men in his company. "I'm proud of you men. You'd all have medals if it were up to me, but I suspect you'd rather have new weapons. Those of you with shotguns and flintlocks get first choice on the Yankee Springfields. They won't need them. Lay out the Union dead behind us. You gave Missouri honor today by the way you fought."

James and Henry searched the three hundred yards behind them and counted seven dead from company H. To their right and left, they saw men from other companies doing the same.

"Help," someone cried out, and then the voice choked and moaning began.

They both ran to their comrade. "It's John McCook," Henry cried. "God, look at his arm."

They knelt by the violinist who had played so sweetly for them last night. The poor man was writhing in pain. James could see that the upper right arm was shattered close to the shoulder and was twisted at a grotesque angle. James was choking up, for he knew no one would ever hear the magic of this man's talent again. He gave his fallen comrade a drink from his own canteen. John's eyes were filled with pain and terror.

"Be brave, John. We'll get litter bearers here. Why, you'll be going home soon, you lucky man." The look John gave him froze his heart. John knew his arm was destroyed, and he still may bleed to death, either here on the ground or in the surgeon's tent. "The doctor will give you some opium for the pain," James said lamely. "Rest easy. You'll soon be out of here."

"Hey, you two. We need help. Here's another litter. Take your friend to the surgeon's tent," a hospital orderly called.

"Where?" James asked, and the man told him it was four hundred yards behind their original line.

It was a long walk to the surgeon's tent and with almost every step, John cried out in pain. It was almost unbearable to hear John's pitiful cries, but there was nothing they could do. A scene from hell greeted them when they reached their destination. At least three hundred men were already lying in front of the tent, and the sounds of pain and suffering overwhelmed them. Some moaned, others begged, and many were obviously delirious, crying for wives, babies, and mothers. The ground was soaked in blood as men's lives drained into the earth before they could see the surgeon.

"Put him over there," an orderly commanded brusquely.

James and Henry carried John to the designated spot. "He needs attention quick," James said. "He's bleeding real bad."

"They all need attention quick," the haggard orderly answered.

"Please, Corporal, please," Henry begged. "Isn't there something to do before the doctors see him?"

The man turned his tired eyes to Henry and James, eyes that had seen too much suffering for two years. "I'll stop the bleeding, but there's only enough pain medicine for surgery. I'll see if I can find a little whiskey."

They thanked the man and walked away.

"Did you see that?" Henry asked. "Now I know why they call surgeon's sawbones."

"What?"

"Turn around and look under the tree on the other side of the tent."

James turned and wished he hadn't. Stacked like cordwood, were the limbs of men—arms, legs, feet, hands. They were bare and porcelain white, stacked neatly and tidily as if some orderly thought there might be an inspection. If not for blood on the ground, they could have been the appendages of broken dolls. One especially stuck in James's memory. It was an arm leaning against a stack of other limbs, its hand spread and reaching for heaven. The sun reflected off a gold wedding band. He could not bear to look any longer and would never speak of it until the spring of 1866. He would tell a young woman who held him as he opened his soul between the rows of a freshly plowed field. No more, Lord, let me see no more death today, he prayed silently. He would. Their grisly chore was not over. They still hadn't checked for dead and wounded at the ramparts, and walking through the horrific results of the Yankee cannon fire was another part of seeing the elephant.

"Ayee"

James turned with alarm to see Henry sprawled on his back. He had slipped and fallen. The boy was trying to get up, but when he did, his foot became entangled in the wet, gray intestines of someone who had been blown to pieces. He fell again and cried out once more. Before he could free himself, his hands and body were wet with viscera matter. He finally tore himself free, only to look down and see he was standing on what might be part of a comrade's liver. Tears ran down Henry's cheeks, and he began to vomit as he slipped and fell once more into gore. James pulled his friend away from the quagmire of horror.

"I'm sorry," he blubbered. "Sorry, James. I, I—"

"It's okay, Henry," James said. "Can't be helped. Don't see any other parts. Guess that counts as one dead, or maybe two." James felt his own strength leaving him.

Henry nodded numbly, and the friends continued looking for others. They found three who were at least recognizable as once being human, but it was hard to say who they were, or had been. Henry found one body he recognized.

"James," Henry said. "It's Lawrence. Looks like he's just asleep."

James walked over to look. There were no marks, but when they turned Lawrence over, they found a small hole in the back of his head. One tiny piece of shrapnel had snuffed out his life. As they looked down, James felt something wet hit his shoulder with a plopping sound. Startled, he jumped and brushed it off. An unrecognizable face, folded and wrinkled, lay on the ground. Someone's entire face had been sheared from the skull. Looking up, they saw the torn upper torso and faceless head of a comrade hanging from the tree branch. One eye ball hung from the bloody skull and starred down at them. James fell to his knees, and spasms of nausea racked him as he emptied his own stomach. Gagging and coughing, he finally rose. Now, he had the dry heaves, and his stomach convulsed in protest. As yet, neither James or Henry were hardened to the repugnant carnage of battle. They would learn.

James wiped his mouth with the back of his hand and mumbled, "Okay, let's finish and get back."

"What about this," Henry said. "Here's three arms and one foot. Do they count as two dead, or three?"

James looked and was confused. First the terror of battle, and after the surgeon's tent, this. He felt fatigued, and it was hard to make a decision. "Oh, let's say it counts for two. See anybody else?"

"No, I think we've covered all the area of our company. Can we go now?"

"Yeah, let's get back to the line."

As they walked back toward the ridge, Henry asked, "James, how does all this make you feel? I just feel empty."

James looked down and thought about the question before answering. "Empty, yes, sick, yes. I know what you mean, and I also feel grief, but I'm mad, mad at our enemies. After all, they came down here. We didn't go north and attack their home. I just want to drive the Yankees out of Missouri."

Within a few minutes they were back to the company's new position and made their report to Pleasant. By late afternoon, the Missourians still held the ridge and waited for reinforcements before making another charge against the Union lines. They were three hundred yards ahead of the rest of the Confederate army, and they waited patiently. In the distance there was occasional firing, and they had a few light skirmishes themselves, but no major attack had been mounted from either side. The Yankees seemed to be probing, testing their strength. As the day wore on, it was apparent that the Yanks were reforming. The men could hear shouted orders and movement of masses of men. The Missourians were worried they were in danger of being cut off. They were also short of ammunition. What they got from the Union dead had not gone far. So, they waited patiently and wondered what their commander had in mind. By sunset, it was apparent neither reinforcements or supplies would be coming.

"James, I've only got three cartridges left for my new Springfield," Henry said, his voice tinged with worry. "What happens if the Yanks come at us again?"

"Throw rocks, I guess." James was a little disgusted with the situation. "I've got four cartridges myself. Seems like the only thing old Jeff Davis has supplied me with so far is tainted beef and hard tack." Then he laughed. "That's an idea. Reach into your haversack. Maybe we'll load our guns with the hard tack."

"No, just throw it at em. Why, it'll probably knock their heads off." Henry began to giggle. "Now we know why they said prepare two days rations. It's all for killing, not eating. We should have known."

"Why didn't I think of that," one of the men close by said. "Why of course, our glorious leaders didn't expect us to eat the swill, just kill Yankees with it." Soon, all the men close to James and Henry were laughing. A couple of the men, like Henry, were in uncontrollable spasms of giggles, which brought even more laughter.

"Sorry I questioned our leader," James said loudly between his own gasping laughter. "Why all this time, leaving us exposed and alone with nothing but hard tack and spoiled beef was for our own good. Yes, sir, General Hindman was just takin' care of his boys. Let's charge now. I'll throw the first volley of food and you boys follow. Yanks won't stop runnin' 'til they're back in Illinois. God save General Hindman. Huzzah! Huzzah!"

Up and down the line, men began breaking up with laughter as the banter spread. Some of the exhausted men were laughing so hard, they wiped tears from their eyes. It was one of those rare moments men share in the middle of combat, poking fun at their leaders and themselves, then breaking into laughter at something, which under normal circumstances might not seem to be especially funny. It was a good thing, this laughter. The exhausted, discouraged, and apprehensive men needed something to break the tension. Even their company commander was laughing hard. When the laughter subsided, Pleasant spoke to his company.

"Listen. These boys we're fighting today aren't from Blunt. They're Herron's men."

"Thought his army was in Missouri!" One of his men said with a curse.

"Was," Pleasant said. "Now he's here. We're outnumbered two to one, and our whole army is short of ammunition. We'll be pulling back quietly after dark. Remember to be silent. We'll form up and rest where we camped last night and from there march to Little Rock. A couple of days, and we'll be in comfortable quarters. Our battle's over."

During a rest period the next day, James found his brother sitting on a small boulder at the side of the road. He was writing in his journal.

"What's the bad news, Brother?" James asked.

"What? Oh, James. Pull up a rock and have a seat. What news are you talking about?"

"Our casualties. Thought you might have the final count by now."

Pleasant looked glum, then checked his journal. The Brigade's casualties were over three hundred wounded, forty-six missing, and ninety-two killed, including Colonel Steen, their best regimental commander. Considering the engagement only lasted a few hours, casualties were heavy.

"Twelve of those killed are my men," Pleasant said.

"I know, I saw the bodies. Have you heard anything about John McCook?"

"Saw him earlier when I checked the hospital wagons. He's alive, barely, but drugged heavily and not making sense. God, they had to take his arm at the shoulder. James, I'm the one who recruited him. Don't know if I can forgive myself. I've been trying to write a lot about my feelings just now. It's hard."

James's heart went out to his brother, for he knew Pleasant's own heart was heavy. He didn't take his responsibilities lightly, and the men of company H were important to him He hadn't come to grips with the fact he could not keep all of his men safe. All of his company would not live to return home, and many of those who did would not return home whole. This was, after all, war. Men die in war, both the good and the bad.

"You carried your responsibilities with honor, Pleasant. I was proud to call you my brother today. The men are with you, and you still have their trust. Put that in your journal."

Pleasant looked into his eyes and gave a faint smile. "Thank you. That helps. I was proud of you today also and of the entire company. They fought well, didn't they? See you saw that Henry survived the elephant too. How is he?"

"He's good. Finally started his whistling again as we marched. He's a little quieter and probably grew a year or two older yesterday, but he'll be fine. Wants me to help him write a letter to his sweetheart when we get to Little Rock."

Pleasant laughed. "Perhaps a little love poem might help."

James smiled and said, "Don't know if I'll do that. By the way, think any mail might catch up with us in Little Rock?"

"Should. We'll probably establish winter quarters there. I doubt if we'll be seeing any action unless there's a threat to Little Rock. Of course, that's just a guess. Can't tell what will happen for sure, but there'll be lots of time for letter writing."

"You mean between marching, drills, digging latrines, marching, foraging, standing guard, marching, standing in line, patching, cleaning the maggots off the meat before we cook it, and what ever else comes down by chain of command?"

Pleasant grinned. "Somebody's got to make decisions to keep you busy. After all, you know an idle mind's the devil's workshop."

"Thought that's where I was. Better get back to my squad."

Within two days, Parsons' Brigade was in camp outside of Little Rock, Arkansas. Within two weeks, trees had been felled, hewed, and crude log huts built for winter quarters. The accommodations were not anything to brag about, James told Bertie in a letter, but they were easier to keep warm than tents. By Christmas, Texas beef arrived on the hoof, and the food became better in both quantity and quality. There were the usual duties that came with soldiering, and at times it seemed to the men they would be marched until they all became several inches shorter. Morale was generally good, but they all discovered what other soldiers of other generations discovered. Being a soldier was ninety-five percent boredom and five percent terror. Spare time was devoted to cleaning, gambling, joking, talking of home, and what would happen after the war. There were also excursions into town. For those who were readers, books were passed around and shared until the covers were falling off. Christmas Day did bring a diversion to the men. It was time to give their officers a "rubbing." This was done by catching one in the dark, and several stout men would hold the man against a tree and literally rub him up and down. The best trees were the ones with the roughest bark.

"James, you gonna help give Pleasant his rubbing?" Henry asked with excitement in his voice.

James laughed. "Guess not, but go ahead with Luke and the others.

They're bigger and stronger. Pleasant's gonna have a very good rub. Does officers good to eat some humble pie." Then with a chuckle, he went back to his book.

That night, several officers in the camp got caught after dark and received the rubbing. Most took things in the right spirit and considered it a harmless way for the men to release tension at their officers' expense. A few threatened court martial, but nothing came of it and was soon forgotten. It would be a Christmas tradition with the Missourians until the end of the war. The next day, James walked over to Pleasant's quarters for a visit. His brother was sitting outside warming himself next to the fire and drinking coffee.

"Hello, Brother," Pleasant said. "Pull up a stool and pour yourself some coffee."

"Thanks, don't mind if I do." He poured a cup and sat next to Pleasant. After a sip, he glanced sideways at his brother with a grin. "How's your back?"

"Hurts, but I'll live. I was hoping the boys would use a pine tree, but they found an oak. The bark was rougher than hell. Got some good news by the way. Hindman is being transferred to the east, and Price will be here by April. There's also a rumor we're finally getting proper uniforms and equipment, including British Enfields and more Richmonds."

James grinned. "That is good news. Things are looking up for the Missourians. I hope we're getting shoes also."

Pleasant nodded yes. "Something else, I'm taking twenty days of leave the first part of May. J.P. will bring Frances to Arkansas, and I'm taking her back to Georgia. I've given this a lot of thought. The war has changed everything. I've got money saved, and I'm going to buy some land that adjoins what I own of grandfather's place. Guess we'll settle there after the war. Frances will feel better with her folks for now. What do you think?"

James thought for a moment and said, "See nothing wrong with it. After all, you grew up working grandfather's land, and you'll do well once this war's over. I know Mother and the girls will miss Frances, but they'll adjust."

"There's something else," Pleasant said. "Frances is with child." He smiled into his cup.

James was taken aback for a moment, then said, "That's wonderful." Then he slapped his brother on the back. "Great news."

"Ouch! Thanks. That's another reason for the move. Frances wants to be with her parents during this time, and I've decided I want my son born where I grew up."

"Son. What if it's a girl?"

"It'll be a son. Wanna take a wager?"

James laughed. "All right. I'll bet you it's a girl. The loser has to buy the other a couple of books."

"Done," Pleasant said, and he shook James's hand.

The winter passed for the Missourians with only a skirmishes with Yankees who were probing Little Rock in January. A severe outbreak of measles in February killed more of the Missourians than the small battles did. Spring and April finally arrived, and just as Pleasant said, General Sterling Price returned to the army from New Orleans. Spring also brought fresh replacements and the new equipment and uniforms. Now when they marched, James thought they not only marched like soldiers, but looked like soldiers. They were no longer the offspring of a back water brigade. They were soldiers, and every man walked a little taller. The men were beginning to feel better about themselves and the army. Price also brought back flags made by the ladies of New Orleans which were given to the regiments. The flags consisted of a white cross on a blue field trimmed with red borders. This new flag became the regimental colors that Missourians would fight under throughout the war. When May came, Pleasant left to meet J.P. and Frances, then took the train for Georgia. He returned before the month ended. One evening, shortly after Pleasant returned from his trip to Georgia, James and Henry talked over their chicory coffee.

"Does your brother know where we'll be fighting when all this drilling and marching is over?" Henry asked.

"He doesn't know for sure, but thinks it'll be on the Mississippi, so we can drive Yankees off this side of the river. Maybe it'll help break their strangle hold on Vicksburg. Looks like we'll be paying dearly for these new uniforms and rifles. Oh, General Holmes will be leading us, not Sterling Price."

"Granny Holmes?" Henry shook his head. The Missourians had little trust in Holmes.

Chapter Eleven
Webfeet

"James, help!" Henry cried.

James looked back to see Henry trying to pull one leg from the mud and walked over to help his friend free himself. He grabbed Henry under the arms and said, "Pull." Finally, Henry came free of the dark brown mud they had been fighting for almost a month. They both fell backwards into more mud and began to laugh. It was the laughter of exhaustion and frustration.

"My shoe's still in the mud," Henry said weakly.

"We better get up before the whole brigade marches over us," James said. "Dig out your shoe."

Henry finally found his shoe. It was an unrecognizable wet glob. His whole sleeve was also coated with the clinging, sucking, wet earth of Arkansas. It had rained on and off since the day they left for Helena, Arkansas, a major port on the Mississippi, and their objective. Each step became a challenge of will for both men and animals, and they were exhausted. What should have been a few days march had turned into a month's ordeal. Their trek was littered with the bodies of mules and abandoned supplies. Much was lost in small streams turned into torrents of churning waters by unusually heavy rains.

"Got an idea, Henry," James said as the company found a resting spot in a grassy meadow. Here, the ground was only soggy, not muddy.

"What?" Henry responded as he cleaned the mud from his shoe.

"Take our shoes off, and tie them around our necks. At least we won't keep losing them."

Henry started laughing again. "Well, guess we're real webfeet. Whoever thought of calling infantrymen webfeet sure knew what he was talking about."

"Yeah, well, at least there's no drizzle today. The sun's out. Maybe it'll start drying out by tomorrow."

"Sure hope you're right. I'm so tired, I just want to lie down and sleep. Don't care if it's in the mud. Just sleep. Wonder if I'll be fit to fight when we get to Helena."

"We'll all be fit. Surely old Granny Holmes will let us rest up before the battle starts. If he don't, we'll be whipped before we start. Get ready, here comes my brother. One more swig of water, a bite of my hard tack, and we're off again." The bite snapped off and James let it dissolve in his mouth with the help of some water.

"Rest break is over men," Captain Pleasant said wearily. "Check for your comrades, and make sure everybody is with us. With luck, we'll be within striking distance of the enemy by tonight." He nodded and smiled at James, who winked back, then Pleasant walked over to speak with him.

"You boys look terrible," Pleasant said with a grin. "Glad you're on grass. Wouldn't know you were here if it was mud you were sitting on."

"So do you," James answered with his own grin. "Shame an officer would get so dirty. Sure that's a Confederate uniform? You could be a Yank underneath all that mud. Are you sure we'll be close enough by tomorrow?"

"Yeah, we'll be there. Don't worry about it," Pleasant answered.

"We gonna rest a day or so when we get there, Capt'n?" Henry asked.

"Don't know, but doubt it. General Holmes wants to attack right away. He thinks surprise will be in our favor if we do."

"Has he thought our exhaustion might be in the Yankees's favor if we don't rest?" James asked with a smile.

Pleasant looked up at the clear sky and smiled slightly. Then he answered. "I would hope he's given it thought. I have. Maybe at least we'll stop and camp early today. That might help us. For now, let's march and don't forget to prepare food for two days when we stop. Maybe we'll make better time today."

The march continued, and by now, most of the men were wearing shoes around their necks. The sun stayed out, and the heat became oppressive. The progress was still slow, but now a drying brown crust was forming over the earth. As the day wore on, James always looked ahead for the large oak trees with their inviting green canopies casting cool shade. The column seemed to slow as it passed beneath the shade trees. James certainly walked a little slower as he savored the small relief from the sun's heat for at least a few seconds. He glanced at the men around him and marveled at their strength. Their faces were blank and tired eyes only stared ahead. The men were marching on will power alone, marching on legs that should have collapsed days ago, marching on stomachs that were never quite full since this ordeal began. Occasionally, there was a curse or grunt as someone stepped into a softer spot in the trail. With a wet sucking sound, a soldier would pull one foot free, curse again and continue his slow plodding march forward. It always seemed to James that when the men thought they could not march another five minutes, a supply wagon would be stuck, and they would be ordered to help the teamsters get their wagon on the move again. Even the mules had a tired and weary look in their eyes. And so it had been for a month. The stream crossings were not only exhausting but dangerous as well, and the snake infested swamps were often waist deep. Several men had drowned during the march, and most of the bodies were swept away by fast moving swollen creeks.

"Another stream ahead," Henry said. "Looks high, but not as bad as the last one."

"I see it, and a wagon's stuck in this one too," James answered. "Looks like more work for us."

Pleasant motioned for his company to come forward and help get the wagon out of the quagmire of water and mud. The weary men waded into the water with Pleasant. The stream was only thigh deep, but they had to struggle against a strong current. Soon, ropes were attached, and men on the other shore pulled as the soldiers of company H grappled with the wagon and its wheels.

"Heave, men, heave," Pleasant shouted as he, James, and Henry tried to roll one stubborn wheel out of its muddy trap. Other men worked at the other wheels, and men on shore pulled with all their might. Suddenly, the wagon lurched forward and stalled in deeper water. Now the water was chest high, and it was harder to help with the wagon. It took all their effort to just hold on and keep from being washed away. All at once, there was a loud creaking noise, and the wagon tilted toward Pleasant and his men.

"Watch out!" Pleasant shouted as he swam out of harm's way.

James heard his brother shout and tried to move, but he was too late as the wagon fell sluggishly on its side. He quickly found himself swallowing muddy water as something pushed him toward the bed of the creek. There was no vision beneath the silty water, and James became disoriented as he struggled beneath the surface. Holding his breath, he tried to fight his way to freedom, but something was heavy on his chest. He knew it couldn't be the wagon holding him down. The weight of a loaded wagon would have crushed him to death instantly. He strained desperately with the weight on his body, and his mind swirled in panic. Just as he began to lose consciousness, hands were groping his face and body. A dream, he thought, and he embraced blackness.

"Is he dead, Capt'n?" Henry cried as he and Pleasant dragged James onto the stream bank.

"Help me turn him over," Pleasant answered. "Pound his back. Get the water out. He can't be dead. Should have just cut the mules free and let the wagon go. Please, James, wake up. Wake up." Both Henry and Pleasant were hitting James on the back as they pleaded with him not to die. Finally there was a cough and some dirty water came bubbling out of James's mouth.

"He's breathing!" Henry said excitedly. "He's alive. My friend's alive."

A few minutes later, James was sitting and coughing up more dirty water, but he was alive. He looked out at the stream. Men were ducking under the water and coming up with boxes to carry ashore. Other men were at work trying to right the overturned wagon. The mules were ashore, shaken, but alive and well.

"What happened?" James asked between coughs.

"There were a couple of large crates holding you down. Fell off the wagon when it tipped," Pleasant said.

"We thought you pegged out on us," Henry said.

"What was in the boxes, lead?" James asked.

"Salt Horse," Pleasant answered.

"Salt Horse! You mean I almost got killed by cases of tinned beef. Why, it's undignified, Pleasant. Down right undignified. Killed by our own vittles. Don't suppose old Jeff Davis would strike a medal for me on that account."

"Maybe," Pleasant said as he and Henry helped James to his feet and led him to a dry spot beneath a large tree. "Might call it the Exalted Order of The Tinned Beef."

"More likely the Exalted Order of the Fly Blown Beef," James retorted and coughed up some more fluid.

"How about Vittles Cross of Courage? Stay here and rest, James," Pleasant said with a chuckle. "We'll help the boys take care of the wagon."

"Brothers!" James said as Pleasant and Henry walked back into the water. "Thank you."

The two men turned and waved off a salute. To James, it looked as if Henry had tears in his eyes. He and his tent mate had become close, and he knew Henry looked up to him like an older brother. James had become very fond of Henry also. Though combat had matured the boy, and at times could be somber, he still had the bright-eyed enthusiasm of a seventeen-year-old, soon to be eighteen. Henry only had a rudimentary education, but with effort, he could read and write, and James spent a lot of time helping the young man improve his skills. He had proven to be an apt student and learned quickly as he became interested in the books James introduced to him. He now only asked for suggestions as he wrote his own letters. The boy had finally used the word "love" in his letters to his sweetheart. Last month, he had gotten the courage to write and ask the girl's father for his daughter's hand. As yet, there was no answer. For the youngster's sake, James hoped the answer would be positive. He thought Henry was a good boy and would grow into a good man to make the young lady in question a fine match. He was a relentless and hard worker with a strong sense of family loyalty and common decency. James leaned back against the tree trunk and looked up into the thick foliage of the oak. Birds sang as they fed their new hatchlings, and the sun's golden rays filtered though the green leaves warming his face. The chill from the cold water gradually leaked from his bones. His ribs felt bruised, and his entire body ached from weariness. He would eat good tonight if he could muster the strength to prepare something. His thinking became fuzzy as the heat made him drowsy.

"Mother, I'm so tired," James mumbled and dozed off sitting upright, his chin resting on his chest. He dreamed and found himself in a strange, foreign place with giant, majestic, southern pine soaring overhead as they pointed toward a blue, cloudless sky. He looked down into an open grave that beckoned him to lie within the good earth's womb and rest, rest his weary body and embrace oblivion. Mourners surrounded him weeping anguished cries of loss. Bertie, Adelaide, and mother were dressed in black and wept as they were held by faceless strangers. Bertie leaned forward, one arm held by a beautiful auburn haired stranger, the other outstretched toward the grave, her mouth open in a cry of sorrow. He watched in fascination and wonder as saliva leaked from the corner of her open mouth. Adelaide was making her terrible mewing sounds again, and a small girl with the face of sweetness stood apart staring at him. Tears ran down the child's cheeks and formed a small pool at her feet which reflected the dark blue of eyes that mirrored his own. She stared at James with hurt in her angelic face and held the hand of a sandy haired boy holding a bouquet of flowers. Mother held a handkerchief to her nose and wept as she watched him. James looked back into the grave and now saw a rough-hewed casket. There were flowers sprinkled across the casket's lid. Far away, someone played *Ashokan Farewell*, and James looked across an open field and saw his cousins, Thomas and David. David's flute made sweet music, and Thomas accompanied him with his violin. A great sadness spread through his body, a sadness he did not understand, just as he could not understand for whom these people were mourning. Who? He wondered.

"James, wake up," Pleasant and Henry called out in unison.

He looked up and was confused. His brother and Henry were standing over him with grins of their faces. "The wagon—" James never finished the sentence as he stood up shakily.

"Taken care of," Pleasant said. "We march now, but we'll stop soon and make camp. No more streams to cross, and tomorrow at first light we attack the Union fortifications at Selena."

In the faint light rising from the eastern hills on July 4th, 1863, the men of Parsons' Brigade could dimly see the earthen breastworks and rifle pits in front of their objective, prophetically called Graveyard Fort. They and their Arkansas comrades were to make a frontal assault, drive the Yankees back, and secure the fort. Other units on their right and left had the job of attacking and securing the other small forts that guarded the entrance to the city of Helena. The Confederates numbered over seven thousand and had high hopes of driving the Federal troops from the city. They were tired men, exhausted men, weary from slogging their way through swamps and swollen streams for a month. However, they were not demoralized men. In their minds, they were struggling to free their state from a foreign occupier and would fight bravely on this day.

"Fourth of July," Henry said. "Celebration and fireworks."

"For them, not us anymore," James answered. "But, there'll be fireworks aimed at us, I'm afraid."

"Think old Granny Holmes is right? They ain't expecting us, and we'll surprise the Yanks after all?" Henry asked.

"No," James said with a grin, and just as he spoke, Federal artillery shells screamed overhead with their own answers to Henry's question.

Shells exploded among the men in gray, and the cries of wounded could be heard up and down the line. The Union artillery had them in range, and now there was no hesitation. Now the only thoughts were to charge the Yanks. Standing in position to be slaughtered by artillery was no option. The familiar rebel yell to prepare for charging rose into a crescendo of deafening noise. Soon the hair-raising screech was all around them, and James was taken by it too as his voice rose with his comrades. There was no thinking of safety, or logic, or families, or why—only a visceral, blind, animal desire to charge the enemy and kill. The men ran forward toward their objective three hundred yards away over rough terrain. First, kill the Union pickets in front of the earthen embankment and keep charging to drive the enemy back into the town. They held their fire, charging with their bayoneted rifles held forward. These were wild men, fierce warriors, screaming war cries as they ran full speed, determined to kill every blue coated soldier they met. Kill them before they themselves were killed. Drive these foreigners from their land. Send them to hell. The thin line of Federal pickets in their rifle pits were the first to fall under the Missourians bayonets, and of course, men in gray fell also. It was the bloodiest of combat—hand to hand, face to face. The enemy was not faceless now. It was toe to toe fighting. Both the men in blue and the rebels were living human beings as their eyes met in this desperate fight for survival. It was the kind of combat that would in later years haunt the dreams of soldiers from both sides as they remembered faces and cries of men they killed. Men, they would later recall, who had mothers, children, and other loved ones never to be held or seen again. But now it was kill or be killed, and those thoughts of shared humanity were driven into their sub-conscience, only to be recalled in the darkness of night when they were alone. Then, they would awaken with cold sweats and stare at a bedroom wall. It was something most combat veterans would try to forget in future wars as well, and it was another subject only combat veterans could understand. A few of the Union troops survived the charge to retreat back up the embankment with the Missourians in quick pursuit. Soon, the Missourians reached the top of the fortifications and were shooting down into the Union trenches. Two volleys, and the men of Parsons' Brigade were in the trenches with the Yanks and the slaughter continued. Bayonets jabbed, and rifles were used as clubs on both sides.

"Look out, James!" Henry cried.

James turned to his left and saw a Yank charging with his bayonet. He dodged to the right and countered with his own bayonet thrust. It caught the soldier in his side, and he went down to one knee. In an upward swing of his rifle butt, the Yank's jaw was smashed, and the enemy fell face first into the mud. James drove his bayonet into the soldier's back, gave a twist and withdrew the bloody blade. "Behind you, Henry!"

Henry turned to see an officer's pistol pointed at his face. He thought it was over, but when the lieutenant pulled the trigger, the hammer fell on an empty chamber. The man cursed and swung his sword. Henry parried with his bayonet, then stumbled backwards and fell. The Union officer grunted with satisfaction seeing his adversary on the ground and went forward with sword raised. Suddenly, there was a hole where his eye should have been. The enemy twisted and slumped to the ground—dead before his body embraced mud.

"Comes in handy sometimes," James yelled at Henry as he re-holstered his Colt revolver. Henry nodded grimly and jumped up to continue the fight. After an hour of hand to hand fighting, the Union troops began to abandon their position and retreat back into the town. The bodies of their comrades were strewn in the trenches they had just surrendered.

Pleasant gathered his exhausted company among the grotesque corpses of Yankee dead and counted heads. "The position is ours. Good work men. I'm proud of you." He walked over to James and Henry and squatted beside them, holding out his canteen to James.

"Thanks," James said and took a long swallow. Henry was already drinking out of his own canteen. "How's it going on either side of us?"

"Don't know for sure," Pleasant responded. "But, I believe we're ahead of the rest of the troops."

"Sounds familiar," James said. "Hope it don't mean trouble for us like Prairie Grove."

"Me too," Pleasant said wearily and took a drink. "Okay, we chase Yankees now."

Five minutes later, Parsons' Brigade was marching into Helena's outskirts, rifles at the ready. There was sporadic firing from the retreating Federal forces as the Missourians continued to follow them toward the town. Suddenly, after climbing into and out of a deep, wide ravine on the edge of town, Pleasant halted his company and motioned them to one knee and spoke.

"Listen, men. I think we're in a dangerous position. Our forces on both flanks are nowhere in sight. Something's wrong. We're way ahead of everybody. If they're stuck and can't move forward, we'll be outflanked and trapped."

"What about our boys already in town? Must be three hundred of them already," his company sergeant said.

"Yeah, and that's got me worried. Who wants to volunteer to be a runner and warn Major Smith about the situation?"

His answer came with Yankee gunfire from both sides. The sergeant fell to the ground, his face blown to red pulp.

"Back to the ravine!" Pleasant shouted. "Back to the ravine and take cover."

The men retreated back to the ravine they had just crossed. There was a problem with the ravine. It only gave protection from the front and back. The bottom was wide and flat, and now Union soldiers were firing from about three hundred yards on each side. Indeed, the Missourians were outflanked. The only cover was scruffy bushes and a few rocks. Soon, other Missourians were stumbling down the ravine walls to join them. They had run a gauntlet of flanking fire to retreat from the city. The sergeant had been right. Over three hundred were left behind and would have no alternative but surrender. The rest of the army had not moved more than a hundred yards from their early morning formation, and the Missourians and Arkansans had been too successful in their attack. They were the only ones to take their objective and as a result were left exposed on both sides. The soldiers were trapped.

"Captain, look!" one of the men said with alarm. They all turned their heads toward the direction of the Mississippi. A Union gun boat had positioned itself where it could fire into the ravine with its cannon, and it didn't take long for the first shot to arrive with thunder and death.

145

The men dug in as much as possible. Now, it was obvious. They may have to consider surrender if they wished to survive. Over three hours of fighting and death for nothing.

After an hour of cannon barrage and volleys from Yankees on both sides, the men of Parsons' Brigade made their decision. No one wanted to surrender, and they had no intention of waiting for death in the ravine. Make a run back to their own lines. Run the gauntlet and take their own chances. The order was given, and the men desperately ran up the ravine's south wall and sprinted for their own lines three hundred yards away. It was a race against death as bullets buzzed overhead, and cannon shot exploded among them. Men screamed in pain around company H and fell to the ground. Fifty yards away from their goal, the exhausted men slowed to a walk as they finally moved beyond the range of Yankee fire. James noticed that Pleasant seemed to be staggering and walked over closer to his brother. He looked down at Pleasant's side and noticed blood seeping through a hole in his coat.

"Pleasant, you're shot!" James said with alarm.

Pleasant turned to James with a puzzled look and stared down at his side. "I'm shot." He immediately fell to the ground unconscious.

"Oh, no, not Pleasant!" James said and knelt at his side. He was in a panic to think about another brother dying. He handed his rifle to Henry and picked up Pleasant. Carrying him over his shoulder, he jogged toward safety and looked for the surgeon's tent. Finding it in the woods, he carried Pleasant inside, ignoring the protest of the orderlies. The surgeon was washing blood off the operating table with a bucket of water and looked up. He was startled to see this private carrying a man into his tent.

"What's this?" Major Smith, surgeon to General Price, asked brusquely.

"This is Captain Pleasant MacEver, and 'this' happens to be my brother," James said just as brusquely as he carefully lay Pleasant on the still wet table. "Fix him! Just fix him." Then, he took a deep breath and pleaded. "Please, sir, please fix him. Please save my brother."

The surgeon gave James a hard look. "Kind of impertinent, aren't you, Private?" Then he sighed and nodded. "All right, help me get his shirt and coat off, but if you faint while I 'fix' him, I'll see you before a court-martial." He looked at James over the spectacles hanging on the end of his nose and smiled. "Your brother's still breathing regular. Don't worry, I'll fix him up real good."

James watched the surgeon intently as he worked. The wound had bled a lot but didn't look too deep. When the doctor began probing inside the wound, James winced but was fascinated with what was going on.

"Well, well, what do we have here?" the surgeon asked rhetorically. He had the forceps clamped on something dark and then with a twist pulled out a piece of shrapnel the size of a silver dollar. He held it up and smiled. "This young man's lucky. Looks like the piece was almost spent before it hit. He'll be just fine in a few days. See this sharp point. It was stuck in his rib. He'll hurt some, but he's just fine. You look a little pale. Now get out of my tent before I have you arrested. I've got to stitch him up."

"Yes, sir, I'm going. Thank you, Doctor. Thank you." James turned toward the entrance and left to find his company.

The army marched back the way they had come, back to Little Rock. Once again, they had suffered defeat. Once again, they were leaving behind their dead to be buried by those who neither knew nor cared that the bodies they buried in common graves were the sons, husbands, friends, and brothers of men not unlike themselves. It was just one of the tragedies of this bloody war between kin and neighbors. Close to four hundred of the men in gray were now prisoners of the Union, who grew stronger as their foe grew weaker. At least the prisoners' war was over, James thought. The march home was hard, but the rains had stopped, and the creeks and rivers were now easier to cross. The swamps were only knee deep, but one man in James's company was bitten by a water mocassin and died. During the third week of the retreat, Pleasant rejoined his company. The men were glad to see their captain, many of them believing he was the reason the whole company wasn't languishing in a Yankee prison. He returned during the men's break beneath the scattered trees of a green meadow.

"Captain's back!" two of the men shouted, and what was left of the company rose and surrounded their company commander with cries of pleasure. The welcome was informal as Pleasant's subordinates crowded around. There were gentle pats on the back and handshakes. His men were truly glad Pleasant was safe, and he returned their friendly banter. After a few minutes, the men went back to their rest, and Pleasant took a seat beside James and Henry.

"How's the side?" James asked.

"It's fine. Healed up real good. I'm just a little weak from too much inactivity. Tell you, I'm glad to be out of that wagon. It's a rough ride."

"Oh, I can just imagine," James said with a laugh. "Every step through the last swamp, I was really worried about you having to ride instead of wade. Felt real sorry for you. We both did, didn't we, Henry?"

"Yes, sir, Capt'n, real sorry you had to ride," Henry added with a smile.

"You should be more sympathetic to your brother," Pleasant said with a chuckle. "And to think I brought apples. Shame on you both." He handed each an apple from his haversack.

As they ate the apples, the three men talked of the battle.

"We took it hard, didn't we?" Henry said. "We've heard nothing but bad news."

"It is bad. There were over 1,600 casualties, and a third of those are from our brigade. Over three hundred of our men are missing, probably prisoners. Another three hundred wounded and a hundred sixty two killed. We lose some of the wounded every day. I woke up one morning to find three men in the wagon with me dead. In my company, there's only twenty-five left. Forty souls gone, I…well, you know." Pleasant couldn't go on. He grieved for his men.

"Rumor has it General Price argued against the attack all along," James offered.

"He did," Pleasant said. "Counseled against it during a meeting before we left Little Rock, but General Holmes thought it would be a quick victory and help give Vicksburg relief. By the way, Vicksburg fell the same day we attacked Helena."

"Any news from the East?" James asked.

"None, we won't know what's going on there until we get back to Little Rock in a couple of days," Pleasant answered. Then he sighed heavily. "Wouldn't be surprised if there's more bad news when we get back. Vicksburg, Helena…well, it's said bad news comes in threes."

At Little Rock they heard about the terrible and bloody battle at a little hamlet in Pennsylvania called Gettysburg. The South's greatest hero, Robert E. Lee, suffered a disastrous defeat on the last day of the battle, the same day of the Missourians' bloody attack on Helena and the fall of Vicksburg. Lee's losses were more than the combined Confederate forces that attacked Helena. They also heard of Quantrill's raid on Lawrence, Kansas—burning the town and butchering civilians, also on July 4th. In James's mind, it was typical partisan behavior. As Helena helped decide the fate of Arkansas and Missouri, Vicksburg and Gettysburg spelled the downward spiral of the Confederacy's hopes of winning and establishing a separate country.

A few weeks after returning to Little Rock, the city was abandoned to Federal occupation, and on September 10th, the men of Parsons' Brigade marched south to winter quarters near the Louisiana border.

"When we gonna get to this camp, James?" Henry asked, wiping his forehead with the back of a sleeve.

"Camp Bragg. We'll be there in two more days. It's by a town called Magnolia. Dang these flies. They been following us for a hundred miles. Grown attached to company H, I guess. Wish the cavalry would ride behind instead of ahead. You're gonna wear that letter out, Henry." James said and smiled as he noticed Henry re-reading the reply from Emilia's father as they took a break. Her father agreed to the match, and his friend had been walking on air since leaving Little Rock. James was happy for him.

"When do you think the war will be over?" Henry asked.

"When we drive the Yankees out of Missouri," James answered and took another swallow of water from his canteen.

Henry swatted flies away and squinted at the pitiless sun. He said, "Looks like we're going in the wrong direction again." There was a bit of frustration in his voice.

"Looks that way," James answered. "Who knows? Maybe Granny

Holmes has a secret plan with all this marching south. He hasn't asked for my advice lately."

"I'll have to speak to the general about his lack of foresight," Pleasant said with a laugh and took a seat next to his brother on the large exposed root of an oak tree.

"Greetings, Captain," James said with a grin. "Glad to know I have a voice in the council of war at the big tent. What's the latest from Frances?

"She's well and sends her love," Pleasant answered.

"When you gonna be a papa, Captain?" One of the other men in company H called from a few feet away.

"November." Pleasant shouted. "Before Christmas, anyway."

"Capt'n, still think it'll be a boy?" Henry asked.

"Of course, it'll be a boy. Has to be. Got a bet on with my brother."

"Which I'll collect in December. Those books are gonna make nice Christmas presents," James said with a laugh. "By the way, rumor has it General Holmes is leaving us."

"Yes, he is. The old gentlemen is being transferred to some fort in Mississippi. Feel sorry for him. He's an honorable gentleman, but too old for this kind of command. You'll like this. Sterling Price will be put in charge of the Arkansas Department."

James grinned. "That should cheer the Missourians. I'm surprised the morale is still high. Every man here still dreams of returning to Missouri and driving the Yankees out of our state."

"And you, Brother. Do share that dream?" Pleasant asked.

James looked at his brother seriously. "I'm beginning to have doubts we'll ever return home. But I still hope for the best as we march in the opposite direction. How about you?"

Pleasant knocked the fire out of his clay pipe and stuck it in his pocket. "You always ask hard questions, Brother. Let's just say I'm cautiously optimistic. God willing, we'll survive winter to return north."

"And God, is he on our side or the Yankees'?" James said and grinned laconically.

"Get thee behind me, Satan," Pleasant answered and grinned back at his brother. "You already know we both feel the same about that age old question. I think God grieves to see kin, neighbors, and countrymen killing each other in this war, but I suspect he's neutral when it comes to politics. Doesn't mean we can't pray for his protection and guidance though, just as I can understand those men in blue sending up the same prayers. Kind of hard to imagine God noticing the color of the uniforms. His creatures can be as mysterious as himself, but to change the subject, James, wish you would reconsider the promotion. We need another good sergeant."

"Thanks, Pleas, but I don't want the responsibility. Just don't want it. I admire those of you who take that kind of responsibility, but it's not for me. Corporal Benton will make a good sergeant. The men respect him, and he'll carry the burden with dedication."

"Okay, but then I'll need a new corporal. How bout it? Your squad respects you. Please, we need you."

James sighed, and said reluctantly, "Okay, I'll take the corporal's job."

"Good!" Pleasant shook James's hand. "It's done then."

"Gosh, James, should I call you sir?" Henry asked.

"Oh, no, guess not." Then he gave his buddy a lopsided grin and continued. "But, you know, 'Your Majesty,' has a very nice ring to it." Then he laughed at himself along with his friend and brother.

"Captain MacEver," Henry cut in. "The good books says to pray for our enemies. Should we be praying for the Yankees?"

"Good question, Henry," Pleasant said and teased his moustache. "Of course, pray for them. Pray they all go home on the quick step." Then he laughed and stood up. "Rest is over men. Let's form up again."

The march to Camp Bragg continued with some grumbling, but the men kept a steady pace in the late summer heat of September. Two days later they arrived at their winter quarters and began the chores of settling in and preparing for the coming winter. Within a few days, the camp took on a semblance of a temporary home. At the entrance to the camp the men erected a large sign to let visitors know this was Missouri City. Rations were good, new clothes arrived, mail showed up, and with drill and discipline, the morale of the Missourians remained high as the oppressive heat of summer gave way to fall and early winter.

The week before Christmas, Pleasant showed up at James's cabin and motioned him outside. He had a package with him.

"Here you are, James," he said. "Congratulations. This is from your new niece, Orazaba." He was smiling broadly.

James was surprised. "Pleas, you mean it's a girl after all?" He shook his head then embraced his brother. "Congratulations. Frances is well, I hope."

"Yes, she's well and says the baby is beautiful. Of course, I'm happy. We named her after Frances's grandmother. Frances got the books for you."

James looked at the new editions of the books they talked about last summer and smiled.

"Okay, Pleas, you must have planned early to have the books for me now. How did that happen?"

Pleasant smiled sheepishly. "Well, back in October, Frances said it would be a girl, and it seems she's always right, so I told her about the bet and asked her to get the books for me just in case."

James laughed and said, "I'm really happy for you. She'll be beautiful just like Frances, and the next one will be a boy. When was she born? Want to come in and share some chicory coffee with us?"

"November 3rd. Thanks, but I can't. I've got an officers' staff meeting. Need to get going. I'm already late."

James congratulated his brother again and went inside to tell the other men. They all ran outside to congratulate their captain. It was good news, and they were happy for their commander. There were slaps on the back and happy words. Then they followed along and serenaded him with lullabies as he walked to his meeting. When he entered the command headquarters with a deep blush, there were some puzzled looks from his superiors.

A few days later, James went into town with four of his roommates. Between the camp and town was a maze of shacks and tents offering every service off duty soldiers might want. Photographers, souvenir and crafts peddlers, barbers, and women who offered washing services hawked their wares and services as they passed by. Some of the women offered themselves.

"Don't even think about it," Abe the oldest said. "These gals are the cheapest, but we'll stop at Lucy's in town. She runs a clean establishment."

After stopping at a spirits establishment and drinking for two hours, the men had a group portrait made. There would be copies ready the next day.

"Want to join us at Lucy's, James?" One of the men asked. "Be good for you."

"Come on, James," another comrade said. "Do you a world of good. Maurice is right. You never have fun. Come on."

James hesitated. He had too much to drink already, which only made him melancholy. What he really wanted was to get something for his stomach at the red medicine wagon, go back to camp, and finish some letters. James had the same urges as every one else, but he was also the son of his mother, and knew he would feel guilty about the experience. What he really wished for was a woman to love and to hold. Someone who would help him shut out the carnage of war for a few minutes. He looked down at the ground and shrugged. I guess that's what my comrades want too, and if they have to pay for it, they will, he thought. He smiled and joined his friends as they walked to Lucy's Place.

"Look at these people in front of us. Must be more than fifty," James said, as they took their place at the end of a long line.

"Don't worry, they work fast," someone chuckled.

"I can only imagine," James mumbled.

As the line slowly moved forward, he noticed men coming out the exit. He estimated about one every five minutes and shook his head. "Don't know if I want this. Don't know if a long wait for five minutes of pleasure and a disease is worth it."

"Ah, be patient, Corporal. We're almost there," Charles said. "Don't worry. All of Lucy's girls are clean."

"How bout all these men in front of us. They clean?" James wondered aloud. But, he stayed and soon was inside, paid his money, and was ushered into a dimly lit room.

"Well, hello, Soldier. Yes, I take tips if you like my service, and you will. My, my, ain't you the handsome warrior though. Don't be bashful. I'm Amanda, and I won't bite, unless you want me to. Take off your clothes, Darling."

James began to get undressed and looked at the young, aging girl lying naked on her cot. She was positioned seductively with her hands folded behind her head. She smiled at him. James guessed her to be in the late teens, but she seemed so much older. Her eyes bothered him. They had seen too much, just as the hundreds of men she serviced had seen far too much. Only partially undressed, he sat on the edge of her bed and a tear slipped off his cheek. It wasn't just guilt for doing something he felt was wrong. He had never been with a prostitute before, and now he was ashamed for taking part in another person's degradation. He thought of the humiliation and degradation of his own sisters, and quickly his desire was gone. Amanda sat up, put her arms around him and nuzzled his neck.

"What's wrong? What's your name?" She reached down and felt his flaccid manhood. "Oh, my. Don't worry bout that none. Amanda can get your gun up real fast."

"I'm James, and don't worry about it. I shouldn't be here, but could I just lie next to you? Would you hold me? I, uh…this must sound strange. You probably think me daft."

"Oh, Honey. You'd be surprised at the requests I get. Come, lie with me, and take me in your arms. I'll take your mind off home and the war, but not for long. After fifteen minutes, Miss Lucy gets upset with us for dawdling too long. Put your head on my breast, and I'll stroke your hair, and you can tell me I ain't no ugly, dirty whore to be spit on by the high and mighty proper women in this town. Come, my mighty warrior, comfort me too. I get sad and tired of smelly men humping over me like panting dogs. Sometimes, I get tired of life."

James took her in his arms gently, and they did give each other comfort with kind words and soft strokes of tenderness. Two strangers, each with their own sorrows and regrets, caressed and kissed away some of the hurt of the other. It was sensual, but not sexual, as two wounded souls, and for a time, two kindred spirits, shared some intimate moments, and they both wept onto the others breast. After twenty-five minutes, a loud rap on the door reminded Amanda she had dawdled with a customer too long, and so ended a pleasurable interlude for both of them. James tried to give Amanda five dollars as he left, but she placed her finger to his lips and shook her head no. She stuck the bill back into his pocket and blew a kiss to him as he walked out. On the way back to camp he whistled *Dixie*. James never returned to a brothel.

At camp, James found a letter from Pineville waiting for him on his bunk. He walked over to share Bertie's letter with Pleasant.

Pleasant read it and said, "Well, perhaps Adelaide is making progress. Bertie sounds hopeful. Thanks for sharing the letter."

"Yeah, she does. Makes me feel a little better about things. I think it's great that Adelaide is helping Bertie with her Sunday school class. Gives her something to do, and she'll be a good teacher. Think we'll be fighting any more this year?"

"Doubt it," Pleasant answered. I don't think there'll be another campaign for us until spring. Not a bad place to winter though, but come spring, I'm sure the Yankees will be marching south, but for now, there's plenty of Texas beef and fat deer to keep us fed."

"Spring," James said. "Yes, spring will be soon enough for me."

Chapter Twelve
Red River Campaign

In early March, Federal forces undertook an ambitious campaign through the valley of the Red River in western Louisiana and Arkansas. General Nathaniel Banks planned to make his way north to Shreveport from the coast, and General Frederick Steel would meet him with a large Union force marching south from Arkansas. Once the combined Confederate forces in Louisiana were crushed, these two Union armies would invade Texas. On the 20th of March, Parsons' Brigade and the Arkansas division of General Thomas Churchill marched south for Shreveport to reinforce the Texas and Louisiana forces already engaging Banks' army. General Price stayed in Arkansas with six thousand cavalry to harass General Steel, who was moving south from Little Rock. Price was having success, and the Union forces were slowed to a crawl. The Arkansans and Missourians moved south quickly to join the Texas and Louisiana troops. By the 23rd, they were marching through Mansfield, Lousiana where the Louisiana and Texas boys had stopped the Yankee advance. What they saw gave them courage. Hundreds of Union commissary wagons were abandoned by the road, and much needed artillery was ready to be turned against its previous owners. There were cheers from the Missourians as they marched by the captured and abandoned Union wagons and cannon.

"Look what's coming," James said to his squad, "Yankee prisoners, and it looks like they've taken a beating."

"Sure a bunch of 'em," Henry said as he watched the Federal troops walking in the opposite direction.

Most of the prisoners kept their eyes straight ahead or downcast. Some looked over at their enemy with as much curiosity as the men in gray had for them. There was no gloating among the Missourians or derisive remarks, just somber looks, and then it was eyes forward again. Every now and then, two enemies would exchange glances, and there would be a nod or even slight smile. The Confederates marched on. Their fight was about to begin, and these Yanks had finished theirs.

"Gawd, James," Henry said. "What's that awful smell? Smells like death."

"It is. Look over yonder," James answered and pointed toward a large open field.

Buzzards circled above, and below the circling scavengers was another face of this war—bloating corpses. Not all were whole, as body parts were also scattered over the terrain. The dead soldiers all wore the blue uniforms of Federal troops. There were more than Henry could count, and the smell was overpowering. Confederate burial details were digging long trenches as common graves for the fallen Yankees. Men who had died for their cause and would never return to families in places like Illinois and Ohio would lie side by side in death as they had marched side by side into battle. The men of the burial details had rags tied across their faces and worked with grim determination in the oppressive heat and odor. More than once, the marching men observed the carrion pecking at the bodies of Union dead, tearing off pieces of flesh before they were chased away by a shovel wielding Confederate.

"James, I ain't never seen nothing like this before in my life," Henry said as he gagged and tried to cover his nose and mouth with his shirt.

"Neither have I," James responded. "This is a vision of hell. It can't be imagined. It has to be seen to be believed, and I'm beginning to have a bellyful of war."

"Not a vision. This is hell!" Matthew, one of their squad members said. "Wish those up ahead would pick up the pace and lead us out of here faster."

"Amen, Brother," someone else called. "Let's get to the battlefield. Think I'd rather face Union bayonets than stay here longer."

"It scares me," Henry said to James.

"It is scary to see piles of dead men as you march to battle," James said.

"No, that's not all," Henry said. "I mean, being buried all together. If I was to be kilt, Paw would have a fit if he couldn't find my grave. Please, James, don't let 'em bury me like that."

"I won't, I promise, but don't think about it," James said "You have to be killed before they bury you, and you won't be shot this day."

"Course not," Henry said with a little too much bravado. "We been through too much to make a mistake and get shot by those Yankees up ahead." He began to whistle Dixie nervously as they continued the march.

Five miles from the village of Pleasant Hill, where the enemy waited, the Missourians and Arkansans parked the wagons and filled their canteens from a clear stream. By one o'clock that afternoon, under a hot sun, the men formed up into a line of battle one mile from the town. Pleasant Hill rested on a low plateau, running a mile from east to west. In front, strung out in the same direction, waited twelve thousand of the enemy. The Yankees were formed in two lines. The second was in full view along the plateau, and the first line occupied a natural ditch running zig-zag in the shallow valley between the town and the Confederates. This time, the Missourians were on the right flank. Stretched out to their left were the divisions from Arkansas, Texas, and Louisiana. The Rebs also numbered twelve thousand and were full of confidence. As usual, it seemed to James, Parsons' Brigade would be fighting up hill again.

"Real pretty town," Henry said. "Think the locals will be glad to see us?"

"I suspect so, from all the plundered homes we saw coming this way. Of course, that's saying we don't have to blow their town to hell driving the Yankees out."

At five o'clock, the attack began with cannon fire and a frontal attack by the Texas cavalry on the Union's center. Three times the cavalry charged and three times were repulsed by heavy musket fire. At each turn, more horses returned with empty saddles. After the final cavalry charge, the entire infantry line was engaged, firing volley after volley. The green carpet of grass and pink wild flowers was strewn with the gray uniformed cavalry men and dead and dying horses. Between the volleys of fire, could be heard the cries of wounded men and animals. James shut it out of his mind and concentrated on firing, reloading, and firing again. Kill the enemy. That's all, kill the enemy before he can kill you. After an hour, orders came down for Parsons' people to charge the long blue line. General Churchill, the corps commander, promised support to insure the Missourians would not be outflanked again.

"Reload and prepare to charge!" Pleasant and other officers shouted to their men.

"Scared?" Henry yelled, trying to make himself heard above the din as he inserted another paper cartridge in the muzzle of his rifle and rammed it home. His eyes were wide and he was breathing heavily.

"If you're not, I'm scared enough for both of us!" James yelled back and pointed his bayoneted rifle forward. He motioned his squad forward. "Steady, here it comes," he yelled.

Once again, the ear splitting screech of the rebel yell arose from the throats of thousands of men, and all logic was replaced with a blind lust to charge headlong into the deadly fire of those who wanted them destroyed. Forget the possibility of a shot crushing the life from their own bodies—kill the enemy and drive him from their land. The Confederates ran screaming toward the Yankees who were firing from their trenches. Disregard their own comrades falling all around them, forget the cries of pain from these fallen men who had shared tents and rancid rations. Vengeance would be theirs once they reached these faceless men in blue who were killing their compatriots. Survive the charge, pounce on their hated enemy, kill, and drive them from this place. Instill in these opposing forces such fear they will regret coming south of the Mason-Dixon line. The sprint across the open meadow quickly carried them to the zig-zag trench. Behind them were now Missourians and Arkansans mixed with the fallen bodies and horses of the Texan cavalry who died earlier. As they charged, some of the Union soldiers were already climbing out of the trench and running back up the slope toward the second Federal line of defense. Two divisions of Confederates pointed their rifles into the trench and fired their saved volley. James aimed his rifle at a young Yankee and could see his wide, brown eyes fill with fear. He fired point blank into the youngster's face. Then, like the rest of the brigade, he jumped into the trench, and the hand-to-hand combat began. It didn't take long to finish the job on those Yanks who were left behind by their comrades. The trench was theirs, but now, the harder part of the attack would begin. Dislodge the long blue line at the edge of the town. Charge again, this time up the slope, and drive the rest of the enemy out of Pleasant Hill.

James turned to his squad and counted noses. All were accounted for. He was relieved to see none of his men were among those killed.

James turned to Henry and asked, "You okay?"

"Yeah," he said. "How bout you? You got blood on your face."

James nodded and wiped his face with the back of his sleeve. They both were bloody—the blood from men they killed. Even their shoes were seeped with blood from stepping in the refuse of killing.

"Get ready, Henry. We're going again," James warned.

"Look!" Henry shouted.

James looked toward the town. He could see civilians, both women and men waving happily at them from an upper story veranda on the front of one of the large homes.

"Guess folks are glad to see us," Henry said.

"Yeah," James said grimly. "What do they think this is, a circus?" He shook his head in disbelief.

Once again, came the rebel yell, and the brigade of men climbed out of their trench and started up the slope. The response was immediate as smoke and thunder came from a thousand rifles in front of them, and Confederates fell backwards into the trench they had just taken.

"Don't hesitate!" Pleasant shouted at his company and charged ahead waving his sword along with other officers. James motioned his squad forward to follow his brother. The flag bearer fell over with a mortal wound to the chest, and another man picked up the Missourian's battle flag, encouraging the men to follow him. The top of his head disappeared with a well placed shot from the Yankee's position, but the flag was picked up by yet another man, this one from James's squad. The exchange of the flag seemed to instill more energy into the rebels, and the warrior's yell reached an even more intense frenzy as they charged even harder up the slippery killing ground.

James tripped once and fell sprawling next to a wounded Union soldier. He found his face inches away from the fallen enemy's. Another boy, James thought.

"Help me," the youngster cried softly. "Help me."

James was shaken and could only say, "I'm sorry," as Henry pulled him to his feet. They charged on.

At only fifty paces, the entire line of charging rebels stopped and returned their own volley at the Yankees. As blue coats fell, and the half crazed Missourians continued their onslaught, the Yanks began to panic and retreated into the town.

"We've got them on the run!" the Missourian officers yelled. "Reload and fire at will!"

All along the gray line, men were firing, reloading and firing again at the retreating enemy. There were wild cheers from the windows and second story balconies of homes lining the streets. Ladies waved their own flags of perfumed lace handkerchiefs.

"Quite a sight," a man on James's left said.

"I think they've all taken leave of their senses," James said. "This is insane. This whole town is full of crazy people."

"Well, it's still nice—" The man fell to the ground, blood pouring from his neck. Simultaneously, James had heard the familiar sound of a bullet whizzing past his nose. He looked to his right. Hundreds of Union soldiers were firing at them from the edge of the woods. More men fell. Then on the left, there was more enemy fire from Yankees in an outward bulge of their line. Evidently they had not been pushed back as far as those directly in front of Parsons' Brigade. Once again, having achieved their objective, the Missourians found themselves in wicked crossfire. They were in the open, without cover and without support.

"Sir, I thought we were getting support once we reached the town," Pleasant yelled at Major Stephens. "Where is it?"

The major shook his head in frustration. "Don't know. Hold your ground til we get orders."

The same conversation was going on between General Parsons and his aides. The general was disgusted and alarmed to see his men dying in a withering crossfire. He would not have his Missourians slaughtered again.

"Have the division pull back to our original position," the general ordered. "We're falling back. It appears there's no relief coming our way."

The brigade began retreating down the slope to the original position they held earlier in the afternoon. As usual, the Missourians had fought bravely and achieved their objective, only to pull back because promised relief had not materialized. There was one plus to this day's fighting. The Union army under Banks was in retreat also, and the Yankees headed back south, giving up the ambitious Red River Campaign. Banks was not Sherman, and he pulled the Union army out, leaving his dead and wounded on the field.

"It happened again, James," Henry said. "And we had the Yanks on the run." Anger rose in his voice.

"I know," James said wearily, "I know. Keep your head down."

"James, the Yanks aren't chasing us. Looks like they're leaving too. Don't see the ladies waving at us anymore either."

James turned with alarm to see Henry standing straight up, shading his eyes and looking back at the town. "Henry! I said keep your head down." There was a dull whacking sound, and Henry fell backward with a cry of surprise. James ran and knelt beside his friend.

"Oh, Gawd, James. I'm kilt. Look at me. I'm ruint." James could see the entrance wound was just to the left of Henry's belly button, and blood was bubbling up from it.

"Don't worry, Henry. I won't leave you. I'll take you to the surgeon's tent myself. You'll be just fine, just fine. I'll take care of you."

James began to crawl back to safety, dragging Henry along by the collar of his coat. It was agonizingly slow progress through a quagmire of torn bodies in blue and gray Up ahead, the Texas cavalry horses were still there also. All were not dead, and the wretched sounds of suffering mounts who carried their masters to death were mingled with the cries of dying men. Pitiful cries of "Mother" rang in his ears. Several times, as he pulled Henry along, dying men reached out to grab his arm and beg for help. He could only jerk himself away, and crawl on. He found himself crawling through blood, and some of the things he crawled through only a surgeon skilled at autopsy would recognize. His hands, knees, arms, and elbows were covered with blood, and what else, he didn't know. What other unmentionable things will I drag my dying brother through? What else do you ask of me, Lord? Once he glanced back toward town and shouted.

"Where are you fine ladies and gentlemen who cheered us? Come, look, and see the real face of war." For a moment he stood and lifted his hands toward the town. "Yes, come with me you gentle people. Come and see the carnage of glory. Walk with me and smell death. Drink in the pungent perfume of blood that men spilled here today. Dip your perfumed handkerchiefs in a hero's gaping wound." Then, in tears, he fell back to his knees beside Henry and continued his slow task. For a fleeting moment, he wished a Minie ball had found its mark between his eyes.

"I'm in hell," James cried out once. "God save me. You've sent me to hell. Please, sweet Jesus, speed me from this awful place. I'm finished with war. Finished."

In what seemed like eternity, James finally reached safety. In the shade of a magnolia tree, he cradled Henry's head in his lap. He was still alive, but moaning loudly in pain, now that the shock was wearing off. James rocked back and forth feeling impotent at his inability to ease the pain of his friend.

"Shhh, Henry. You'll be fine. I promise. Just hold on a little longer."

He said a silent prayer and rose with Henry in his arms. Now his friend's blood soaked into his own uniform as he walked toward the area where he hoped to find help. Seeing orderlies pulling hand-carts toward the battlefield, he stopped to ask directions. They pointed in the direction he was already headed.

When he got there, he was greeted with a fresh vision from hell. Hundreds of men lay around the large surgeon's tent, and again he was surrounded with pitiful cries of men dying in pain, both Yankees and Confederates. A surgeon and orderlies were going among the men checking to see which ones might be saved. Those they thought had the best chance would be given priority and taken inside. Those that could not be saved would be left to die. James knew what was going on. These weary men were making God-like decisions. There were also some women volunteers giving comfort.

"My friend needs help," James said to the surgeon wearing a red stained leather apron and walking among the wounded. "Please."

The doctor took one look at Henry and shook his head. "Soldier, put your friend down. There's nothing we can do. Inside, his bowels are shredded. He'll bleed to death while his body poisons itself. Sorry, we can't do much for him." The surgeon continued his weary search.

James knew the truth, but walked in circles for a few minutes asking orderlies, and the answer was the same. Finally, he carried Henry over by a tree and laid him down in the shade. He sat beside Henry, and once again cradled his friend's head in his lap. He would not let this young man die alone among strangers. As darkness fell on the encampment, James still held Henry. The dying was slow and painful. All during the night, Henry's moans and cries were mingled with those of other fallen soldiers who suffered only a few yards away. Like this farm boy from McDonald County, who had never been more than twenty miles from home, other farm boys from other states, both north and south, would die far from home in a land of strangers. Throughout the ordeal of Henry's dying, James would wipe his friend's face with the wet sponge one of the orderlies had given him. The orderly had warned him not to give his friend a drink, so when Henry asked for water, James would wet the sponge and press it against his friend's parched lips. Just before dawn Henry became delirious from high fever and pain, mumbling and crying incoherently. Finally, as an orange sun rose behind the trees, Henry looked up at James and smiled. For just a moment he was lucid.

"James, Brother James," he said weakly. "I see heaven. Mama waits for me." The light went out of his eyes. It was over, and James wept.

Two hours later, Pleasant found his brother. He had been in a panic since the men had fallen back the previous evening, and he couldn't find him. He knelt beside James.

"James, it's over. Come with me. You need to eat something."

James looked up at Pleasant. His face was lined with grief. "No, I've got to bury him."

"The burial detail will take care of him," Pleasant said gently. "Let them do it."

"No," James said evenly. "He won't rest in a common grave with others. I'll dig his grave myself so his father can find it after the war. It was my word, and I won't break it. I just need to rest a little, that's all."

Pleasant nodded. "I understand. I've got to get back. By the way, the Union army has abandoned Pleasant Hill and is marching in retreat to the south again. We've done our job here. They won't be back." Pleasant would not make an issue of James's guardianship over his friend's body. He knew the full story from Helena about James carrying him to the surgeon's tent and demanding his brother be cared for.

James understood and nodded his head, but said nothing. Pleasant left, his heart heavy with worry over his brother, and he was afraid there was a look of defeat in his eyes now.

James finally laid Henry down and folded the boy's hands over his chest. He tenderly straightened the body and cleansed Henry's face and hands. Around mid-morning, one of the women volunteers, who had watched James all morning, walked over with a basket of food and gave him some small sweet cakes and cheese to eat. He thanked the young woman for her kindness and ate slowly as he watched the continuing panorama of the tragic aftermath of battle still unfolding in front of the surgeon's tent. Men on burial detail went about the prostrate bodies looking for dead. When finding one, the body would be loaded into a hand-cart and taken to the burial area a few hundred yards away, where they were stacked like cordwood to be buried by the men assigned to the grisly task.

"Soldier, you want us to take your friend to the burial ground?"

James was startled and looked up. Soldiers from the burial detail were standing in front of him with empty handcarts.

"No, but let me borrow a shovel. I'm burying him beneath this tree," James said.

"Don't know if you can do that," one man said with a puzzled look. Then he looked down at Henry and back into James's grief stricken face. "Suit yourself," he said and handed James a shovel.

James finished his meal and began to dig Henry's grave on the other side of the tree. He was a man possessed as he dug, seeing nothing but the damp earth yielding to his shovel and hearing nothing except his own labored breathing as he bent his back to the task. A lieutenant from company F noticed James working and asked him what he was doing. There was no answer or even acknowledgment an officer was talking to him, just the mechanical movements of James at his work. The lieutenant knew the corporal was Pleasant's brother. He thought about reporting the incident, but after a few moments of watching, he recognized the look in James's eyes. It was the same look other American soldiers, in another great bloodletting of another century, in lands far from American shores, would call the "thousand-yard stare." Shaking his head, the officer walked on, and James kept digging. Finally, he collapsed onto the pile of dirt he had excavated. His breaths came in great heaving gasps, and he labored to suck in enough air to replenish his starving lungs. He closed his eyes and rested. After a few minutes, he picked himself up and gathered what he needed. He wrapped Henry tightly in his half of the dog-tent and gently placed the body in the grave he had just dug. What he didn't know was he had an audience. Off and on during the past two hours, the women volunteers and three of the orderlies had been watching him at his work. They were moved by the dedication of this war-weary soldier putting his friend to rest. Just as he started to spade the dirt back into Henry's grave, a hand reached out to take the shovel from him. James was startled and looked up.

"Rest, Soldier," one of the orderlies said gently. "We're here to help."

James let the shovel be taken from his hands. Two other orderlies were already spading the dirt over Henry. He nodded and rested against the tree trunk. He was too tired to argue. Soon, the grave was filled, and the men were patting the soil down into a neat mound.

"Thank you," James said. "Is there a plank around I can use for a marker?"

"I'll find something," one of the men said and went to fetch a suitable board.

In a few minutes, James was carving Henry's name deeply into the plank. When it was finished, a few hammers with a shovel planted it firmly into the soft earth at the head of the grave. One last swing of the shovel, and he looked up. Two of the women volunteers were standing with the orderlies. They each carried a bouquet of pink, blue, and red wild flowers.

One reached out and touched the back of James's hand. It was the same girl who had brought him food earlier.

"We thought you shouldn't have to lay your friend to rest alone," she said with compassion and concern. "We know you've been here since yesterday and stood guard with him all through the night. We prayed for you."

James choked back a sob. He was deeply touched by the kindness of these strangers and said simply, "Thank you. I know Henry appreciates your kindness too."

Both women placed their offerings of condolences on Henry's grave and embraced James. He held back the tears he thought would either choke him or flood in an embarrassing torrent. It was almost too much to bear, feeling the compassionate touch of heartfelt tenderness in this brutal killing field. He returned the embraces and shook hands with the men who were resting on their shovels. They visited for a few minutes as the strangers asked about his friend, and he told them about the boy who grew into a man. Before they parted, he asked another favor from the ladies.

"I would very much appreciate your help," James said. "I want to mail a letter along with a few personal things from Henry's haversack to his father in Missouri, but I have nothing to mail them in. Could you help me?"

"Of course," Julia said. "Do you need paper and pen?"

"No, I've got writing materials. I'm going to write the letter and draw a map showing where his grave is. I'll make quick work of it."

"Go ahead and do it. We'll return in a few minutes, but you have to promise to eat. We'll bring something back."

James quickly wrote a letter to Henry's father and drew a map with directions to Henry's grave. In the letter, James included Bertie's name and address in Pineville. From what Henry had told him, his home wasn't far from there. From Henry's haversack, he gathered his friend's few personal belongings, including letters from his parents and sweetheart. James also found Henry's white shaving mug with a hand painted stag's head on the side, razor, hunting knife, wallet, a hand made quilt, and photograph of his family. James knew Henry was the only son and had two older sisters. He looked up. The women had returned with a box about the right size for Henry's belongings.

"Don't worry," Julia said. "We'll wrap everything carefully so the shaving mug doesn't get broken, and we'll post it tomorrow. Just give us his address."

"Now, eat," the older volunteer said as she handed him a paper wrapped lunch. There was cheese, sausage, bread, and fruit.

To make sure he ate, the two women took a seat on the grass facing him as he ate his meal. He was famished and savored every bite. The women were gratified and chatted as he ate. As the hunger disappeared, he realized Julia was a beautiful young woman. Long, shiny, black hair framed her delicate features with a small straight nose, white teeth that showed when she smiled, expressive eyes, and a wide mouth with full lips. She wore a brown dress, and her hair was tied back with a pretty, green ribbon matching the color of her laughing eyes that seemed to flirt with James. Once, she blushed as he smiled back, and the red rising in her high cheek bones as she cast her eyes downward made his heart beat a little faster. Her smile was warm and inviting, and James marveled at her long eye lashes when she blinked. Lashes of lace, he thought to himself. He was taken by this beautiful, tenderhearted girl, who had shown him kindness and taken his mind away from the carnage around them both. She wore no wedding ring, and James wished he had no place to go, wished this war was over, wished Henry was on his way home to see his sweet Emilia instead of under the mound on his right, wished Henry's father had not lost his only son so far from his side, wished all of the dead from this day's slaughter were safely home where they belonged. He noticed Julia clutched a book of Coleridge's poems in her hand.

"Is Coleridge your favorite poet?" he asked.

Her face brightened, "No, not my favorite, but a favorite of one of the men in the hospital tent. I promised to read to him later. My favorite is Browning. Do you love poetry?"

"Yes, I do. So, is it Robert or Elizabeth?"

"Oh, Elizabeth," she answered with a laugh. Her laughter was the tinkle of crystal wind chimes swinging in a gentle breeze. "Who's your favorite?"

"English would be Tennyson or Coleridge," James answered. "My favorite American poet is Poe. I like the musical quality of his poetry."

"Where did you get your love of poetry and books, James?" Julia asked.

"Parents and sisters," he answered. "Father built the first school in my county back home."

The conversation drifted from books to family, and the horror of the past two days began to dissipate from James's heart. He had enjoyed his discussions of books with Henry, but that was teaching, and this was pure pleasure. Finding kindred spirits unexpectedly in this killing place who loved reading as much as he lifted his spirits, and the conversation gave him solace. But soon, too soon, it seemed to James, he was finished with his meal, and it was time to get back to his company.

"Good-by, ladies," James said and kissed the hand of each as he gave his thanks for their kindness. "God bless you both."

"Good-by," they said. "Stay safe and alive," Julia added. Her eyes were brimming with tears.

He waved and watched them walk away. As he was about to turn and go his way, Julia suddenly turned and ran back to him. She put her arms around his neck, then kissed him full on the mouth.

"Walk with God, James," she said. "Return safely to your home and family." There were tears in her eyes as she ran back to her friend.

James was in pleasant shock and reached up to touch his lips as if to hold the warmth of her kiss there, to hold this sweet, fleeting moment just a little longer. For the rest of his life, he would recall this special time with a smile. As he stood watching the departing women and savoring the sweetness of Julia's tender gift, he heard Margaret speak.

"Julia! Your mother would skin you alive if she saw such brazen behavior from you." Leaning against Julia's shoulder, she chuckled and said, "Don't worry, I won't tell. He is handsome, isn't he?"

James turned, grinning broadly as he did. Walking away to find his company, he began whistling *Dixie*, and there was a spring in his step as he moved away from death and despair. Where his steps would take him tomorrow, he didn't ponder. His mind was with the tenderness of the past hour. There would be other times to think of the terror, the grief, and the carnage of this war, but for now, he pushed it from his mind and whistled as he walked back to reality.

Chapter Thirteen
Chasing Steele

After resting a few days near Mansfield, the combined army of Missourians, Texans, and Arkansans departed on a forced march for Camden, Arkansas. General Price and his Confederate cavalry had successfully stopped the Union force's advance south and driven the Yankees under General Steele into this city on the Quashita River. If the Confederates could reinforce Price in time, there was a chance to destroy this threat from the north. It would be a hard two hundred miles, but after forcing Banks and his Union army from the south to retreat, the men of Parsons' Brigade left in good spirits and still had visions of returning home to drive the Yankees from their soil. The Missourians left with high hopes on April 14.

"James, I think all you pie eaters love this marching," Willard said, using the derisive name city dwellers often used for farm boys. He laughed and plopped himself down next to James under the shade tree.

"That's Corporal Pie Eater to you," James answered with a grin. "Why, a simple plow boy like myself thinks it's all just hunky-dory. Wish I had a mule and plow to walk behind," James continued, and closed his eyes as he folded his hands behind his head.

Willard was his new possum, or buddy, and carried half the dog-tent he and James would share when needed. He had arrived with other replacements to replenish Parsons' decimated brigade just before the army began this march north. James considered him a blow-hard and full of himself, but tried to be tolerant. Perhaps, he thought, it was only nervous bravado, because the man was a fresh fish never having seen action before. Pleasant had assigned him to James's squad, and he accepted this new responsibility with aplomb, but was beginning to have doubts he could teach the new man anything. How can you teach anything to someone who knows it all, he began to think after five days of hard marching. Willard seemed to have a good education and had been a law clerk in St. Louis before following a recruiter across the border into Arkansas. However, for the last year and a half, he had done nothing but run errands for officers at headquarters in Shreveport. Must have gained the ire of some colonel to end up here, James surmised, because from all his complaining, he certainly didn't volunteer for action.

"Got any more of those goobers?" Willard asked. "Need some water too. Never been so thirsty in my life. Why can't we ride in a wagon? We got plenty. Don't need all those Yankee rations they left behind anyway. We'll make short work of them Yanks in Camden. You just wait."

"Should have filled your canteen back at that last stream like everybody else," James said and poured some peanuts into Willard's out stretched hand. He then poured half of his own canteen of water into his partner's. The man chugged most of it down in one drink.

"Ahhh," Willard groaned with satisfaction after draining the last of the water. Then he began to eat the peanuts, not thinking they would make him thirsty again. "What we need is some bark juice," then with a chortle added, "suppose you don't drink either, do you?"

"Not much," James responded with a mock chortle. He closed his eyes again and thought of the warm interlude back at Pleasant Hill. He smiled as he remembered soft lips pressed against his.

"Can't wait til we meet those Yanks," Willard said, interrupting James's reverie. "They'll see a real fighter now. Chase em' back to kingdom come."

"I can only imagine," James said and sighed. He stood up and got his squad back on the march. Two hours later, Pleasant called James out of line.

"How are you getting along with the new man?" Pleasant asked.

James shook his head slowly. "Hard to say. We ain't fighting, but he's hard- headed and a braggart. If he fights as tough as he goes on about, the whole war will be over by nightfall, maybe sooner. He'll show them ornery Yankees."

Pleasant began to laugh. "Struck me that way too. Been thinking about transferring him to Company A. Captain York's replacement strikes me the same way. They'd make a good match. Sorry it had to be you. I wasn't aware how bad he was that first day."

"Maybe it's penance for teasing my sisters all those years," James said. "I've already heard about Reynolds. The men of company A are fit to be tied, and their new company commander may not last past the first ten minutes of the battle. Killed in action, not by a Union Springfield but a Confederate Enfield. My own suggestion is that the entire army take a rest when we get there and send those two charging after the Yankees. Why, it'll change the course of history."

Pleasant laughed again. "I'm sure! Oh, Brother, I gotta come and see you after every staff meeting. Listening to all that stuffiness, I need to hear someone with common sense and humor. Don't spread this to the men, because I don't want our sterling Lieutenant Reynolds dying before the battle starts. At the last staff meeting, when asked about his new command, he offered this. 'Enlisted men are ignorant, but crafty beasts who bear watching at all times, and I must report that too many of our officers are altogether too familiar with the enlisted ranks to suit my pleasure.' But, I'll have them disciplined before we go into battle.'"

"Ignorant, but crafty beasts? Too familiar to suit his pleasure? What under God's heaven does that mean?" James began laughing. "Don't know if I can hold this nugget of wisdom in or not, but I'll try. What did Colonel Monroe have to say?"

"You'll like this," Pleasant said, then filled out his stomach and talked in a deep voice. "Lieutenant, these company officers and other field commanders, including yours truly, have shared the same rotten beef, faced the same shot and shell, watched comrades blown to pieces, stepped in the same blood of patriots as we charged the enemy, and eaten the same dust enlisted troops swallow on this march. That sort of thing is rather intimate and probably creates a smidgen of familiarity. You'll have to live with it."

James began to laugh so hard, tears ran. When he finally stopped laughing, he wiped the tears that had turned to mud globs off his cheeks. "I think we should vote the good Colonel a generalship. I liked the man from that first day we met when he took my horse. He was still Major Monroe then, a good man and a brave soldier."

"Yeah, he's a top drawer officer, that's for sure, but he'll never make general. He's too outspoken for his own good. Besides, both Parsons and Price know he's too valuable as a divisional field officer."

"Think any mail will be catching up to us soon?" James asked.

"Doubt it. So, how's it going with Willard this afternoon? Did you give him anymore water?"

James shook his head. "Afraid I gave in. Let him have one swallow as I held the canteen. Had to jerk it away before he gulped all of what little I had. I just took my last swallow half hour ago. He's been bellyaching ever since."

"Well, there's good water within two hours. We'll bivouac there tonight. We'll talk later. I better get back and take a lead."

James waved to his brother and rejoined his squad.

"Must be swell having your brother as a captain," Willard said through parched and cracked lips. To no avail, James had warned him not to lick his lips.

"We enlisted together," James replied. "Yes, it is nice."

"Bet you get officer's rations and extra things, don't you?"

"Afraid not. In fact, his rations aren't any better than ours."

"Could he get us some water? Nobody around will share any more with me."

"His canteen's empty too. We're only two hours from fresh water. You'll make it. Here, roll this around in your mouth and stop licking your lips." He took a small round pebble from his pocket and handed it to Willard.

Willard did as he was told, but the grumbling didn't stop. He just couldn't get it through his head that the talking would make him thirsty also, or even cause him to swallow the pebble. James already knew what to do to keep his mind off thirst and the march. He daydreamed of happy times. Willard didn't get it, but within two hours, they finally heard cheers up ahead.

"What's that all about?" Willard asked.

"We're there," James answered. "We'll soon have water and stop for the day."

Company H reached the bivouac area along a clear running stream and broke ranks to gather in their designated area. First order of business was to fill canteens and find a sleeping area. The men began lining the creek and filling canteens. Willard fell face down into the water. A stream of curses from the men downstream filled the air as he stirred silt with his big splash. James shook his head with disgust and moved a few feet upstream from Willard. Duly scolded, Willard returned to the bank, stirring up more silt and filled his canteen. Like the other men, James drank slowly to slack his thirst and watched Willard gulp down most of his canteen in one long drink.

"Willard! Slow down, or you'll make yourself sick." The warning was ignored, and James shrugged. Why waste my breath, he thought and continued to sip his water. When his thirst was gone, James stood to stretch as Willard staggered past him and began vomiting while leaning against a tree. Within a few minutes, the men had finished refilling their canteens and were face down in the water washing themselves. There was laughter and joking up and down the line. Some were splashing and playing like school boys, releasing the tension and tiredness of the day's march. James joined in the frolic for a few minutes and then went to the tree where Willard was sitting. His companion was whipped, and for a moment, there was some pity in James's heart. He hung his shirt to dry from one of the lower branches and took a seat by Willard.

"Okay, now listen," James said, "drink a little water, just a little, and when we eat tonight, some more. Refill your canteen first thing tomorrow morning."

"I will. Learned my lesson today."

"Good. Hey, go join in the fun for awhile."

"Everybody's mad at me," Willard said. "Never had so much cussin' out in my life."

"It's forgotten now. Just remember next time. Go on. I'll get our camp site ready. Rations will be coming along anytime."

James swung both their back packs and bed rolls over his shoulder and walked a few yards where other men from company H were already gathering. Pleasant and a detail of men had already returned from the commissary wagons with the company's rations. James got two tins of Yankee preserved beef, two potatoes, an onion, and dried fruit. He scooped some flour into his small cooking pot. Wouldn't be a bad meal tonight, he thought, but right now he wanted to rest. After laying out both bed rolls, and arranging things, he lay on his and stared into the sky which was beginning to show the coming of twilight. The sun would be down soon, and the bottom of the clouds were already reflecting yellow. It would be another starlit night and no need for a tent. He thought if he were cooped up in the small tent with Willard till morning listening to his jawing, he might go mad and garrote the man in his sleep. He watched the beauty of the departing sun for a while and decided to get supper ready. As the sun surrendered to darkness, Willard showed up. He didn't look so green now.

"Feeling better?" James asked.

"Whatcha cookin'? Smells good," Willard responded.

"Stew. We'll have supper in a few minutes. It's already boiling. Won't take long."

"Is that bread?" Willard said pointing to the rifle ramrod sticking in the ground next to the fire. James had made bread dough, rolled it into the diameter of a cigar and wrapped it around the ramrod. It was already smelling like fresh baked bread and in a few minutes would be golden brown and ready to eat.

James smiled. "It's called ramrod bread. You'll see a lot of the men making it around campfires when we have the flour. Guarantee you'll like it better than the hardtack."

"I'm starving," was Willard's only response.

"Chew on these," James said and handed him some dried peaches.

After supper, James volunteered to wash the mess kits and cooking pots. Actually, he preferred a little solitude by the creek. In the dark, James worked at cleaning and was content. In the distance, he could occasionally here the noise of someone at the same chore. Moonlight was reflected in the dark waters as he worked, and James whistled softly to himself. The coming battle was kept in its private compartment at the back of his mind, and he didn't dwell on it. He heard a splash and looked up. A stag froze in the middle of the cool water and stared at him. James froze also and held his breath as he concentrated. Now, he was the stag with all his senses alert for danger. Cold water swirled around strong legs that were tensed and ready to bolt for freedom out of harm's way. It was a moment of magic as James imagined himself as the stag.

"Beautiful, isn't he," a voice whispered behind him.

James turned and saw Jeremy Collins standing behind him. At that moment, the stag made the other bank of the stream in one leap and disappeared into darkness.

"Sorry, James. I wouldn't have interrupted if I had known he was here. My mess kit needs cleaning too."

"Don't worry about it, Jeremy. He wouldn't have stayed long anyway." James liked Jeremy. Like Willard, he was one of the replacements, but unlike his new possum, he was a steadfast soldier, who listened and learned without complaint. James didn't know his age, but thought he was close to sixty. His craggy face, full of lines and character, was softened by deep-set hazel eyes that held a person's attention. There was both character and humor in his face, the face of a trustworthy person.

"You have family back in Dunklin County, Jeremy?" James asked.

"No, not anymore. My wife, Mary, died last winter of pneumonia, my daughter is married and living in Kansas City. Both my boys lie at Shiloh. Killed the first day of battle. Mary seemed to give up when we got the news. Don't think she wanted to live much. The fight was kicked out of her, so I sold my land and came south to join up. No, nothin' left for me in Missouri's boot heel anymore."

"You going to Kansas City when the war's over?"

"Yes, think I will," Jeremy answered. Then he blinked back some tears, and a smile broke the lines of his face. "Got a grandson waitin' for me. I'll have somebody, won't I? So, God has given me blessings."

"That's something to go home for. When the battle comes, keep your head down. You've already given two sons to this cause. That's enough. You stay alive."

James finished his chore, said goodnight, and walked back to the sleeping area. Willard was already snoring when he reached the campsite, and James got between his own covers. He stared into the heavens with hands folded behind his head. Alone, in the dark, he thought of Jeremy's wounded soul, his own, and contemplated the countless stars above him. He knew this bleeding country was full of untold wounded souls who grieved over lost loved ones, grieved over dashed dreams, grieved over bodies maimed and crippled. And we fight on, James thought, and wondered what the God both sides prayed to thought when he looked down on this bloody ground. James was a believer and felt the Lord must also grieve to see the killing. Must be getting tired of us—really tired of us. Restful sleep finally overcame him, and like uncounted thousands across this tortured land, both Union and Confederate, from Virginia to Arkansas, he dreamed of home.

Two days later, on April 22, the army arrived at the outskirts of Camden. The fighting was limited to skirmishes, mainly by Shelby's Texas Cavalry and General Price's mounted troops. Steele and his Union soldiers were trapped in the city. Fighting was sporadic, but Steele knew he had to move his troops out of Camden or be destroyed. He chose the former and on the 27th, burned all his surplus camp supplies, destroying one hundred wagons. At 3:00 o'clock in the morning, the Federals abandoned Camden and crossed the Quashita River in their pontoons. Within an hour, the Confederates marched into the city amidst the cheers of a grateful population, happy to be rid of the Yankee occupiers. The troops were gratified to see happy civilians, cheering and thrusting snacks and water at them. However, there was no time for rest. General Price was in charge and determined to catch up with Steele and destroy the Federal army. The engineer battalion would build a floating bridge across the river, but first they needed planks—lots of planks. Along with others, Parsons' Brigade was given the task of tearing down the long cotton warehouses at the outskirts of Camden for their planks. A deafening noise of shouting, hammering, tearing, and chopping rang over the city. As thousands of men tore the warehouses apart, thousands more carried wood to the engineers who were constructing the bridge. In the middle of this din of activity could also be heard laughter and singing as the men made light of their heavy work.

"Give me a hand with this beam!" James shouted at Willard and another man.

"Hold your horses," Willard called back with a curse. "I'm a soldier, not a carpenter. I joined to kill Yankees not do this."

"You won't live long enough to cross this bridge we're building if you don't put your shoulder into the job!" Sergeant Perkins yelled at him. "We cross the bridge, and then we'll see if you're the fighter you claim to be. But first, we build the bridge."

"You sergeants ever think we might need a rest?" Willard retorted with a snarl.

Sergeant Perkins moved so close their noses were almost touching. His voice was cold and even. "I'm tired of your whining, Private. That's all you've done. Look at Jeremy. More than twice your age and half your weight. Thing is, he's done twice the work as you. So, move it, or you'll cross the bridge in chains. Get my drift, Private?"

Willard nodded and got to work. He grumbled no more and pulled his own weight. By daybreak, the bridge was finished.

Before the sun was very high, the infantry began crossing in single file. At the same time, artillery and freight wagons were ferried across on flats. As soon as companies and brigades were formed up on the opposite shore, the pursuit for Steele began. There was no rest through that day and into the night as the army marched eastward. During that night's long march, the procession of men and arms was an eerie sight. The cloud-covered night was pitch black, and every third wagon carried torch lights. The bayonets of the marching soldiers between the wagons reflected the light from torches and glistened with an unearthly aura. It seemed to James, the army had the ghostly appearance of a terrifying brigade from hell marching through the forest, and the teamsters looked like demons sitting in the glare of their wagons' torches. He was glad when light from another day began to leak through the dark forest, and the marching men were no longer apparitions from the netherworld.

As the army left the forest and moved across a prairie, the men's resolve to catch the Yankees and punish them deepened. The Federals had left a wasteland in their wake as Steele practiced a scorched earth policy between the Quashita and Saline rivers. Homes and businesses were ransacked, fields of young green wheat destroyed, smokehouses emptied. Even fences were torn up and burned. They saw circling buzzards over ruined fields where draft animals lay dead and bloating in the sun. As they continued the march through devastation, the adrenaline of anger replaced the men's fatigue, and the pace was quickened.

"Hope we catch 'em soon," Jeremy said grimly. "No sense to this, no sense or reason at all to kill dumb brutes whose only crime was pulling a plow. Don't Yankees plow their land with mules and horses too?"

"Suspect they do," James said and shook his head. "If they were hungry enough to eat 'em, I'd understand, but this...this is senseless."

"Philistines!" yelled a voice from behind. "They be Philistines and whore mongers, not honorable soldiers!"

James smiled. He recognized the voice. It was Abraham McCall, or Preacher Abe as most of the men called him. He turned and yelled back at Abraham, "And we'll smite them hip and thigh with our terrible swift sword!"

"Amen, Brother, amen!" came the answer.

"Oh, Lordy, James, don't get old Abraham started," Samuel Johnston said, marching in line behind James.

"Oh, he's harmless," James answered.

"Yeah, but you don't share a tent with him," Samuel answered. "I try to sleep every night with him preaching and praying at me."

"And nobody needs it worse than you, Samuel," a comrade called. "Preacher Abe caught you mongering after some whores back in Shreveport. Knows you need the preaching."

"Yeah, Samuel. Hope you been listening to your tent mate. You need all the help he can give you," another soldier teased. Up and down the line there was laughter until one of the sergeants gave the order for quiet in the ranks.

On April 29, they finally caught up with the Union forces at Jenkins Ferry on the Saline River. A heavy rain had fallen all that day and turned the land along the Saline River into a large, flooded swamp. General Steele had his 12,000 Union troops in a good defensive position on the bank in preparation for flight across the river. Both flanks were guarded by impassable bayous, and the land in front of him was flooded in knee-deep water. The condition of the battle field prevented the Confederates from engaging with an extensive line of battle. The cavalry charged into the Federal lines time after time, drawing heavy fire, but the wet terrain was not suited for cavalry charges. The horses kept bogging down and could not mount good speed, so General Churchill's Arkansas infantry was ordered forward. After two hours of fighting in knee-deep water, exhaustion slowed the advance to a crawl, and Price ordered the Arkansans to withdraw from the field to be relieved by Parsons' Missourians. Company H was on the right, and Pleasant waved his men forward into the quagmire of muddy water that was now turning a murky red in places. The men whooped as they plunged into the fray, but soon their charge turned into agonizingly slow progress toward an enemy that was laying down a withering fire.

"Keep your heads down," James yelled at Willard and Jeremy. "Low as possible. Make yourself a small target and keep moving."

Willard's eyes were wild with fear, and he was gasping for breath before they moved twenty yards. James had doubts the man would make it. If he didn't collapse from exhaustion or die from a well-placed bullet, he might be shot in the back by one of the sergeants as he ran away. Willard probably didn't know that in both Union and Confederate armies, one of the jobs a sergeant was assigned was to shoot men who turned and ran from the face of the enemy. James hadn't seen it happen, but there was always a first time. The Missourians struggled and plunged ahead, stopping to fire their own volleys every few yards. But the enemy had the advantage. They fired from good cover made from cut timber.

In front of them was a Negro regiment. They were apparently good marksmen and well disciplined, sending volley after volley into the ranks of the Missourians. It took a while for James to realize these Yankees had a different color, but hadn't given it much thought. They were only more Yanks trying to kill him.

"My God, they've sent darkies to kill us," Willard yelled. He stopped and started to turn.

Sergeant Perkins slammed his rifle into Willard's back. "Keep moving, Private. They're all Yankees. Keep moving and keep firing." Willard staggered forward with a curse.

Drawing close enough for one final charge into the Colored division's lines, the exhausted Missourians managed one more rebel yell and went splashing forward as fast as the mud and water would let them. At almost point blank range, they fired a volley, lowered their bayonets, and splashed ahead with another scream. With their knees pumping almost chest high as they struggled through the water, James thought the men looked like crazed deer bounding through a river. The blue coats began to fall back as these crazy men leapt onto their breastworks, fired another volley and began swinging rifles like clubs. The fighting was fierce and the Yanks began an orderly and disciplined withdrawal. A few steps backwards, fire at the enemy, cut his ranks down, and then retreat some more. Even in retreat, the Union division was taking its toll on the Missourians. Somehow, in the confusion, James and part of his squad were separated from the others. They were several yards to the right, and the water was deeper here, making the forward progress slower. The Union troops regrouped and began to counterattack.

"Where's everybody?" Willard asked in a panic.

"On our left," James answered. "Just keep moving forward. Look out ahead. Yankees."

There were half a dozen of the Negro troops up ahead of them. They were firing to their right at other Missourians, and it was hard to see in the thick smoke.

"Quick, take aim and fire," James told the others. "They haven't seen us yet, so fire before they do."

They all fired in a volley and three of the men in blue fell. The Yankees swung their rifles and returned fire. Now, only Willard and James were left standing, and the three Yanks charged with their bayonets pointed forward. Willard turned and fled. James wanted to shoot the coward down himself, but pulled his revolver and carefully aimed at the largest target. The big man fell backwards, but the other two kept coming. He aimed again and his gun misfired. Twice more, he tried with the same results. James re-holstered the pistol and waited with his own bayoneted rifle at the ready. There was no time to reload, and he waited as two of the enemy bore down on him. His only thought was of Honey Creek and the day that brought him down this path to death. I will die and rot here in a Godforsaken, nameless swamp. The first soldier plunged at him. James successfully parried the stab, and with an upward thrust, his rifle's butt caught the enemy's jaw. The Yank fell backward into the water. James turned but knew he was too slow. The other Union man had already begun the downward thrust of his bayonet toward James's chest. James dodged and tried to maneuver backward, but stumbled and was now prone at the enemy's feet. Simultaneously a shot rang out, and the Yankee dropped his rifle and fell to his knees. He stared blankly at James, and his dark eyes were full of agony as he fell face forward into the muddy water. James turned and saw Sergeant Perkins.

"Second man I killed today. At least I didn't shoot this one in the back."

James nodded with understanding and said, "Thanks, Sergeant. Willard?"

"Yeah, your brother sent me this way to look for you when he noticed a few of his men moving too far to the right. We've been ordered to pull back. The Texans are relieving us. I saw that cowardly scum run and leave you to be killed. Told him to halt twice after he threw his rifle down, but he kept running. God, I knew I might have to do this someday, but never really thought about it much. Didn't want to think about it I guess, and today...may God damn this war to hell."

"You did what you were ordered to do. Thank you for my life, Sergeant. I'd be face down in this swamp instead of these men if not for you." He waved his arm at the dead Union soldiers. "Thank you."

"Well, I'll say this for the Colored troops. They're good soldiers. So much for all the talk they wouldn't be. They fought like hellions, and they're still fighting against our fresh troops."

James shrugged as they splashed back toward their unit. "Maybe they fight like hellions, because they know why they fight."

"Good point," the sergeant said. "And you, James. Don't you know what you're fighting for anymore?"

"For a Confederate States of America? Not anymore. I gave up that dream at Pleasant Hill watching old men and boys die with us. But, I'd still like to run the Yanks out of my state."

"And you still fight. I'll tell you something, James. If not the best, you're one of the best soldiers I've ever seen." Then he sighed. "Yeah, I've had some of the same feelings as you."

"And you still fight," James said as they found themselves back with their division, still splashing toward higher ground. They waved at the Texans wading in the opposite direction.

"Don't know no better," Perkins said with a grin. "Besides, like you, I signed on for the duration, and it ain't over yet, officially anyhow."

Unknown to the Missourians, while the Colored division fought the men in gray, Steele was already moving his other troops across the Saline River in their Indian rubber pontoons as the division of Negroes fought a rearguard action. Steele burned the rest of his supply wagons and with infantry mounted on mules, he made a fast retreat to Little Rock. The Missourians and their allies had achieved the major goals, stop the Red River campaign and drive Steel from southern Arkansas. They had force marched more than four hundred fifty miles and fought three major battles in just over a month. At Jenkins Ferry, the Confederates lost more than a thousand men. It was an expensive victory.

The next days were spent retrieving bodies of the wounded and dead. For the first time during the war, James was on burial detail. This time, he was one of the men who picked up the mangled bodies of both comrades and enemies, to be taken to the burial area. Thankfully, though the battleground was still muddy, it was drying out, and the men didn't have to wade in knee-deep water to complete the job. It was James who found Willard's body. After all, he thought, he had been James's possum, his tent partner. He felt it was fitting and harbored no anger toward Willard, only pity. It took three days to bury all the Confederate and Union dead in common graves. By the third day, the smell of the bloated, twisted bodies became over-powering, and once again James felt he was in hell—another memory to haunt his dreams. On the second day, Pleasant joined him, and over the protest of senior officers, helped with the grisly task. James's brother told his superior that he would resign his commission if it would make him feel better. The major shook his head, but made no more protest about Pleasant's decision. What James knew was the company would now follow his brother into hell if need be.

By late May, the Missourians were camped in southern Arkansas, and for the first time, James felt resentment against his commanding officers. He wasn't the only man in Parsons' Brigade to harbor these feelings. While ladies from the town of El Dorado gave balls and parties for the central staff, consisting of the generals and thirty other senior officers, the enlisted men were detailed by companies and assigned to surrounding plantations as farm laborers. One evening, as James rested by his campfire, Pleasant stopped by to see his brother.

"Going to the ball tonight?" James asked with a smile as Pleasant took a seat next to him.

Pleasant laughed. "Afraid not, the invitations don't filter down to my level. Today, they kept me busy taking inventory in the commissary office. Frankly, I'd just as soon plow. How was your day in the fields?"

"It went. I don't mind farm work. Just resent doing it for the people I am. Didn't believe this is what I would be doing when we signed up."

"How the rest of the men taking it?" Pleasant asked.

"Grumbling. They don't like it much either, especially the city boys.

They're not used to the work. First time I ever heard men say they wish we were back to drilling and marching. Well, you hear the same grumbling I do. You know."

Pleasant took a firebrand from the fire and lit his pipe. Taking a puff, he thought a moment. "Neither did I, Brother, and I'm a little disgusted also. Back at Jenkins Ferry, we had a chance to either destroy or capture Steele's army, but were too slow with the pursuit."

"So, those men we buried last month made the supreme sacrifice for nothing," James said. "And now, we work as slaves for these plantation owners. I'm beginning to suspect the only reason we fought was to save their peculiar institution."

"That wasn't the reason you and I or the others enlisted. You know that. Neither of us ever owned slaves."

"Oh, I know, Pleasant," James said wearily. "I'm tired, just tired and discouraged. Can things turn around for us?"

"I have my doubts," Pleasant said. "Just between us, I think Lee will have to come up with a miracle, but I don't see how his men can do it. They have to be in worse shape than we are. At least we still get beef and other supplies from Texas. But what can we do? Neither of us would desert. So, we harbor our doubts and carry out orders."

"Think we'll leave here anytime soon?" James asked

"Doubt it. There's a rumor from headquarters we'll move south to Shreveport come fall." With a sheepish grin he added, "After the harvest."

"But, of course," James said as his brother stood and waved good-by.

And the army did stay, and the men did their duty. The plantation owners in that part of Arkansas had bumper crops of everything that year, including cotton, but with the blockade, there was no place to ship except to local markets that were saturated. They didn't make as much as they first hoped with the windfall of unlimited free labor. The Missourians and Arkansans were not unhappy when they marched south and took up residence with their old comrades-in-arms, the Louisianans and Texans at winter quarters near Shreveport. The only excitement while in southern Arkansas had been the appearance of a

Union force marching south toward their encampment. General Parsons took the lead in front of his brigade and after a few volleys, the Yankees dispersed and were driven back north by the cavalry. There were no casualties. James missed the action. He was working in the fields of a plantation.

One day in November, after drill and inspection, Sergeant Perkins brought the men mail.

"Mail, James. The mail's here!" Jeremy shouted excitedly at James. James smiled broadly, his spirits suddenly lifted as he walked quickly with the other men toward Sergeant Perkins, who was standing in the back of a mail wagon shouting names as he sorted through letters and packages.

It took half an hour of waiting before the sergeant gave him four letters, one from Aunt Judith in Indian Territory and three from Bertie. He rushed back to his shebang. It was the name of affection the men gave to the log cabin quarters they had hastily built earlier in the fall. He shared it with the six men left in his squad, including Jeremy. He sat on his bunk and greedily read the letters several times. The letter from Aunt Judith had been written over a year ago. His cousins serving with Stand Watie were all well. There was tragic news concerning Chief John Ross. Though a wealthy plantation owner and slaveholder himself, Chief Ross had sided with the Union. Watie's men had burned his mansion to the ground in retaliation, but Ross did escape with his life. Another tragedy of this war, James thought. He knew Stand Waite and John Ross were not only both chiefs who served on the same Cherokee governing council, but had also been close friends for years. There was also a letter from little Frances included. He read her childish scrawl and smiled.

Dear Cousin Newton,

I miss you a whole bunch. Mama misses you too. We send kisses and hugs. I wish you were here to hug me and hold me. I get sad when I know you are far away. I hope you come back to us very soon. It's been hot, but I still do my chores. When will the war be over? Have they told you yet? I want my brothers and you to come back with us. I miss Bertie too.

I love you,
Cousin Frances
P.S. Mama helps me with the spelling, but I knew most of the words. I work hard at my lessons like you said. I say my prayers for you too.

He smiled again and opened one of Bertie's letters. This one had a date eight months old and was puzzled why it had taken so long. The others were posted only last summer and this fall.

My Darling brother,
I am afraid this letter brings tragic news. We have heard from Honey Creek in Indian Territory. Our dear and sweet Aunt Judith is dead. She died before the year began. A group of Union men, including some Pin Indians, arrested and tortured her. She was kept in squalor for several days and died of fevers three days after she was released. They did unmentionable things to her. The cowards tortured Judith trying to make her tell where her boys and Stand Watie's men were. I doubt if she even knew. When they finished with their unspeakable horrors, they left our aunt in a filthy pig sty for several days where she caught the fevers. The girls are safe. For now, they are living with Uncle Larkin and his family. He writes that he has plenty of room. Our generous friend, J.P., wrote to Uncle Larkin and offered his help. I cannot bear to write anymore, but will try again tomorrow. As always, you and Pleasant are in our constant prayers. Pray for us also.
Your loving sister,
Bertie

Tears streamed down James's face, and he held his head in his hands as he grieved for his aunt and cousins. The thought of sweet, angelic, Frances suffering the loss of her mother brought a soft sob from his throat.

The door swung open, and four of his squad members walked in with their own mail. Jeremy was with them.

"James, there was a package for you," Jeremy said with a smile.

James regained his composure quickly and said, "Thanks, Jeremy. I wasn't expecting a package. Wonder who it's from." He quickly opened it.

He was surprised and a little puzzled. Inside were two letters—one from Bertie and one from Henry's father. Carefully wrapped was Henry's shaving mug and razor. He read the letter from Henry's father first.

Dear Mr. MacEver,

My daughter writes this for me. I'm afraid I wasn't schooled much. She read your very kind letter to me, and I thank you for sending it along with Henry's things. We are very thankful for your map and will travel to Arkansas to see our son when the war is over. I talked it over with my daughters, and we all are alike in this thought. My only son spoke of you like his brother, and he done told us how you took care of him and gave him lessons in writing and reading. So, we will think of you as his brother and another part of our family. That is the reason for Henry's shaving mug and razor. I have no other son. We want you to have it as a memory of your adopted brother. With this, maybe you will remember Henry's family with affection.

God bless you.

We are respectfully yours,

Franklin Henry O'Brian

James looked at the painfully written scrawl. He wanted to weep, but fought and choked back the sobs that were choking him.

"Are you okay, my friend?" Jeremy whispered. The other men were also watching James carefully. Everyone he shared the shebang with were his friends.

James shook his head and passed the letter around. Except for Jeremy, all the men knew Henry and remembered him with affection. They understood James's feelings and knew the shaving mug and razor were important and poignant gifts. They were right, and as he admired the mug, he wondered if some day, he might have a son to pass it on to.

James hoped so, just as he hoped to have a daughter like his sweet cousin, Frances. He finished reading his mail. The other letters were cheerful, and he was glad to read his mother and sisters were doing well. For the next two evenings, he would be busy answering the letters, including a long one to his little cousin, Frances. The following day, he would write to her, but for now, he joined in with the happy chatter of his comrades who were discussing news from home. As he listened, his mind wandered, and he wondered how tall Frances would be the next time he saw her, or if he ever would. Then he stood. Suddenly, he needed to get away from the confines of the cabin.

"Where you going, James?" Jeremy asked.

"For a walk in the woods," he answered. "Just want to walk a little. Hey, any news about that grandson?"

Jeremy beamed. "Yep, growing like a weed. Daughter says he favors me in the eyes."

James slapped his new possum on the shoulder and laughed as he walked out the door. He wanted to breathe the fresh, cold air and walk alone. Maybe the coldness and dark of the woods would cleanse him and wash away some of the fresh sorrow. Twenty minutes later he was deep into the tall southern pines of the forest. The trees stretched upward more than a hundred feet, and a full moon shone from above, orange, bright, and huge. Harvest moon, he thought to himself and smiled toward the heavens. The crisp air invigorated him as he walked, the smell of pine and earth filled his lungs, and he breathed deeply. He was right. It was cleansing him. He stopped beneath the tallest tree he found and rested. When he looked up, he heard the high-pitched scream of a cougar. He learned against his tree and watched across a small clearing. He could not see clearly into the forest on the other side of the clearing but by straining finally saw two yellow eyes. The cougar, he thought, prowling for prey. He watched for a few minutes. Neither the cat nor he moved. They were both frozen in this moment of chance meeting. The man wondered if he was to become the prey, and the cougar wondered if he was the man's. Finally, James picked up a rock and with a shout threw it in the cougar's direction. The cat vanished, and James walked back to his shebang.

That night, he dreamed of his walk in the dark forest. Again, he stood against a tall pine and watched yellow eyes staring at him. But this time, the yellow eyes rose from the ground and shone from the height of a man. They came closer, and he could only speculate whether or not the cougar had taken to walking on his hind legs. Cold sweat trickled down his spine, and the hair on the back of his neck rose. The cougar had red fur. James knew of no bright, red cougars. But then, it wasn't a cougar. It was Jonah Quigley holding a noose. Under one arm, he carried his cousin Frances, who reached out toward James crying for help. Jonah's yellow eyes glowed with fire and hatred. Brown, tobacco stained teeth were bared in a snarl. James's nemesis opened his mouth wide, and a scream from the bowels of hell screeched through the forest. James reached for his gun, but his hand came up holding a decaying, naked arm. One of the out stretched fingers of the hand wore a gold wedding band he had seen before. He cast it away with a cry. Following Jonah was a vision of horror, dead soldiers wearing blue, and one of them had the innocent face of a youngster who looked vaguely familiar. The boy in blue pointed one gray finger at him, opened his mouth, and screamed the same blood curdling cry Jonah had emitted from his throat. The boy was dragging a body part with his free hand. It was the torn upper torso of a man. The head had no face— only bloody underlying muscle tissue. The thing helped itself along with one arm as it made pitiful mewing sounds. James awoke and sat straight up in his bunk gasping for breath. For two hours he lay in bed and stared at the door where moonlight filtered through the cracks between the door and its frame. He didn't doze off again until almost dawn, and as he did, a chill that didn't come from the cold night raced up his spine. He had a feeling that Jonah Quigley was close by. It was an irrational thought, but James couldn't get it out of his mind. He remembered the line from a letter written to Bertie two years before. "Wouldn't it be funny if Quigley was the one to end up running away to Texas instead of me?"

Chapter Fourteen

Drovers
October 1864,
Throckmorton County, Texas

"So, you've worked as a drover before? Where? Never heard the name, and I been in this part of Texas most of my life." Charles Goodnight looked hard at the man standing in front of him. He needed experienced hands, and most of his men were working across the state, rounding up longhorns scattered and gone wild the last years of the war. After his own three years serving with a Texas frontier unit for the war effort, it was time to rebuild his herd and take care of business.

"Up Missouri way. My uncle had a cattle spread. Worked for 'em seven years." the man answered. "I been working as a teamster close to Tyler. Decided to see what the west was like."

"Well, longhorns are ornery critters. Think you can handle them? These cows you'll be working with are half wild. The pay's passable, the food's filling, the work's hard, the days long, and the nights are short. There will be no gambling, fighting, or drinking during the drive. You're new, so you'll be riding drag and eating longhorn dust for three hundred miles. Be in the saddle more than a month. Want the job?" Charles Goodnight didn't smile as he made the offer.

"Where we takin' these critters, Mr. Goodnight?" the man asked.

"Shreveport. I'm keeping a promise to an old friend."

"You goin'?"

"No, I've got too much work getting the main herd together." For the first time, the rancher who would become a legend, smiled. "Robert Clay's the boss on this drive. You just met him. He's my foreman and the best drover in Texas." The smile disappeared. "He's a hard man, but fair. He'll work you till your tail drags, but he'll outwork you and the rest. Oh, he won't abide drunks and fighters either and expects strict discipline. He'll enforce the rules with fists or his gun if necessary. Anymore questions?"

"No sir, guess I'll sign on."

Goodnight turned the ledger around so the new man could sign or put his mark. "Put your mark here."

The man stiffened ever so slightly and said, "I can read and write."

Charles Goodnight raised one eyebrow slightly as the man signed his name slowly in the company ledger. After the ledger was signed, Goodnight turned it around to look at the signature. It was legible.

"Jonah Quigley," Goodnight read aloud. "Good, Jonah. Go on over to the chuck wagon and grab supper. The herd leaves tomorrow at sunrise. By the way, you been in the army?"

"I was," Jonah answered.

"Texas 22nd? They're in Shreveport now, part of the army waiting for these beeves."

"No. I was with…a partisan group…uh, back in Missouri for two years…disbanded, so I came to Texas," Quigley stammered.

The rancher nodded and waved him off as his foreman walked over. He followed the unkempt redhead with his eyes and stroked his chin thoughtfully. Partisans? He rolled the word around in his head with distaste. The bloody affairs going on in Missouri and Kansas were not unknown to him, or most Texans, who read the papers or listened to war gossip.

"Signed him on, I see," Robert Clay said as he noticed his boss staring after the new man. "So, what's your measure, Mr. Goodnight?"

"Don't know right now. Have some doubts, but you need another hand. We got to get started early tomorrow, and you'll be short handed the way it is. Ahh, I doubt he'll cause you trouble, but keep an eye on him. Tell Martine to do the same. Something about the man's eyes and way about him. Won't look you in the face, and he has the bearing of a coyote. I suspect he's a coward at heart. How 'bout you?"

Robert laughed. "That about sums it up. He looks a little soft too, everywhere but his eyes. They're hard, not a strong hard, just mean. But, he sets a horse good, and when I showed him around, he seemed to be comfortable with the herd. Little sloppy with roping. He's got a lot to learn, but don't worry, I'll break him in real good. By the time we get to Shreveport, he may want to join up with Jeb Stuart's boys and forget about steers."

"Doubt that," Goodnight said with a chuckle. "But I never worry when you're in charge of the herd. The drive should go as scheduled. Haven't had any frost yet, and the weather's still warm. In fact, it's been downright hot for October."

Robert nodded and walked toward the chuck wagon. The men were gathering around to eat and chat. They had already put in a long day. Tomorrow would be longer.

Goodnight went back to his crude dugout to write a letter to his friend and fellow rancher, Oliver Loving. He was also rebuilding his herd. Loving and Goodnight had first worked together before the war when they took their longhorns through Indian Territory and Kansas, then west to the mining camps in the Rockies. After the war, these two friends would pioneer a new cattle trail to Colorado that would later be called the Goodnight-Loving Trail. He pondered his reluctant decision to send cattle to the Confederate army in Louisiana. The only reason he accepted the contract was because of an old friend, Henry Willis, who commanded a brigade of Texas infantry licking their wounds in Louisiana. A personal letter from him had accompanied the contract offer, and he wasn't the kind of man to turn down a friend's plea. He knew the beef was needed just as he knew the Confederate money he would be paid with would soon be worthless. *I might as well divide all of it among the drovers and tell them to spend it quick.* He chuckled to himself. *It's over for the Confederacy. Old Sam Houston was right. We*

194

should have stayed with the Union. We should have listened. He sighed and finished the letter. Tomorrow, he would leave to join others working to build the herd west of Throckmorton County. There were lots of cattle in West Texas, wild and scruffy, but once gathered they would become the foundations for cattle empires. In the future, fortunes and legends would be made by men in this hardscrabble land—those few men with a unique blend of grit and vision.

Jonah watched the drovers around him carefully as he ate his stew. At least, he thought to himself, the chow would be fitting to eat. The outfit's cook was good and not stingy with the servings. Eight men sat in a circle around the campfire, talking quietly as they ate. Laughter occasionally punctuated the conversations. Most had their bedrolls behind them, ready to use. Jonah would find on the trail that men didn't linger over conversation very late into the night. He would discover the reason by the following day. They were friendly enough and had given him warm welcomes as he was introduced as the new hand. Jonah also knew his measure was being taken and would continue to be as the days went by. He was not a fool and was careful with his words and behavior. He not only needed the payday, but a new start. Things had gone wrong down by Jefferson, where he and a partner had taken to watching trails along the Texas border with Louisiana and bushwhacking lone soldiers coming back to visit home. They figured some were probably deserters too. The money wasn't a lot, but safer and easier than robbing banks. It kept him in enough money to get by on as he nursed his determination to find MacEver and kill him. He was patient. One of their victims turned out not to be so easy, pulled a gun hidden under his shirt and shot his partner dead. Jonah was fast enough to shoot the soldier before he could be shot himself, but decided it was time to leave that part of Texas, and he began to drift west onto the expansive prairie.

"So, where you from, Jonah?" a newcomer asked as he squatted next to Jonah with a plate of stew. "My name's Martine," he continued with a broad smile and stuck his right hand forward. Martine had a thick, Mexican accent.

Jonah took the hand and managed a slight smile. Martine's dark eyes were wide and expressive. His swarthy, lined face held an open and friendly expression. Like all the men around him, Jonah thought this one also had a lean and hard look about him. He had never met a Mexican before. "Jonah Quigley," he answered, and went back to his second helping of stew.

"Where you from, Jonah? " Martine continued, still showing his toothy grin.

"Missouri. I come from Missouri."

"Never been to Missouri myself. What's it like?"

"Trees and hills," was the short answer. Quigley didn't mind the eastern part of Texas, with the thick forests of pine and oak, but this treeless prairie was new and strange. He always had a feeling of nakedness and exposure that created a constant uneasiness in the back of his mind. He continued eating. A conversationalist, he wasn't. Martine took the hint, shrugged, and moved next to someone else and was soon laughing and nodding as he ate.

The next morning, still dark, Jonah woke wide-eyed and with a start, his ears ringing from the noise of a large pot being banged on with a ladle. The cook was rewarded with curses for his earlier rising to have breakfast ready for the hands when they awoke. But it wasn't long before the men were talking and laughing over their scrambled eggs, bacon, and biscuits. There was also plenty of hot coffee that steamed into the early, crisp, morning air.

Martine nudged Jonah to look eastward toward the dawn. "You're about to see the closest thing to a sunrise at sea, Amigo," he said.

"Sea? I ain't never been at sea," Jonah said. "Where did you see one?"

"Gulf, with my father. I'm from a fishing village."

The sun came up slowly and dominated the eastern sky with its majestic entry into a new day, glowing red and large, magnified a dozen times the normal size, it seemed. Darkness began to slowly pull back from the sun, and light enveloped the men sitting around the chuck wagon in the middle of a sea of short grass and scrubby brush. Buzzards in the distance were silhouetted against the sun, black on red, then orange, then they vanished into blinding white as Goodnight's foreman began leading the men toward the herd. They were moving out. Jonah was introduced to the three men who would be riding drag with him behind the herd, and the long day of moving longhorns eastward to Louisiana began. It would be an exhausting day of heat, dust, and frustration as Jonah learned the hard way about being a drover. Thirty more days awaited him, each much like the first. However, sometimes there was a surprise, usually unpleasant.

"Storm!" Lawrence screamed at Jonah above the din of herd noise. He pointed toward the southwest. "Movin' fast. Coming our way."

Jonah looked over his right shoulder. The entire sky was black with roiling, heavy clouds moving toward them. There was an ominous, green tint to the dark clouds, and thunder was already rumbling in his ears. The clouds turned almost purple and pulsated with light. The naked feeling moved to the surface of Jonah's mind. "Now what?" he screamed back.

"Be ready if the herd runs. Have to stay ahead and turn 'em back. Just pray there ain't hail with this."

Within a few short minutes the darkness of the storm was on them, and rain came in horizontal sheets that stung the skin. Lightning streaked across the sky in frightening zigzags of white death. The thunder was immediate and deafening, rolling over the men and their wards with the cracking sound of heaven splitting apart. The driving rain and the darkness of the sky cut his vision to a few yards. Only when the lightning streaked down at them from the ominous, angry clouds would the scene be lighted for a moment. During these flashes of light, Jonah caught glimpses of the other men trying to keep the frightened longhorns from bolting. Each time it happened, the hair raised on the back of his head and arms. The steers were braying and stamping back and forth, their eyes wild with fright, and as hail mixed with rain, Jonah felt real terror. Blue fire flashed across spans of horns, giving the cattle ghostly, demonic countenances, and his blood ran cold. He turned his face downwind as the pelting rain and hail stung him. The horse was feeling pain also and became hard to control. Jonah cursed and tightened his grip on the reins, trying to steady this animal who felt the same terror as he, smelled the same ozone and danger as he. Suddenly, blinding light from hell flashed only a few yards away within the herd, and the sound of heated and expanded air collapsing back on itself exploded in his ears. Surely I'll never hear again, Jonah thought as his horse reared on two legs, throwing him from the saddle onto the wet earth. With a thud, the breath left his lungs and he gasped to breathe. Catching his breath, he staggered to his feet and looked around for his horse. Now, I am naked, he thought and the terror deepened. Then he heard it, the noise of the herd beginning to stampede. Jonah turned to face death, when suddenly, he was grabbed by the arm and jerked upward. He looked up to see Martine, and with the drover's help, jumped behind the Mexican onto his horse and held on for life. Both men rode at headlong speed, trying to stay ahead of the longhorns driven mad by the storm. They gradually pulled safely ahead and began to slant toward the outer edge of the herd. It was the most horrific five minutes of Jonah's life. Suddenly, both men were plummeting head first over the mare's head. She had stumbled, going to her knees. Jonah rolled three times and came up on his feet. He grabbed the reins of Martine's horse. Terror pumped adrenaline through his veins, and with one leap he was in the saddle. He heard a yell. Martine was trying to stand, but his leg was twisted, broken. Jonah looked at the longhorn coming, cursed, then turned the horse and headed out of harm's way and left the man who saved him to be trampled to death. Martine's horse seemed to be gimpy on one leg, but he and his rider found their way to refuge behind an outcrop of rock and sagebrush. Jonah dismounted and waited for the herd and drovers to thunder by as he hid. As soon as he was alone, he mounted and began looking for his own horse. After half an hour of searching, he found him grazing quietly. The worst of the storm had passed. Jonah thought about what to do, made a decision, and mounted his own horse. After a few minutes of back tracking with Martine's horse in tow, he found the mangled body lying in the mud. Throwing Martine's body over the saddle of his horse, Jonah began to follow the herd, refining his story as he walked.

Up ahead, the storm had passed, and the longhorns had finally slowed. The drovers were getting them calmed down and under control. Robert Clay had counted heads and knew two of his men were missing, Martine and Jonah.

"Lawrence," Robert said. "Have you seen Jonah or Martine?"

"No, sir. One minute during the storm, Jonah was a few yards away, then the next time lightning lit up the place, he was gone. The same with Martine."

Robert went around to all the men asking if they had seen the missing men. The answers were the same. No one knew what happened to them. He was worried. Jonah was a tenderfoot, but Martine was seasoned and savvy. He knew how to take care of himself. He sighed and began to ride back the way they came. He could only hope to find them alive, but had a bad feeling.

Two miles away, Jonah was riding toward Robert. He held the reins of Martine's horse in his hand. There was no remorse in his heart for the dead man who saved his life. He was just glad the man did save him before dying. Jonah only knew three things about Mexicans. They came from Mexico, they spoke Spanish, and they were breeds. He detested breeds almost as much as he detested Indians. But he had been smart enough to at least be civil to all the drovers on this trip, and that included Martine. Jonah would be contrite and sorrowful when he told the tragedy of Martine's death. That afternoon, Jonah would insist on digging Martine's grave himself. He managed a couple of tears as he stood before the grave and told the others how he saw Martine's horse stumble and fall, throwing him to the ground. He spurred his own horse into danger, but was too late. The other men nodded sympathetically, but Robert only stared at Jonah with a hard look in his eyes. He didn't believe the story. He felt something was missing but had no proof, so he let it go. When the drive ended, Jonah wouldn't be invited to join the outfit on a permanent basis.

When Jonah told his story, he knew the foreman didn't believe him and was suspicious, but he didn't really care. Anything could have happened during the stampede, and there was no proof of his cowardly behavior, only suspicion. Besides, he thought, I didn't break no laws. His only thought was to work as a drover until they reached Shreveport and hopefully find Newton MacEver. Two of his kin had snooped around Pineville and Indian Territory for him and written that MacEver and his brother were serving with Missourians under Generals Price and Parsons. Rumors along the border in East Texas told of the Missourians, Arkansans, and Texans camped at Shreveport. He knew one thing for sure, he never wanted to see the prairies of West Texas again. But this job gave him an opportunity to ride into the Confederate army camp, find MacEver and cut his throat. His dreams for the rest of the trip were pleasant.

Chapter Fifteen
Beeves

The following day, James sat at the small communal table in his cabin writing letters. The other men had taken the opportunity to go fishing or walk into Shreveport. It was Friday afternoon, and except for those on guard duty, the men were free for the weekend. He had just finished two letters when Pleasant walked in and took a seat opposite of his brother.

"Who you writing to, James?" Pleasant asked.

"Bertie and Frances." James glanced up at his brother and then looked closer. "You've got something on your mind, Pleas. I recognize the look. What is it?"

Pleasant smiled. "Nothing bad, I don't think. You'll probably enjoy the break. The division needs a couple of new teamsters, and you're the only one in my company that's got the experience with mules. How would you like some temporary duty hauling supplies?"

James looked up. "Well, maybe." He studied Pleasant's face a few more moments and smiled. "There's something else, isn't there?"

Pleasant nodded in the affirmative. "The Texas 22nd is sending a man they want out of harm's way. Think he was a drummer boy really. He'll be your possum. You gotta train him to handle a team."

"Uh, just how old is this boy?"

"Sixteen."

"Sixteen." James smiled sadly and shook his head. "And we were speaking not long ago of old men and young boys." Then he grinned. "Sure, why not. Be glad to show the boy how to handle mules."

"Thanks, James. I knew you'd do it. Hey, there's a good side. No drill while you're on that duty, and I hear the teamsters eat good. You'll be working with the commissary people."

"Colonel Young?"

"Yeah, he's okay," Pleasant said. "You know your business, so you'll be left alone."

"Where will we be hauling things from mostly?" James asked.

"Oh, sometimes just to Shreveport and back, so you'll only be gone a day at a time. They'll also be some hauls from Texas. On those trips, you'll be gone for a few days or more. Other than that I'm not sure. Of course, if the army marches to action, your assignment is with the wagons."

"Sleeping arrangements?"

"Here, while we're in camp. I've heard some of the teamsters sleep in their wagons on the move if they're covered. This isn't permanent. Your shebang is here, and the bunk is still yours."

"When should I report?"

"Monday. You don't have to wait for muster. Just go on after you get up. Report to Sergeant Williams." Pleasant said good-by and left James alone.

Midmorning the next day, James squatted on a large, flat rock washing clothes in the river that ran through the edge of camp. Jeremy was next to him and at least a hundred other men were doing the same. James looked up from his chore. There was noise in the air, shouts, the sound of hooves, and braying of cattle.

"Beeves!" someone shouted. "Beeves comin'! We eat good tonight, boys!"

Cheers rose from the soldiers lining the bank as the longhorns came into view stirring up clouds of dust. The Texas drovers worked to keep the herd moving toward the water. It would have to be crossed to get the animals into their grazing area. But, at the stream's edge, the cattle balked and began to bunch up, hesitating to cross. Many were drinking and showed no inclination to move. There were shouts and curses from the drovers as they tried to get their herd across, but the longhorns had their own minds. It was a stalemate between drovers who wanted the job finished and the rangy steers with their own priorities.

"Don't know bout you, James, but I'm ready for beef steaks," Jeremy shouted at James. "Let's give those boys a hand. Quicker those beeves cross, the quicker they end up over the fire."

James grinned. "Let's do it," he shouted back. Both men removed their shoes and trousers. Suddenly, there were almost a hundred others joining them as the soldiers splashed into the waist-high water with shouts and laugher. This wasn't work. They were schoolboys again, these soldiers who were ready for a break in their routine, whooping and hollering at the tops of their voices. The cattle didn't stand a chance against these crazy men, now boys, having fun helping the drovers accomplish a mission. Soon the drovers were laughing and hollering also. They hadn't expected this from the soldiers and were joining in the fun themselves. They also had some tension to release. Even Jonah Quigley was laughing at the sight of a hundred soldiers, half naked, splashing, hooting, and throwing rocks at the longhorns who were now beginning to ford the river. As Jonah laughed, he watched the closest soldiers, and suddenly froze and stared hard at one. Like the others, this one was having a good time. He nudged his horse forward and moved closer to make sure. He couldn't believe his good fortune, for it was Newton MacEver, no mistaking that. The hatred he had nurtured for almost three years boiled to the surface, and he burned with desire to grab Newton by the hair and slash his throat. His common sense told him where he was, in the middle of an army camp with thousands of armed men, but his brother's words of patience slowly vanished as his irrational thirst for revenge took over his emotions. He lost all reason and applied spurs sharply to his horse.

"James, look out!" Jeremy shouted.

James turned to see a horse and rider almost on him. He twisted to the right, but it was too late. With a wet smack, the horse's shoulder collided hard, knocking the breath from him, and he went under. Jeremy and another man began to splash toward James. He still hadn't come up. Then, the crazed drover jumped from his horse and unsheathed a knife. He bent over and groped in the water. With a whoop of triumph, the man pulled James to the surface by his hair.

"Open your eyes, Newt MacEver," Jonah shouted. "I want you to see who's killin' you."

James was still unconscious and gave no response. With a shrug, Jonah raised his knife overhead. Just as he began the downward plunge that would drive the knife into James's throat, a boot smashed into the side of his head. Jonah dropped the knife and fell backward into the water. He came up sputtering and cursing, then looked up into the flinty eyes of Robert, the trail boss, who had a pistol pointed at his head. Jeremy and two others pulled James from the water and carried him ashore.

"I ought to shoot you right now, Jonah," Robert yelled. "Have you gone loco? Gimme your gun, and get back to work."

Jonah handed his gun to Robert. His eyes were cold. "The man killed my brother."

"We'll see. You can tell your story later, but now get to work. I want our money for the job and get back to Texas today." He watched Jonah ride back to his position and then rode to the bank to see if some sense could be made of the incident. He noticed there were a dozen soldiers on the shore seeing to their comrade. There was also a tall officer bent over the coughing soldier Jonah had tried to kill. The officer looked up at Robert as he dismounted.

"I'm Robert Clay, the trail boss," he said and offered his hand to Pleasant. "I'm sorry this happened and don't know what it's about, but my drover says this man killed his brother."

Pleasant took the drover's hand and nodded. "Pleasant MacEver. This is my brother and he's no murderer. Your drover's name must be Quigley."

Robert was taken aback. "Well, yes, it is. Jonah Quigley. You know him?"

"Yeah, we've met. Your hand's wanted for murder in McDonald

County, Missouri. He and another brother murdered a postman there. The other was hanged two years ago."

"I see," Robert said. "And his story about your brother killing his brother, what's that about?"

Pleasant shook his head and explained. "Amos Quigley was the captain of a Union guerilla band. In January of '62, they attacked our home, burned it to the ground, and killed our brother and sister, then beat and raped two other sisters. This is James. He killed Amos Quigley during the raid, something anyone would do under those circumstances. It wasn't murder, just a man defending his home and family. You would have done the same, I suspect."

"I see," Robert said. "Well, Jonah did admit being in a partisan group before coming to Texas. Didn't say which side." He shook his head. "Not surprised. Had a bad feeling about him. Now, I don't know what to do. I'm not too anxious to take the man back to Missouri. Believe it's in the hands of the Yankees now."

Pleasant nodded. By now, James was standing and obviously fine. "So, it was Quigley," he said.

"Yeah, Mr. MacEver, Jonah Quigley," Robert said. "Sorry about all this. Real sorry I brought this man along. Didn't know of course. You gonna be all right?"

"Yeah, I'm okay. Never knew what hit me," James said as he shook the drover's hand. "So, now what?"

"Don't know for sure. You or your brother have any suggestions?"

"Hang him, like he tried to hang me," James answered as he rubbed his neck and remembered his last meeting with the Quigley brothers.

Robert's eyes widened. "He tried to hang you?"

"Yeah, in Indian Territory." Then James told Robert the entire story of his near fatal meeting with the Quigleys. Robert listened intently.

"I'd like to hang him myself," Robert said when James finished. "Don't have the authority though. Don't think any sheriff in Texas has the authority either. How 'bout the Confederate army?"

Pleasant teased his moustache in thought. "No, might get him locked in the stockade a few days for assault. But for what he's done in another state? Matter of fact, it's in another country and not much concern to this army I'm afraid." He shook his head. "Don't rightly know what to do. Do want him out of here though."

"That's easily done," Robert said. "I've already got his gun, and he won't get it back, but it's not an hour's ride to the Texas border. I can try to put a good scare in him, I suppose. You boys got a suggestion?"

Pleasant thought a moment and then with a sly smile said, "Hmmm, a good scare, you say. Do you mind a little escort, Mr. Clay?"

"Got something in mind?" Robert asked.

"Yeah, believe I do," Pleasant said. "I've got some friends with the Texas cavalry here. Why don't I call in a favor and arrange an escort. They'll convince Quigley to stay out of Louisiana."

Robert grinned broadly. "Believe I like the way you think, Mr. MacEver. It'll be a pleasure. Looks like all the beeves have crossed the river. We should have them pastured in an hour and have our money in less time than that. Why don't we meet them on the far side of the stream. Would three hours be okay?"

James and Pleasant looked at each other and grinned. Soon, all the men standing around began to laugh. This is something they wanted to see.

Three hours later, as soldiers sat along the bank of the stream and watched, Robert Clay gathered his drovers around him on the other side of the creek. They all had dismounted, and he was taking his time counting out their money.

"Where's my gun?" Jonah asked as Robert handed him his wages.

"You're lucky to have the money," was the answer. "If it was up to me, you wouldn't be paid, but Mr. Goodnight always keeps his word. You helped get the herd here. You get paid, but you don't get the gun back until we're out of Louisiana. I know all about you now. The only reason I don't shoot you myself is because it's against the law."

Jonah was seething with anger and wished he could shoot the trail boss. He looked around for support among the other drovers, but found none. They had heard the story also.

After stalling for a few more minutes, Robert mounted his horse. As his crew began to mount, the splashing of horses turned their heads and they saw twenty mounted troopers headed their way. In front, the captain was shouting for the drovers to stop. From across the shallow river, two hundred soldiers cheered.

"Captain Smith, at your service, sir," the cavalry officer said to Robert with a salute.

"What can I do for you, Captain?" Robert said with a mock serious expression.

"We're looking for Jonah Quigley. Understand he rides with you. We intend to see he gets to Texas where we're gonna hang the sorry bastard."

Jonah's jaw dropped with disbelief. "Boss, you can't let…why, they ain't got no right to—" He was cut off as the Captain's gloved hand slapped him hard across the face.

"Shut up. Don't even speak, or Sergeant Major O'Donnell will cut your tongue out." To make sure he got the message, the sergeant hit Quigley in the jaw, knocking him from his horse. The sergeant jumped down from his own horse, quickly tied Jonah's hands together, and then the powerfully built man swung him back into his saddle. He mounted his own horse, and to emphasize what they had in store for Quigley, the sergeant shook a coil of rope in his face. As the drovers rode off with their cavalry escort, the infantrymen began hollering and waving their caps. A few, who had their rifles, discharged them into the air. Jonah Quigley was frightened, very frightened as the troopers began talking about Quigley being a murderer, trying to kill one of their own, even saying he was a Union spy.

"Yeah, didn't tell Mr. Goodnight it was Yankee troops you rode with in Missouri, did you?" One trooper yelled at Jonah and whacked him across the shoulders with his hat.

"Came here as a spy, didn't you?" another trooper accused him. "We hang spies.

That's why we're taking you to Texas. This is a Texas Cavalry unit, and we're gonna hang you there. Only fitting, and this way we don't waste time at camp with no court-martial."

"Robert," Jonah pleaded. "You gotta help me. You know I ain't no spy. Don't let em hang me. Please—" He never finished as another trooper slapped him.

"Don't know what I can do, Jonah," Clay said over his shoulder. "We're out gunned."

Within an hour, the riders were across the border into Texas, and by a grove of large live oak, the men halted. The sergeant major threw one end of the rope over a large branch of one of the trees. A hangman's noose hung limply from the end. One trooper led Jonah's horse to the tree, and another slipped the noose over his neck. As the trooper tightened the noose, he leaned close to Jonah's face and snarled, "How does it feel, Yankee? This is what you tried to do to one of our own."

"For the love of God, please do something to stop it, boys. I rode with you. I ain't no spy. Help me."

Finally, Robert walked over to the captain and took him away from the other men. He talked out of Jonah's hearing range.

"Think he's had enough to keep him out of Louisiana?" Robert asked the Captain.

"I suspect so," the captain said with a grin. "Really would like to hang him after what Pleasant told me. When you get back, give Charles Goodnight my best. Know him from years back, and he's a good man. Nope, I think this Quigley fella won't be going back to Louisiana. I'll have a little parting chat with the scalawag first."

They both walked back to the tree where the captain gave orders. "Take the noose off, but leave it hanging from the tree in case this sorry, murdering thief comes this way again. Pull him down, Sergeant."

There was a din of protest from the cavalry troops as the sergeant pulled Jonah off his horse and cut the rope binding his hands. The captain walked close to Jonah and got in his face.

"You better get down on your knees and thank God for your good fortune. Your foreman just reminded me of something. The only ones with proper authority to hang you are the Yankees, and it's a long ride to Missouri. We ain't Union partisans like you rode with, so we're not gonna hang you. We're not murderers, but don't try our patience. If you ever come back here, we'll kill you. They're six thousand men in our camp, and they'll all have a description of you with orders to shoot on sight. Do you get my drift, you piece of dog dung?"

"Yes, sir, yes, sir," Jonah said as he nodded his head up and down frantically. Then he began to blubber. He just wanted to get away from these crazy Texans. It was the second time in a month he thought he was going to die, and he wanted to be gone. He looked around at the troopers with mucus running over his quivering lips, and saw the contempt in their hard, unflinching eyes. The one closest to him spat a long stream of tobacco juice that hit the toe of his boot. He walked closer.

"Sure hope I'm the first to see you if you come back. I want to be the one to shoot you, so please, come back," he said with his nose almost touching Jonah's.

Then, with waves to the drovers, the cavalrymen rode back to Louisiana. The cowboys headed west, and Jonah followed his crew at a distance. He could feel their contempt. Late that evening, they reached the outskirts of Tyler where the drovers intended to spend the night. They all dismounted

"Here's your gun," Clay said to Jonah and tossed it onto the ground at his feet. "You got your money, and now you have your gun. There's not a man here who wants to ride with you, so get on with you now. If you want to live don't ever show your face in Throckmorton County, and don't go back to Louisiana. I'm already regretting that I got you out of that well deserved hanging. Can't say it's been a pleasure knowing you."

Jonah looked around at the other men, and they all turned their backs. He picked his gun out of the dust and got on his horse. As he rode away, he was raging inside, but kept his peace. He didn't want a fight with any of the drovers, especially Robert Clay. It was an incident in his life he would just have to put behind him. He rode northeast, but had no intention of crossing the border into Louisiana again. He would have to be patient. Someday, Newton MacEver would leave Louisiana, and that day would probably be soon. Jonah knew it was just about over for the Confederacy, and Newt wouldn't be hiding in an army camp forever. Yes, he was determined now. He would be patient. He would remember the vow to avenge his brothers' deaths. Newton MacEver would still pay. Jonah would have his revenge, not only for his brothers, but for the humiliation he had gone through from these crazed

Texans. I've suffered humiliation and shame in this Godforsaken state trying to find Newton MacEver, he thought to himself. By God, I'll see him dead at my hands no matter how long it takes. Because of you, I can't go home, and I'll be patient. "I'll have my justice! You hear me, Newton MacEver?" he shouted to the heavens with his fist raised. "I'll have my justice!"

And he would be patient. He had learned some hard lessons, and his resolve was strengthened. Over the next few years as he drifted north and south in the eastern part of Texas, he would always focus on his only purpose in life.

"You're dead, Newton MacEver, or James, or whatever other bastardized name you try to hide behind," he mused aloud. "No matter what name you go by, I'll find you. I've got all the time in the world, and I'm a patient man."

Chapter Sixteen
Teamsters

Monday had come and gone quickly, and by Thursday, James was acquainted with his new comrades. He enjoyed working with the teamsters, and certainly wasn't new to being around mules or other draft animals. He had picked up a lot of experience when working with his uncles. That same afternoon, as he helped hitch up six mules to a wagon in preparation for a pickup in Shreveport, the new boy from the Texas unit finally showed up.

"I'm lookin' for Corporal MacEver," James heard the boy say to one of the other men. "He's gonna teach me how to be a teamster."

The man smiled, pointed at James, and the boy walked toward him grinning broadly. A real towhead, James thought as he noticed the straw colored hair sticking out from the boy's hat. With bright green eyes and an oval face that was open and friendly, James thought he should be sitting at a school desk, not wearing a uniform.

"Mr. MacEver?" the youngster asked and held out his hand.

James took the hand and the boy's grip was firm. A good sign, he thought to himself, but my Lord, he looks fourteen, not sixteen. He also took note of his enthusiastic grin. Finally, James returned the boy's smile and said, "Yeah, I'm James MacEver. So, you want to learn the teamster trade."

"Yes, sir. I'm with the Texas 22nd Infantry. We fought beside you Missourians at Jenkin's Ferry. Yes, sir, I was proud to fight with Parsons' Brigade. Real proud."

"You Texas boys did yourselves proud too. Call me James."

"Yes, sir, James. What do I do first? When do we start hauling things? Do you like being a teamster?"

James laughed and said, "Help me get the rest of the mules hitched, today, and yes, it beats marching. Oh, you don't have to say sir to me. I'm not that old, and I'm only a corporal. What's your name?"

"Benjamin Franklin Bankes. Most people call me Frank. It's easier."

"Okay, Benjamin Franklin Bankes, hitch up this mule to the lead bar while I work on the one behind. Check the collar and see that the tug chains are fastened to these single trees. No shame in asking for help, so ask if you're not sure. Ever worked with mules before?"

"Sure, when I was plowing on my pap's farm, but that was just one mule. I didn't have no problems handling one. Got along good with old Lick. Called him Lick cause he was always licking his nose with that long tongue of his. Never worked with a team, but I'll learn."

"Sure, you'll learn. By the way, you did that just right. Now, let's follow the main chain and make sure everything is correct. I'll show you what to look for as we go along."

"This side's done, James," the other teamster called over the mules. "Gonna leave you and Frank to finish. You takin' the haul to Shreveport today?"

"Yeah. It'll give Frank a little experience. Thanks for your help."

Fifteen minutes later, Frank and James were leaving the camp on the road to Shreveport. James drove the team, giving Frank pointers as he did.

"What we picking up in town?" Frank asked.

"Horseshoes, blankets, oats, and hay. Oh, some eggs for the officers' mess too."

"Hope them eggs are packed real good. This old wagon rides pretty bumpy," Frank said.

"Me too. The generals don't like their eggs scrambled," James responded and they both laughed.

"Do you have a wife, James?"

"Nope, do you?"

Frank laughed. "No, you know I don't. I just turned seventeen last week. Wouldn't know what to do with a wife. Sounds like big trouble. I come from a large family. Do you?"

James thought a moment. "Well, it used to be bigger. My mother and sisters are in Missouri. Believe you met Pleasant."

"Yeah, Captain MacEver. I met him. My sister and I are the oldest. I got six more younger brothers and sisters at home. Elvira, she's the oldest, twenty now. Here's some pictures." Frank handed James photographs of his family.

James looked through the pictures, smiling and complimenting Frank on his family. The last one was an individual picture of a beautiful young lady staring boldly into the camera's lens. It was a strong face, he thought, feminine, with an oval face, a generous mouth, and straight nose, but strong. She stood straight, her shoulders back, and chin high.

"This Elvira?" James asked.

"Yep, my sister Elvira. Pretty, ain't she? Been lots of suitors, but pap ran them off."

James laughed. "Sounds like your pap's a hard man. What color are her eyes and hair?"

"She's got green eyes like mine, but her hair's well, red, but not bright red. It's dark and...don't know how to describe it."

"Auburn?"

"Yeah, that's it, auburn. She's got long, auburn hair, just like ma used to have."

James looked at the photograph again and added color with his mind's eye. "She's beautiful. No wonder your pap's kept busy chasin' men off."

"Well, she's not sweet on anybody, and she's marrying age. You want to meet her? I think you two would be a good match. You'll like my sister. She's smart too. She's had the most schoolin' of the whole family. She's always reading books."

James began to laugh. "Whoa, partner. Don't know if I want to face your pap's wrath."

"Oh, no. They'll both take to you. Believe me, I know. You'll see when you meet my family. You really ought to write my sister. She'll write back too."

James began to laugh and slapped his new ward on the back. "Okay, my young friend, I'll take your word for it, but sounds like you want to get her out of the house bad like."

"Well, she'll soon be twenty-one. I'd hate to see her become an old maid like my aunt, who's she's named after."

James laughed even harder. "Twenty-one, imagine that. Why, she is getting old, and here I already turned twenty- five this month. It's kinda scary."

"Yes, sir, it's something to think about," Frank said dead serious. "You ain't gettin' any younger either. Twenty-five is one quarter of a century. I always been good at figuring."

James smiled. "Well, Frank, you've given me a lot to think about. Tell me now. You said your sister likes to read books. Do you?"

"Yes, sir, I do read books. I read the Scriptures too. In fact, I read the Bible a lot. I do believe, someday, when I'm deserving and more versed in the Good Book, I want to be a preacher. We're all Baptist, don't you know. Do you belong to a church, James?"

"I usually go to the camp chapel on Sundays. I was raised in the Methodist church. So, guess I'm a Methodist. Tell you the truth though, for a long time, it was the only church in town. So, if church going was on your mind, it was your only choice."

Frank was quiet for a moment before saying, "You know, I never met a Methodist before. Why, you're the first one. Once met a Hebrew man named Marcus over in Tyler. He owned the dry goods store there. Nice fella, but you're the first Methodist."

James was laughing again as they pulled the wagon next to the loading dock of the warehouse. The boy was without guile, and in some ways, he reminded James of both Henry and his brother Jasper. "Okay, Frank, here's the hard part of the job, loading up. This is a lucky day though. Warehousemen already got our stuff sorted and stacked on the loading dock. We'll get the eggs when we finish here. The general store will have some in from local farmers."

Within the hour, with some help from a couple of warehousemen, they were on their way. At the general store, James and Frank carefully placed the eggs between them in the front seat. The crate of eggs rested on two blankets, and Frank put another blanket over the crate.

"Think they'll ride okay?" Frank asked.

"They're packed in straw. Yeah, they'll be okay, Frank, and don't worry, if any break, I'll sit right behind you at your court martial."

Frank looked up quickly, then grinned. He liked James's humor and patient way of teaching him things. He also seemed to be kind. Yes, James should meet his sister.

"Why we stopping here at the Venanda Hotel?" Frank asked as he reined in the mules and set the brake. "Never been in here before. The folks in the porch rocking chairs sure are dressed fancy. Think they'll let us in."

"Yep," James answered with a chuckle. "Don't worry. We're meeting my brother and a friend at the restaurant inside. He's buying us steak dinners to celebrate my birthday."

"Well, happy birthday," Frank said with surprise.

"Thanks. Actually, it was yesterday. Come on. You're in for a treat."

Inside, Frank gawked at the high ceiling of the lobby and the furniture. Plush maroon chairs and divans were situated in front of a large, stone fireplace. Finely dressed ladies and gentlemen conversed quietly and nodded to the two soldiers as they walked by.

"This is right fancy," Frank said as they walked into the dining area. "Sure your brother can afford to feed us in a place like this? Don't think I could afford it."

"He's an officer and makes lots more money than us lowly enlisted men. There they are."

Pleasant stood from a corner table and waved them over. James grinned. He recognized Major Smith, the surgeon he met at the Battle of Helena when he barged into the hospital tent with Pleasant. The major smiled back and rose with his hand outstretched.

"Good to see you again, James," the surgeon said. "Hope you haven't brought this young fellow for me to fix." James laughed and introduced Frank.

"James," Pleasant said. "After dinner, the major and I are going to a planter's home just outside of town. Has a good selection of brandy and cigars, I might add. Want to join us for a friendly game of chess?"

James looked up with interest, but said, "Tell your friend thanks, but we can't make it tonight. Frank and I have to get the supplies back to camp and deliver the generals' eggs."

Within a few minutes their orders arrived, thick beef steaks with greens and yams in a sweet, spicy, Creole sauce. The smell of the fresh baked bread accompanying the meal wafted around the table, and James inhaled deeply and sighed. Then, to James's surprise, Pleasant stood and tapped his wineglass with a spoon for attention.

"Gentlemen," he said, then turned to other diners and bowed slightly with a smile. "And ladies." He put his hand on James's shoulder. His brother blushed. "This is Corporal James Newton MacEver. It's his birthday. So, here's a toast to my brother, the most fearsome soldier in Parsons' Brigade and a most reputable poet, I might add. Give me ten thousand like him, and we'll chase the Yankees into Canada."

"Hear, hear," the major and some other men called. There was a round of polite applause, and James blushed a deeper red.

"Thanks, Brother," James mumbled, still blushing. Then he grinned broadly. "That was nice, Pleas, real nice. I'll never be able to show my face here again, but thanks anyway."

"This is good," Frank said, taking another swallow of his wine. "Don't know if I'm supposed to drink it or not, but it's good. The preacher's always talkin' about demon rum and whiskey, but never heard him say anything about wine. Guess I'll drink it."

"Take a little wine for thy stomach's sake," the Surgeon said with a chuckle. "That was the apostle Paul's advice to the young Timothy."

"Any news from the East?" James asked.

"Well, Lee's holding his own," the doctor answered. "Richmond is still ours, but the Yankees are pressing hard."

Pleasant added that Sherman was still moving through Georgia and was unopposed. The road to Savannah would be open for him. The garrison there was only 10,000 and wouldn't be able to stand against Sherman's seventy thousand. The news reports were grim as Sherman left a trail of destruction and made war on civilians. Atlanta had already fallen.

"It looks like a bleak Christmas for the citizens of Savannah and the rest of Georgia," Pleasant said.

"Sherman can be in Savannah by Christmas? That's only a month off, Pleas," James said incredulously.

"What's to stop him?" the major said. "Farmers with pitchforks and women with their parasols? Lee certainly can't help. He's got his hands full holding his own against Grant and protecting Richmond."

"Sherman sounds as bad as a partisan," James said as he chewed another bite of steak.

"He is. Worse as far as I'm concerned. Why, the man's a West Point graduate, supposedly a gentleman, but he's given his men carte blanche to plunder and murder their way through Georgia. Disgusting behavior!" the major said emphatically.

"Any news from home?" James asked Pleasant. He was growing depressed with talk of war and wanted the subject changed.

Pleasant brightened. "Yes, Frances sends her love again. Our daughter is beginning to walk, and she has my eyes. Lord, I want to see her." Suddenly, there was a distant look in his eyes. "I'll be glad when this war is over. Sometimes, I think we should just…oh, well."

"It will, Pleas," Newton said. "You'll be back at Spring Place by next Christmas."

"And you, Frank," Major Smith said. "Where's your family? Are they well?"

"Yes, sir. My family's good. Our farm's in Hood County, Texas, only a long day's ride from here. I want James to meet my sister. Told him to write her. She's real pretty and almost twenty-one."

Pleasant looked at the earnest expression on the boy's face, smiled, and said, "Why, that's a good idea, Frank. So, why don't you write the young lady in question, James. You're not gettin' any younger."

"Yes, sir, Captain," Frank broke in excitedly. "I done told him that very thing. Why, he's one quarter of a century old. Yes, sir, told him that." He drank the last of his wine.

"Goodness," the major said and laughed as he splashed a little more wine in Frank's glass. "Why, James, you'll be in your dotage soon." He clucked his tongue with exaggeration.

James joined the laughter. "Perhaps you're right, Major. Maybe I can talk Frank into writing his sister first and introduce me before I write. Of course, after she does meet me, she might chase him out of his home with a wet rope."

"Or worse," Pleasant offered. "James, have you met any pretty ladies at all since you left Indian Territory? Surely, there's been some damsel who sparked an interest."

James thought a moment, and remembered that touching moment under the sweet gum tree at Pleasant Hill, where for a brief, fleeting moment, a beautiful and tenderhearted young woman washed the horror of that ghastly day from his mind with her crystal laughter, kindness, and intelligence. Yes, he thought, for at least one short hour, I was in love and forgot about war and killing. I'm not dead, he thought. The three men listened carefully as James told his short story. It was the first time Pleasant had heard of the tender part of why James was late to muster that day. He knew about the burial of Henry.

"Ah, she was beautiful then?" the major said. "She sounds like a vision from heaven, and she must have been after that bloody day. Well, James, think of this. It's only a two day ride to Pleasant Hill. Have you thought about that?"

"What was her name?" Pleasant asked.

"Oh, yes, she was quite beautiful, even her name. It was Julia. She embraced me and kissed me on the lips. Did I tell you? Oh well, it's impossible to think about going now unless I desert. Who knows, after the war perhaps." He touched his lips and smiled, then shrugged.

Pleasant laughed, tapped his wineglass again and stood. "Gentlemen! Gentlemen! Here's to all the beautiful women in Louisiana." All four men stood and raised their glasses to the other customers, which included several very pretty ladies. There was laughter and applause.

"I'm sure that lady in Pleasant Hill was beautiful," Frank said. "I bet she ain't as beautiful as my sister who you're gonna marry someday."

"Bravo," the major said. "That calls for another toast." All four men began laughing. At nearby tables other diners joined them.

The meal and conversation continued with more pleasant banter. At the end of the meal, James noticed they were served real coffee. The waiter also brought a small cake for dessert.

"Ahh, I see your fine hand in this, Pleas. What a treat. Thank you. This has been a most memorable evening. Good food, good company, good conversation. I can't think of a better way to spend a birthday. Thank you for coming also, Major Smith. I'm honored."

"The honor's all mine. I'm happy Pleasant invited me, and I'm certainly glad you brought Pleasant to me that day at Helena so I could 'fix' him. It's been a pleasure to become acquainted with both of you." Then, he looked at Frank. "And you also, young man. I suspect you and James will make an outstanding team."

"Thank you, Major sir, my pleasure, sir," Frank said with a toothy grin.

The men parted at the door. Pleasant left with the doctor in his buggy. James and Frank climbed into the wagon and drove back to camp. They delivered the eggs to the commissary first, and it was quite late by the time everything else was unloaded. James smiled as he crawled under the covers. It had been a good day, and Frank wouldn't face a court-martial. Not a single egg was broken. He chuckled silently to himself as he drifted off to sleep. He slept soundly that night, a night that passed without nightmares.

Christmas came and went as winter's cold grip came even to Shreveport, Louisiana. There was little snow, but mornings greeted the men with a frosting of ice. On some mornings, James and the others would be woken by the sounds of limbs, heavy with ice, snapping and falling in the forest around them. General Parsons was a stickler for keeping a tidy camp and when that happened, the men would be in for a day of cutting and cleaning up the debris from the night's ice storm. In January, the camp heard the news of Savannah's fall shortly before Christmas, and stories of more outrages visited on the civilians of Georgia. Lee still showed brilliance in maneuvering his troops and inflicted heavy casualties on Grant's army, but it was a holding action, only stalling the inevitable. Grant could handle the loss of thousands of more men, but not the Confederacy. There was much talk of forming volunteer units and marching east. Of course, the only problem was Federal forces now controlled the Mississippi from New Orleans to Saint Louis, and the Union blockade was complete. It was another impossible dream for Parsons' Brigade. But still, the men drilled, morale was high, and the Missourians kept their cohesiveness as a viable fighting unit. Other units of the army from Texas, Louisiana, and Arkansas lost men to desertion daily. Many simply gave up hope and went home to their farms and families. They weren't cowards or shirkers. They just simply went home with a feeling it was over, and James really couldn't fault them, even the few Missourians who left. He had given it thought himself, but he had no place to go.

At mail call one day that January, he was shocked to receive a letter from Elvira, Frank's sister. He read it with great interest.

Dear Mr. MacEver, or may I call you James?

Frank has told us so many wonderful things about you, I feel compelled to take pen in hand and write to his new friend. His letters constantly sing your praises, and you should know his family is grateful you have taken Frank under your wing and keep him safely away from danger. Frank writes enthusiastically of his teamster work, and is proud of how he can now handle a team of many mules or even oxen. So, apparently, along with your other virtues, you are a good tutor also. The family is happy Frank has you as both teacher and friend. Goodness, you must be a patient man too. Although, I know my brother is a good and kind boy, his energetic enthusiasm and forwardness can try a person's patience at times. You must have a good and warm heart.

Frank also tells us of your love of books and how you share them. It's good to know he is becoming more interested in the written word. Perhaps you should become a teacher, because it's apparent you enjoy sharing knowledge with others. I am a lover of books also, and I enjoy correspondence, so please do write to me if you are so inclined. Now, I must confess something. Frank sent me a copy of one of your poems. I don't know if my impulsive brother asked permission or not. I hope he did, but he may not have. If he didn't ask you, please forgive him, for I loved the poem and hope to read more of your poetry some day. This one touched my heart, and I felt the anguish of the writer. I must assume this is something heart felt. There are so many families suffering from this awful war. I especially loved this quatrain.

Search for innocence but not in me, for mine is gone as you can see.
Look to the silent ashes, smothering laughter at Honey Creek.
Press your ear to that ground, so damp and cold at Honey Creek,
There with dear Jasper and Florence, you will find that best part of me.

You do have a gift with the language, and I certainly hope you continue with your writing when you have time. Frank tells us also of the long hours you soldiers work. Again, thank you for helping my brother and becoming his friend. Believe me when I tell you your friendship is returned. You've become an important part of his life. I hope we meet one day, but if our eyes don't meet, perhaps our thoughts can through the written word. Please do write. Oh, by the way, my favorite poet is Longfellow, and yours?
Most sincerely yours,
Elvira Bankes

James read the letter twice, folded and placed it back in the envelope. Storing it away with his other letters, he smiled and immediately answered her's. He chuckled thinking about Frank copying one of his poems and mailing it to his sister. He's a determined matchmaker, he thought to himself, but he was pleased at the result. Elvira sounded like a very intelligent, thoughtful lady, and he already knew she was a striking beauty. Now, he was anxious to meet her. "Yes," he mumbled. "You certainly may call me James." He was glad it was the weekend. He needed to catch up on his correspondence.

The rest of the winter went routinely. There had been trips south near Alexandria to remove what stores were left there. What few troops were in the area were going to move closer to Shreveport, and the command didn't want to leave supplies for the Union. They were gone nearly three weeks on this mission, and it was the closest they came to combat. A Yankee troop of cavalry tried to seize the wagons, but were driven away after a brief skirmish with their own cavalry escort. There had been no casualties. James was pleased with Frank's progress. He was now handling the oxen and mules as well as the other teamsters. The boy worked hard and with enthusiasm. They were a good team, and James enjoyed working with animals himself. It was one of those jobs that he was good at, and it gave him satisfaction. Pleasant had been correct. As long as he did his work, no one bothered him.

In March, Frank and James had orders to accompany other teamsters into Texas. They were hauling many of the supplies they had removed from Alexandria only a few weeks before. James didn't really understand the rational, but accepted the orders. In the third week of March, a dozen wagons left camp accompanied by a small contingent of Texas cavalry. Spring was early, with pleasant weather as they left for a depot in a town Frank had talked of, Whitman, in Hood County.

"Yeah, James, Whitman's walking distance to my family's home. Think Captain Edwards will give us time to visit before we come back?"

"Oh, yeah, he and a few of his cavalry troopers intend to ride on to Tyler and see family while we're there. How far's Tyler from this Whitman town anyway?"

"About twenty miles. Won't take them long on horses. Sure hope we get to go. The folks want to meet you, especially Elvira," he added with a grin.

James grinned also. He felt a little skip to his heart thinking of her. There had been several letters between them since that first one two months ago. At mail call, there were usually two or three at a time. They were not that far from Whitman, and so mail from East Texas was frequent.

"Getting warm already," Frank said.

"Just right," James answered. "Sure love it. It's good to see spring again. Believe we're in Texas already."

"Yep 'bout twenty minutes ago," Frank said. "We'll be there by tomorrow. Are you anxious to meet Elvira?"

"Yeah, I am. Hope she likes me."

They continued in silence for a long while. James smiled as he noticed Frank occasionally nodding off. He looked around and enjoyed the scenery. The road took them through a forest, lush green with massive pines reaching toward the clouds floating lazily above. Oak, sweet gum, sycamore, and cedar were scattered through the evergreens. Azaleas with their bright pink and red blossoms dotted the road side, and the colors seemed even brighter surrounded by the deep green of the forest. An occasional dogwood stood out with its distinctive four-petaled flowers, some pure white, others a soft pink. Wild flowers were in season also, and patches of clearings were carpeted with bluebonnets and the red of Indian paint brush. Life is good, he thought. The war will soon be over, and life will be even better.

"Are you tired, James? Want me to drive for a while?" Frank asked as he stretched and yawned.

"Sure, Partner. I'll dig us out some snacks while you take over. We should be stopping soon to water the animals."

As they continued, both chewed on the venison jerky James smoked himself a few days before. The road began to parallel a wide stream, and within a few minutes, the teamsters and cavalry men were letting their animals drink and rest. They would camp here for the night.

"This is the Sabine River," Frank said, as they prepared their bed rolls beneath the wagon. "Pa and I catch some big cat fish out of this river where it runs close to our farm."

"Really? I like to fish," James said. "Now, let's get some sleep. Tomorrow will be a long day."

By three o'clock the next afternoon, the convoy of wagons had reached the town of Whitman, and the men were unloading the supplies into a barn on the edge of town that would serve as a warehouse. Six of the cavalry men would be left in town as temporary guards for the impromptu storage facility. The six volunteers were very happy with their assignment. Their families lived in the county, and they relished being close to loved ones, and besides, it was choice duty with no drills and no inspections for awhile. The captain had no problem with James and Frank taking twenty-four hours to visit family and only told them to be back at the warehouse by nightfall the next day. He also said they could take a couple of mules to ride if they wished. Save time he had said. All the men worked frantically to unload and get the mules into the adjoining corral. They all would have twenty-four hours of free time.

"How's your mule, Partner?" James asked with a laugh. They both rode bareback and butts slapped mule hide as their mounts trotted down the road.

"I—I—I—d-d-d-d-o-n-t know for sure," Frank answered in a mock stutter to exaggerate the effect of the mule's gait. "Guess I'm excited some. My heart feels like it's coming up in my throat. Lordy, I'm ready to see everybody again."

"And they'll be anxious to see you," James answered.

"Yeah, they will. Elvira and me are the oldest. Robert's the youngest. He's only four. So, I got four younger brothers and two younger sisters. The other girls are too young for you."

"Got it all figured out, don't you, Frank?" James said with a grin. "What if your sister thinks I'm warthog ugly?"

"She won't. Look, we're there!" Frank shouted and kicked his mule into a faster pace as they approached the farm house.

James looked over Frank's home. Everything looked in good repair, and it was a large house. He held back, waiting for Frank to greet his family who was streaming out the door, faces wreathed in smiles over this happy surprise. Frank's mother was in tears as she hugged and kissed her boy. The toddler's arms were wrapped around his brother's leg as Frank's father solemnly shook his son's hand. His left hand was placed on Frank's shoulder. It reminded James of his own father's formal attitude toward his boys after they grew up. The girls were making much ado over Frank's uniform, telling him what a handsome soldier he had grown up to be.

"You're too thin, Frank," his mother commented. "Don't they feed you soldier boys enough? Why, you're skin and bones."

"No, Thursa, he's not a boy anymore," his father, Ezekiel said.

"He's growed into a man. That's all. You look fit, son."

"Frank!" another sister shouted as she came out the door, and with tears of joy embraced her brother and held on for several moments.

James recognized the striking, young lady immediately. This was Elvira, and even in the fading light of the sunset behind him, he could see the photograph did not give her justice. She was beautiful, and her auburn hair framed a delicate face with classic features. Frank turned around and motioned for James to come forward. He did, and now was nervous about meeting this family and charming woman who smiled warmly at him. Up close, he was even more enthralled and felt like a foolish schoolboy. There was not a flaw in her peaches and cream complexion, and the smile captivated him. I'm gone, he thought to himself as he greeted other family members. As he picked up Robert, the baby, Elvira laughed, and his heart leapt. It was Julia's laughter— crystal wind chimes in a soft breeze.

"Enough of the formalities, James," the father said. "Let's all get inside now."

James followed the family through the front door carrying Robert, who was still hanging on tightly and giggling. Elvira turned her head around as she walked in front of him and smiled again. He swallowed hard. Ellen, the twelve year old, guided him to a chair.

"This one's for company, Mother says," Ellen informed James. "Sit down. Robert's heavy. I know. I carry him a lot. I'm afraid all of us spoil him."

As the women and girls prepared supper, James bounced Robert on his knee and visited with Zeke, who was full of questions about Missouri and the war. As they talked, James looked around the large living area of the home. The high ceiling beams were of cypress. It was an expansive room with a kitchen in the rear, partly separated by a latticed partition. Halfway between the kitchen and front of the house was the dining area. The large dining table looked as it might seat a dozen people. It was nicely crafted in red oak and polished to a beautiful shine. James thought it was either made in a furniture shop or custom built by a good craftsman. The ten chairs were of the same wood. A large, oval, brown rug set off the dining area. To James, the house had a comfortable and warm feeling and invited one to make himself at home.

"You still got family in Missouri? " Zeke asked.

"Yes, sir, I do. My mother and two sisters are living in Pineville. A good friend of my late father watches after them. Father passed on in '57 of consumption."

"So, your family's city folk?"

"No, sir, Father and his friend pioneered the southeastern corner of Missouri in '38. Father was in the trade business also, but first and foremost he was a farmer. That was his first love." James paused a moment. "Union guerrillas burned us out in '62. That's why Mother and the girls are in Pineville."

Zeke nodded and didn't push the matter any farther. He wasn't a nosy person and would never make a guest uncomfortable, so he simply asked if the family originally came from Missouri.

"No, Mr. Bankes, only my youngest sister was born in Missouri. Our family came from Spring Place, Georgia."

"Spring Place," Zeke said with interest as he leaned forward. "Of course, I know Spring Place. It's up in Murray County. Why, we come from Coweta County. Now ain't that something."

James grinned and said, "Why, Frank never told me. Sure, I know where Coweta County is. It's southwest of Atlanta."

Zeke began to chuckle and shake his head. "Now that's something ain't it. Almost neighbors back home, and we meet here in Texas." Then he turned somber for a moment. "In the hands of the Yankees now. Sherman burned Atlanta to the ground after they surrendered. May he rot in hell."

In the kitchen, Elvira, Ellen, and Thursa Bankes chatted quietly as the youngsters got the table ready for supper.

"Well, I for one like this young man very much," Thursa said to Elvira. "He's quite handsome too and has kind eyes. I like that. See the way he still plays with Robert. Shows patience and fondness for children. That's a good sign."

Elvira smiled and glanced across the room, and for a moment, James caught her eye. She blushed and turned to her mother again. "Yes,

Mama. I think he's a very nice looking young man. And did you hear what he said? His family's from Georgia too, not far from Coweta. Now isn't that something?"

"Fate!" Ellen said loud enough that her father turned with a question on his face. "Fate, Elvira. It's fate." Ellen had learned a new word at school and liked to use it whenever she could. Elvira laughed and shooed her sister into the dining room.

"When's the last time you went back?" Frank asked. "I never knew you came from Georgia."

"Back in the spring of '55," he answered, still playing with Robert as he talked. "The whole family returned when my grandfather died."

"Ellen, come and take Robert," Zeke interrupted. "Why the boy's wearing down our guest. Bet his knee's plumb wore out."

James protested and laughed, but Ellen took her little brother and carried him to the dining room where he found a toy to play with. At the same time, Thursa announced that supper was ready, and the whole family gathered around the table and waited for their father to say the blessings. When the patriarch finished, and the amens were said, he announced, "Eat."

"I do hope you like fried chicken, James," Thursa said, as she passed the platter piled high with steaming, golden brown chicken pieces.

"Love it," he said and forked a drumsticks and breast into his plate. " It all looks delicious, Mrs. Bankes. Thank you. This is a real treat for me."

"Gravy?" Elvira asked, smiling as she held out the gravy dish to him.

James nodded and smiled back as he took the gravy. As he ate, the conversation around the table was mostly directed at Frank. Both his brothers and sisters wanted to hear about his adventures in Louisiana and Arkansas. James smiled as he listened. It was obvious the siblings were proud of Frank, as they should be, he thought.

"James," Thursa said, "Elvira has shared your poems with me, and I enjoyed reading them. They're beautiful. Have you always enjoyed writing?"

James blushed and said, "Why, thank you, Mrs. Bankes. That's very kind. Yes, Ma'am, I've kept a journal and written poetry since I was a school boy."

"Well, you must write more," Elvira said as she smiled and then caste her eyes downward to the plate.

James watched her and felt his chest tighten again. For the rest of the meal, he mainly tried not to stare at Elvira. Don't want to scare her off by gawking like some moon-struck sixteen year old, he thought. After dinner, Frank, James, and Zeke retreated to the chairs around the fireplace. This time, Robert sat on his father's lap and began to nod off. James noticed all the children seemed to have a job at clearing the table and cleaning up after supper. Both boys and girls went about their assigned tasks quietly without orders or direction, and the nightly chore went quickly and efficiently. After supper, the children returned to the table with their books and did school lessons. Again, he was impressed with how Frank's brothers and sisters quietly worked. At times, one would ask for help, and it was quickly given. Only when the schoolwork was finished did the youngsters join the family. Tonight, Elvira was going to read another chapter of *The Deerslayer*. Her mother and she took turns at this pleasurable task. Sometimes, whatever book was being read would be passed to the younger children to read passages aloud. The whole scene that evening reminded James of home which brought bittersweet memories. It was obvious to him the written word was considered important in this family, and that pleased him very much.

"Maybe James already read this book," Thursa said. "He might want to hear something else."

"Oh, no, please," James said. "Elvira, go ahead and read. It's a great story and I don't mind hearing it again."

Elvira read, and her clear voice floated across and touched James. With her head tilted slightly toward the lamp by her side, she read. The dim light gave the right side of her face a soft, golden, romantic glow contrasting with the shadow on her left side. As she read, her little brother crawled into her lap and was soon asleep. Thursa quietly picked up the boy from Elvira's lap and took him to his bed. As James listened and watched, he was glad for this time, for now he could watch Elvira closely without feeling awkward. Seeing her face in the lamp's light with eyes downcast toward the pages of the book, he could see her eyelashes were long. He remembered Julia's and thought again about lashes of lace. Elvira was a good reader, adding emphasis with her voice at correct moments, raising and lowering the tone at times. The children listened intently. The words drifted through James's mind, but mainly he just wanted to watch Elvira and hear her voice. He was beginning to believe he was falling deeply in love with this young woman and only hoped he wouldn't do something foolish to chase her away. Within an hour, she was finished and the children were in bed. The adults stayed up for a while and visited until they were ready for sleep. A feather mattress was laid out in the parlor for James, and it was just fine with him. He had slept on the floor many times, and the feather bed was snug and comfortable. As he drifted off to sleep, he was happy. It had been a good day, and he looked forward to the next morning. His dreams were pleasant.

"This is great, Mrs Bankes," James said, as he swallowed another bite of his biscuit smeared with strawberry preserves.

"Thank you, James, but I didn't make the biscuits. Elvira did. She also made the strawberry preserves. In fact, she did most of the canning last year."

James looked across the table at Elvira and grinned as he lifted his coffee cup in a salute. He said, "Sorry, Elvira. You're a good cook just like your mom. Should have known. These may be the best biscuits I've ever had, and the strawberries are wonderful."

She blushed as she chewed her own breakfast and lifted her long tapered fingers to cover her lips as she mumbled a thank you. James noticed she had changed dresses and put up her hair. The dress looked so new, he guessed it might be something usually reserved for church. It was a pretty forest green that was tightly fitted above the waist then flowed out over her hips and hung to the heels of her shoes. It was set off by a row of brass buttons down the front and white lace at the cuffs and neck. A bright yellow ribbon held her long hair in place. Yes, she's beautiful, he thought to himself, and she has a perfect figure.

"Elvira, why don't you take James for a walk, and show him around the place when we're finished with our coffee," Zeke suggested. "You'd like that, wouldn't you, James? I'll help Mother clean up, and we'll have some time alone with Frank."

"Yes, sir, I would, if Elvira doesn't mind. I'm finished with my coffee." He looked at Elvira with the question in his eyes.

Elvira looked up and smiled. "Yes, I would love to walk."

James was so happy he wanted to shout, but only nodded and said, "I'm ready." He took the last swallow of coffee and followed Elvira outside. As he glanced at Frank, he noticed his partner's cheeks were full, and he had a wide grin for him. He believes his plan is working out just right, James thought and smiled. It probably is, thankfully. At first, Elvira showed him their farm and land. James could see the spring plowing and planting were already done. The large garden was in also. It was a decent spread, and James figured about five hundred acres, maybe less. The two milk cows looked healthy with full bags and were ready to be milked. There were also hogs and a few goats in separate pens. The chicken yard was full of squawking hens, and a purple plumed rooster strutted among them. Apple, peach, and pear trees in the orchard were heavy with blossoms. After seeing the farm, Elvira led James down a favorite walking path. She loved it in spring with the colors of wild flowers and flowering trees.

"Aren't the red buds pretty this year, James?" she said and pointed to a bushy tree blooming with thick clusters of small pinkish-red flowers.

"Yes, very pretty. We saw a lot of them on the way here. It was a beautiful trip. I do love spring with its colors. Sometimes I get feeling down and blue in the winter after a lot of dark cold days."

"Yes, I'm glad winter is over too. Well, here we are. I wanted you to see my hideaway."

In front of them was a wide area in the trail that obviously had been kept clean of weeds and brush. The little hideaway was about twenty by twenty yards. A magnificent live oak tree grew on the western edge, its heavy, gnarled branches spreading out to cover the area with shade. Beneath the tree's outstretched limbs was a gazebo, and inside were two benches facing each other. Outside were two more benches and a chair. Swings hung from sturdy branches facing a small grove of dogwoods and azaleas. Colorful wild flowers, green grass, and clover carpeted the ground.

Elvira watched James as he looked at this small wonderful spot in the woods and asked, "Do you like it?"

"Elvira, it's absolutely beautiful. Someone's put in a lot of work here. Are we still on your land?"

"Oh, yes, Father left almost a hundred acres of the farm in forest. He didn't want all of it cleared. This is my secret place." Then she laughed. "Well, it's the family's of course and no secret. Father built the little gazebo for Mother and cleared this spot when I was only a child. We still come here at times for family picnics. Mother and I come here to read and talk about books. When the weather's nice, it's so pleasant to just relax, visit, or read. I read your letters sitting in the bench swing."

They both stepped in and sat opposite of each other on the benches. There was an awkward moment, and then Elvira said, "James, I am so glad you came to see us. Everyone in the family is glad."

"Oh, Elvira, if you only knew, but thank you for saying that. I was nervous the whole time riding here. I love your family and admire the way everyone helps each other. There's much love on this land. And you...well...I" James stammered and paused as he looked deeply into those expressive eyes that looked boldly into his. "It's hard to explain what your letters have meant to me, and now that we've met, I want to come back to this place. I want to know you better and have you know me better. I wish and hope we can share our thoughts, our dreams, and become closer. Sorry, I didn't mean to be so bold."

She laughed, and he was enraptured again. Then she reached out, touched his knee and said, "James, I feel the same way. I love your charm, the way you give of your heart. You're a good man, and yes, I want to see more of you also. I hate this war. It's separated too many people. If something happened to you, and I never saw you again, it would break my heart. So, James, before you is a woman who wants to have you come a courting" Then she began laughing and said, "Oh, my, what a shameless woman you've turned me into."

James laughed, then stood, took her hand, and pressed it to his lips.

231

"Shameless, no. You honor me, and I promise, no one will be as careful to stay out of harm's way as I will. Don't worry, with your father's permission, I'll return to court you."

Elvira stood and stepped closer. Her emerald eyes glistened, and her expression was serious as she tilted her head slightly and reached up to touch his face. She left the hand against his cheek until James took it in his own and kissed the palm once, twice, three times.

"James, I—"

"Shhhhh," James whispered and shook his head. He took Elvira in his arms lightly and kissed her, and she kissed him back. The kiss was warm, soft, and lingering.

After the kiss, they each stepped back, the fingers of both intertwined, and James said, "Thank you, Elvira. Thank you for your words and for the sweet kiss. It means so much. I do believe I'm falling in love with you. Oh, don't you worry one bit, I'll come a courting."

"Why, I enjoyed the kiss also," she said blushing. A grin passed her lips and she continued, "I do confess that I like kissing you." She led him out of the gazebo, and they sat in the bench swing. Sitting side by side, the two held hands as they talked and gently swung back and forth. Their conversation was accompanied by a rhythmic creak as the rope sang its own song to accompany the mockingbird mimicking the yellow finches nesting in the oak tree. They talked of family and friends, the past, and dreams of the future.

"And Bertie, how old is she?" Elvira asked at one point.

"Let's see," James replied. "Why, she's nineteen now." He shook his head with the realization of it.

"So, three years ago," Elvira said, "at the tender age of sixteen, she took on the responsibility of caring for Adelaide and your mother. Then she sent her remaining brothers off to war. This responsibility she handles alone. I must meet her, James. What strength of character and maturity she must have. Would you give me her address? I would like to correspond with her if you think she wouldn't mind. Tell me about Honey Creek."

James told of growing up in his own large family and spoke softly of Honey Creek. As he spoke, Elvira listened intently, because she wanted to know and understand the people and events that molded James into the person who was sitting beside her. From first looking into his eyes, she had sensed some sadness within. And now, as he spoke of the land he grew up on, the land and home he certainly loved, she sensed something was missing from the story. She didn't think he was lying, he was simply leaving something out, and the subject wasn't pressed. What he did tell was obviously painful, and she did not want to open a raw wound. She only squeezed his hand and listened. She knew about Pleasant, but hearing more of him and his wife Frances, her curiosity was piqued.

"Oh, James, I believe I love your Pleasant and Frances and do want to meet them so. All of your family, I must meet them all. They sound perfectly wonderful. Goodness, look at the sun, it's getting close to lunch. We really should get back."

Still holding his hand as they stood, she leaned close to his face and kissed him softly, sweetly, and with meaning. Then she laughed again, took his hand, and they walked slowly back down the path toward her home smiling and chatting. As they walked, James's heart beat happily within his breast, and he was filled with hope for the future with the realization that he may have met his soul mate in this beautiful, tenderhearted girl walking beside him. He began whistling *The Yellow Rose of Texas,* and the sound of those crystal wind chimes accompanied him as Elvira laughed softly and leaned her head against his shoulder. After lunch, Frank and James spent much of the afternoon helping Zeke repair the wagon and mend the fences. As they worked, talked, and joked, the formality loosened, and Elvira's father told James to just call him Zeke. As the younger siblings came walking down the trail from school, Elvira and Thursa prepared a picnic supper. Thursa wanted the entire family to ride back to Whitman with James and Frank. It would be a chance to have a family outing in town. They usually went once a week anyway, and it was Friday. Thursa could put off saying good-by to her soldier boy son just a little longer.

Two days later, Frank and James were back in Shreveport, and the routine of camp life returned. James only had the rest of March to serve as a teamster and would return to his regular duties with company H.

Frank would stay with the teamsters. He would be fine, James decided. The other teamsters liked Frank, and he had learned the job quickly.

The first night on returning from Texas, James wrote Elvira a long letter and wrote another one to her parents, thanking them for their hospitality and asking permission to visit again to court their daughter. He included another poem in Elvira's letter. He also wrote a letter to Bertie, sharing his feelings about Elvira. It was a letter filled with hope about the future. He knew he could not return to Missouri until the murder charge was straightened out, so he also included the Bankes's address. As he finished the last letter, Pleasant walked into the cabin.

"Okay, Brother, tell me about your adventures in Texas. From the grin on your face, I suspect you had a good time." Pleasant stood by the table with his hands on his hips smiling broadly.

"Sit down, Captain, and I'll tell you. To begin with, it may have been the happiest twenty-four hours of my life."

"Great news, James," Pleasant said as he slapped him on the back and sat down. "Tell me more."

"Elvira's not only more beautiful than I thought, but she's a warm, tender, and understanding young woman. I believe I've fallen in love, Pleas. No, I have fallen in love. This is the person I want to spend the rest of my life with, the person I can share my hopes, my fears, my inner soul with. It's hard for me to explain. She's, well, she's perfect for me and certainly inspires me to become a better person."

"Nothing wrong with your character now," Pleasant said. "The whole family is proud of you. You know that, but excuse me for interrupting. Go on."

James blushed and continued. "Anyway, her family sort of embraced me with their hospitality and warmth. They're all good people. Her father told me to drop the mister and just call him by his first name, Zeke. That's a good sign, don't you think?"

"Very good sign. It was over a year before Frances's father gave me permission to call him by his first name."

So, James told his brother of the perfect morning with Elvira, the secret place and their conversation in the gazebo. Everything had been beautiful, the weather, flowering trees, wild flowers, Elvira, the birds.

As James continued his enthusiastic monologue of the twenty-four hour experience, Pleasant listened carefully. With each word, a little more of the worry about his brother was peeled away layer by layer, and his spirit lifted while James talked. He knew he must write Frances tonight and give her the good news about James.

When James paused, Pleasant said, "Okay, now answer the important question. Was your affection returned?"

His brother grinned. "Yes, I kissed her, and she kissed me back— twice. Not only that, she told me she liked kissing me very much, and yes, she wants me back for courting."

Pleasant laughed. "My gosh, James. I've underestimated your debonair man of the world charm. You have potential."

Finally, James continued. "Her parents also invited me to come back. If I return there after the war, I may use their postal address to receive mail. That was kind of them, don't you think?"

"Yes, it was. So how far is this Whitman?"

"About seventy miles east of us. It's not a bad trip."

Pleasant nodded, "Well, I have some more good news for you. Got a letter from Marcus Murray. J. P.'s been in contact with the state representative from our district. Representative Cowers is a good friend of his. First of all, no one has taken the murder charge against you very seriously. In fact, Sheriff Smith threw all three of the wanted circulars on you away. He hasn't gotten one since last June, and no one in southern Missouri seems to be actively looking for Newton MacEver."

"Does that mean I can go home?" James interrupted.

"No, not yet." Then, Pleasant finished explaining what was happening. After the war,

Cowers would put in a petition for Newton's pardon. There was already a plan for doing it for many men who were caught in the middle of partisan activities and charged with crimes, both Union and Confederate supporters. Newton's name would be added, and J.P. was already collecting affidavits and eyewitness accounts. Half the people in Pineville were ready to testify as character witnesses, including the sheriff and county judge.

"You just have to be patient," Pleasant said. "Either a dismissal of charges or pardon will eventually come for you."

James shook his head and said, "Our father certainly knew how to pick friends, didn't he? J.P. has been so good to us. He's a good man of high character."

"Yes, he is," Pleasant said. Then he stood and said goodnight to James.

The rest of March went swiftly, and James returned to his regular duties with company H the first week of April. It didn't take long for him to fall back into the routine of drills and inspections. The Missourians seemed to be the best disciplined part of the Trans Mississippi Department as far as James was concerned. Their desertions remained low, and morale was high. General Price had some success with cavalry raids as far north as Missouri, but was now back in camp, and Old Pap could still inspire his men. The Missourians maintained regimental discipline, and even as others lost hope, Parsons' Brigade still had dreams of returning home to drive the Yankees from their state. However, April brought the news Richmond fell to Grant's army on the third day of that month. President Davis and members of the government had abandoned the capital on the previous day at General Lee's advice. There would be more bad news a few days later.

In the middle of April, after the day's duties and supper were finished, Pleasant came looking for James and found him sitting on the bench outside his cabin. He was reading a letter from Elvira.

"You're smiling, so it must be from Elvira," Pleasant said and sat next to him. "Nice day to relax outside."

"Yeah, it is," James said as he put the letter away.

"Go ahead and finish it, James. I can wait."

"No, I've read it three times anyway. So, what's the latest from officer country?"

Pleasant took a deep breath and said, "More bad news, the worst of news, James. Lee has surrendered the Army of Virginia to Grant. Happened a few days ago."

James was silent and stared down at his folded hands for several moments. Then, he spoke. "Where did this happen?"

"A little place in Virginia called Appomattox."

"Well, then it's over," James said quietly.

"Think you're right, but there's no official word our government has surrendered. We still have troops in the field, but...yeah, it's about over."

"In the meantime, we just wait," James said.

"That's about it," Pleasant said sadly. "We just wait until someone else from the east makes a decision for us. If the Yankees make a move against Shreveport, we'll fight, but I suspect there'll be no kind of spring offensive for us or the Yanks."

James nodded. "Just as well. It's strange, but you know, I've had a feeling the past few months the Yankees here in the west have been doing the same thing, just waiting around to see what happens back east."

A few days later, Frank stopped by to see James and say good-by.

"Good-by? What's going on, Frank?"

"The Texas 22nd is marching to Texas. We're going home and disband soon as we get there. No one sees any sense in staying. It's all over, and we're just going home. That's all."

James nodded sadly and said, "Can't blame you boys. We know it's over too but won't move til there's an official surrender or something." Then he smiled. "Maybe we're just stubborn like our mules. Today, we did another day of routine drills like always."

Frank laughed and said, "Us boys from Texas been talking about how you Missouri fellows not only fight like demons, but march the same way."

"So, when you leaving?" James asked.

"Tomorrow. That's why I came straight over to tell you."

"Well, let me give you two letters for your sister. Appreciate it if you'll take them to her for me."

"Of course, be glad to. I'll miss seeing you, James. Are you still coming to Hood County when Parsons' Brigade gives it up?"

"Oh, yes. Don't have anyplace else to go anyhow, and you know I'm in love with Elvira. I'll be there soon as it's over. It can't be too far off."

James got the letters for Frank and also had something in a cloth sack. "I just thought of something. If we surrender, we'll have to surrender our arms, won't we?"

"Yep, believe you do. According to what I was told, it's one of the reasons we're going to Texas and disband. None of us want to give anything to the Yankees, including guns and horses. We also don't want to give them our colors." James hefted the sack. "Heavy, what's in it?"

"My colt revolver. Would you mind putting it in your haversack and taking it home with you? The rifle and bayonet will be enough for the Yankees. I want to keep this."

"Don't worry. I'll keep it safe for you." Then he grinned. "Any message for my sister?"

"Give her the letters, tell her I love and miss her terribly, and I can't wait to be with her again." With a grin, he slapped Frank on the shoulder and shook his hand. "Good-by, Frank. Go with God."

The next six weeks went about the same as the previous six weeks with rumors, gossip, and occasional official word. Finally, in early June, General Kirby Smith surrendered the Confederate armies of the Trans-Mississippi Department to the Union. The war was officially over for all the troops west of the Mississippi. On June 7, men of Parsons' Brigade waited for the inevitable, the arrival of a Yankee regiment the next day to officially accept their surrender. There had been a heated discussion among the men about burning the colors. No one wanted to surrender the flags, and armies would often burn their flags rather than have the colors they fought under become souvenirs of the enemy. Finally, someone came up with a better alternative. The flags would be cut up into small squares and divided among the men who wanted them. General Price and Parsons were each given a flag. The men would march behind the colors one last time to the neutral field between themselves and the Yanks where weapons would be surrendered. The companies had drawn lots, and company H would be the proud color bearer carrying the lone, uncut flag. As soon as rifles were stacked, this last flag would be cut and divided among the men of company H. Everyone liked the idea, a final act of rebellion.

The men of company H stood around their captain discussing

tomorrow's plan. They all took solemn pride in their company's role during the surrender.

"One last thing," Pleasant said. "You men decide this. Who will carry our flag for the last time?"

"Your brother!" Came a shout from the rear. "James MacEver." There were shouts of approval, and no other names were called.

"James, do you accept the honor?" Pleasant asked.

"Yes, sir, with gratitude and thanks."

On the next morning, the men were rousted out early and formed up. James intended to say his good-byes and start for Texas after the surrender. His backpack was filled with what he needed on the trip. He kept his large knife, mess kit, some tins of beef, pemmican he had made himself, hardtack, and dried fruit. Fellow Missourians would be walking in other directions. They were also ready to leave immediately after the surrender.

"Company H, attention!" Captain MacEver shouted, and the men snapped to. "Forward, march!"

The Missourians began a short march across the meadow where the Illinois 88th Infantry awaited their surrender. Generals Price and Parsons, along with other staff officers rode in front of the long column of gray, sitting their mounts tall and straight. At the head of the column was company H with James carrying the flag proudly . His brother marched with purpose, left hand on the sword scabbard, sword in the right hand, blade on his right shoulder. Suddenly, James was proud to have been part of this army and proud of his comrades-in-arms now. They had kept their cohesiveness as a unit the past months while others began to fall apart. In every battle, these men always achieved their battle assignments with efficiency and suffered much for their bravery. They marched with their heads held high, eyes straight ahead. There were no downcast eyes, no slouched shoulders of despair. These were proud men who had done their best and done it with honor. They had no reason to be ashamed, and they weren't. Like the other men, James would carry his small piece of the battle flag for the rest of his life. As they marched into the field of surrender, a thousand blue coats snapped to attention, Union officers saluted with swords swung to the side smartly, and the brave men of Parson's Brigade marched a little taller at this gesture of goodwill from their former enemies.

The ceremony was short and informal. The arms were stacked, and the men of company H cut their flag as planned, and each had their own memento of Parsons' Brigade. An hour later, James and other Missourians were still talking and visiting with members of the Illinois regiment. The meetings had been tentative at first as some of the men in blue walked toward the men in gray. But soon, the fraternization of former enemies was in full swing with handshakes, joking, and bartering. Yankees trading their tins of real coffee for Confederate tobacco had replaced the exchange of rifle and cannon fire. Finally, James began walking west along the road with Jeremy and other friends. They stopped at their former parade ground and chatted. Finally, his friends began to drift off while he waited for Pleasant. The last to leave was Jeremy. The two men looked at each other awkwardly and then embraced. It was a sad parting for them both. James waved his final farewell and walked to a shade tree. He waited there for Pleasant, who like all officers, was signing a pardon, swearing never to take up arms against the union again. James soon nodded off as he waited.

"Well, how's it feel to be a civilian?" Pleasant asked. "Gonna sleep the peace away?"

James woke with a start and stood up. He rubbed his eyes and said, "Looks like it. Didn't mean to sleep, just dozed off before I knew it. So, what's your plan?"

"Going home to Georgia. I'll make my way to Mississippi first and either find a train or horse. Just wanted to visit some more before I leave."

"I'm about ready too. Sure glad Parsons kept us in good shape. It's a long walk, but I'll be a good piece into Texas before I have to stop and camp."

"Need anything?"

"No. Got everything I would take on a march into battle except a rifle, including food and bedroll. I'll be just fine. Maybe—"

"Newton? Pleasant?

Both men looked behind them, startled by the questioning voice. A

Yankee soldier was dismounting his horse. It was an officer, a major in plumed hat. He walked toward them quickly wearing a big grin, and they finally recognized their brother-in-law. It was their sister Josephine's husband, Andrew J. Caulfield, now Major Caulfield. Neither men waited for a hand shake, but walked forward to embrace Andrew and pound his back. After friendly and warm greetings, they stood back. All three were grinning and happy to see each other alive, but not quite knowing what to say after years of war.

"How's our sister?" both brothers blurted at the same time and then began laughing. "And our new nephew?" Pleasant added.

"They're both great," he said. "Little Burton looks just like me, and Josephine is with child again. I knew you were here somewhere. Bertie keeps me informed through Josephine."

"Oh, so you've had leave," James said with a laugh and slapped his brother-in-law on the back again. "Congratulations. Oh, congratulations on your promotion. Last I heard, you were still a captain."

"Thanks," Andrew said with an embarrassed grin. "Well, I assume you're going to Georgia, Pleasant, but what about you, Newton, or should I call you James? Yes, I know all about Honey Creek and the name change, just as I know a great injustice has happened. You should be returning to Missouri with your head held high. Damn this war! What can I do?"

"Oh, it doesn't matter much, but Newton is fine. I can't think of anything unless you wanna give me your horse." James laughed and continued, "I'm headed west to Texas. Gotten to know a family there, and I'm sweet on their daughter. Yeah, damn this war." Then he brightened. "Oh, I know. Got any coffee?"

"Ah, that's easy." Andrew walked to his horse and took two cans of coffee out of his saddlebags. He pitched them to James and Pleasant.

"Thank you!" Both men exclaimed. "Real coffee! You Yanks have no idea how we missed this."

The three in-laws sat under the shade tree for another hour reminiscing and exchanging family gossip. Finally, James looked up at the sun and said, "Close to noon, and I've got a long walk. It's time to get started."

It was a very difficult good-by for all three men, and Pleasant was worried about his brother being alone on the road. He knew brigands were about, and the incident with Quigley had shaken him.

"You have the addresses?" Pleasant asked, prolonging the parting a few more seconds.

"Yes, I do. Don't forget to give Frances my poetry. I'll be safe, really I will. You take care of yourself." Then he embraced both men and turned to go. He did hate partings.

"Go with God, James. Go with God."

James turned, waved, and said, "I always try, Brothers. God go with you both."

It was a two hour walk to the Texas border, and once there, he rested under a shade tree to eat his late lunch in solitude, reflecting on the past three years. During the half hour rest, he noticed not a single person, either walking or riding, passed by. He wondered if he had made a mistake by not hiding his gun somewhere in camp. As it turned out, there were no searches anyway. He could have put it in his back pack, and none of the Federal authorities would have known. He was beginning to feel a little naked. All this past year, there had been rumors about soldiers being murdered and robbed on these lonely roads as they tried to make their way home.

"Enough," he finally said as he stood and started down the road. "No brigands on the road or monsters in the forest." He began to whistle as he walked at the quickstep. As he did so, he daydreamed pleasant thoughts of Elvira and fell back into the routine he learned on many marches. Keep your mind on pleasant things and forget the trials of the march. His pace quickened, and he began to make good time. The afternoon sun was glaring now and the heat oppressive. There were no clouds, and the trees gave little shade, for the sun was in front of him as he walked westward. He pulled the bill of his hat down to shade his eyes. Twice that hot afternoon, he stopped for short rests and drank from his canteen. There was one thing he was thankful for—there weren't a thousand feet of marching soldiers, cavalry, or wagons to stir up the choking dust he had eaten on other marches. Relief came as the sun's furnace gradually began to burn out.

"My God, what beauty," he said aloud, then stopped. Suddenly, it occurred to him to find a place to camp quickly before the light was gone. He took another glance at the setting sun, then walked into the forest and found a likely camping spot beneath a post oak. There was a nice carpet of grass to make a comfortable bed, and he quickly gathered some dead branches and leaves for the fire. Just as the last of the sun's light vanished, he had a small fire going.

Within a few minutes, James had his bedroll laid out and arranged the backpack as a pillow. He opened a tin of beef and heated it over the fire, deciding to eat from the can. He didn't want to waste water cleaning his mess kit. From the firelight, he gathered more dead branches and laid back on his bed roll to look at the night sky, now brilliant with stars. A time for dreams, he thought to himself and tuned his hearing for the sounds of a forest covered with the cloak of night. In the high branches of the tree he rested under, the hoot of an owl sounded. Abruptly, there came the beat of heavy wings and whoosh of the winged predator swooping down close to the ground. He heard the faint, high pitched squeal of a prey and then nothing but the beat of wings. A second later the owl was back in the tree. "One mouse gone," he said to the owl. There was a hoot in answer. Once, James heard a horse and buggy, and he turned toward the road. As the buggy went by, all he could see were two golden, ghostly, dancing orbs floating beyond the trees. He stared until the buggy's lanterns were out of sight and flinched from the chilling scream of a cougar close by. It screamed again later, but the sound was much farther away this time. He was glad and threw some more branches on the flames. As the coyotes serenaded him, he regretted again not having his weapon. Finally, he drifted off to sleep and three hours later awoke in a cold sweat. His nightmare of Quigley and the cougar had returned to haunt his dreams once more. He sat up shivering, and it was not the coolness of the dark morning that made him shiver. He wrapped the blanket around him and sat starring into the darkness until dawn. Will I meet Quigley on this road? Is that my destiny? Is that why I survived bloody battles? Newton wondered if Quigley hadn't been frightened off by the cavalry last fall after all. Enough, he finally thought and stood.

"The name's Newton John. Do you hear me? I'm Newton John MacEver, and I'm hard to kill," he said loudly as he relieved himself against a tree. "Hear me, Jonah? I'm hard to kill. Better men than you tried and failed. They were all better men than you. They failed, and so will you. I won't shrink from my quest. I won't live in fear. Damn you to hell, Jonah Quigley, I'll build a new life, a clean life, a life full of love and family, and you or any other beast from hell won't keep me from that love. Go to Hades and rot with your sorry brothers! I am not afraid of you. I've kept the faith and my honor!"

The catharsis over, James got his fire started and prepared breakfast. Whistling, he heated a makeshift cereal of crushed hardtack and dried fruit, sprinkled with sugar. He didn't linger long at his camping place, for there were many miles to go. Scraping the mess kit clean, he rinsed sparingly with the water in his canteen, packed up, and made his way to the road. He turned and looked in the direction he had come. The sun was still low in the early morning sky and would be at his back for a few hours. He smiled, turned westward and began his quickstep down the forest-lined road.

"I'm coming, Elvira! God willing, I'll see you soon," he shouted with a grin and continued his march. He whistled and walked with confidence, his hands balled into fists as they gripped the straps of his backpack.

Part III
Elvira

Chapter Seventeen
Reunion

Supper was finished, and the family gathered on the porch to catch the early evening breeze as the sun set. The sun hadn't quite reached the horizon yet, and so was still too bright to try and look into directly. But in a few short minutes, it would gradually sink and become less glaring as it loomed ever larger to brush the western horizon with color. The girls held the back of their hair up, letting bare necks feel relief as the dampness evaporated in the breeze.

"Pa, I think someone's comin," John Thomas, his fourteen year old son said.

"See who it is?" Zeke asked.

"Nope, just a speck, but someone's walking this way."

Frank strained to see, shading his eyes with his hand. "Too far away to tell."

Within minutes, the sun touched the road leading into Whitman, and the blinding glare was dissipated. The family continued their watch as the figure marched toward their home. Whoever walked their way was now silhouetted by orange magnificence and slowly became discernable. Puffs of dust swirled around the walker's knees as he gradually drew closer, and Frank rose with anticipation.

"I think it's a soldier," Zeke said.

"Yep," Abram agreed.

Elvira stood and strained her eyes. Her heart beat faster, and she prayed it was Newton. The entire family had worried since Frank returned home and told them Newton planned to walk from Shreveport after the surrender.

"It must be James, I mean Newton," Frank said. "I'm sure it is, Elvira."

Elvira turned to her parents with tears in her eyes. Zeke and Thursa looked at each other knowingly and at their daughter with love.

"Go to him, Elvira," Thursa said. "He's come such a long way. We know you love him, so go."

Zeke smiled at his oldest child and said, "Well, child, go ahead and run. Don't keep the boy waiting."

Elvira kissed both parents, darted down the steps and ran, her heart pounding with each step. On the porch, her siblings clapped and laughed their support. Tears flowed unabashedly. Within seconds, she knew it was Newton. He stopped and waited, standing tall in his dust and sweat stained gray uniform. Removing his hat, he smiled, a smile tinged with weariness. He said only three words before she was in his arms. "Elvira, my heart."

Zeke and Thursa watched the reunion with mixed emotions. Thursa silently shed tears of her own as she held her husband's arm and clutched the brooch at her neck.

"There, there, Mother," Zeke said and patted his wife's hand. "She's happy and I suspect we'll be havin' us a wedding."

"Fate," Ellen said laughing. "Told Elvira so, yes, it's her fate and destiny." The other siblings began repeating the words and laughing.

"Now stop it!" Thursa demanded. "Don't you children be teasing your sister and spoil things."

"You heard your mother," Zeke said. "Here they come, straighten up now."

Elvira hung onto Newton's arm tightly and smiled into his face as they walked back to the house. Newton's newly adopted family waited on the steps.

"Welcome home, Newton," Thursa said as she embraced him. "God bless you."

Zeke took Newton's hand warmly and shook it. "We've been worried, Newton. It's a long walk from Louisiana."

With their parent's formal welcome over, Elvira's brothers and sisters were clamoring around Newton with excited chatter, handshakes, and embraces of their own. Finally, he was led to one of the porch rockers where he gratefully removed his backpack and plopped into a resting position. Suddenly, the exhaustion hit him. It had been a long walk, and by his stubbornness, he had pushed himself almost to the point of collapse. He fumbled with his canteen, but Thursa interrupted.

"Frank," Thursa said. "Fetch this boy some fresh water. No telling how warm that canteen water is. Get him some fresh, cool water from the well and bring a glass for him.

Soon, he was washing the taste of dust from his parched throat with a tall glass of cool, sweet, spring water. Surely, he thought, it was the best tasting liquid that ever passed between his lips. "Thank you. Best glass of water I ever had."

"Bless your heart, Newton," Thursa continued. "Are you hungry? We have some leftover ham, fresh bread, and peach cobbler. I'm afraid all the greens and peas are gone. Would you eat a sandwich? Elvira baked today."

"A sandwich sounds wonderful, Mrs. Bankes. Thank you. Do you have any milk?"

"Of course. Ellen, fetch the milk from the spring house. Elvira, help me fix this poor thing supper."

The first thing James attacked when his supper was brought was the milk. He loved milk, and he was still thirsty. He savored the sandwich with generous pieces of smoked ham between thick slices of freshly baked bread. As he ate, James fielded questions about his trip and the Missourians' surrender at Shreveport.

"Did the Yankees do anything to ya?" Abram asked. "They wanna get revenge or anything?"

James shook his head with a smile. "No, we just marched into the field, put our guns down and that was it. Wasn't long till we were talking, joking, and trading with the Yanks They were glad the fighting was over too."

"Trade? What did you trade?" John Thomas asked.

"Mostly our tobacco for their coffee," he answered. "Oh, that reminds me. I've got some things for you." James opened his haversack.

He smiled and handed the can of coffee to Thursa. "Thought you might like this. I know coffee's been hard to come by since the blockade."

"My goodness, Newton," Thursa said. "Real coffee." She kissed him on the cheek. "Tomorrow's breakfast comes with real coffee."

He dug into his haversack again. "Come here, Robert. Look what I found." The youngster ran to him excitedly. "Close your eyes and hold out your hand." Newton placed a hand crafted model sailboat in his chubby hands. It was bright green with C.S.A. printed on the sail. He had bought it from one of the peddlers at camp, and Robert gave an appreciative squeal.

"Now, Robert, say thank you," Thursa demanded. The little one climbed onto Newton's lap and squeezed his neck.

There were some other things, trinkets and tins of hard candy for the other children and black lace scarfs for Thursa and Elvira. For Zeke and Frank, he had pocket knives. There were protests from Thursa for spending his money on the family, but the gifts were appreciated and everyone took delight.

"So, the Yankees treated you boys with dignity then," Zeke said. "I'm glad to hear that. No use rubbing your faces in the dirt."

"No, no one lorded it over us, Zeke. I was proud of Parsons' Brigade and proud of the Yankees too. Oh, almost forgot. Pleasant and I got to see our sister's husband. He's a major with the Union regiment we surrendered to and the one who gave me your coffee. My sister, Josephine, is expecting another baby soon. It was good to see him again."

"Have you heard from Bertie?" Elvira asked.

"No, I hope the last letter with your address got to her before she wrote. If she sent it to Shreveport, I'll never see it, but I'll be writing to her again with your post number. Sure appreciate you doing that till I get settled here."

"Newton, you've got a home here long as you need it," Thursa said and patted his shoulder. "No need to worry. Now, I've got to get these younguns ready for bed. I'll get your pallet ready in the parlor."

"Oh, no. I'm too dirty, and I'd just soon sleep here on the porch now that it's warm. Got my bed roll and I'll be fine, really I will."

"Well, suit yourself." Then she turned to Frank. "Get Newton two buckets of water, the soap, and towels. He can clean up when he's ready to sleep. Now the rest of you inside. Let Elvira and Newton have some time to talk alone."

There were protests, but in a few minutes, Newton and Elvira were visiting quietly alone as they rocked side by side in separate chairs. He reached out to hold her hand as they talked.

"Can't tell you how much I've missed you," he said. "Guess it's the closest I ever came to deserting. Never even thought of it going into battle, but wanting to be with you about drove me to it. Oh, thanks for telling the family I wanted to go by my given name."

"Oh, Newton, I missed you too. Your letters helped, but sometimes reading your words made me miss you even more. But, you're here now, you're safe, and I'm grateful."

"Elvira, I love you. I love you with all my heart and soul. I've wondered for years if I would ever find someone to share my life. The day Frank showed me your photograph, my heart told me it was you. And then, with your letters, that belief became stronger until finally those wonderful hours with you confirmed those feelings. I want to ask your father permission for us to marry."

Tears were streaming down Elvira's face, and as she squeezed his hand tighter, she was silent for a long time, or so it seemed to Newton. She turned her face to his and smiled brightly through her tears. "Yes, I love you, and yes, I'll marry you, but let's wait and make sure." Then she leaned closer and placed her lips against his.

"You honor me, Elvira, and I understand. I don't expect to marry right away. I need to find a piece of land to farm, and in the meantime,

I should find work. I know I can't afford to marry now, but knowing you're waiting, I'll work hard enough to make it happen soon. I've only got about three hundred dollars left from my inheritance, but soon we'll marry. It's my promise."

"Don't worry," Elvira said and kissed him again. "I'll be waiting. You're the one I've always waited for. Guess Ellen's right. It's fate." They both laughed.

Late into the night, they talked about their hopes for the future and their love for each other. Finally, as Elvira stood to go inside, they heard's Zeke's voice.

"Elvira, it's bedtime. Say goodnight to Newton."

A few minutes later, Newton undressed, rolled his dirty clothes into a ball, and bathed in the moonlight. Washing the grime of his long march from Shreveport seemed to wash away much of the fatigue he felt. When finished, he sat on the porch stoop and listened to the night for a while. Knowing that he would not be going back to war, and knowing Elvira would be here gave him comfort. He was still a little nervous about talking to Zeke on the morrow, but tomorrow would take care of itself. Suddenly, the fatigue and exhaustion of the trip hit him, and he snuggled into his bedroll. As he drifted off, his last thoughts were about how he should ask Zeke for Elvira's hand.

"Yes, Newton, you have our permission to marry Elvira," Zeke said and slapped his future son-in-law on the shoulder. "What took you so long to ask? I think Elvira was getting worried. Why, you've been back a week already."

Newton grinned and took another drink from the burlap wrapped water jug setting between them. "Afraid you might say no, I guess. Admit I was a little nervous about asking. Seemed like I could never find the right time to be alone with you. Glad you needed help with the fence today."

"So, when will the wedding take place?" Zeke asked.

Newton thought a moment and said, "Not till I have my own land. I want to provide Elvira a home first. The problem is I only got three hundred dollars left from my savings and no income."

"Why, Newton. That's more money than most people start with."

Zeke looked at the field of young, green cotton plants and thought a moment. "You know, the Murchison place is for sale, and you could make it into a nice home for Elvira. The lady's all alone now. Her husband was killed at Vicksburg, and she's living in town with a brother, so it's empty. Needs work, but we all could help get it ready for living in."

"How much land and how much money?" Newton asked.

"Not a large place, but close to three hundred acres. I'd suspect around nine hundred to a thousand dollars would buy it. We could make an offer and go to Tyler to meet my banker. Suspect you'd get your loan if you have a hundred dollars to put down. Oh, I hope your savings ain't Confederate dollars."

Newton laughed and said, "No, it's all in Union gold. My needs weren't much during the war, and I spent the Confederate dollars I got paid in. I kept all my original savings. When can we see this place?"

"Don't see anything wrong with today. The place is only two miles from here and then another mile into Whitman, in case you want to meet the widow Murchison and make an offer. We could hitch up the buggy and take Thursa and Elvira if you want."

"Sounds good, Zeke." Suddenly, Newton was excited with the prospect of finding his own place.

Two hours later, Zeke, Thursa, Elvira, and Newton were checking out the empty home on Widow Murchison's property. The house faced the prevailing breeze and a breeze way ran completely through the structure. Main bedroom, parlor, and dining room were on the left. Kitchen, with eating area, and two more bedrooms on the right. There was also another small storage room. During hot weather, the doors could be propped open, and evening breezes would be forced into the rooms to cool things. Good thinking on the builder's part, Newton thought.

Newton smiled. "I like it, Zeke. If Elvira likes it, I'm happy. Make a good home for us. I'd like to add a corral for a couple of horses."

"Got a suggestion for you Newton. But remember it's only a suggestion. When we talk to the banker, borrow enough not only for the property, but some extra for your stock and other things you're gonna need to get started. You can save money by getting colts and breaking them yourself when they're grown. Same thing for any other stock. Of course, it's your business. Just something to think about. Here come the women, and Elvira's smiling."

"I love it, Newton," Elvira said excitedly. "When can we move in? Think I'm ready right now if you are."

Newton laughed and said, "Well, I don't suppose we better do that till we're properly married. You really like it? If this is where you want to live, your pa and I will go to Tyler this week and see about a loan to buy it. I could live here and work to fix things up with some help from your brothers. When it's finished, we'll get married and move in together. How's that?"

"Wonderful." She threw her arms around his neck and held on a long time. Then she stood back to look at him closely. "Ma and I could come and help with things too. It needs a woman's touch again, beginning with a good scrub down. How long will it take to be ready?"

"By fall," Newton answered. "We can be married and in our new home by fall."

True to his word, by November, they were married and living in their home. Their vows were given at the little Clover Hill Baptist Church they attended with Elvira's parents. It was only a mile from home. The repairs and additions to the property were the easiest part of the job; the hardest part was preparing the neglected land for spring plowing and planting. Newton was happy, for it seemed to him his hopes were coming true. He had the woman of his dreams by his side, and they both wanted children soon. Newton had never known a woman physically, so he and Elvira learned the exquisite pleasures of sex by exploring each others' bodies upon the marriage bed. It seemed to them both, some new exciting secret was uncovered each time they made love.

As the months went by, Elvira began to know more of Newton through her correspondence with Bertie. She wrote on a regular basis to her, and sometimes a letter from Pleasant and Frances would arrive to be answered. Elvira had come to love Newton's family from their letters, and she felt a special bond with his youngest sister. She would read Bertie's letters several times and kept them all just as she kept all of Newton's letters. That first Christmas, she spent without Newton, for he and Frank were gone December, January, and February working as teamsters for a freight company in Jefferson. She was sad, but understood. At two dollars a day, the pay was good, and they needed the money. He wrote more than twenty letters to her during those three months, and she read them over and over. At times, Elvira worried when Newton would have dark periods and walk alone. She knew there were things he kept locked inside and didn't share with her, so she waited patiently for him to open his soul. It would come. She would just have to be patient.

Chapter Eighteen
The Journal

"Another biscuit?" Elvira asked as she filled Newton's coffee cup again.

"Sure," he answered

"You're welcome," she said.

"Oh, I'm sorry. Thank you. Like always, breakfast was good. Your biscuits are better than my mother's, and that's the truth. The wild plum jelly's great."

"Bet you said that to your other wives too." Elvira said as she sipped her coffee and studied Newton closely over the rim of her cup. She knew something was bothering him. He had spent most of the breakfast hour playing with his eggs until they were cold and didn't show any real appetite until there was sweet jelly for the biscuits. He wasn't his bright talkative self, and her questions had only been answered in monosyllables. Well, she thought, I know he's got a large sweet tooth, but something's bothering him. He's gone someplace again and doesn't want to take me with him, but he will when he's ready.

"We'll only be gone a month, Elvira," he finally said. This is the last time we'll be separated. Frank doesn't want to drive again, and this is his last haul too. By tomorrow, I'll have the corn planted. The garden's done, and the cotton field is finished. It bothers me to leave you again, but we'll have a little more money to bank. Mr. Babcock's paying us a bonus this time. I'm feeling guilty about leaving again, especially now."

"Newton, don't worry about it. Both John Thomas and Ellen are staying with me while you're gone, and it's only half an hour by buggy to my parents house. I'm not helpless, Newton John MacEver, and pregnant women aren't as fragile as you think. Now, what's really bothering you?" Then she leaned over the table and kissed him.

He brightened and said, "Oh, nothing really. I love you so much, really I do. If it's a boy, are you sure we shouldn't name him after your father?"

Elvira laughed and Newton's spirits rose. "Heavens no. Father told all of us years ago, he wouldn't wish the name Ezekiel Mordecai on anyone. We'll stay with our original plan. If it's a boy, we'll name him John Henry after you and your friend."

Newton smiled and said, "Well, no disrespect to your father, who I love, but I'm relieved." Then Newton got that distant look in his eyes again as he sipped his coffee.

"How did the Grange meeting go?" Elvira asked.

"Hmmm, it went."

"My Dear Heart," Elvira said, "ever since last night when I shook you awake because you were tossing and crying out in your sleep, you've been distant. Don't you trust me?"

Newton looked at Elvira and his heart swelled with emotion. He stood and walked around the table, pulled her chair out to face him, then knelt. He kissed her hands, and placed another on her swollen stomach. With his head on her lap, he said, "Yes, I trust you, and forgive me. I love you more than my own life." Then he kissed her extended belly again. "And I love you, John Henry, or Thursa, or whoever you may be."

Elvira wiped a tear from her eye and said, "Stand up, hold me close, and kiss me the way you did that first time in the gazebo."

He did, and they held on tightly. Newton cupped her face in his hands and said, "I'm going to the corn field and finish plowing. While

I do that, stay inside, get my journal out of the trunk, and read it. I'm sorry I haven't shared it before. When you're finished, I'll answer your questions. I promise."

Elvira kissed him deeply, and with a wicked smile said, "All right, my warrior, but come with me first." She guided him into the bedroom.

A few hours later, Newton had finished plowing the corn field and returned his mule to the barn. After checking on the two young horses and giving them some oats, he returned to survey his day's work. He thought both horses would be ready to break by fall. The pungent smell of freshly plowed damp earth still gave him great satisfaction, and he had high hopes for the cotton and corn, his two cash crops. Green sprouts were already appearing in Elvira's large garden and melon patch. Newton squinted, smiled up at the blue sky and sat down to rest on the ridge of black earth he had just plowed. With his feet in the furrow, he watched the two horses running around the corral. He was anxious for the time both would be ready to ride. It gave him pleasure to think of riding side by side with his bride. It won't be long, he thought. After the harvest, we'll have a little more money in the bank, and a young one around our feet, God willing.

"Newton!" Elvira called.

"Here," he shouted back and waved to get her attention. She saw and began walking toward him carrying a water bottle. As she came closer, he marveled at her pregnant beauty. She complained to him that she looked fat and ungainly, but to Newton, she was even more beautiful. "I'm a most fortunate man," he said to himself.

"Well, aren't you going to stand in the presence of a portly lady?" Elvira asked.

"No, I'm too tired, my turtledove. Take a seat next to me and we'll watch the sun go down." He stood and helped her sit.

"Oh, Newton," she said with a gasp. "I wonder if I'll even be able to get up and down by next month. Here, drink some water. You never drink enough when you're working. Don't know what I'll do after John Henry's born, and I've got two boys to chase after."

She watched her husband tilt the bottle up and drink greedily of the cool water. She had finished the journal. As she read, there were times she had to turn from the pain and horror in places and shed tears. After a short reprieve, she would return and continue reading. She knew in a general way about the partisan raid on Newton's home, the war, and the loss of his friend. But reading of the atrocities visited on his family and the horror of war in Newton's lyrical style had been almost too much to bear. The descriptions of battle overwhelmed her, and at times, she would turn from the carnage to walk about the room. There were other subjects in the journal also, and much of those brought smiles and even laughter. She was touched by Newton's interlude with the tender-hearted girl named Julia, and felt fortunate Newton met Frank before he had a chance to go back and look for her. She thought of her sister's word—fate, and she smiled. Toward the end, the journal was full of his thoughts about her, beginning with the day Frank showed Newton her photograph. By the time she was finished, tears streamed down her face, and her heart filled with the affirmation she had her soul mate.

"Lay your head in my lap," she said, and he did. And now, there were some more tears.

"Please don't cry, Elvira. The thought of giving you pain is unbearable." He sat up and kissed her tears away.

"Oh, Newton. You didn't give me pain. Don't you know as I read your journal you were opening your soul for me to touch? For over a year, you've kept part of yourself from me, and I prayed for the day you would explain those dark moments you have when you walk alone in the woods. I never complained because you didn't share, but now that you have, I'm happy. You're not only my best friend and husband, you're truly my soul mate."

"And you, mine," he responded.

They embraced and kissed with the passion of two young people deeply in love. When it was over, she continued. "Now put your head in my lap again, and I'll massage your temples."

Newton looked into Elvira's face as her fingers worked their magic and his throat tightened with the love he felt. "Any questions for me?" he asked.

She thought a moment. "To begin with, do you think Quigley is still here in Texas? Could he be close by?"

"Truthfully, I don't know. He's wanted for murder in Missouri, so I doubt if he would go back. I think he's probably still somewhere in Texas, but it's a big state. I've decided not to worry."

"Are you afraid?"

"No longer," he said. "Quigley no longer haunts my dreams, and if we meet again, I'll kill him. That's all."

Sorrow rose in Elvira's heart and she said, "Is your heart filled with so much hate?"

Newton thought about the question before answering. "No, it's not hate, and I try not to feed the evil, but surely God wouldn't punish me for defending myself. Do you think so?"

"No, I don't," she said with relief. "But I hope you don't have to kill him. Let's pray he's arrested and punished by the law."

"That might happen too. He's probably still following his murderous ways, and I hope he gets caught, because I want to be finished with killing." He paused, then continued. "It's hard to explain, Elvira, but I…I feel unclean and it haunts me. Do you understand?"

She leaned down to kiss him and said, "Yes, I understand, but you're not unclean. Your soul isn't dirty. What you have is a conscience, so you're not comfortable with the things you have done to stay alive and protect your family. I understand, and so does God. Did Jesus condemn the Roman centurion because he was a soldier?"

"No. My head feels better now. Let's go to the porch and watch the sunset."

"And your heart?" Elvira asked.

"Clean and wonderful. Wouldn't want you to have a dirty soul mate." They laughed and walked back to the house hand in hand. In the next few days, James would share more of his soul.

A few evenings later, Elvira's family came for supper to visit before Newton and Frank left for Jefferson and the teamster jobs. After eating, Newton, Zeke, and Frank talked politics.

"Seems I can't vote. First they say I can, but now I can't. I'm a little disgusted with the Union and their reconstruction," Newton said.

Zeke took a draw on his pipe and said, "Gotta understand, Newton, they want their carpetbagger Republican friends elected, and by keeping Confederate veterans out of the poll booths, they can control the whole state."

"And looks like they'll get their way, Pa," Frank said. "The governor and most of the legislators will be Union lap dogs."

"Reconstruction! Just what do the Yankees mean by it?" Frank asked.

"Line the pockets of their friends, I suspect, while they keep us under their boot heel," Newton said. Then he thought a moment. "You know, Lee said something about not only surrendering to Grant's army but also to Lincoln's goodness. Guess the worst thing that happened to the South was Lincoln's murder by that cowardly Booth. Lincoln talked reconciliation, and now we have occupation and rule by the Union army."

"Yeah, you're right," Zeke said. "And don't forget, Sam Houston fought tooth and nail against Texas seceding from the Union. Fought hard both as a senator in the legislature and later as governor. When the hot heads in the legislature got their way, he refused to take the oath of Confederate allegiance and got booted out of office. Died broken-hearted, I suspect." He sighed. "Old Sam was right."

"Oh, did I tell you my aunt knew Houston?" Newton asked.

"No, you didn't," Zeke said.

"Well, she did. My Aunt Judith's full blood Cherokee, and her second husband's my father's brother. Anyway, before he kinda became a hero and legend in Texas, Houston lived with the Cherokees and even took a Cherokee wife once. My aunt met him in those days, and after he became famous in Texas, she remembered who he was."

"Did she know him good, like a friend?" Frank asked.

"Oh, no, she just knew who he was. He was married to a Cherokee woman her family knew when she was young is all. When I came to Texas, I thought it was interesting. Anyway, Zeke, how long do you think the occupation will last?"

Zeke shook his head and leaned over the porch rail to spit into the dust. "When they've ruined Texas with their carpetbaggers and other scalawag Republicans. And we're the lucky ones. Everywhere east of the Mississippi is even worse."

Newton nodded and said, "It's all a shame, a bloody shame, and bloody confusing what this war's done to all of us. Say what you will about that rascal Sherman, he was right. War is hell."

"Yep," Zeke said, "both confusing and bloody. The bones of thousands of boys from Texas are resting in places like Vicksburg, Shiloh, Cold Harbor, Gettysburg, and Lord knows where else. It's so dang sad." Zeke blinked back a tear and continued. "Think on it. Before the war, those poor boys never heard of such places, and most never been out of the state. Some local boys never been out of the county, and they go so far away to die. I wonder if they knew what they were dying for."

Newton thought a second and said, "Maybe it's like one my friends told Yankees at the surrender. Said he was fighting so hard cause they were down here."

Zeke smiled and said, "Maybe that's reason enough. As good a reason as I can think of, if there is a good reason for war. Still wish the damn Yankees would go home though. There's more bitterness with this occupation than the war caused."

"I think you're right, Pa," Frank said.

"Maybe," Zeke said. "Maybe, but I'm no genius. Still confused about what really happened. Ahh, let's talk about something else. Newton, the Grange work you're doing is helping farmers in this county. You're getting quite a reputation around these parts, and it's bringing in fresh ideas."

"Thanks, Zeke, but there's more work to do. At least the county commissioners are starting to listen, but we need a voice in Austin."

The men talked for another hour about the growing Grange movement throughout the country. The National Grange was started by a Minnesotan and spread quickly across the country as farmers became angry at falling prices and lack of control over their destiny. Newton had started the first lodge in East Texas and worked hard for the past year spreading the word. Finally, Zeke gathered his family. It was time to go home.

"Eight's early enough, Frank," Newton said as he and Elvira waved good-by to the family. "Jefferson's not far, and we'll be there by noon."

Later, in bed, Elvira thought of something that had been nagging the back of her mind.

"Newton," she said. "You mentioned a bonus if you went back to work with the freight company. Why are they willing to pay you a bonus?"

It was a question he hoped wouldn't be asked but answered truthfully. "Because of my military experience. Guess there was an incident couple of months ago. A small band of renegades attacked the wagons out west, mixed whites and Kiowas. I'm glad they got confidence in me."

"Newton, that worries me," she said with alarm in her voice.

"It's nothing to worry about. I doubt if the thieves would try again. Besides, we'll be equipped with Henry repeating rifles. Really, Elvira, there's nothing to worry about. I know what to do to protect myself and the others."

She held him close and kissed his ear. "Please, Newton, please be so very careful and promised me when this is over, you'll never work for the freight company again."

"Never, it's my promise. I won't be working for the freight company again. My future is here with you and the land."

Chapter Nineteen
Snake Oil

"Here's your tobacco. No sir, don't recollect meeting a Newt or James MacEver around Jefferson. You might check with Abraham at the feed store. An old war friend you say? What outfit did you boys serve with?"

"Parsons' Brigade, Missouri 16th. Someone told me my friend came to this part of Texas after the surrender. Thought I'd check while I was in town."

"What brings you to Jefferson?"

"I'm part owner of Doctor Bingham Presswood's Medicine Show. We'll be in town a couple of days. Drop on by. Can't miss our red wagon at the fair. Got the best line of patent medicines in Texas. Got a good fiddler too. He's a real Cherokee chief and medicine man. Best fiddler I ever heard."

"Well, sounds interesting. I'm getting a little rheumatism myself. Could use something on my shoulders. Didn't catch your name."

"Quigley, Jonah Quigley's the name. Yeah, drop on by at the fair this afternoon. We'll be there."

Outside, Quigley, stuffed a plug of tobacco in his mouth and slowly worked it around the inside of his cheek as he watched a line of freight wagons lumber by. He vaguely wondered what they were carrying west when he noticed the teamsters were armed with Henry rifles. This city of thirty thousand was equal to the coastal city of Galveston in population and the only port city of north Texas. Galveston and Jefferson were the largest cities in Texas now, and Jefferson was alive with noise and activity. Stern wheelers carried cargo and immigrants to Jefferson all the way from New Orleans via the Mississippi and Red Rivers to Caddo Lake and Big Cypress Bayou. The city billed itself as river port to the Southwest, and had become rich as a port city, second only to Galveston for total yearly freight tonnage. All this would change within five years when the U.S. Corps of Engineers would remove the natural fallen tree damn above Shreveport, and the water level of Big Cypress would drop, making river boat travel to Jefferson impractical. The city would shrink to a sleepy rural town of less than two thousand, and it's glory days would live only in the local museum.

Quigley spat a stream of brown tobacco juice into the street as the last wagon drove by. He returned a wave from one teamster and crossed to the Excelsior Hotel. The hotel was a little fancy for his taste and so was the saloon, but that's where his partner would be.

"His excellency, Doctor Bingham J. Presswood's got mighty refined taste in food, liquor, and women," he said to himself. He smiled at his good fortune. The doctor was also a bad poker player, and for a year, he had owned half of a tidy little business.

Jonah walked through the large lobby of the white two story hotel and into the saloon. A long, dark, walnut bar with a brass rail ran the entire length of the north end of the room, and several brass spittoons rested on the floor. Mirrors lined the wall behind the bar. Stacked neatly on the long, wide shelf in front of the mirrors were bottles of every type of spirits. Most were liquors Quigley had never heard of, but he kept his ignorance to himself. The bartender was well dressed in dark brown trousers and a vest over a ruffled yellow shirt. He smiled and nodded at the barkeep, then looked around the room for his partner. He was sitting at a table in the back.

"Well, Doc, drinking alone, I see," Quigley said and pulled out a chair for himself.

As Quigley sat down, Bingham raised one eyebrow and said, "Please, Jonah, either Bingham, Mr. Presswood, or Doctor Presswood. Doc, has no dignity. Remember, we are businessmen, men of substance, not commoners."

Quigley nodded solemnly. "Sorry, Doc. No one else at the table to hear us. What difference does it make anyhow?"

"Ahhh, but don't you see? It's practice. You make practice at speaking intelligently, and it becomes a habit. But, excuse my manners. You're without refreshment." With that, he motioned the bartender over. "Drinks are on me, my dear Quigley. I would recommend the establishment's brandy. They have a fine selection."

"A beer," Quigley yelled out at the bartender before he reached them. His business partner shook his head and rolled his eyes. Quigley grinned. He knew the good doctor was already on his way to being drunk, which was good. By the afternoon, the old man would be in perfect form to make his pitch to the plow boys and others who would gather round the wagon at the fair. He didn't dislike the old man. He had been generous to Jonah since taking him as a partner. He only grew weary of his talk of manners, books, poetry, and what he called the finer things in life. After all, Jonah thought to himself, he always had good money in his pockets, and it was easy money. He was rather amazed at how simple it was to make money without breaking any laws, legal laws anyway. Quigley had never given much thought to moral laws. Besides, as they made their way south, they stopped at every town on the way to Houston and Galveston, and Quigley could continue his search for MacEver without being obvious. It was the perfect situation for him, and he had decided to let the good doctor live a little longer. The Cherokee, he would keep. As much as he detested Indians, the man was useful

"Thanks, Partner," Quigley said as he raised his beer mug in a salute.

"Yes," Bingham replied, "A toast is called for. I believe we'll do well at the fair. I'm doubling the price of our precious bottles. By the way, Mr. Quigley, the goatee and hair cut give you a most respectable and debonair appearance. My compliments to you and Jefferson's barber."

"Debonair?"

"Never mind. You look quite handsome. You work the crowd today and work on the ladies. Remember, no chawing or spitting, and no cussin'. Most of these farm women think they have the vapors. Probably do. I'd feel blue all the time too if I had their hard row to plow." The old man got a faraway look in his eyes. "Now when I was younger, I loved to work the ladies in the crowd. I cut a dashing figure then and had lots of energy. Yes, sir, many pretty things lost more than a dollar to me in those days."

"Think the elixir helped in that department?" Jonah asked with a leer.

The old man winked. "Well, it might have. I suppose opium mixed with alcohol and the Cherokee herbal formula certainly perks one up, so to speak. But then, charm and flattery will go a long way. Remember that."

Quigley took another gulp of his beer and studied Bingham closely. As usual, he was dressed quite dapperly. His dark olive suit was sharply pressed, and the brown silk tie was tucked smartly into his vest. A diamond stud set off the tie. His partner's pale, lined face and wispy, thinning, white hair reflected his advanced age. The gray eyes were now dull and had a myopic and watery look to them. The more he thought about it, he believed the good doctor probably was a handsome fellow in his youth, but now the years and alcohol had done their damage.

"So, where's the Injun?" Jonah asked.

"Please," Bingham answered. "The man's name is Jefferson Dragging Canoe, and I'm quite attached to him. He's a real Cherokee chief and medicine man who deserves respect. A man of dignity, he is, and much of the medicine I sell comes from his own formulas. I gladly pay him twenty percent of our profits. He's earned it. To answer your question, he's taking care of the horses and guarding the wagon as he always does. If something happens to me, you will be well advised to keep him happy."

"No disrespect meant. Matter of fact I was just bragging on him as I spread the word in town. I don't harbor any hatred for Injuns, at least not Cherokees," he continued with a lie.

"I'm glad to hear that. Jonah, you have potential. You're grammar and dress have certainly improved over the past months. I'll make a good salesman out of you yet."

"You've never told me. Are you a real doctor?"

The old man sighed and shook his head. "I'll have you know, I took my medical training at the College of Physicians in Philadelphia. My father was a wealthy planter in Virginia and wanted his oldest son to be a doctor. I did actually practice medicine for a few years in Richmond."

"What happened? Why are you doing this now?" Quigley asked.

"Ahh, my good fellow. The fortunes of womanizing. Women have been my weakness.

You see, one of my patients was the daughter of Virginia's governor. I couldn't help myself. The lovely thing was quite beautiful and quite married. I impregnated her, and after the birth of a son, the good Christian lady, in a fit of remorse and guilt, confessed her sin. Naturally, the husband came after me. I had no recourse but to kill him and flee westward into the wilderness. I practiced medicine in Tennessee and Georgia for a few years, receiving little or nothing for my efforts in small hamlets. I ended up following the Cherokees on their unfortunate Trail of Tears, and it was there that I met a seller of patent medicines and became interested in the enterprise. It soon became apparent there was money to be made in this business, so with my medical background, and what I learned of patent medicines, I started my own medicine show. In the new Cherokee Territory, I met Jefferson, so we put our two talents together and came to Texas in '53."

"That's quite a story, Bingham. Any regrets?"

"Regrets? Yes, I'm not proud of killing a man or leaving that poor woman with my child and without a husband. I'm not proud of shaming my family and never being able to see them again, but I make the best of my life. It's all I can do. I make a good living, and so do you, I might add."

Jonah nodded solemnly. "Yep, we ain't breaking no laws, and we make good money." And you use our own elixir too much, he thought to himself. He was quite aware, though legal, the opium based elixir could draw a person into depending on it too much, and his partner drank a bottle a day along with his normal amount of whiskey and brandy. He thought the good doctor did it because of guilt. He felt no guilt about the men he had robbed and killed or the women he had raped, no guilt at all for his life. He only regretted he hadn't found Newt yet. Guilt was a waste of time and for weaklings. A hundred years hence, Jonah would have been labeled a sociopath.

"Ah, my friend. Just when I think you're polished, you revert back to the speech pattern of a rube. Avoid the word ain't and don't use double negatives. It makes you sound like an ignorant plow boy."

Jonah laughed. "Well, my fine doctor friend, I am a plow boy, and I didn't have much schooling. But, I'll remember, especially with the customers." He drained his beer and wondered when and how he would kill his partner. Somewhere between here and Galveston, he thought. It would have to look like either an accident or natural death. He would need the Cherokee and didn't mind the idea of giving him his normal twenty percent, especially when he would be getting eighty percent instead of forty. "Patience," he said aloud.

"What's that?" Bingham asked.

"Patience, Mr. Presswood. You need to practice patience with me. You have to admit, I talk a lot better than when you met me a year ago. I look better too."

"Yes, you do, my young friend, you certainly do. Now, let's have a bite of lunch. I notice the barkeep has placed some sandwiches and boiled eggs on the bar. Then we'll get to the fair grounds. Our customers will be arriving soon."

The crowd was lively that afternoon with lots of people milling around the garish red wagon. The folding platform that served as a stage was set up, and Jefferson was in good form with his fiddle. Doctor Bingham Presswood Esq. was even in better form as he made his pitch in between Jefferson's fiddle tunes. After a short spirited pledge of the wonderful benefits within the amber bottles for sale, Bingham would ask the crowd for a tune request. If someone wanted to whistle or hum part of a tune they couldn't name, Jefferson would begin playing that song also. As Bingham took money from the stage's edge, Jonah worked the crowd. He didn't ask if people wanted one of their patent medicines, he would approach with his best smile and manners, then simply ask whether they needed the elixir, cough medicine, or liniment. As he moved among the people, he too, was impressed with the Cherokee's talent. Though secretly, he detested him as he did all people of color, he gave the man his due. Jefferson was muscularly built with broad shoulders and a flat stomach. His dark face, with high cheek bones and rugged good looks, was framed by shoulder length black hair streaked with gray. Wide, dark eyes looked out over the crowd as he made his music with feeling, and a broad smile charmed the customers. Like his white partners, Jefferson was well dressed. His choice of suit with vest was a butterscotch color. There was an eagle feather in his hatband. Like Bingham, I'll use you till I no longer need you, Jonah thought.

"Mister."

Jonah turned as someone tugged at his coat sleeve, and he faced a young man. A few steps behind the man was a young mother holding her baby. Two small children clung to her dress. With his best smile, Jonah said, "And how may we help you today. My, what a beautiful family. Yours?"

"Yes, sir, thank you," the young man said and guided Jonah a few steps farther away. "I'm wondering if you have something for my wife. Ever since our last baby, she hasn't been herself. Mary just sits in the rocker and stares out the window, letting the house go and herself too. The last couple of days, she cries when she nurses the baby. Don't know what to do."

"Aha. You're fortunate, young man. Doctor Presswood diagnosed a young woman with those same symptoms this morning. She's just got a bad case of the vapors. His new elixir will bring her back in no time. Three dollars a bottle and worth every penny."

"Three dollars?" The young man gulped. "Well, if it'll help her, it's worth it."

"Of course, your wife's health and welfare are worth it, and we've reduced the price for the good people of Jefferson. Over in Tyler, we charged four dollars." With that lie said, he passed a bottle of Doctor Bingham Presswood's miraculous elixir to the young man with instructions to give his wife two good swallows right away.

As Jefferson played on, Jonah continued working the crowd and extolling the virtues of his wares. Sales were brisk. On stage, the good doctor was selling even more. As the sun began to set and the crowd dispersed, they had taken in over five hundred dollars, the best day Jonah remembered.

"Yes, sir, my boys. We've had us a blue ribbon day. Tomorrow, we leave this fair city and head south. Lots of small hamlets and towns between here and Galveston. In Galveston, we can restock and rest. Then, we'll head back north moving a little to the west. East Texas is just a large ripe fruit waiting to be plucked again."

"I'll drink to that," Jonah said. "But right now, my body's craving something else. Think I'll walk down to the dock area and find me a saloon with some good rye and accommodating whores."

"Don't you know the rot gut whiskey will eat your insides out, and the whore will give you syphilis? No good cure for it by the way. It's also a place ruffians hang about to rob gentlemen dressed like you of their money."

Jonah laughed as he left. A few minutes later he returned and changed into his rough clothes, then left again. The thought of being robbed and beaten got his attention.

"I don't like that man," Jefferson said. "He's got dead eyes. Even when he laughs, his eyes never change. He's fed that evil wolf all his life, and it's taken his soul. I met white men like him in Georgia, when they drove us from our home. Be careful, Bingham. He's dangerous."

"Oh, now, Jefferson. I know he's got rough edges, but I've brought him a long way. He's a good salesman and did good today."

"Just be careful, Bingham. I don't trust him. I could be wrong, but I don't trust him. It's none of my business when he asks about this MacEver fellow every place we go, but I just don't believe it's all about looking up an old war friend. Can't picture him with a close friend."

"You worry too much, my old friend." Bingham stretched and

yawned. "I'm tired. Sure you won't join me at the Excelsior?"

"No, I'll sleep in the wagon. You know they wouldn't let a dirty Injun in their fancy hotel anyway. I suspect even our new partner would throw a fit if I tried to get a room."

The doctor sighed. "I know. I know, and it's a dirty shame. I've met no better man than you, and I mean that. Goodnight, Jefferson, sleep well."

"Goodnight, Bingham."

As he dozed off in the wagon, Jefferson hoped a whore did give Jonah a disease. He shivered. The thought of some poor woman having Jonah on top of her with his dead eyes drilling into hers made his skin crawl. "Even a whore don't deserve that," he said to his companion, the darkness.

A few months later the medicine show was in the small town of Liberty. Sales had been good among the farmers coming into the small community, and Bingham was satisfied with their profits for such a small place. There were only a few stops left before reaching Galveston, where they would restock and settle in for the winter season. The men camped in the forest a half day's ride outside of Liberty. Over the campfire, the two white men drank and talked late into the night, long after Jefferson had retired to his tent.

"We've had a good season, Jonah, a very good season. We'll soon be in Galveston where we'll only have a few days hard work restocking. Then we'll have a much deserved rest, and come March, we'll move west along the coast, then north into ranch country."

"West? I thought we were staying in East Texas. What's wrong with that. I been in West Texas. Hated it. Besides, we've made good money in the eastern part of the state."

"Time for a change, that's all. Thought about going north on the western edge of the Big Piney region, but it's only been two years since I made that circuit. Trust me. I know what I'm doing. Jefferson and I haven't taken the show into West Texas in almost four years. It'll be like virgin territory again. Pass the bottle."

"I still say we stay in East Texas." Jonah was falling into a dark mood, because he was convinced that next season, he would finally find a town in East Texas where someone knew MacEver. He had paid someone to snoop around the troops in Shreveport before the surrender, and found out Newton MacEver had gone home with a friend from Texas.

"Well, my friend," Bingham said, "you're out voted by your partners. Don't forget, Jefferson has a percentage in the business too, and he agrees with me." His words were slurred.

Jonah nodded in agreement glumly, but his thoughts were not in agreement. He had reached a decision in his mind. Jefferson and Jonah had already talked of the old man's declining strength and health. Jefferson wanted their partner under the care of a good doctor when they reached Galveston. Jonah knew the liquor was killing Bingham and never tried to stop him. In fact he encouraged it. Partners, he thought. The bones of the traveling photographer, who spied for him, were buried in the deep forest of East Texas, near a hamlet called Alba. Jonah took care of him when the photographer thought his partner didn't deserve half the profits from his work because he hadn't helped. Tonight, Jonah would take care of this partner also.

"Well, you know best, Bingham. What ever you think we should do, we'll do it. Just so we're making money. That's all that counts."

The old man nodded and grinned. His rummy eyes were watering.

"Good, my friend. You're learning, and in Galveston, we'll have us a good time and a good rest. It's a nice city, and the fresh gulf breezes will do me a world of good."

"Why, it'll do us all a world of good," Jonah said. "Bout ready for bed? I'm kinda tired myself."

"Yes, but you better help me into the wagon. I'm a little shaky."

"Sure."

Inside his small tent, Jefferson could hear the two white men talking and stumbling into the wagon. "The sorry son-of-a-bitch let Bingham drink himself into a stupor again," he mumbled to himself. "He wants the doctor to drink himself to death."

Within a few minutes, Bingham was snoring loudly with his mouth open. Jonah lay on his own pallet next to him and listened for almost an hour before killing this man who had shown kindness and taught him much. When it was time, he quietly mounted Bingham's chest and used his knees to pin down the doctor's shoulders. Simultaneously, Jonah pressed his own pillow across Bingham's face. The doctor's struggles were weak and his moans muffled by the pillow. Jonah kept the pillow over the man's face for a full five minutes after the struggle was over. Then he calmly lay beside the man he had just murdered and went to sleep. He rested peacefully.

"AAAhhhhhhhh! My God, he's dead!"

Jefferson rose with a start, and as he came running out of his tent, Jonah leapt out of the wagon visibly shaken.

"My God, Jefferson. I think Bingham's dead. He won't move, and I can't wake him up. Lordy, I slept by a dead man all night."

Jefferson glared at Jonah and jumped into the wagon. In a few moments he climbed out. "He's dead, that's for sure. So, what happened?"

"Well, I don't know. Like always, he was still snoring when I went to sleep. When I woke, I told him to get up, and when he didn't, I shook him. He didn't move. That's all." Jonah's tone of voice was defensive and belligerent, but Jefferson's eyes never left his and didn't flinch.

"Told you lots of times not to let him drink so much. You wouldn't listen."

"I tried. He's the one who wouldn't listen. Hey, I liked the old man too. Did a lot for me. I was finally making a good living with the medicine show."

"I'll bury him," Jefferson said, and his eyes drilled into Jonah's. Jonah looked away.

"Want go back to town and find the undertaker?" Jonah asked, still avoiding those eyes.

"No, he told me a long time ago what do to if he died."

"I'll help you bury him."

Jefferson picked up the shovel and turned to Jonah. "No, you won't help bury him. This is a job for his friend. Just stay here and make breakfast. By the way, his will's at the bank in Galveston. I'll show it to you when we get there. He names me as his only beneficiary, and both our names are on the account. So, with my twenty percent and his forty percent, I own sixty percent of the business. His horse and saddle are mine too, and we go down the coast like he wanted. Another year or so, we'll move back to East Texas, and you can look for your friend again." He emphasized the word friend with sarcasm, then continued. "Look, I know you don't like me because I'm Cherokee. I don't care. I've had business in the past with men who didn't like me. It's not important. You see, I don't like you either. I certainly don't trust you. I can tell you this much. I'm hard to kill. If I even get the smallest suspicion from your eyes you might be thinking something, you'll be dead before you can blink."

Jonah got the fire started and began making breakfast. He was so angry his hands shook. He had no intention of trying to take on Jefferson. He knew the Indian was savvy, strong, and always alert. Jonah was a coward. For the first time in his life, an Indian had given him orders, and without a single word of protest, he obliged. As Jonah worked, he could hear the Cherokee chanting. He watched the bacon sizzle and pulled up his shirt to look at the rash that had started on his back and spread to one side. It wasn't painful, it was just ugly, and it worried him some. A few days after they left Jefferson, he had noticed an ugly canker sore when he urinated. It went away, and he was relieved, but now this rash had appeared. If it didn't go away, he'd see a doctor in Galveston. Unfortunately for Jonah, it did go away before they reached Galveston, but he would live long enough to return to Hood County.

Chapter Twenty
Iron Hands

"Don't worry, Newton", Thursa said reassuringly. "Zeke will be back with the doctor shortly." She turned and hurried back into the bedroom.

Newton nodded and prayed hard that Elvira and the baby would be safe. In spite of his mother-in-law's assurances, he was terribly worried, and the moans he had listened to for the past two hours pierced his heart like a hot poker. Thursa had been midwife to many women in Hood County and delivered John Henry without problems. Her neighbor had also assisted at many births, but now, something was wrong. Even with the mulled wine, Elvira was having more pain than last time. He was sick with worry, but continued to rock four year old John Henry as he read.

"Papa," John Henry said, "what's wrong with Mama?"

"She's just hurting a little, son. Like grandmother said, don't worry. The doctor's coming fast. Soon, you'll have a baby brother or sister. Now then, uh, where was I?"

"Right here," John Henry said excitedly and pointed to a picture of the wolf. "Will he eat the little girl?"

"Well, Son. Let's finish reading and see what happens." Newton continued reading, adding his own embellishments. Soon the boy was asleep, and Newton gently kept rocking as he carefully brushed the hair from John Henry's face. When he saw his son like this, he was enraptured with what Elvira and he had made. Was I ever that pure and vulnerable, he wondered to himself? Finally, with relief, he heard Zeke and the doctor ride up. He nodded to Doctor Black as he walked in. Zeke took John Henry from Newton's arms.

"It's gonna be okay now, Newton. You'll see. Now go and help comfort Elvira while the doctor delivers your new child. He has no objections to you being there."

As he and the doctor walked into the room, Thursa and Melinda, the neighbor lady, were draping a sheet over Elvira's spread knees and legs for the purpose of modesty. As customary in the mid-19th century, the male doctor would deliver by touch, not sight.

Elvira held her hand out to Newton, and said in a weak voice, "Forgive me, I'm afraid I've been such a weakling today."

"Shhhh," Newton said. "You're not a weakling. As always, you show more courage than me. Don't talk, save your energy." He squeezed her hand and placed a soft kiss on her lips. "I love you, and I'm here. I'll always be here for you." Newton was frightened. Elvira's voice was extremely weak when she tried to talk. His wife's face felt clammy and had a deathly pallor as he cradled her head in one arm. He was not comforted when he saw Doctor Black take the large forceps from his bag. Hands of iron, someone called them. Then the doctor went to work, feeling his way with his head turned toward the wall.

"Push," the doctor ordered, and Elvira's face contorted with the effort, and she screeched with pain.

"I can feel the head, Elvira. Be strong, and give me another push."

Elvira panted as she turned her tear streaked face to Newton. "I'm so weak," she whispered in an almost inaudible voice.

Newton's eyes were now full of their own tears. "I'm here, Elvira. I'm here. Try again."

"Aiiieee," came another painful cry as the open forceps were pushed into the birth canal.

"My God!" Newton cried. "Can't you look at your job and forget custom? You can't even know what you're doing with that god-awful tool of yours if you can't see. You're killing her!"

"Shut up, Newton. I know what I'm doing. Do your job and I'll do mine," was the doctor's reply. "Now push, Elvira, push."

Three more times the order for Elvira came from the doctor and each time, Elvira screwed up her face and pushed with another cry of pain. Then her head would fall back against Newton's arm again. Each time, her eyes looked into Newton's pleadingly. He felt as impotent as he did when his friend Henry lay dying in his arms. It seemed to him that with every push, Elvira looked closer to death.

"Am I going to die?" Elvira asked weakly.

Newton's tears fell on Elvira's forehead, and he promised, "No, you're not going to die. I won't allow it. Look at me and know how much I love you, and what a long life we'll have together. Some day, you'll be playing with our grandchildren. You can't die."

"One more time, Elvira. One more time, gather your strength and push with all your might. Now!" Doctor Black ordered again.

Newton held on to her hand and whispered in Elvira's ear. "Push, my darling. Show the doctor your strength. Push."

Again, Elvira lifted her head and with a contorted face that was almost purple, pushed and pushed. With a scream of pain and relief, it was over as the doctor pulled the baby from the birth canal.

"Oh, God," Elvira said weakly, "I did it. It's over."

"Yes, it's over," Newton said.

Newton embraced his wife and kissed her gently. They held on to each other and waited. There was silence as the doctor and two women worked over the baby. Finally, after what seemed to be hours, they heard the cry of a newborn. Soon, Thursa had the baby swaddled and placed it in Elvira's arms.

"Newton, you have a daughter," she said.

Elvira burst into tears as she peeled back a corner of the blanket to peek at her daughter's face. Newton's eyes watered also. He looked up at his mother-in-law and said, "Meet your namesake, Mother Bankes. We shall call her Thursa."

Thursa beamed as the doctor said, "Good choice, Newton. She's sure earned it. Knowing her, if she'd had the forceps, she could have finished the delivery."

Newton stood and shook the doctor's hand. "Thanks for coming so soon, Dr. Black. I'll come to town tomorrow and draw a bank draft to pay you."

"No problem. Now then, both of you listen. This has been a hard delivery. I want Elvira bedfast for a week. Newton can do the cooking and cleaning for a while. Be good for him. I'll drop by tomorrow. Don't worry about the bruising and swelling of little Thursa's head. It'll disappear in time. She's a strong, healthy child with good lungs."

"Yes, sir. There's no problem. I'll take good care of Elvira and the baby," Newton said. "Would you care for coffee or other refreshments?"

"No, sounds tempting and thanks for the offer." The doctor chuckled and continued. "I've got to get back to our good sheriff and finish lancing a boil off his bottom."

Newton walked Doctor Black to the door, waved good-by, and turned to his father-in-law, who was now crawling around the floor giving John Henry a ride on his back.

"Well, Grandpa, you've got a granddaughter to give rides to now," Newton said.

"Good," Zeke said and picked John Henry up and held him. "I knew it would be just fine. Had confidence in both Elvira and the doctor. A couple of prayers might have helped too. Let's give the ladies a few minutes to straighten up, and we'll take John Henry in to see his baby sister."

Newton nodded and sat heavily in the rocking chair. He held his head for a few moments and then said, "I'm tired. Must be getting old. This whole thing has drained me."

"Papa," John Henry said as he crawled onto Newton's lap. "Do I really have a baby sister?"

"You got a beautiful baby sister. Her name's Thursa. She'll be someone else for you to love."

"Good. Sisters are good, I think."

"You think right, Son, you think right. Just remember, you'll have to be careful with her."

"I will, Papa. Promise."

About that time, Thursa and Melinda came out of the bedroom.

"Newton," Melinda said. "I've got to get home. Daniel and the boys need me there. Congratulations on a beautiful girl."

Newton escorted their neighbor to the door and thanked her for the help. He watched her pull away and walked back inside.

Thursa said, "Zeke, you and Newton can come in now, but don't stay long. Elvira's very weak and needs rest." The men followed Thursa back into the bedroom. Newton held back for a few moments while Zeke embraced his daughter and cooed over his new granddaughter. After a few minutes, Zeke nodded at Thursa and both left the room.

"John Henry," Elvira said. "Come here and meet your new sister."

Newton placed the boy next to Elvira, and John Henry embraced his mother's neck. "Love you, Mama. It scared me when you cried. You won't go to your grave yet, will you?"

"Of course not, my darling. Not for a long, long time. Look at little Thursa. She loves you too, just like I do." She uncovered the baby's face and John Henry looked at his baby sister solemnly.

"She's little. Can I kiss her?"

"Of course. She'd like that."

The boy kissed his sister on the forehead and smiled. "I'll take good care of her. Promise, Mama. I promise."

"I know you will. You're a good boy, and Mama loves you."

"Okay, John Henry," Newton said. "Your mother and sister need rest now." Then he embraced his wife and kissed her softly. "I love you, my dearest. Thank you for your courage and the gift of a daughter."

"Love you too. Yes, I'm tired. I'll sleep for a while."

Newton picked up his daughter and placed her in the crib he had made two months earlier. Father and son left the bedroom quietly, shutting the door behind them.

In the living room, he embraced Thursa, and said, "Thank you, Mother Bankes. Thank you so much. I love you."

"Oh, my goodness, Newton. We love you too. I just did what I've done for others. Go on with you now. I didn't do that much. Zeke's going back home, but I'll stay tonight. Tomorrow, the girls will drop by to help."

"That's wonderful. Don't worry, I can cook too. I'll cook tonight. You just see about Elvira, and I'll take care of supper."

Thursa nodded and went back to the bedroom. Newton sat back and reflected. '71 had been a good year for them. The harvest had been abundant this fall, and with the birth of his daughter, Newton was happy. He wasn't sure he wanted Elvira to go though childbirth again, but for now, he was content. The past few years had gone quickly, and he was blessed. It would soon be Christmas, and then another year would be upon them. He sighed. It was time to make dinner. 1872 could take care of itself.

Chapter Twenty-One
Fulfillment

"Heeyah, Mule, steady now," Newton commanded as he plowed the last row for spring planting.

"Heeya, Mule, steady now," John Henry yelled in his high pitched voice to mimic his father. He held on to the cross bar of the plow in front of Newton. In his mind, he was plowing also.

"Woah, Mule," Newton said.

"Woah, Mule," John Henry said.

Newton laughed and picked his son up. "That's it, son. The spring plowing's over. Time for a water break. Thirsty?"

"Yeah, Papa. Plowin's hard work."

"Here's what I like to do when I'm finished plowing." He sat John Henry down on the edge of the freshly plowed earth and unhooked the burlap covered water bottle from the plow. He sat beside the boy. "Whew," Newton continued and wiped his forehead with his handkerchief. Then he lifted the water jug to his mouth and drank deeply.

"Whew," John Henry said. "Plowing's hard work, Papa."

"Yep, sure is," Newton answered and passed the water jug to his son. He grinned as the boy raised the heavy bottle to his mouth and drank. Most of it spilled onto his shirt.

"Taste good?"

"Yep, sure does. Did I help good, Papa."

"You helped good, John Henry. You surely did. Why, don't think I could of done this by myself, do you?"

"Nope," John Henry answered with a serious expression. "Sure glad I was here. Mama wouldn't like it if we didn't plow."

"That's for sure, Son. Women don't like the ground unplowed. Makes 'em nervous like."

"Yep," the boy said solemnly. "Mama would be mad at us."

"Yep. A man has to work hard to keep a woman happy."

"Whew, we sure do."

Newton laughed again and pointed to the place they started. "You see what we've done, John Henry. Now then, think about the coming growing season. Sprouts will be growing up, then by the end of summer, corn will be taller than your papa."

"Yep," John Henry said with a serious expression and slowly nodded his head. "Papa, how come our mule don't have a name."

"Why, he does. It's Mule."

"Papa, you're teasing. I know that's what he is. It's not his name."

"Well, what do you want to call him?"

John Henry put his serious face on and thought. "Methusa. He was the oldest man in the Bible. Grandma told me."

Newton smiled at the way his boy pronounced Methuselah, and said "Methuselah it shall be."

"Hey, you men!" Elvira called from the porch. "Come in and eat." Thursa was cradled on her hip.

Newton smiled at Elvira and swallowed hard. She never looked more beautiful or desirable to him. Her figure was back, and standing like she was, with Thursa straddling her out thrust hip, she seemed extremely seductive.

"Mama didn't sound mad," the boy said as they walked back to the house hand in hand.

"Nope, not at all. You see, John Henry, we done good. Yes, sir. We kept Mama happy."

"I'm glad, Papa."

Newton laughed and swept his son up and carried him the rest of the way as he told him, "So am I. Now, don't forget, wash your face and hands good. That keeps Mama happy too. Get ready for supper while I unhitch the mule and put him away."

"Did you wash your hands and face good, John Henry?" Elvira asked.

"Yes, Mama. Papa said men gotta work hard to keep Mama happy and stay clean too."

Elvira laughed. "Well, your papa's right, and I'm proud of you both. Oh, Newton, we've got a letter from Bertie. Why don't you read it to us? It's on the fireplace mantel."

"Bertie? Good. It's been two months since we heard from her." After putting the mule away, Newton went into the house and retrieved the letter from the mantel. Then he read.

My Dearest Brother and Sister,

First of all, I have wonderful news. All charges against you have been dropped. J.P. said it was only a formality of paper work, and should never have taken this long. You just got lost in all the mess of the war, and it's taken a long time to straighten things out. Nobody in McDonald County took the charges seriously anyway. So, you can come back to Pineville whenever you want. Oh, before I forget, the family wants to have a big family reunion next May after the spring planting. Pleasant and Frances plan on being here, and of course, our sisters and their families. Our uncles and cousins in Indian Territory will join us too. But, we'll talk of that later.

Mother is over seventy and worries she won't see you again before she dies. We try to reassure her, but you know how she is. She seems so frail now, and like Adelaide, she hasn't recovered from that awful day at Honey Creek. So, she wants us to catch a train and come to Texas. I've already been to the depot. We can ride the train all the way to Mineola. The Station Master says that it's also in Hood County and only a few miles from your Whitman. We plan to do so next fall. Our Cherokee cousins will be joining us. You're in for a shock when you see cousin Frances. She's seventeen now and has turned into quite a beauty.

Adelaide will turn thirty-five this July. She's about the same, so pretty, and now and then, some man will show interest, but it only frightens her when that happens. The poor thing still has dark periods and retreats into that hidden world of hers, but she functions most of the time. On bad days, I still have to spend two hours just to get her up, fed, dressed, and into the day. Please don't think I'm complaining. It's just the way it is, and I do my best to take care of her and mother. I do love them so. I only thank our Lord that the church is here for us. When Adelaide goes to her classroom, the children help her open up like a beautiful blossom, and she is probably the best Sunday School teacher we have for the youngest ones. It's her whole life, and I'm happy she has that. And me? I enjoy teaching my classes also. I have older children, and they bring me so much joy. Oh, my, I'll be 26 in April. Goodness, Elvira, will I become an old maid? I hope not. Some day, I want to meet a good man, but for now, I'm much too busy to think about such things. I pray there's a good man with a big heart who will accept me as I am with my shame. I won't go into a marriage without my partner knowing the whole ugly truth of Honey Creek. By now, you've noticed the bank draft for three hundred dollars. It's your share of Father's land. We finally have the settlement. J.P. Took care of it for us. None of us have returned to Honey Creek or ever will. The dear man also arranged for the bones of our loved ones to be removed from both sides of Honey Creek and brought to Pineville. Now they lie close by. Things do rest a little better with mother now. We're having nice stone markers made with part of our share of the land sale, and after constant pleading, J.P. is finally accepting a rental fee.

Thank you for sending the photograph. It thrilled us to see our brother with his family. Elvira, you are a great beauty, and my brother is fortunate. Newton, John Henry favors you so much, and little Thursa is such a precious thing. We are all looking forward to seeing all of you in October. We will count the months, weeks, and days till that happy time arrives. Newton, it's been ten years since my big brother hugged me or teased me. I have missed you so much, and of course, our mother and Adelaide have also. All of you have been in our constant prayers

for these long, lonely years. Now, I am in tears and cannot write anymore. Pray for us too, Dear Ones. I hope the time flies.
All my love and kisses,
Bertie

Elvira reached out to hold Newton's hand. He was in tears, and Elvira shed her own.

"Papa, don't cry," John Henry pleaded. "Don't be sad."

Newton hugged his son and wiped away the tears. "I'm sorry. Papa's got something in his eye, that's all. I'm not sad, just happy to know my family is safe, and we'll all be seeing them soon."

Elvira wiped her eyes and said, "Oh, Newton, does the poor thing really think she's guilty of doing wrong. It's not her shame, but the shame of those monsters who attacked your home. Bless her tender heart. If you wish, we can go to Missouri right away. Oh, how I want to hold Bertie. You know I've learned to love your sister just through her letters alone."

Newton thought a moment, then said, "Yes, I would like that. But, let's wait. We'll need the money for going to the big reunion. Or, if it's possible for all the family, maybe we could talk them into having it in the fall instead. We could return with Bertie and the rest when they go back after the October visit. The harvest would be over by then."

"Papa, can we go riding tomorrow?" John Henry asked.

"Elvira?" Newton said with a raised eyebrow and smile.

"Yes, what a wonderful idea. I'll pack a picnic lunch. We'll all ride through the woods on the way back from town and have lunch at grandpa's gazebo. Papa has to deposit the bank draft anyway." She winked at Newton and said, "Maybe Papa will buy us a surprise while we're in town."

"Will you, Papa?" John Henry asked with excitement. "Please."

"Hmmmm, let's see now. You did work awful hard plowing today, and you're mama didn't have to remind you to wash before supper. Guess that deserves something."

"No, Papa, Mama didn't have to remind me. You did!"

"Aha," Elvira said, "So someone did have to remind you."

"Oh, oh," he said and covered his mouth.

The next morning after breakfast, Newton was in the barn saddling the two horses. The sun was out, and the coolness of this April morning was perfect. It would be a great day, he thought. They hadn't been riding in quite a while, and today would be a good outing for his family.

"Hand me Rebel's bridle," he said to John Henry, and his son gave the bridle to his father.

"Can I help, Papa?"

Newton looked down at his son's excited face and said, "Sure you can." He dragged a box next to Rebel and placed John Henry on it to give him a better reach.

"Okay now, this is the bit. See how it goes in his mouth?"

"Yes, Papa."

"You men ready yet?" Elvira shouted from the porch. "Thursa and I are."

"Almost," Newton shouted back over his shoulder, and within a couple of minutes, he and John Henry led Rebel and Dancer out of the barn.

Newton grinned at his wife, and thought she looked quite fetching in boots, his old gray army pants, shirt, and floppy campaign hat. It was her usual riding apparel. She had told him early on not to buy a side saddle, for she preferred a standard one. Around her front, rested his old back pack which he had modified to be worn in front as a carrier for first, John Henry, and now for Thursa.

"Easy, Dancer, easy," Elvira said to her horse as she stroked its head. "That's a good baby. Yes, we're going for a ride."

"Need some help?" Newton asked from his saddle. John Henry sat in front of him holding on to the saddle horn.

"No, I can still mount by myself." She did so, and continued, "You brushed her this morning, didn't you? Thank you."

"We're off," Newton said, and they turned the horses toward Whitman. He was a little envious of Dancer's beautiful coloring. Like his, the mare was also was a quarter horse, but with the chestnut color and white markings on the face, it stood out. Rebel was a gelding with a solid brown coat and only a little white in its tail.

They rode the short distance to town in only twenty minutes, and after depositing the bank draft, Newton withdrew a little cash and took the family to the general store. He already knew what surprise to get Elvira. As she walked around looking at cloth and children's clothing, Newton talked to the proprietor.

"Hi, Newton. Out for a ride?" Harold, the owner asked.

"Yeah, it's a nice day for one, and I need to buy a few things too. Still got those earrings you showed me a month ago?"

Harold smiled. "Yep, put em away for you." Then he reached under the counter and brought out the little box.

Newton looked at the earrings carefully. They were expensive, but solid gold with a simple design, just heavy tapered loops about two inches in diameter.

"I think Elvira will love these. My wife calls them elegant. You want me to wrap them?"

"No, I'm gonna give them to her today. Give me a little of the candy for John Henry."

"And for you," Harold said with a laugh.

Newton laughed. He was well known for his sweet tooth. "Well, make sure there's enough in John Henry's bag for his papa too. Could use some shaving soap and two bars of that fancy perfumed soap for Elvira. I'll take the rag doll also."

"You got 'em."

Newton paid for his purchases and walked over to see what Elvira was looking at. John Henry was trying on new shoes as Thursa sat on the floor and played with his old ones.

"Find what you want?" Newton mumbled around a large piece of candy.

"Yes, shoes for John Henry and three yards of calico. Did you? I see your surprise, but save some for John Henry. So, where's my surprise?"

"Later, at the gazebo," he said and bent down to give Thursa her doll. "Better stop making fun of me or you won't get it."

"Papa, can I wear my new shoes?"

"Why not?" he answered. Newton bent down, tied the laces of John Henry's old shoes together and hung them around the boy's neck.

"There, you got a necklace. We'll save these for work shoes."

"Boys don't wear necklaces," John Henry said.

"Only when necessary." There was a flash back. Helena, Newton remembered and swallowed hard. "Here, have a piece of candy. Put the sack in your pocket before I eat all of it."

John Henry grinned and thanked his father.

An hour later, after visiting with some neighbors, they left town. It took another hour before they arrived at the gazebo and garden on the Bankes' land. Elvira unpacked the picnic while Newton took Thursa and John Henry for a short walk. Soon, they were back and eating.

"The venison sausage is good, Newton."

"Thanks. Did turn out good, didn't it? So are the biscuits, even cold, your biscuits are good. Aren't they, John Henry?"

"Yep, Mama makes the best biscuits."

After they had eaten, Newton led Elvira down to the swing. "John Henry, stay in the gazebo and play with your sister," he said.

As the swing creaked back and forth, Elvira said, "Has it really been seven years since we swung here, and you kissed me for the first time?"

Yes, it has, and I have something for you to celebrate that day. He opened the jewelry box and gave her the earrings.

"Oh, Newton. They're beautiful. Thank you." She turned her head to him and placed a wet kiss on his mouth, once, then twice. "Thank you. I do love you so. You don't think others might think them too much, do you?"

"I don't care what others think. It's a gift of love, and they look beautiful on you," he said and kissed her again.

"I'll wear them always." She returned his kiss.

"Mama, Papa," Thursa and me want to swing too."

They looked down at their son. He was holding Thursa off the ground with his arms locked tightly around her waist. He leaned backwards with the effort. Elvira grinned at Newton and said, "Well, it was nice while it lasted." They both laughed, then leaned down and picked their children up.

"Papa, when will Thursa be able to walk? She's heavy."

"It won't be long, probably about the time your aunts and other

289

grandmother arrive. Yeah, I bet she can walk by then."

"Who goes there in our garden?"

Elvira and Newton looked up with a start to see Zeke and Thursa walking toward them.

"Grandpa, Grandma!" John Henry said with delight and jumped down to run toward his grandparents' outstretched arms.

"Hi Zeke, hi Mother Bankes," Newton called. "We're just enjoying the colors of spring in your hideout. Join us."

"Don't mind if we do," Zeke said as he patted Rebel on the rump. " Did you hear? The last of the Union troops pulled out of Austin last week. They're on their way back north where they belong."

"Yeah, we heard," Newton said. " About time. Looking forward to voting this year."

"Good, we'll be able to clean house in Austin with all the veterans voting again, and we can get rid of that nest of vipers."

As Newton and Zeke talked politics in the swing, Thursa and Elvira visited and played with little Thursa and John Henry in the gazebo.

"Newton, you still going to run for the legislature this fall?"

"Yes, I've talked to Judge Parker, and I'm running. He thinks I have a good chance to win, and he's putting together a committee."

"Good plan. Look, Newton. You've become very well known and popular in this area from all the work you've done with the National Grange movement the past few years. You can speak for the farmers here in East Texas and get some legislation passed to help us. "

"That's my dream, Zeke. I want to make a difference. Too many others, like the railroads, are determining our future. The people in this district deserve someone who works for them. "

"Well," Zeke said. "You got my vote. Any news from Missouri?"

"Yeah, had a letter from Bertie yesterday. All the charges were dropped against me, and mother, my sisters, and a couple of cousins will be here in the fall. Coming by train. We'll pick them up in Mineola, and we'll return with them for a family reunion when they go back."

"That is good news." Zeke slapped his son-in-law on the back. "Very good news indeed. I'm happy for you. We're anxious to meet your family."

"Papa," Elvira said. "Mother says you wouldn't mind watching the baby and John Henry for a while if Newton and I went for a ride."

"Course not. We'll watch them. Come back by the house when you're finished. What fella gave you the fancy ear rings?"

"Newton, and you know it Pa," Elvira said as she mounted Dancer and raced away. "Come on slow poke," she shouted over her shoulder. "Race you to the live oak tree on the Old Mill Road."

Newton grinned broadly and raced after her. She had a head start, but Rebel was the faster of the two horses, and within a few minutes he was pulling abreast of her 100 yards from the magnificent old live oak tree that was close to a thousand years old. He raced ahead and by the time she reached him, he was lying in the field of bluebonnets at the base of the tree. His back was propped against one of the huge limbs that now grew on top of the ground. He yawned with exaggeration as Elvira reined up and dismounted.

She sat beside him and snuggled into his shoulder. "You really should let the woman who sleeps with you and cooks your food win now and then. Might improve both the lovin' and the cooking." Then she turned her face to his and kissed him long and passionately.

"I do love you, Elvira. By God, you're irresistible in my old uniform."

"Then don't resist," she said hoarsely. "Don't resist."

Their kisses and fondling became intense. Newton rose and pulled her up after him. They led the horses to the other side of the tree and tethered them. He picked Elvira up and carried her between two more large branches growing along the ground and lay her in the bluebonnets. He fell to his knees and unbuttoned his old shirt she wore. Her eyes were clouded with desire.

"Newton."

An hour later, they rode side by side holding hands, as they took a different trail leading back to her parents' home.

"It's been a good day, Newton."

"Yes, it's been a very good day. Well, tomorrow back to work. I need to get the corn planted."

"Hush, you brute. How can you talk about planting corn ten minutes after having your way with me?"

Newton laughed. "Sorry, my turtle dove. My only thoughts are of my heart's desire. How crude of me to bring up the corn. Please forgive me. I should be shot."

"Well, at least thrashed," she said.

"Wait till we get home and the babies are asleep. Then you can thrash me all you want."

She laughed and leaned over for a kiss. "You're such a divine man. I do believe I'll keep loving you till the day I die."

"I certainly hope so. 'Love me pure, as musers do,/Up the woodlands shady;/ Love me gaily, fast, and true,/As a winsome lady.'"

"Elizabeth Barrett Browning, but I can't remember the name of the poem. I'll never be able to remember enough to play the game you, Pleasant, and Frances do."

"A Man's Requirements. Doesn't matter, no telling how many perfectly happy and successful people there are who can't remember one line of any poem."

"Well, here we are. Let's visit with your folks for awhile and head on home. I'm tired."

"My, my, did I wear my mighty warrior out this afternoon?" Elvira said with a raised eyebrow and wicked smile.

Later, on the way home, John Henry looked up at his father and asked, "Papa, why do you have Mama's shirt on?"

"What?" Newton answered and looked down at his shirt. It was the same one Elvira was wearing when they started the day. It was like the other old one, but now, he was wearing the gray and Elvira the butterscotch.

Elvira started laughing as Newton stammered. "Well, mine got wet, so I had to wear Mama's."

John Henry looked puzzled, but only said, "Oh."

"Understand?" Newton asked.

"I guess so, Papa. Mama doesn't care if her shirt is wet."

"Well, yeah, Son, that's it." He looked at Elvira for help.

She grinned broadly and said, "Afraid I can't help you. I just wonder if my parents noticed."

"Noticed what, Papa?" John Henry asked.

"Oh, nothing," Newton said. "Mama's just thinking out loud. Hey, how bout sharing a piece of your candy. I'm hungry."

"Okay," John Henry said. "Papa, when is Birdy coming?"

"In October. It's Bertie, Son. Her name's Bertie, not Birdy."

"I know. I said Birdy. I'll be glad when October gets here. I want to see my Aunt Birdy."

Newton sighed. "Me too. I'll be glad when October is here, and we see Aunt Birdy."

Chapter Twenty-Two
Family

"Do you see them yet, Newton," Elvira asked as she swayed Thursa back and forth. "Hope Thursa's over her crying spell. She's been cranky since leaving the house."

"Not yet. Don't worry, she'll be fine. She's just a little tired from the long ride. Why don't you put her down and let her walk a little." Newton carefully scanned the people disembarking the train while he held John Henry's hand. The boy was excited, and his own heart seemed to be rising in his throat as he anticipated seeing his family again.

"Papa, where's Aunt Birdy? Can we take a train ride? I want to ride a train too. Look, it's green except the engine. Why didn't they paint it green too?"

"No, I don't see Bertie yet, Son, and I don't know why they didn't paint the engine green. Yes, in two weeks, we're taking a train ride to Missouri, and you'll see lots of cousins."

Newton walked back into the depot to see if they had missed them. It was empty, except for the station master and the musty smell of dust. Walking back to the platform, his heel caught on a loose nail in one of the boards. He mumbled and stomped the nail back into place with his boot heel, then he smiled and thought of Elvira's comment about him worrying too much about everything having to be in its proper place. A worrywart, she had called him.

"There they are!" he exclaimed as he saw cousin Thomas helping his mother step from the last car."

"Is that your Cherokee cousin?" Elvira asked. " My goodness, Newton, he's a big, handsome fellow."

Newton smiled as he quickly led his family down to the other end of the platform with his heart pounding in his chest. "Yes, that's Thomas helping my mother." He waved and shouted as they drew closer.

Barthenia looked up and cried, "Newton!" Tears of joy streamed down her face as she walked to meet him with her arms stretched out. Elvira took John Henry's hand and held back while Newton greeted his family. Her own eyes were filling with tears. She knew how important this day was for her husband and waited patiently while he embraced his mother for a long time. Two other women stepped from the train. She knew immediately it was Bertie and Adelaide. Adelaide was the older and taller of the two—a handsome woman, she thought to herself. Her fair complexion and blue eyes were complimented by the blue dress she wore. Soon, Bertie and Adelaide were both hugging and kissing Newton also. There were more terms of endearment and tears. Elvira wiped her own face with a handkerchief and waited to greet Newton's family.

"Elvira," Barthenia said as she embraced her daughter-in-law and kissed her on both cheeks. "How beautiful you are. Now we know what kept our Newton in Texas. Thank you for loving our son. And this must be Thursa. She favors you Elvira. She'll be a beauty some day just like her mother. Goodness, and who is this handsome young man?" She continued, smiling down at John Henry.

John Henry looked up and smiled at his new grandmother. With a little difficulty, she knelt and took him in her arms.

"Are you Aunt Birdy?" John Henry asked.

Barthenia laughed. "Well, I'm big Bertie. It's rather confusing at times, so why don't you just call me Grandma."

Elvira embraced and kissed her two sisters-in-law. While Adelaide seemed shy, Bertie bubbled with personality, and Elvira realized she was a striking looking young lady. Her Scotch-Irish features were unblemished, and like Adelaide's, she was also a strawberry blonde. Her large blue eyes were luminous, and they looked directly and boldly at the person she talked to. Elvira looked up as Thomas approached.

"Elvira, we've heard so much. By thunder, my homely cousin did good for himself. You're a beauty all right. Hope the scalawag didn't ply you with hard drink to make you say yes." Elvira blushed as he embraced her.

She immediately took to this cousin and replied, "Oh, no, Thomas, I just felt sorry for the poor thing. I've always had a soft spot for stray dogs no matter how homely."

Thomas tilted his head back and laughed. "You did good, Newton. Sure enough, you did good."

Newton embraced his cousin, and they pounded each other on the back. "God, it's good to see you, Thomas," he said. "You don't know how good it is. Wish you'd brought the family."

"They were coming, but since plans for the reunion have changed, they'll wait for all of us to return in two weeks. It'll be a great time. Pleasant and his family will be there. Guess we're having it at Uncle Larkin's place. He's got the most room."

"Hello, Cousin. Am I still written in your heart?" A voice from behind startled Newton, and he turned around quickly. Behind him, smiling broadly, was a beautiful young woman with shiny raven hair to her waist. The hair framed a beautiful olive complexioned face with high cheek bones and large, soulful, dark eyes.

"Frances!" he cried with delight. "Good Lord, it's my little Frances all grown up. He grabbed her under the arm and lifted her over his head as she laughed through tears. "Yes, yes, you're still written in my heart. I told you, always!" Then he embraced her and held on tightly. Standing aside, Elvira shed more tears. She had read the loving words about Frances in Newton's journal, and another piece of the puzzle about Newton's life fell into place.

"Who's this?" Newton said as he saw a tall, dark, young man coming forward carrying suitcases. Then he recognized David, an adult with his own family now. He still had the sensitive features, but he had grown into a man who also saw war as a member of his brothers' cavalry company.

David released the suit cases and held his hand out. "Hi, Newton. It's been too long, much too long." Newton took the hand and shook it vigorously, then embraced this cousin also.

The family stood on the platform and visited for a few more minutes. To John Henry, it was like bedlam as everyone seemed to be talking at once. Finally, the tall lady came forward and picked him up. "Hello, John Henry. I'm your Aunt Adelaide. My, you're handsome and big."

"Yep," he said. "Everybody says I look like Papa."

"Why, you certainly do," Adelaide said and kissed him with a large smack on the cheek.

John Henry looked at his new aunt solemnly and then squeezed her neck hard. I like my new aunts, he thought. I like both of them a lot. He watched his Aunt Bertie playing with Thursa and decided this would be fun. Everyone seemed to be laughing a lot.

"Well, we better get going," Newton said. "Glad I brought the wagon instead of the buggy. It's got two seats and room in the back."

Soon, the men had all the luggage in the back of the wagon, and they were off. Barthenia and Elvira sat in the front with Newton, and the back seat was taken by Adelaide, Bertie, and Frances. Bertie held Thursa, while Adelaide held John Henry in her lap and told him Bible stories. David and Thomas sat on an improvised bench behind the back seat. Barthenia hugged Newton's arm tightly and leaned against his shoulder as he drove.

"How far is it?" Thomas asked.

"Not far," Newton said. "It's about twelve miles to Whitman, and our place is only a mile outside of town. We'll be there in an hour or less. Did you bring your fiddle?"

"If you mean my violin, I sure did. Albert sends his best, and says he'll see you in two weeks. Told me wild horses couldn't drag him to Texas even if you are his cousin."

"Hasn't changed much has he," Newton retorted with a laugh.

"No," Thomas said. "Still the same, and ornery as ever. Poor Mother, she never could make a lot of headway with Albert."

"Now stop that, you two," Bertie said. "Cousin Albert has a good heart. He just has a few rough edges. Cathleen will polish him."

"That's why we call her Saint Cathleen," Thomas said, laughing again. "Yes, Bertie, my brother's a good man, but he wouldn't be Albert, if I couldn't tease him."

Within the hour, the wagon full of family members lumbered through the outskirts of Whitman, and Bertie said, "Newton, did you see the red medicine wagon in the field? Seems there's lots of activity. What's going on?"

"No, didn't notice it, but we're having the fair here tomorrow. Whitman's the county seat, and there'll be lots of things going on, booths with games, craftsmen, and artists. Lots of fun things to do, even music and dancing. I've talked Elvira into entering her preserves and pecan pie in the baking contest. We'll come back tomorrow. I think you'll enjoy the fun. No cooking tomorrow either, there's a big barbecue right after the fiddling contest."

Thomas looked back and said, "Looks like a Cherokee standing by the medicine wagon."

"Don't know," Newton said. "We'll find out tomorrow. Maybe he is. Hey, Thomas, bring your violin. You might get invited to play too."

"Good idea. Show these Texas boys how it's done."

Within a few minutes, they were home. "This is it," Newton said. "Welcome to our home. Elvira's already got most of the things ready for supper. Hope you like beans, corn bread, sweet potatoes, and fried chicken."

"Oh, no, not again." Thomas said. "Probably won't be able to eat more than two or three helpings."

"Well, Thomas," Elvira said. "You can join the horses in the barn and share their oats. That is, if they let you. They're mighty picky who eats with them." By now, she was into Thomas's character and banter.

"Good for you, Elvira," David said, and they all chuckled.

An hour later, the entire family stood around the dining table holding hands. As requested, Bertie said grace.

"Well said, Bertie," Newton responded when she finished. "Now, everybody, let's eat."

"Everything looks delicious," Thomas said as he began his supper. "Wonderful."

"Thank you, Thomas. I'm glad you like it," Elvira said with a wink. She looked around the table and was happy. Newton was obviously ecstatic having these important people around him, and it made her happy to see Newton so animated and content. Now, even more, she looked forward to the Missouri trip. She was thrilled she would finally meet Pleasant and his wife. She knew from their letters, she would love them also. In fact, from reading Newton's journal, she had learned to love all the important people in her husband's life. She was beginning to understand where his intelligence and goodness came from. The dark beauty of little Frances took her breath away. She seemed to be as sweet and innocent as Newton described her in his journal and almost choked up thinking of the poor thing being a witness to her mother's terrible death. As she watched Adelaide feed Thursa and talk to John Henry, she understood what Bertie and Newton meant about her having a childlike quality that children were drawn to. It was obvious that John Henry was enraptured and hung onto every word. It was rather the same with Bertie, but she could tell Adelaide was already growing special to her son. Elvira's heart swelled, and for a moment, she wished she was alone and could cry with happiness.

"Oh, my parents will drop by later," Elvira said. "They want to meet you. Newton has told them so much about his family. So, if you don't mind, we'll put off coffee and dessert til they come."

"Of course, we don't mind," Bertie said. "Why don't you enter the pies in the contest at the fair?"

"Oh, I'm getting up early and bake two fresh ones for the fair. Maybe I'll get a blue ribbon this year."

"If dessert is as good as the main course, you'll get two blue ribbons," David said.

"Why, thank you. How sweet. We'll see what happens."

"Oh, my goodness," Barthenia said. "I almost forgot. We've brought some books for you, Newton, and the children. I'll get them unpacked later. Don't let me forget. It seems I forget so much lately."

"Thank you, Mother," Newton said. "We're already reading to Thursa, but could use a couple of more suitable ones for her age." He smiled at his son. "John Henry's already reading. He's got a head start at school this year. Closest place with a real book store is Tyler, and that's a half day's ride from here."

"Why, John Henry," Adelaide said. "What a smart little boy. You can read also."

"Yep," he said solemnly. "I know all my letters already and can write them too. Want to hear me read?"

"Why, yes, we all do. After supper you must read one of your new books we brought for you."

"I like it when someone reads to me too. Will you and Aunt Birdy read to me?"

"Of course," she said and squeezed him.

An hour later, Elvira's family arrived, and the two families merged into one. Both sides of the family took to the other which pleased Elvira very much. As it grew crowded, the men withdrew to the front porch and talked while Thomas smoked his pipe. Later that night, Newton felt truly blessed, and slept peacefully.

Chapter Twenty-Three
Dark Heart

"Well, how was your old army friend?" Jefferson asked as Jonah rode up.

"Ahh, he's got company," Jonah said, and dismounted. "Didn't want to disturb him. I can go back tomorrow."

"What took you so long? Thought his place was just a mile away."

"My, you're full of questions, ain't you?" Jonah snarled.

"Just curious. What are you so riled about?"

"Nothing. I just decided to go for a ride and see the country side."

"Well, there's some beans and bacon left. Better eat something, we've got a long day tomorrow. Looks like we'll have a good crowd."

"Sheriff give you any guff bout the permit."

"No, a real congenial fella, for a white man," Jefferson answered. He watched Jonah gobble down his beans. He had bad feelings about Jonah's search. In every town and hamlet in East Texas, Jonah would ask around about a Newton MacEver. This morning, his reluctant partner was almost choking with excitement when the blacksmith told him where MacEver lived. He even described the man. He'd taken right off, and Jefferson's suspicions had risen when Jonah took his rifle and pistol. Might do a little hunting, he told Jefferson. Sure, Jefferson thought. Going hunting dressed in his best suit. The Cherokee had already made up his mind. Tomorrow would be a good day, and his other cash was hidden in the secret compartment he and Bingham built in the wagon twenty years ago. So far, Jonah hadn't found it. He also had his savings in the Galveston bank. He could draw a draft on it at the bank in Tahleguah, the Cherokee capital in Indian Territory. Day after tomorrow, I leave without notice. It's time to go home. I don't want to die in Texas, so it's time to return to the Nations. I've got enough money to last what's left of my life, and I'm tired of white people and their ways.

As he ate, Jonah watched the Cherokee watch him. Wonder what the sorry Injuns thinking up. After I take care of Newton, I take care of him. Got plans for you. For three years I've swallowed my pride and let you run this business. I've got a belly full of taking orders from a low life Cherokee who thinks he's good as a white man. Your time's coming. You got a small tent. That's why I bought the shotgun. Don't have to try and sneak into your tent at night. I know you're a crafty one. But with both barrels of the scatter gun, I'll get you. Two days north of here is the perfect place. There's already one fellow's bones in that thicket, and soon, yours will molder beside his. Jonah took another bite of his beans and reflected on his day. When he found Newton's home, it was empty. There was no lock on the door, and he just walked in. His nerves and senses were sharpened with the knowledge he was prowling in the home of the man he intended to kill. As he walked through the rooms, he would reach out and touch things—a hair brush with strands of auburn hair, the framed photograph of Newton and Elvira, Newton's shaving mug. He took the wooden spoon out of the pot of beans on the stove and savored the taste of Newton's supper. He found the closet with Elvira's clothes and pulled them to his face and inhaled her fragrance. He decided he would take her after killing Newton. He ran his fingers lightly over the family portrait. A small boy and baby girl smiled at him. Think I'll kill them too. Let the bitch watch as I do, then I'll take her. As he did his prowling and defiling of Newton's home, he never felt better or stronger in his life. The excitement in his heart was almost sexual. The pain in his joints was gone, and he was never more

302

alive. It was almost the feeling he thought he would have when he killed Newton and his family. Finally, he was finished with his dark search and carefully checked to see he left nothing out of place. He walked from the house and took his horse deep into the woods, then returned to the edge of the tree line and waited behind some thick brush. Yeah, old Newt's wife's a looker, he had cackled to himself before having a coughing fit. It wasn't long before Newton arrived, but to his dismay, there was a large group of people. He looked closely. By God, it's that pretty Bertie. This is even better he thought. Then, he noticed the beautiful Frances. Now there's one that's ripe for plucking. Gawd, look at those two big breeds in back, he thought. Must be the Cherokee kin. He waited longer, but after an hour, another wagon pulled up with more people. When that happened, he gave up and came back to town. Now, he grinned broadly at Jefferson and lifted his spoon.

"Hey, good beans, Jefferson. Best I ever ate. Thanks. Tomorrow, I'll pay for our food. There'll be lots at the fair. Hear tell they're having a barbecue."

Chapter Twenty-Four
The Fair

"Good morning, Mother," Newton said as he gave Barthenia a kiss. He poured a cup of coffee and sat across from her. Smiling after the first sip, he said, "Do you know how long it's been since we shared coffee across the table. At home, you and I were always the first ones up and would start our day with conversation over coffee. God, Mother, how I've missed those days."

Barthenia blinked back tears and reached out to grasp his hand. "Oh, Son, me too. I was hoping you were still an early riser, and we would have a few quiet moments together. I love your family. Elvira is a treasure, and what two lovely grandchildren you've given me. Are you happy? Have you finally put that awful day and the war behind you?"

"Yes, Mother," he said and leaned over the table, took his mother's face in his hand and kissed her tenderly. "I'm very happy. Honey Creek is behind me, thanks to Elvira. And you. Are you well? Are you really well?"

"Yes, I'm well, Newton. There are days when I miss your father and his strength terribly, but having Bertie and Adelaide with me has been a great help. Both Adelaide and I draw strength from Bertie. She is such a strong and good person and much like you, she took on great responsibility at a young age. I know Adelaide will never marry, but

Bertie should find a good man. I know she wants to, but—" She stopped, choked back some tears and continued. "The people at church are wonderful to us, and my faith keeps me steady. Anyway, I have faith that your father and my babies wait for me. I'm ready for that day. The material things of this tired old earth are so fleeting. And you, do you keep your faith?"

Newton chuckled. "Yes, I do. Guess I'm a Baptist now. We attend the little Baptist church Elvira grew up in. We'll all go together next Sunday. It's a little different than the Methodist Church, but it's full of good people."

"Grandma, I'm thirsty," John Henry mumbled as he tugged at her dress."

"Why, bless your heart," Barthenia said and picked her grandson up. He snuggled into her lap, rested his head on her bosom, and was quickly asleep again. Barthenia chuckled and brushed the boy's hair away from his eyes. "Reminds me of another MacEver so many years ago. Looks like John Henry's going to be an early riser like his father and grandfather."

"Yeah, he is. He usually shows up a few minutes after I start my coffee every morning. Elvira wakes up a little later than I do, so it's my job to get the fire started and coffee going every morning. Sometimes, when I'm ambitious, I'll get some biscuits ready, which I'll do now. Thought we would eat light this morning, biscuits, jam, and fruit. There'll be plenty to eat at the fair. The town fathers are hosting a barbecue."

"Hey, Grandma, we're thirsty too," Thomas said as he rose from the pallet he and David were sharing in the corner.

"Well, bless your heart also, Thomas," Barthenia said as she laughed. "Both you boys get up, and I'll pour you some coffee."

"Newton," Elvira said as she came into the room. "I slept late again. I need to get those pies ready."

"Elvira, you just do what you need to. I'll help Newton get everyone fed as they get up," Barthenia said.

"I'm working on the biscuits now," Newton said. "They'll be in the oven in a minute. Have a cup of coffee. Pot's on the stove. Just relax and visit a few minutes. We don't need to be there before noon. You got time."

"Mother Barthenia, sit still," Thomas said. "Newton, where's the frying pan and eggs? I'll scramble up eggs. I can hear Bertie and Adelaide out in the breeze way, so it's time to get a little breakfast ready. Elvira, we're all used to waiting on ourselves, so relax. Your husband and cousins mostly fed themselves during the war, and we're not helpless. We'll clean up, and before long, the kitchen will be yours."

Thomas was right, and before noon, the family was on the way to the fair. Elvira drove the buggy, while Newton and Thomas rode behind on Rebel and Dancer. John Henry rode with Newton as usual. As they rode into the fair grounds, the area was bustling with activity. It was Saturday, and farmers from all over the county were there to sell, trade, shop, have a good time, and take a break from the routine of farming. Excited children laughed and ran from one adventure to the next.

"What a beautiful day for a fair," Bertie said. "Blue skies and sunshine."

"Yes," Elvira said. "It should last through November."

"Winter comes a little earlier in Missouri," Adelaide said.

"That's what Newton says," Elvira responded as she carefully picked up the box holding pies and peach preserves for the food judging. "Let's take these things to the judging booth, and then we can walk around. Oh, there's mother and father." They all waved at Zeke and his family as they followed Elvira.

Newton, Thomas, and John Henry walked around looking at the wares and crafts for sale. John Henry held on to his cousin's hand. It excited him to be with his father's Cherokee cousin.

"Newton," Frances said as she caught up with them and grabbed his arm. "Can I walk with you?"

"Of course, be proud to be seen with such a beautiful young lady." She grinned and took his hand as they walked.

Someone else watched the group carefully as they stopped to chat with the local sheriff. What was left of his few remaining wisps of red hair were covered by his hat, and his face clean shaven. Corroded joints gave him constant pain, which he alleviated with his own medicine, and his eyes burned with the fire of fever and hatred. He wasn't as heavy as he once was and had little appetite. Jonah's body was ravaged from the disease he garnered from a prostitute years ago. At times, his thinking was fuzzy, but his grim resolve to keep his promise was sharp and focused as ever.

"Yeah, he mumbled to himself from the medicine wagon's stage platform, that's Newt for sure, and today he dies. I'll take that pretty thing he walks with too." He began to cackle, then went into another coughing frenzy, spitting up large amounts of dirty looking phlegm.

"What's that?" Jefferson ask, as he prepared things for their day's work.

"Nothing," Jonah answered and coughed up some more. "Just talking to myself. Don't feel so good either." He knew he had a problem and couldn't be standing up on the stage to give the medicine pitch. He might be a little harder to recognize now, but he would stand out on the stage, and Newton couldn't have forgotten him. Looking eyeball to eyeball with a man who was trying to hang you would leave a life time impression, he figured.

"Well, don't worry bout today," Jefferson said. "I can take care of the sales and the music. Walk around, find a shade tree and rest. Don't really need you here anyway. You might even see your old friend in the crowd." As his partner walked down the steps of their fold up stage, he watched him with disgust. Jefferson would just as soon not have him around potential customers. He didn't like to be with Jonah himself, and he certainly couldn't use him as an example of what wonderful things their wares could do for people.

Jonah retrieved his pistol and rifle from the wagon, then saddled his horse. He wasn't ready to ride out at the moment but wanted to be prepared. He stuck the pistol in his belt and checked to make sure it was hidden by his coat. "I'm coming, Newt," he said to himself, and pulling the brim of his hat down to cover his eyes, he joined the milling crowd. As he left, he could hear Jefferson playing his violin.

"Papa, look!" John Henry said excitedly. "Juggles."

"Yeah, son, let's watch the juggler." They joined the crowd

watching the jugglers and acrobats. As the entertainers went through their routines, they were rewarded with appreciative sounds of delight and applause from the crowd.

In the back ground, Jonah watched as Newton placed his son on his shoulders for a better view of the show. He had been following Newton around for an hour and was beginning to become frustrated. He realized he couldn't shoot Newton in this crowd and wondered when he would have an opportunity. But, fortune smiled on him as he saw Bertie and Adelaide approach Newton.

"Newton, Adelaide doesn't feel good," Bertie said. "I'm afraid the excitement of the crowd has been too much for her."

Newton looked at Adelaide and saw the old fear in her eyes again. "It's all right, Adelaide, I'll drive you back to the house in the buggy and stay with you."

"Oh, no, Newton." Frances said, "I'll go with Adelaide. Bertie, stay here. I know you're having fun."

Bertie looked worried. "Frances, are you sure? I don't mind going."

"Not at all. I might take a nap with Adelaide after I read to her."

"Come on, girls, I'll take you back and stay a while myself," Newton said. "Adelaide, if you feel like it after you rest, we can all come back together."

"Okay," Adelaide said. "Maybe I just need to rest for a time."

Jonah followed at a distance. Adrenaline was now coursing through his veins, and he forgot his ills. After ten years, he was almost there. He waited a few minutes and walked back to get his horse. As he mounted, Jefferson gave him a hard look while taking money from a customer. Jonah waved a little salute and turned his horse toward Newton's home. He was in no hurry.

"What would you like me to read, Adelaide," Frances asked as Adelaide reclined on the sofa.

"My brother's poetry," she said, and as Newton walked to the porch, Frances read. Newton sat in one of the porch rockers and whittled. As he did, the afternoon sun dipped below the rim of one corner of the porch roof and warmed the right side of his face. He was happy, happier than he ever remembered being in his life. Elvira and the children were the constant anchors of his life. Every morning when she sat across from him with her coffee, he was thankful for Parson's Brigade for no other reason than his decision to join up brought him to Hood County, Texas. Now, his mother, sisters, and cousins were here also, and soon, he would be with all his family. Yes, he thought, God has smiled on me. I'm the luckiest man alive, and wonder if I'm worthy to have such good fortune with so many good people who love me.

"Well," he said to himself. "I've got a tooth pick." He stuck it in his mouth and leaned back in the rocker with his hands folded behind his head. He smiled and closed his eyes while a yellow finch perched on the porch rail serenaded him.

"Newt MacEver?"

Newton jumped up, startled from his doze, and before him was a man dressed in a dapper looking green suit and brown felt hat. The fellow looked emaciated and only faintly familiar, but there was no mistaking the business end of a 44-caliber Colt revolver leveled at his chest.

"Don't recognize me, Newt?" Then the man took off his hat. The wisps of red hair that were once thick and long was one giveaway, but when the killer came closer, it was the eyes that told Newton that Jonah Quigley had finally found him.

At the fair grounds, Thomas and the rest of the family were standing around the medicine show listening to the Cherokee play his violin, and with the performer's encouragement, Thomas had joined in to play also. No one wanted any patent medicine, but the music was lively and entertaining. Thomas kept staring at the Indian as he played.

"Now, I remember this man," Thomas said and lowered his own violin. The Indian looked at him puzzled and walked to the edge of the stage where Thomas stood. "Cha-quat-te-he?" Thomas asked.

The Indian jumped down and looked at Thomas closer and nodded his head. "Judith's boy. Good Lord, it's Ambrose MacEver's boy, Thomas. I haven't seen you since I worked a spell for your father." Then he slapped Thomas on the shoulder and shook his hand vigorously. "What are you doing in Texas?" Jefferson asked.

"We're all her visiting my cousin, Newton MacEver and his family.

Matter of fact, he just took my cousin and sister back to the house."

Blood drained from the old Cherokee's face. "Thomas you get back to your cousin's place now and find the sheriff too. God, I never made the connection. The good for nothing man I work with went looking for him. Always told me he was an old army friend. Thought it was a fishy story, but didn't make the connection with the MacEver I knew. Think he means to do harm."

"What's his name?"

"Jonah Quigley."

Barthenia, Elvira, and Bertie, cried out in alarm together, and Thomas asked one question, before shouting orders. "What's he wearing?"

"Fancy green suit and brown hat. Skinny man, close to six feet."

"David, get the horses. Zeke, find the sheriff and tell him what's going on."

"Don't you want me to go with you?" Zeke asked.

"No, Zeke, find the sheriff fast. Oh, you have a gun?"

"No."

"I do," Jefferson said and reached behind him to pull out a new colt revolver. He tossed it to Thomas, who smiled tightly as he checked the full chambers. With a salute, he ran toward the horses. He and David mounted quickly and rode hard for Newton's home.

Back at the house, Newton stared contemptuously at the man who once tried to hang him. He had no fear for his life, but the thought of this man being alone with Frances and Adelaide made his blood run cold.

"So, you finally found me," Newton said. "I'll go with you, and you can do what you want."

"Not that easy, Newt. I want to see you beg for mercy and crawl in the mud. Want to have a little fun with those two pretty ladies inside." His laughter was mirthless and evil, then he choked and began to have a gut wrenching spasm of coughs.

The man is mad, Newton thought and wondered how he knew Frances and Adelaide were inside. He didn't think anymore and made his move. No matter about his own safety, he didn't want this pile of dung attacking his sister and cousin. He lunged forward when he noticed the gun waver in Jonah's hand as he wheezed. There was a loud explosion. Newton staggered back and fell. Blood spilled from a hole in his right side, below the ribs. The bullet had gone completely through.

"You ruined it!" Jonah screamed and shot again. The second shot hit Newton in the chest below his left shoulder as he staggered to his feet, and he was knocked to the floor again. He coughed blood as he heard Adelaide scream.

"The shotgun," Frances shouted and ran toward the fireplace mantel where it rested on two pegs.

Jonah heard the shout with alarm and stormed into the house. He grabbed Frances by the arm and threw her down before she reached the shot gun. He looked around and saw Adelaide lying on the sofa. Her eyes were wide and filled with terror as she made pitiful mewing sounds. He looked at her carefully and said, "Why, you're crazy. You must really be touched in the head." Then he jerked Frances up by the arm.

"You're comin' with me, you little Cherokee harlot. I got something you'll love."

Frances fought and raked her nails across Jonah's face. He yelled in pain and slapped her hard with the back of his hand. Blood ran from her mouth, and she was subdued as he jerked her toward the door and outside. She screamed when she saw Newton on the porch, bleeding from two wounds. Now, Jonah's mind was clouded as lust rose in his loins. The screams of this beautiful young girl increased his lust and carelessness. Instead of leaving the house immediately on horseback, he dragged Frances toward the barn.

"Ever done it in the hay, gal? You're gonna have a real man, not some Injun buck. Yeah, you'll thank me later." Inside the barn, he tore at her dress as she struggled and pleaded, which only aroused Jonah more. He had become completely irrational. Frances's dress was torn and the top hung from her shoulder. In a frenzy, he pushed her to the ground and ripped off his own coat. His eyes were wild. Frances looked up at this pitiful apparition from hell with disgust.

"You're nothing but an ugly, cowardly son-of-a-bitch!" she screamed and spat at him.

Jonah only cackled and coughed again. Mucus spilled from his mouth as the spasm of coughing hit him hard.

"Like she said, you're nothing but an ugly, cowardly son-of-a-bitch," came a soft voice behind him. "Turn around."

"Huh," was all that Jonah said as he turned. His eyes showed surprise and disbelief as the thunder of Newton's shotgun exploded in his ears. He was blasted into one of the stalls and looked down at his blood-soaked shirt as he fell back, his head hitting something wet, soft, and foul smelling. The overwhelming odor of Rebel's feces and the stench of his own hate filled soul carried him into eternity as the light left his eyes. They were no longer hard, just sightless, just soulless. Dead men's eyes, Bertie once said.

"Stand up, Frances, he can't hurt you anymore."

Frances stood up. Adelaide dropped the shotgun and put an arm around her cousin, then led her back to the house where they both looked after Newton who was bleeding badly.

Adelaide knelt by her brother. "He's still alive. Frances, go in the house and bring towels. Wet a couple of them." Her voice was soft, calm, and steady, and Frances ran to do her bidding. This was an Adelaide she had never seen. Never before had she seen this cousin with resolve and determination in her eyes.

Adelaide cradled Newton's head in her lap and bent down to kiss him. "I'm here, Newton. I'm here to take care of my little brother. I love you."

He looked up at his oldest sister with wonder—the same Adelaide who had spoiled him when he was a child. "Love you too, Adelaide," he said weakly. "Hard to breathe. Don't think my lungs are working." Then some blood bubbled from his lips. It was frothy.

"Shhh, my darling brother," she said as Frances returned with the towels.

"Frances, press down with the towel on his chest and try to stop the bleeding," she told her cousin. "Stuff one under his side where the other wound is bleeding underneath."

Thomas and David rode up as Adelaide wiped Newton's mouth and face with a wet towel.

"Oh, my God," Thomas said as they ran to the porch and knelt beside this cousin they both loved like a brother.

"Elvira," Newton whispered and coughed up more blood.

"Zeke's behind us with the whole family, Newton. The sheriff's coming with a doctor just in case he's needed."

Newton blinked his eyes and smiled. He knew his life was draining away and wondered what the doctor could do about a lung shot. He wasn't a fool and had seen many men die from such wounds. By the time Zeke's wagon arrived, and the family was all gathered on the porch, his vision was blurring.

Elvira put her arms around him and kissed his lips softly. "Please don't go, Newton. We have too many years ahead of us." She motioned for John Henry to come and kiss his father. He did. He wasn't crying yet, just confused about why his papa was bleeding so badly.

"Papa, Mama got a blue ribbon for her pies."

Newton smiled. Tears were welling up in his eyes, and he wanted so much to tell John Henry to take care of his mother and little sister, say how much his father loved him. He wanted to tell all his family how much he loved them, but there was no strength in his throat or wind in his lungs to do so. He managed to whisper to Elvira that he loved her. Then, as the light faded from his eyes, he managed two words: "Honey Creek." It was over, and Newton carried love into eternity.

The family stood in shock. None of them could believe how quickly a wonderfully happy day filled with laughter and fun had changed into such gut wrenching shock and grief within moments. Each of the women went to Newton and held his face a moment as they kissed him good-by. Bertie was beside herself with uncontrollable grief and wept with great agonizing cries that rang through the surrounding woods. Adelaide comforted her baby sister. Two days later, Newton John MacEver was buried behind the little Baptist church at Clover Hill, not far from home.

There were more than two hundred mourners at the grave side funeral service. Newton was well known and much loved. Their pastor deferred to Thomas and let him deliver the eulogy after reading the 23rd Psalm and offering a prayer.

"Mama," John Henry asked. "Will we see Papa again?"

"Yes, Darling, someday, we will all meet again. Your father waits for us in heaven and remember, he's written in your heart. And yours too, Baby." She kissed Thursa who clung to her neck and reached out to touch her mother's tears in wonder and confusion.

The boy nodded and looked down at the bouquet of wild flowers he held in his hand. Then he looked up at the towering stand of virgin pine, and thought surely they reached up to heaven where his father could touch the tops. That pleased him in some way. It pleased him very much to know the trees reached from where he was all the way to heaven where his father waited for him. Then he turned and looked up at Thomas.

Thomas was finishing up his eulogy as he said, "...and my cousin, Newton John MacEver was the sweetest mortal man who ever walked this good earth. As he told my sister Frances, so many years ago when she was a child, he has written in our hearts, and his words are still there. I carry those words, and everyone who loved him carries those words of love. We were written in his heart also, and no man carried a braver and kinder heart than he. Newton, I know you're waiting for us in heaven, and you must know your Cherokee cousins will always be here for your family when they need us. Now, hear our tribute." Thomas picked up his violin and David walked to his brother's side with his flute. The strains of *Ashokan Farewell* floated around those who loved Newton, and it moved their hearts. Great beads of sweat rose on Thomas's face as he played like he had never played before. The sad refrain affected everyone, and even men shed tears unabashedly. Thomas seemed to be in physical agony as he nursed every sweet note he could from his violin. David's efforts were just as intense and emotional, and when it was over, both men were physically and emotionally spent. Thomas dropped to one knee and wept without shame. David patted his older brother's shoulder.

There was silence for a few short moments, and then the mourners were startled to hear the clear and beautiful soprano voice of Adelaide singing "Amazing Grace". She too, sang with emotion, and the words of the English spiritual stayed true and clear as a bell when her voice grew in strength and volume. John Henry looked up at the towering trees again, and when he thought his father surely must hear his sister singing, he shed his own tears. The finality of his father's passing was finally settling in for this boy, who like his father, would mature early with responsibility. Elvira fell to her knees, still holding Thursa, and put her free arm around John Henry to share his anguish.

After the funeral, there was a house full of people coming and going, leaving condolences and gifts of food, a common gesture of the time. Elvira and the family greeted every person with dignity and grace. She would save her catharsis for the night as she reached out and touched only a sheet in the dark of her bedroom. It would be a long time before Elvira gave up her side of the bed to sleep in the middle with both pillows propped under her head. Grateful for the support of neighbors and friends, Elvira was relieved when she was alone with just Newton's family. She wanted them to stay the full two weeks. It had become important to her having the loved ones of Newton close.

Later, Elvira retreated to the bedroom. She could be heard crying, and after an hour, Bertie, Barthenia, and Adelaide decided to see about her.

They rapped softly on the door, and Elvira said, "Come in."

Elvira was sitting on the edge of her bed. She clutched some of Newton's clothes to her breast, and great sobs racked her body. Barthenia and Bertie sat on opposite sides of Elvira and wrapped their arms around her heaving shoulders. Adelaide kneeled in front of her.

"We're here to share your grief," Barthenia said. "Grief for your loss of a husband and ours for a son and brother."

"Yes," Elvira said between sobs. "You dear ones have lost much too, and part of my grief is for you. Newton was never so happy as the day we went to Mineola and got you. For six months, he's planned this reunion. Lord, my heart is breaking. I never knew anything could hurt so much." Then the flood came, a flood not only of tears, but soul wrenching agony tearing at their insides and bringing physical pain. Bertie also clutched some of Newton's clothes to her breast and buried her face in them as she wept.

Outside on the porch, Thomas and David rocked and visited quietly while Frances entertained the children. Most of the day, their sister had kept her grief inside as she tried to keep the children entertained. She would release her pain later as the children slept.

"What happened to Quigley's body?" David asked.

"Sheriff said they buried him in an unmarked grave outside town. Good enough for him, and may he be rotting in hell this very moment." Thomas knocked the fire out of his pipe and blinked back tears.

"Oh, almost forgot. Did you return Jefferson's pistol?"

"Yeah, did that early this morning before the funeral. He was packed and ready to leave.

I told him to go home, and he said that's where he was headed, back to the Nations. He's had enough of both Texas and white people. Wants to go home to die. When he said that, he just waved and rode off headed north."

"What about the wagon?"

Thomas chuckled. "Said I could have it if I wanted, but I declined. Guess he don't care what happens to it. Seems like it's part of his life he wants to forget."

"Sun's going down, and I'm really tired," David said as he stretched and yawned. "Didn't sleep any last night. Think I'll make out the pallet and go to bed."

"Me too, soon as I take care of business."

Inside, Frances sat on the sofa staring into space with tears running down her cheeks. She had already put the two little ones in bed. David sat beside Frances and put his arms around her. She cried into his chest, and her fingers clutched him so hard, it was painful. She sobbed and her cries broke David's heart. He knew how much Newton meant to her, how much she loved him, just as he did. But with Frances, it was probably even stronger. He remembered that day, so long ago, when Newton rode off toward his destiny with Frances calling and running after him. For days, no one could console her. He also remembered reading his letters to her before she could read them herself, and how ecstatic she would be for days when Newton wrote. She finally quieted down and wiped her face with a handkerchief.

"David," she said. "I've been sitting here remembering Newton the way he was after that awful day in '62. It always seemed he would put aside his own grief just to keep me entertained. I was too young to really understand what was going on at the funeral, but Newton was so patient and kind. He always made time for me, and I thought he walked on water. And he could make me laugh. I guess I miss his teasing too, always telling me I would be an old maid because I was seven years old already with no prospects for a husband." She laughed and wiped her nose. "Think I should marry a Cherokee or a white man?"

David laughed. "I don't care whether he's white or Cherokee, just so he's rich enough to keep your brother in comfort too."

She chuckled into her brother's shoulder and said, "See, you're just like Newton. You're terrible. Oh, Lord, David, I'm glad I still have the verses and letters Newton wrote those years when I was growing up. I have that part of him to treasure all my life."

"Yes, you do. Guess I am like Newton in many ways. Thank you, I take that as a compliment. Now, little sister, go to bed. I know you're tired. Thomas and I are."

Soon, the lamps were out, and darkness enveloped the house. Outside, the moon slipped behind clouds, and the rooms became even darker. Family members were alone with their grief, their memories, and their pain.

A few days before Newton's family members were scheduled to return home, everyone sat around the dining table and talked of a subject that had been broached before. They urged Elvira to return with them.

Zeke said, "Elvira, it might be good for you to get away and meet the rest of Newton's family. I know you were excited about this reunion, and everyone will be there anyway."

"It would be good for you and the children," Thursa added. "It will be an exciting adventure for you and the children, especially John Henry."

Elvira smiled slightly and reached down to tousle John Henry's hair who looked up with pleading eyes. "What do you think, Son? Should we go?"

"Please, Mama, I wanna go. Please."

"Well, then, we'll go. Yes, we'll go to Honey Creek and Pineville. I still want to see and touch those who loved your father and see the places that shaped him into the man I fell in love with. It will be exciting, and you'll have fun with lots of cousins. Your mama's never taken a train ride either. We'll have us a grand adventure, won't we?" She smiled through some tears and continued, "Yes, we're going. We have the money and we're going."

Chapter Twenty-Five
Honey Creek Farewell

"Elvira, Elvira, wake up my sister," Bertie said softly to her sister-in-law as she shook her shoulder. "Uncle Marshall's ready to leave." Elvira woke up with a start and smiled sheepishly. She had nodded off on Uncle Larkin's porch while rocking. Her mind had drifted off in the warm autumn afternoon as the others whispered and let her rest.

"Oh, I'm sorry Bertie. What everyone must think of me. One minute I was answering questions, and the next moment I'm asleep."

Bertie laughed and said, "Everyone understands, Elvira. You and the children had an exhausting trip, and it's been a whirlwind with all these cousins, uncles, and their broods around you for the last few days."

Elvira nodded. It had been a whirlwind here at Uncle Larkin's spacious home, but a wind she had immersed herself in with pleasure. There had been much grieving the first few days when all heard the bad news, but for the rest of their stay, all the family members did their best to keep Newton's family busy and entertained. They hid their own grief to help Elvira keep her mind on other things, and soon, she was caught up in the warmth and pleasure of enjoying the family's hospitality. John Henry was beside himself with happiness playing with his

Cherokee and other cousins. And today, his Cherokee Uncle Marshall was taking him to the place where his father had spent much of his own childhood. The house was empty now and the land overgrown, but as Marshall and Bertie guided Elvira and John Henry around Ambrose and Judith's homestead, more pieces of Newton's puzzle fell into place for Elvira.

Before leaving, Bertie said, "Wait, Uncle Marshall, I want to show them one other place." She led the family down a path to the beautiful spot she hadn't seen in ten years.

"Oh, what beauty is here," Elvira said, as she sat on one of the large rocks by the clear waters of Honey Creek. She lifted her face to catch the autumn sun and said, "The fall colors are so vivid. I've never seen such bright reds and yellows. Thank you for bringing me."

"I thought you would enjoy taking a little rest here. It is beautiful, but there's another reason," she said as she held on to Thursa's hand, who was now walking. Then, she told Elvira about the day her husband's family gathered by this same stream before burying Florence and Jasper.

"And you were sixteen," Elvira said and wiped a tear away. "I hope you've put those doubts about yourself and your God away."

"Oh, yes, and Newton helped. He gave me such strength. Even his letters gave me strength after we were separated." She glanced over at John Henry, who was sitting on Marshall's knee and peeking under his coat. "John Henry MacEver, what are you doing?"

The boy looked up like a child caught with his hand in a cookie jar. "Nothing. Well, I just looked to see if Uncle Marshall had any scalps on his belt."

Elvira was mortified, but Marshall just waved his hand at her as he burst out laughing. When the laughter was over, he said, "I'll explain, Elvira. You see, when Newton was about this lad's age, he once crawled onto my knee, looked under my coat, and asked me about scalps. From that day on, he became my favorite nephew. Don't worry about this one, he has much of his father in him. He'll grow into a good and gentle man some day, just like Newton."

"Well, Uncle Marshall, do you have scalps?"

"John Henry!" Elvira exclaimed. "Mind your manners now."

Marshall and Bertie were both laughing, and Marshall said, "No, John Henry. I don't have any scalps. Like I told your father, I never did take up the habit—promise."

John Henry stood up in Marshall's lap, hugged his neck and said, "I love you anyway, Uncle Marshall, even if you don't have any scalps." With that, they all laughed again.

"On that note, let's leave," Marshall said shaking his head, and hand in hand with John Henry, he led the women back to his buggy. They visited some more as they rode back to Larkin's home.

"Bertie, Pleasant and Frances are taking me to the Missouri side of Honey Creek tomorrow," Elvira said. "Would it be a bother leaving Thursa and John Henry while we're gone?"

"Heavens no," Bertie said. "They're a delight and no bother. Besides, Adelaide is usually the one they cling too. It's strange, but something inside of Adelaide changed on that day at her brother's home. She's never spoken of it, but of course, we all know from Francis what happened. My sister's stronger somehow."

"Yes, you're right," Elvira said. "It's hard to explain, but somehow, she seems less afraid. I would have thought something like that would destroy her, but she's stronger."

"Oh, Elvira," Bertie said. " I'm sorry we didn't take you by our old home on the Missouri side of Honey Creek when we went to Pineville, but—"

Elvira reached out to hold her hand. "No, please. You don't have to explain. Newton told me none of you would ever return, and I understand. It'll be fun going with Pleasant and Frances tomorrow. I'll enjoy being alone with Newton's brother and sister-in-law. What beautiful people they are!"

"Aren't they though," Bertie said. "They're both intelligent, and certainly, Frances radiates beauty. Pleasant has had such an interesting and fascinating life. Newton probably told you about his brother's travels and adventures in the west. You must ask Pleasant to tell you more. He's certainly entertained John Henry and the other children with his tales. Last night, the child was absolutely spell bound as he listened."

"So was I," Elvira said with a smile. "Yes, tomorrow will be fun being alone with them. I'm looking forward to my day with Pleasant and Frances."

The next day, at noon, Frances, Pleasant, and Elvira were at Cowskin Prairie on the Missouri side of Honey Creek. Elvira had already seen Honey Springs, and now they stood before the ruins of her husband's old home. She carried a bouquet of flowers in her hands.

"The chimney and fireplace still stand, but that'll come down soon," Pleasant said. "The main street of the town will pass though this spot, and so the ruins will be gone soon."

Elvira looked around her. From Newton's descriptions, she could picture the barn, fence and other out buildings in her mind as she stood in what was once the center of the MacEver's home. There were no ashes now, just grass and weeds where once was a plank floor and rooms with furniture—rooms filled with laughter, voices, and other noises of life. Newton played on this spot as a child and grew up in these rooms to take the responsibilities of a household after his father's death. She looked past the chimney to the hills beyond and the place where Newton fought a desperate battle for his life. Turning, she pointed at a spot close to the east side of the house.

"It was there, wasn't it, Pleasant? The place where Florence was shot."

"Yes, Elvira, that's where the wood pile was. Florence came out to get more wood for the fire. And you're standing where Quigley and his men broke into the house and killed Jasper."

Elvira turned and pointed to the ground where Frances and Pleasant stood. "And there. I know what happened there. That's where Bertie and Adelaide were violated."

"Yes, Elvira, that's where it happened, and where Quigley and his man met Newton's justice," Pleasant said. Frances shed her own tears watching Elvira relive parts of Newton's life.

Elvira turned slowly in a circle to take in the scope of this Honey Creek, this long ago home of her soul mate. She thought of his journal with the description of that terrible day, and she could hear the thunder of galloping horses, gunshots, screams, and shouts of anger. She looked down and imagined the terrible animal scream of Barthenia's rage and pain at seeing her babies killed and shamed. Suddenly, she fell to the ground, dropped her flowers, and clutched the dormant grass and earth with her fingers digging deeply. Tears were wetting the grass beneath her face, and in a muffled voice, she cried hoarsely, "Newton, God, Newton, I never felt your pain till now. Are you listening? I love you, God, I love you so. Forgive me, but I need you more than God does. Do you hear me, God? I need him more than you! Why, my God, why? Have you no pity?"

The gut wrenching cries were more than Pleasant could bear, and he started forward, but Frances grabbed his arm and said, "No, Pleasant, not now. This is something she must do alone."

After a few minutes, Elvira composed herself and stood. She wiped her eyes and brushed off her dress. Picking up the flowers, she walked to the fireplace hearth. The limestone was clean and white now, cleansed of the soot by ten years of snow and rain. She dropped to her knees with the flowers clutched in both hands and prayed silently as Frances and Pleasant watched. After a few minutes, she stood and bent down to tenderly place the bouquet on the hearth, and with her fingers she placed a kiss on the chimney. Her fingers lingered on the cold stone while she bowed her head. Raising her eyes toward heaven, she said loudly, "Good-by, my heart, my soul, my love, my life. Good-by Honey Creek and farewell." She broke down again. Great sobs wracked her chest as she rubbed her hands across the chimney's surface and finally leaned her face against the white limestone. Rivulets of tears ran down the rough cut stone as she pressed her lips against the cold surface. It was all Frances could do to keep from running to Elvira as her own tears flowed again while she desperately clutched Pleasant's arm. Finally, Elvira composed herself, turned with a Mona Lisa smile, and walked to the buggy. The catharsis was over. Frances and Pleasant followed. Elvira didn't bring the subject of Honey Creek up again, and neither did they.

THE END

Epilogue

Elvira was twenty-eight when widowed and never remarried. She did keep the farm going, and under her management, it continued to grow and prosper. The bank note was paid off, and the MacEver farm became one of the most prosperous in the county. She took on a live-in hired hand to help until John Henry came of age. There were sometimes rumors about the quiet, handsome farm worker and Elvira, but her only response to questions would be a slight smile. Unfortunately, little Thursa died of cholera the year after Newton's death and is buried next to her father at the Clover Hill cemetery in Hood County. When he came of age, Elvira sent John Henry to the fledgling university in Austin where he studied law. After marrying, he moved his family onto his mother's farm, and Elvira was content to help raise her grandchildren. She took pride watching her son become a respected judge and fulfill Newton's dream by also being elected as a state senator. She knew his father would have been proud. In 1919, when John Henry died, Elvira sold the farm and moved in with her oldest granddaughter, Nellie. Part of the money from the land sale was used to help educate her grandchildren, and Newton's only surviving grandson and namesake became a history teacher who taught school in

Tyler for many years. The end came quietly for Newton's widow in 1927. She died in her sleep after losing a battle with cancer. Elvira had outlived not only a husband and children, but all of Newton's siblings. She is buried next to John Henry at Myrtle Springs cemetery outside of Whitman. Newton's widow was much loved in Hood County and commonly known as "Grandma MacEver." It was enough for her as she took delight in all children. Elvira was not without an income during her last twenty five years. The state of Texas passed the Confederate Widow's Pension act in 1899, and she drew thirty-seven dollars a quarter. At her death in 1927, Nellie, the granddaughter she lived with, received the gold earrings Newton bought Elvira in 1872. Nellie Mae McGhee Kirkland was Elvira's caretaker and nurse for ten years.

Pleasant and Frances spent the rest of their lives at Spring Place, Georgia. Their farm prospered, and both became prominent members of the community. Pleasant was active in local politics and also served as a state senator. They had three boys and two girls, and they named one of the girls Florence. Pleasant died in 1915, and Frances passed on five years later. They both are buried in the Spring Place cemetery.

In1881, Barthenia died. Afterwards, Bertie and Adelaide lived together until finally, in 1890, Bertie met the good man she hoped for. James Caldwell was a Methodist preacher who came to the Pineville congregation from Arkansas, and by all reports was a good and decent person. Bertie was forty-two and James forty-four when they married, and no children resulted from this union. Bertie returned to Hood County several times during her life and always remained a devoted correspondent, not only to Elvira and John Henry, but later to John Henry's children. Much was heard about "Aunt Bertie" among those children and grandchildren. Sadly, Bertie's namesake, Mary Bertie, daughter of John Henry, died at the age of two. She is buried at the Clover Hill cemetery close to her grandfather Newton and little Thursa. In 1922, Bertie became the last of Newton's family to die. According to her husband's letter to Bertie's grand-niece, Nellie, one of John Henry's daughters from his first marriage, it was a peaceful death. Nellie was the granddaughter who cared for Elvira. Bertie lies next to her husband at the same cemetery in Pineville, Missouri, where her other family members are buried. She had lived a long, active, and fulfilling life. Besides her involvement in the church as a teacher, leader in the mission league, and Sunday school director, she also worked with missionary zeal as an early advocate of women's suffrage.

After Bertie married James Caldwell, Adelaide lived with her sister and brother-in-law until she died in 1917. Though never married, Adelaide's life was not without joy and fulfilment, for she loved children, and that love was returned in full measure as Pineville's youngsters received nurturing and love in her church classroom. Three generations of former students mourned at her funeral service. Most of those present had benefitted from Adelaide's gifts of teaching and nurturing.

Newton's shaving mug and razor were passed on to John Henry, who used them all of his life. When his only surviving son, Clarence Newton, turned eighteen, it was passed to him. Today, Newton's great grandson still whips up a lather in the shaving mug his great grandfather carried in the Civil War. However, he confesses to using the straight razor only once, when he was young, resulting in a bad cut with the first stroke of the blade he so carefully stropped to a gleaming sharp edge.

Frank, Elvira's brother, did enter the ministry and established several Baptist congregations in East Texas. He performed the wedding ceremony of his friend's son, John Henry. He also officiated at the funeral services for two of John Henry's children, Morris Wilson and Mary Bertie, who died so very young.

Newton's cousin, little Frances, married a Scotch-Irish man within a year after Elvira's visit to Honey Creek. She bore twelve children, outlived two husbands, lived a long life, and died in 1930. It seems the destiny of the Scotch-Irish and Cherokees were intertwined. Her many descendants are spread throughout America, and today, several are excellent genealogists who still research both her Scotch-Irish and Cherokee roots. Frances is buried at Olympus Cemetery in Grove, Delaware County, Oklahoma.

Ironically, the commander of the same Illinois regiment that accepted the surrender of Parsons' Brigade at Shreveport, was escorted to Indian Territory by a Missouri cavalry company where he negotiated the surrender of Indians fighting for the Confederacy. On June 23, 1865, near Doaksville, Choctaw Nation, General Stand Watie, commander of the Cherokee Mounted Rifles, became the last Confederate General to surrender his forces. The great hemorrhaging of America was over.

In Whitman, the town fathers puzzled for several months about what to do with the garish, red medicine wagon, Jefferson Dragging Canoe left. Then, one day, the sheriff took a prisoner to Tyler and came back with an idea. He had noticed the modern pump wagon the fire department in the big city had. So, with some help from experts in Tyler, the medicine wagon was converted to a pump wagon and replaced Whitman's bucket brigade. It became the pride of Hood County for a while. Unfortunately, while the volunteers had good intentions and kept the wagon looking shiny and clean, mechanically it fell into disrepair. It really wasn't all their fault, for they received little training and no pay. The court house caught fire in 1876, and in spite of their best efforts, the court house burned to the ground.

In 1897, a few months after John Henry's first wife died, he returned to Missouri with his mother and two daughters for a visit with his aunts in Pineville. While there, he took a buggy ride to the MacEver homestead at Honey Creek. The town of Southwest City covered most of the land his father once plowed, and on the main street bridge crossing Honey Creek, John Henry threw a rose into the water and said his own farewell.

Today, a strip mall and parking lot covers most of Newton's farm in Texas, and the house was demolished decades ago. However, the pear tree John Henry planted in 1910, still grows on the empty land at the edge of the woods behind the mall. A few years ago, according to Newton's great grandson, it was still bearing fruit, but today the area is being cleared to make room for a new supermarket. The virgin stand of towering pine at Clover Hill is also gone. And just as the great forest of East Texas shrank to small reserves, the new Cherokee Territory was gradually chipped away to a fraction of what it was when the Cherokees arrived during the winter of 1838. And their new land in what would become Oklahoma, was only a fraction of what they once controlled in Georgia, where they started their long march on the Trail of Tears. Chief Stand Watie's fear that the Union would open up the new Cherokee Territory to white settlement after the Civil war helped prompt him to throw his loyalty to the Confederacy. His fears were well founded, and precious little remains of the proud Cherokees' land. It seems the past always surrenders to the present just as age surrenders to youth. It has always been that way. It is the way of progress. It is the way of the world, and precious little in this world is permanent.

Newton John (aka James) b. Nov. 1841, Georgia d. Oct. 1873 near Quitman, Texas. Wife: Mary Elvira: b. 10 Dec. 1844 d. 20 July 1927 Quitman, Texas. Newton and Elvira were introduced by Mary Elvira's brother, Levi Franklin, a friend and comrade in arms during the Civil War.

Adelaide "Addie" Photo about 1880. She was Newton's oldest sibling.

Nellie Mae b. 10, Nov., 1893, Wood County, Texas d. May 1985, Quitman, Texas. She was Newton John and Elvira's oldest grandchild. Picture taken in 1910 when Nellie was 16. Seven years later, her father, John Henry, would be dead, and she and her husband would become the caretakers of Newton's widow. Nellie took care of Mary Elvira until her death of cancer in 1927.

The family of John Henry, Newton and Mary Elvira's only surviving child. Picture taken in 1910. Upper left to right: Nellie Mae, Mary Elvira (Newton's widow), Vallie Ree, second grandchild. Next to John Henry is Newton's daughter-in-law, Tennie Mae Cathy. In front, holding toy gun is Newton's only grandson and his name sake, Clarence Newton. Next to Tennie Mae is Newton's youngest granddaughter, Winnie Jane.

The "Sterling Price Flag." This is the flag Newton and other Missourians fought under for the Confederacy during the Civil War.

The grave marker of Newton's youngest sister, Bertie. Pineville, Missouri cemetery July of 2004. Jennifer Dawn, the great, great, great granddaughter of Newton and Mary Elvira, kneels beside the marker.

Printed in the United States
72365LV00005B/10-18